for Terri Lynn
my Soulmate and Best Friend

Contents

BEYOND HER TOUCH

PDMAC

Trimble Hollow Press

Beyond Her Touch is a work of fiction. Though actual locations and historical individuals may be mentioned, they are used in a fictitious manner and the events and occurrences were created/invented in the mind and imagination of the author, except for the inclusion of actual historical fact. Similarities of characters or names used within for any person – past, present, or future – are coincidental except where actual historical characters are purposely interwoven. The actions, thoughts, and dialogue of the historical characters featured in this story are fictional and not meant to reflect actual personalities and behavior.

Published by Trimble Hollow Press, Acworth, Georgia

Cover Art by Merwin Loquias

ISBN: 978-1-946495-24-2

Prologue

I am a coward. It is not something I lightly admit, but as God is my witness, I confess my shame. I now pay the price for my absence of bravery. But then, the logical part of me says I would be dead had I not acted as I did.

I was young when I chose the cowl, not yet 14. Old enough to be a man, yet not old enough to act as one. I was born into a good and honest wealthy Saxon family then sent away to another's household to be raised in a scholarly environment where I learned to read and write, amongst other things.

I have little recollection of my parents and I doubt I shall ever see them again, if they still live.

Being by nature of somber and reflective temperament, I chose the spiritual path as being more worthy. Renouncing the vices of riches and carnal pleasure, I joined the monastery at Lindisfarne in the year 789 Anno Domini (using the calendar of Saint Bede). Higbald was the Bishop and welcomed me to the small community of brothers whose lives were dedicated to the care and reverence of Saint Cuthbert.

My life was tranquil. In addition to the daily ritual amongst the brothers, we provided for pilgrims seeking the miraculous powers of the holy relics. My days were idyllic. Not only did I learn the skills of illuminating manuscripts, my ability as a farmer improved, as did, I dare say, my cooking talents.

Though the winds off the seas could blow cold, our monastery was a refuge for all my needs. Those days when the sun parted the clouds and warmth and brightness filled the skies, the aching green of the island and the wonder of

God's handiwork made one wonder if this wasn't a heaven on earth.

But that changed in an instant. Even now I do not understand why I am being punished.

I remember the day too vividly, four years after my arrival at Lindisfarne.

The Norsemen came.

So engrossed in my weeding, I knew nothing until I heard the shouts.

Then I saw them, fearsome warriors with swords and axes swarming over the land and ravaging the monastery. Too shocked to move, it wasn't until I witnessed one of the savages thrusting a sword into Brother Garvin's stomach that fear then gave strength to my legs and I fled.

I ran like a man possessed, yet it is troublesome to run quickly wearing a robe. Still, I managed to get to where the currachs were beached before misfortune found me. I had barely thrust my craft into the water when three of the savages came upon me and prevented my escape.

I will not retell the violation they did to me as I begged for my life, but I was weeping inconsolably as they dragged me back to the monastery. My abject desolation grew when I saw them ravaging and pillaging everything I held dear. Some brothers they simply slew where they stood. Others were dragged out to the sea and held under the water until drowned. But many more were stripped naked and violated then chained.

One thing of curiosity I will mention is the presence of a man who was not one of the invaders and whose presence I do not remember as being a pilgrim. He fought against the savages like something I have never seen. They too were impressed, for after he had defeated a great number of them, they ceased their combat against him and spoke to him. I do not know the words exchanged, but it is my belief that they wished to use his skills for no one fought him again and he went willingly onto another ship.

I stood as the desecration proceeded and watched as all the treasures of our monastery were hauled down to the ships. Then those of us in bondage were forced onto other ships.

My last memory of Lindisfarne is the bodies of my blood stained brothers scattered around the grounds.

I spent three days on that horrible ship, begging God to answer my prayers. Instead, we suffered the insults and taunts of the Heathens. Too fearful for my life, I remember little of the voyage other than, despite the season, I was cold, as though I had descended into a private hell.

We landed in a heathen market center called Kaupang in Skiringssal. My brothers and I were then marched off and put on the auction block. I was one of the fortunate ones, for I was bought by a wealthy trade merchant.

I have been a slave ever since.

Chapter 1

April 2031
Corydon University

Professor Erik Jonsson stood outside the Dean's office, pausing to once again admire the thick mahogany door and the craftsmanship, the intricate swirls and flow of the patterns. Twisting his head to gaze back down the hallway, he felt a warm comfort. On one side of the hallway, late afternoon sunlight filtered through tall arched windows, the lazy dust motes within the light slowly swirling towards the heavy paneled walls opposite the windows. The vision reminded him of a medieval cloister. It was while he was momentarily lost in his reverie that he heard them inside the office, the voices muffled but distinct.

"I'm sorry, but there's nothing more I can do," a man's voice said. Erik recognized it as Paul Atchison, the Dean of Academic Affairs.

"But he's tenured," another voice argued. Erik nodded with a smile. That was Sara Vaughn, Dean of the College of Arts and Humanities.

"I know that," Paul replied, "which makes it all the more difficult."

"But he's well respected in his field," Sara countered. "He's been peer reviewed on at least half a dozen articles he's written and they always say the same thing. They think he's the best."

"Sara," Paul said with a hint of exasperation. "That all may be true, but the fact of the matter is, the numbers just don't support keeping the courses or the program. There has been a steady decline in enrollment for the past several years. We're having a hard time filling those courses and most don't make.   You're having the same problem in the Archaeology department. Let's face it. No one cares about archaeology anymore."

"I do," she objected.

"That's because it's in your college," he sighed. "Let's be realistic. We're paying good money to a professor whose class sizes rarely average above five students. How can I justify his salary against a technology professor with an average class size of 35 students?"

"You also pay technology profs more," she pointed out.

"It's called supply and demand," Paul answered. "We need to put our money where the demand is."

"So you're going to eliminate all his courses?"

"I have no other choice."

There was a pause before Sara said, "I've no other place to put him. That means he'll have to be let go."

"Unfortunately, yes."

"But we've had courses in Anglo-Saxon and Nordic history since this university was founded."

Erik's eyes blinked wide as he suddenly realized they were talking about him. He knocked on the door and pushed it open without waiting to be acknowledged. He knew his fears were confirmed when he saw the looks of surprised guilt, like they had just been caught having an affair.

"You wanted to see me, Paul?" Erik said, mustering calmness as he glanced between the two.

Paul cleared his throat and straightened up, assuming a bravado of authority. "Um, ah, yes, yes I did. Have a seat. Sara and I were just discussing your situation." He sat down behind his large desk, the act reminding Erik of someone hiding behind a protective wall.

"My situation?" Erik sat in the chair in front of the desk, while Sara remained standing, her arms folded. Though she did her best to appear pleasant, her look said she was not happy.

Paul looked at Erik for a moment before saying, "Look, there's no easy way of saying this, but based upon the dwindling enrollment in certain fields of the history department, especially in the English and Nordic History courses, it has been determined that those courses will no longer be offered at the university starting the next academic year."

Erik stared at him, the weight of his career abruptly ending pressing on his chest. He then realized that this was the middle of April and there were maybe four more weeks of classes before the present academic year ended. "But I'm tenured," he frowned.

"You'll be offered a nice severance package," Paul kindly explained.

Erik looked at Sara who gave him a helpless shrug saying it was out of her hands. "But I'm qualified to teach other courses," he countered.

"We already have a full complement of faculty," Paul answered then quietly added, "You're not the only one affected by the declining enrollment. We're having to make some hard decisions here that unfortunately affect certain departments. It's like I was telling Sara, no one is majoring in history anymore and the fact that history is no longer required for graduation means even fewer students are taking those courses. Whether it's any consolation to you or not, the Board is looking at eliminating the history department all together."

"The entire department?" Erik's mouth gaped open in disbelief.

"I'm afraid so. Let's face it. All the jobs are in business and technology. The University is going to put its money where the jobs are. I'm sorry."

Erik recognized the 'end-of-discussion' tone. Pursing his lips, he stood up. "You're making a mistake."

"It's out of my hands," he firmly replied. "Why don't you stop by HR and begin your transition?"

Erik wanted to say something pithy, something to make them remember him for a long time, but nothing came to mind and with a loud and heavy sigh, he walked out of the office and slowly headed down the hallway, oblivious to the warm sunlight and cloistered ambiance.

Once outside in the quad, the warm spring afternoon momentarily distracted him. The air was laden with the bouquet of lilacs and the trees and shrubs were thick with ebullient green leaves. Students discussing classes, love interests and summer plans, lounged beneath the wide-spread branches of oaks and maples. The thought that he would no longer be a part of this filled him with a numb sadness. Looking across the quad at the administration building, he decided the last place he wanted to go to was HR. Instead, he slowly made his way back to his office, noting that it was the rare student these days who called out a cheery "Hi, Professor Jonsson." And it dawned on him that there was a reason no one greeted him; very few students took his classes.

Pausing at the worn heavy door to the faculty building, he also realized very few faculty knew who he was. He knew part of the problem was his own. He found most of his peers uninteresting, especially the Tech professors who seemed constantly enraptured with the latest advancements in design and processing, talking in terms that might as well have been a foreign language. Not that he couldn't speak a foreign

8

language… it's just that it was exceedingly difficult to find anyone who spoke Old Norse.

Pushing the door open, he climbed the stairs to the top floor, eschewing the elevator both for its tacky modern inconsistency with the 19th century building, and because he liked the worn mahogany handrails used by erudite professors for almost two centuries. The stairwell smelled like the past and he reveled in the ambiance and solitude, for few professors used the stairs, preferring to race along in their lives in an elevator that allowed them to "save time."

Standing in the doorway to his office, he quietly gazed around the small room. Two cushioned chairs faced his desk which occupied most of the room. There was a large window opposite the door and Erik had positioned his desk so that he would have to turn his head to the right to look out. Behind the chairs, bookshelves lined the wall from floor to ceiling. Noting the number of books on the shelves, he decided it would take more, a lot more, than one trip to carry them all down. Maybe this would be a time to use the elevator…

Collecting his leather satchel with student papers, he cast one last wistful look around then closed and locked the door.

Erik lived in a townhouse a few blocks off campus and the trudge back home was anything but joyous. He compared the emotion from the day before when the weather and fragrance of spring had filled him with a zest for living. Today, the world was oppressive and meaningless.

Picking up the remote, Erik plopped down on the couch and turned on the TV. He mindlessly flipped though channels while ruminating about his future. At 42 years old, the likelihood of him finding a job requiring his skills was virtually non-existent. Silently deliberating at his uncertain future prospects, he paid little attention to the various shows as he clicked on one channel after the other. Abruptly he realized what he was doing and shook his head in frustration. Was his future so bleak that he was now reduced to wasting his life watching the idiotic shows on television, shows that the moronic masses found so entertaining?

The plethora of reality shows caused him to wonder what it was that people found so fascinating in others' lives? Were their own lives so pitiful that they could only find pleasure in living vicariously for one hour each week watching someone else live his or her life? Yet he knew it didn't stop there, for whatever happened in that hour would be discussed and expanded and deliberated and mocked or envied the rest of the week between shows.

And then there were the competition shows – cook offs, bake offs, haircuts, landscape, tire changing, and far more than anyone could watch in a lifetime. Life had devolved to comedies, reality shows and cook offs.

He stared at the remote in his hand and then at the TV and realized the absurdity. Here he was chastising the mindless myrmidons for being mesmerized by TV and he was sitting doing the same thing. He chuckled at the incongruity for he rarely watched TV. He'd much rather read or play his guitar or anything other than sitting in front of the TV and have his brain turned off while being entertained by some lame show that did nothing to enhance his life.

He pointed the remote at the TV and paused just as he was about to turn it off. By chance, he had flipped though enough channels and was now on the latest popular show, the Time Travel channel. Time Travel. His plight was made all the more insulting. It seemed absurdly ironic that no one took history courses anymore, but everyone wanted to go back in time.

For some reason, he decided to listen and turned up the sound. The announcer, a man in a loud suit, perfectly coiffured blond hair, and overemphasized gestures that reminded him of a carnival barker, was talking to the latest winner, a plump middle aged woman in her 50s.

"Congratulations, Jane," he broadly grinned. "After one month of no winners, you picked the lucky numbers for this week's lottery. Have you decided where and when you want to go?"

"Well Bud," she jiggled with excitement. "I talked with my husband and we decided to go to Hawaii in 1961, just when Elvis was making *Blue Hawaii*."

Bud beamed as he grandly spread his arms. "Wow! What an exciting time you're going to have. Just imagine seeing the King of Rock and Roll, alive in Hawaii." He placed a hand on her shoulder and gently, though firmly, turned her to face the cameras. Speaking directly to the cameras, he said, "Jane here is living the dream. What are your dreams?" Stepping to the side to face her, he motioned with his hand for her to turn around and follow a lab technician. He then returned his attention to the studio audience and the cameras. "While Jane gets ready for her adventure, let me remind everyone out in our listening audience that the Time Travel program is brought to you by the National Lottery. Not only do we give you your dreams, a portion of each lottery ticket purchased in the Time Travel Lottery goes to fund healthcare and after-school programs. And now, let's hear what Alex has to say about Jane's trip."

The screen shot changed to a well-dressed man in his early 30s with a deep broadcaster's voice. "Thanks Bud. As this week's lottery winner, Jane is going to be sent back in time to the year 1961. She is allowed one guest to travel with her and she chose her husband Ryan as her travel companion. Now remember the rules. Each Time Machine winner is allowed one day of time travel to a period and place of their choosing. They may take one other guest with them. Also

11

remember, you are not allowed to interfere with the events of the past. You may take pictures, with a recording device appropriate to the time, and collect souvenirs, but you are not allowed to participate in any event or events that might alter the time continuum. In order to protect you and Time Travel Incorporated, two Time Travel escorts are provided at no cost to you. The escorts are there to protect you and to make sure you return to the portal on time. Back to you, Bud."

"Thanks, Alex. Now, while Jane gets ready, let's visit with another Time Traveler and hear what she has to say about her trip." Behind him, a large screen filled with an attractive woman in her early 40s, standing in a room filled with American Southwestern paraphernalia. "This is Marilyn from Chicago, here to share with us her wonderful trip to Tombstone, Arizona in 1881. Hi, Marilyn. How are you?"

"I am in heaven right now because I just had the experience of a lifetime," she replied, stiffly reading off a cue card.

"I'm sure you are. So what was it about Tombstone in 1881 that made you want to visit then?"

"O my God, Bud," she gushed, going off script. "It was living the dream. I wanted to see and meet the real Wyatt Earp. O my God, O my God it was more than a dream. Ever since I saw the movie *Tombstone*, I was hooked on the Old West. It was amazing, more than amazing… the people, the streets of Tombstone, the saloons, and restaurants."

"Now correct me if I'm wrong, Marilyn, but somehow I remember a certain gunfight in Tombstone in 1881."

"You're talking about the gunfight at the OK Corral," she said, interrupting him. "That happened October 26th. I went there in June, because after the gunfight, things get a little crazy, if you know what I mean."

"Well," he turned to give a knowing smile at the camera then back to Marilyn. "Since you only had two days, what else did you see?"

"O my God," she burst. "We landed far enough away from all the silver mines, somewhere in between Tombstone and Bisbee. I don't mind saying that it gets mighty hot in Tombstone in June... and it was an uphill walk to get there. But when we got there, I was like a little girl in a candy store. You can imagine the looks we got when we passed all the hooker cribs on the east side of town near the Bird Cage Theater, which wasn't open yet. It wasn't open until December of that year."

"Fascinating," Bud said. He pushed the ear piece firmer into his left ear to hear the producers telling him to keep up the rolling dialogue. The audience numbers were improving, most likely due to Marilyn's excitement. "So you got into town. Then what?"

"O my God. We're walking down Allen Street and since it was early, we had breakfast at the Cosmopolitan. It was stunning inside. I had steak and eggs."

"Go on," he encouraged.

Seeing she had an attentive audience, Marilyn enthusiastically continued. "That town never sleeps. With the miners working shifts and the Faro games running nonstop and the saloons open all the time, it didn't matter what time of day or night, something was always happening. So after breakfast, I figured it was still cool enough being it was still morning, I wanted to take a peek at Boot Hill. So used to seeing what it looks like now, I was surprised at the fewer number of graves, which makes sense because it was only 1881."

Bud heard a voice in his ear piece and he nodded. "Very interesting, Marilyn. So, did you get to see Wyatt Earp?"

"O my God, O my God," she instantly spouted. "So we're walking back from the cemetery and I take us over to Fremont Street and as we're just about to First Street where Wyatt's house is and who do you think is sitting on the porch, sipping a cup of coffee and smoking a cigar?"

"Wyatt Earp?"

"O my God, yes. He's sitting there and I'm like "Good morning Mister Earp." And he's like, "Good morning, Miss. Lovely day for a stroll." Can you imagine that? He actually spoke to me. So I stop and ask him how his business was doing. He owned the gambling concession in the Oriental Saloon, you know. So he says, "It's doing fine." So I say, "You're up awfully early for a man who owns part of the Oriental Saloon." He laughs and says, "Yeah, I suppose I am." So I'm trying to think of something clever to say, but I was just so overwhelmed and I figured he'd be around so I'd meet him again, so I say, "You have a nice day." And he says to me, "You too."

Bud heard the voice in is earpiece again, this time telling him to wrap it up. "So you met Wyatt Earp. Anyone else?"

"O my God it was unbelievable. We're walking along Fremont and we pass by Fly's Photo Shop and I'm thinking it would be incredible to have my picture taken. So I stop and walk into the shop and Buck, that's the nickname Mister Fly used, was in the shop. You may not know this, but Fly's photographs are legendary and very highly prized. He's the one who took the pictures of Wyatt and his wife Josephine."

"Did you get your picture taken?"

"I did." Her face brightened with overt pride as she held up a framed sepia-toned picture of herself.

"So, Marilyn, now that you've had a chance to experience the thrill of a lifetime, what can you tell the viewing audience about your adventure?"

The camera zoomed closer to Marilyn, whose excitement had not quenched. "O my God, Bud. This was the best time of my entire life. There is nothing to compare it to. There will never be another experience that can match that. Well, maybe there will be if I can win again. I'm buying tickets like crazy these days."

The camera zoomed away and faded. Bud turned to the main camera, his perfect smile exposing perfect teeth. "While we like hearing enthusiasm like Marilyn's, remember to play responsibly. And that wraps up another day in the lives of Time Travelers. Tune in next week to hear Chet Simpson talk about his trip to the first World Series in Baseball!"

Erik switched off the TV when the commercial came on. Standing, he placed the remote by the TV and looked around the living room. It was neat and tidy, everything in its place, dusted and clean. The books in the bookshelves were arranged by subject and author's last name. Wall decorations consisted of antique pages from medieval books and scriptoriums. Carefully nestled into one corner was his prized possession, a classical guitar he had bought while in college. A Cordoba C10S, he got it for a steal because the music store was going out of business.

But everything was too neat and tidy. Friends would come over and jokingly complain that there was no place to sit because the couch was too clean and their clothes would leave a speck of dust on it. Could he help it that he liked things clean and in order? Once a friend had come by and by the time he left, all the pictures were just slightly askew and the TV remote was nowhere to be found. Erik immediately corrected all the pictures but hadn't noticed the remote missing until two days later when he decided to watch a program on Vikings.

He didn't search long, already knowing who was responsible. "Very funny Allan. Where did you put it?" he asked over the phone.

"You're just *now* realizing it's missing? What have you been doing these past couple of days?"

"Other things than baking my brain on TV. Where did you put it?"

"Other things? You mean like you've had a date?"

Erik sighed. "No. Just other things. OK?"

"Listen, my friend. You need to move on. Linda isn't going to show up and suddenly say, 'Oops, my mistake. I was a fool. Marry me again.' Move on. Go have some fun."

Erik listened then said, "Thanks for your input Doctor Freud. I'll think about it. Now where's the remote?"

Allan paused just long enough for Erik to ask again when he said, "It's in the closet by the front door behind the hats."

Still on the phone, Erik walked to the closet and found the remote in the corner on the shelf, just behind his favorite fedora. "OK. I got it. Why do you do these things?"

"Because I'm trying to put a little excitement into your life. All you do is teach, grade papers, clean your apartment and that mixed martial arts thing. You never go anywhere and you haven't had a date in how long?"

Erik thought a moment and shrugged. "It's been a while."

"The divorce was final over a year ago. When are you going to accept it and get a life?"

Ignoring the question, Erik said, "Thanks for letting me know where the remote was. I'll talk to you later."

"You're hopeless," Allan answered and hung up.

Erik looked down at his phone and pushed the 'end call' button then at the remote in his hand. Allan was right. He needed some excitement in his life. That was one of the reasons Linda left – she said he was boring.

He was born at the wrong time was another accusation. Who in their right mind, she would fuss, would rather sit at home reading a book, listening to classical music when there was a whole world out there just jumping with excitement? Parties and pubs and people, the three 'P's', she reminded him. Life was more than books. If ever she needed to know anything, there was that thing called the internet that had been around since before they were born. Besides, who had time to read when there was the job and then the three 'P's.'?

One time she looked over his shoulder at the book he was reading. It was a book on the medieval history of the Nordic countries. "My god," she said. "What's with you and all these dead people? You were born at the wrong time." From then on, she started calling him 'Captain Anachronism.'

He had lamely explained that he enjoyed studying history, that the study of history was the study of the essence of man. He had wanted to add that her view of life was banal. He thought of a line from Hemingway's short story, *Hills Like White Elephants:* "That's all we do, isn't it – look at things and try new drinks." It seemed to fit her. Her existence was superficial, a veneer of imparting meaning to the trivial. The problem was, she wouldn't understand it. For her, drinking with her friends held far more fascination than being married and living with him.

With a resigned sigh, Erik shook his head, frustrated that he had thought through all this before, too many times. How many more times was he going to justify who he was and why he was divorced? Yet he couldn't shake the emotion that he was now damaged goods.

Looking at the mantel clock, he saw it was time to get ready for his training. At least that was one thing he did that wasn't normal.

Erik was not himself in the evening's mixed martial arts class and the instructor noticed it. "Your mind is elsewhere, Master Erik," he said as he rapped him on the arm with a bo staff.

"I apologize, Sensei," he sheepishly replied, giving him a respectful bow, realizing the rap on the arm hurt. "I have learned today that I will no longer have a job at the end of May."

The Sensei, an older man with tight skin and taut muscles, stared paternally at him. "In here, the world outside does not exist. You had your problems when you entered the dojo, and your problems will still be there when you leave. You must release yourself of outside cares and focus on what is in front of you... here... now. An attacker cares little about your worries. In fact, it is better for him that you *are* distracted, for then you are easily defeated."

"Yes, Sensei," he replied and again bowed.

"Good. Now defend yourself." Without so much as an 'Are you ready?' the Sensei launched an attack of rapid thrusts, spins, and strikes with his bo staff, which Erik parried. After more than a minute of intense combat, the Sensei added kicks and spinning foot blocks. As the two sparred across the mat, the rest of the dojo paused in their workouts to watch. It was after more than ten minutes of concentrated and extreme physical contact that the Sensei held up his hand to stop the contest. The two opponents faced each other and bowed.

With a serene smile, the Sensei said, "You are ready, Grasshopper."

His sweat-soaked Hee-fu uniform matted against his skin, Erik smiled despite himself. "Thank you, Sensei."

It was after the class, as Erik was stuffing his gear into his equipment bag, that Seth Primuth, a fellow student and aspiring actor came up to him. "That was incredible," he gushed. "The way you two went at it. Fast, like lightening. I'm talking real fast. There were a couple of times I thought he had you, but each time you blocked just in time." He swirled and jabbed his hands in imitation. "It was awesome."

"Thank you," he replied, "but I think the Sensei was being kind to me today."

"No way," Seth argued. "I was watching the whole time and I think he was glad to end it." He abruptly stiffened and bowed as the Sensei walked up, dabbing his face with a hand towel.

"Do you have a minute?" he asked Erik.

"Certainly." He followed him into the office.

The Sensei sat behind a small desk. Behind him were numerous pictures and trophies extoling the man's supremacy. "Please, sit down." He waited until Erik was comfortable. "You fought very well today. I am pleased with your progress."

"Thank you, Sensei."

"Now tell me what it is that distracts you so?"

Erik related the news from the Dean, ending with, "I don't know what I'm going to do. I've taught Anglo-Saxon and Nordic history for almost fourteen years. It's what I went to school for, both masters and Ph.D. It's my passion. But now what do I do?" he shrugged helplessly. "All that education and experience and they tell me I'm no longer needed, like a kickstand on a horse."

The Sensei smiled at the analogy. "You cannot find employment elsewhere?"

"It's like the Dean said, there's not a big demand for history professors anymore, especially ones teaching Anglo-Saxon and Nordic history."

"What will you do?"

"That's just it. I don't know. I don't know how to do anything else."

There was a lull in the conversation when the Sensei said, "Until you find your passion again, perhaps you would consider teaching here."

Erik furrowed his brows at the thought. "I... I would be honored. Are you sure?"

With a resigned sigh, he said, "I am getting older and it is time someone younger steps in to take charge. Besides, I could use a vacation," he added with a wry smile.

"But I still have so much to learn," he objected.

"I'm not dead yet," he sniffed. "I will be here to assist you and to teach you."

"Thank you. I would like that." He stood up and bowed.

Seth was waiting outside for him. "Hey. You wanna get something to eat?" He nodded at the pizza place across the street.

Erik was about to say 'no' but realized he had nowhere else he had to be and there wasn't anyone waiting for him at home. "Sure. Why not."

As they walked across the street, Seth handed him something. "Here. I got a ticket for you."

"A ticket for what?" He looked down at the shiny gilded edged National Lottery ticket. "You got me a Time Travel ticket?"

"Yeah. Thought you could use some cheerin' up."

"You do realize you have a better chance of being struck by an asteroid than winning the lottery."

"People win the lottery all the time," Seth countered, holding the door open for him.

"You actually have to play it to win."

"I just did," he grinned, "for you. It's a lucky ticket. I can feel it in my bones. Your life is about to change."

"If you're so lucky, why don't you use it?"

"I only get a feeling when it's about someone else."

Folding the ticket and stuffing it in his shirt pocket, Erik grinned and shook his head then looked around the restaurant. Inside was the buzz of conversation and pungent aroma of oven baked pizza. Finding a free table, they sat down and ordered.

"So when and where would you go if you did win?" Seth asked, arranging the spice shakers.

"I don't know. Can't say that I ever thought about it."

Seth looked at him with a raised eyebrow of doubt. "You mean to say you've never wished you lived somewhere else in another time? Everyone does that."

"That's not what I meant," he smiled. "Sure, if I had the opportunity to live in another time, I would probably want to go back to the time of King Alfred or when Iceland was settled by Vikings."

"Who?"

"King Alfred the Great, the 9th century, in England. It's part of what I teach in college... or what I used to teach in college."

Seth frowned at him. "People actually study that stuff? What's it good for? I mean, like, what's the use of it?"

"That's pretty much what my dean said," he sighed.

"Meaning no disrespect, but what can a guy do learning stuff like that? I don't see how it's practical."

Erik looked at him and shrugged. "Again, that's what my dean said." He looked around at the other customers happily chatting and laughing, wondering what was it about a pizza place that caused people to relax and enjoy themselves so much? "So where would *you* go?" he asked, making conversation.

"I've thought long and hard about it," Seth replied with some gravitas. "I'd like to go back to 1959 when John

Wayne was filming *Rio Bravo* in Old Tucson. Man, I'd love to have had a part in that film."

"John Wayne, eh?"

"Yeah," he grinned. "The Duke." He paused when the waitress came up. Her name was Lisa. She was a pretty buxom woman in her mid-twenties, her blond hair tied in a bun on the back of her head. A loose strand of hair had escaped and dangled over her ear. Giving him the once over with a wink of approval, she took their order and sashayed away.

"She's hot for me," Seth grinned, leaning forward on the table.

"Well you're a very handsome man," Erik observed with feigned disinterest. "I'm sure she'd love to go out with an aspiring actor."

"Yeah, well, maybe one of these days?" He flopped back, resting one arm on the table.

"What play are you in now?"

"I'm playing Mitch in Tennessee Williams' *Streetcar Named Desire*," he said. "It's running for another couple of weeks. I'm already looking to audition for another show." The conversation dropped to a lull when he said, "Hey, y'know you're allowed to bring another person with you when you win."

"Win what?" Erik frowned.

"The Time Travel lottery."

"Back to that, eh? So who would you take?"

"Don't know. You interested?" He tilted his head waiting for a response.

"You sure you don't want to take Miss Blond there," he said, nodding to where their waitress was taking another order."

"Hmmm. That might be fun. What about you? Who would you take?"

"I haven't the foggiest idea," he replied. "It's not something I've ever thought about. Though now that I do think about it, the person would need one very particular requirement."

"Oh?" he asked, hoping it was something sensual.

"Yes. The person would have to speak Old Norse."

"Old Norse?" he blinked then raised an eyebrow. "In other words, you wouldn't take anyone else."

"Not by choice," he spread his hands.

"So… you don't think that perhaps you ought to choose another time where everyone spoke English?"

"You asked me where and when I wanted to go," he countered. "Is it my fault there are complications?"

"You might as well go back to the Romans," he griped.

"What an excellent idea. I could take someone from the Vatican with me," he said with mock seriousness.

"The Vatican? You'd take a priest with you?"

"They speak Latin and that's the lingua franca of the day. Now that I think about it, going to the coliseum in Rome would be an experience. Gladiators, chariot races, throwing Christians to the lions… what an exciting time. I wonder if they'd let me keep the toga as a keepsake?"

Seth studied him for a moment before realizing he was joking. "Very funny."

"Think about the research they'd have to do before they sent you back to Rome. Something simple like coinage. Can you imagine going back to the time of Augustus and have coins from Nerva's reign? One look at those and you might be fed to the lions yourself. Though in your case, once they found out you were an actor, Nero would demand your friendship and together, the two of you could play the amphitheaters."

"Nero? Who's he?"

"A Roman emperor," he answered. "Though you'll want to do it prior to 59 CE because he gets rather weird after that."

"CE? What's that?"

"It means Common Era. It's like AD except it's secular, which is sort of humorous in that they use the same dating but merely call it something different."

"So this Nero guy was weird how?"

"Oh, things like executing his mother and his wife. And then there's that little conflagration in Rome and the reprisals against Christians and Jews."

Seth studied him for a bit then shook his head. "I like 1959 much better. It's easier and I don't have to worry about crazy emperors."

"And you don't have to speak Latin," Erik added.

"Yeah. English is plenty good enough for me."

The waitress returned with their beers, pausing long enough to smile at Seth.

"Seth wants to know," Erik spoke up, "if, after he wins the Time Travel lottery, you'll go back to 1959 with him to see John Wayne making *Rio Bravo*."

"*Rio Bravo*," she brightened. "I love that movie. I love John Wayne."

"You do?" Seth blinked in surprise, his initial irritation with Erik quickly forgotten.

"Of course," she said. "Who wouldn't? Though one of my favorites isn't a western, it's sort of a romance comedy. Have you ever seen *The Quiet Man*?"

"Takes place in Ireland," Seth answered. "Great movie."

"Looks like you two have a lot in common," Erik interjected.

Lisa did a quick look over her shoulder to check on other customers. Satisfied no one needed immediate attention, she placed both hands on the table and leaned forward, focusing her gaze on Seth. "So if you won the lottery you would take me? I don't even know you."

"That can be fixed," he suavely replied.

"Not in one date it won't." She then popped up, "Better check on your order," and was gone in an instant.

The two men watched her as she walked away. "She's very pretty. Great personality," Erik observed.

"Yeah," Seth replied, not quite listening. "What did she mean, 'Not in one date'?"

"I think she wants you to ask her out," Erik answered. "But then, I've been known to misread people before, so I wouldn't trust my input."

Seth turned back with a grin. "Guess we'll find out."

Lisa returned with their pizza and placed it on the table.

"So, will you go out with me?" Seth ventured.

"Of course," she replied as though the answer was obvious. "Here's my phone number." She handed him a scrap of paper folded over. "Guard it with your life. I'm off on Monday and Tuesdays."

"How about this coming Monday?"

"Works for me. Call me." She spun around and went to attend other tables.

Erik smiled at him. "Looks like you have your partner for your time travel adventure. Hope you get to see John Wayne."

"Me too," he grinned, pleased with the evening's success. "But what about you? Who would you take?"

"Actually, I was thinking about that and thought about taking my ex."

"Your ex?" He cocked an eyebrow in consternation.

"Yeah. I could take her to 9th century Denmark and then leave her there. She always wanted an exciting life and Vikings would be a good start for her."

Seth snorted a laugh while staring down at the paper and memorizing Lisa's phone number.

"But," Erik continued, "the likelihood of that happening is what? Eight billion to one? I think I'll save my money."

"You don't have to," Seth smiled. "You got your very own Time Travel ticket."

Erik reached in and pulled out the ticket. "This is a twenty dollar ticket."

"Which means you got four chances to win," he confidently grinned.

Erik gazed back at him. "Which means you probably want me to pay for dinner," he said with a smile.

"Now, now. Don't be so suspicious. Just gotta feeling your life's gonna change and thought I'd help it along."

"By buying me a lottery ticket?" he said, his doubt obvious. "Why not just give me the twenty dollars. At least in the end, I'd have twenty dollars."

"You're such an unbeliever," Seth said, wagging his head. "Have some faith and be thankful someone cares enough about you to give you a lottery ticket."

"You're absolutely right," he replied, chagrined. "I apologize. Thank you."

"No problem," he inclined his head in a regal nod. He looked back to watch Lisa for a bit then turned to look at Erik. "Um... about tonight's dinner..." He spread his hands in a helpless appeal. "I'm just a poor actor lookin' forward to Monday night. Gotta conserve my resources and all. Know what I mean?"

"Be happy to," he smiled. "Hope you have a great evening."

Erik was midway through his lecture of Icelandic Sagas when he saw the student raise her hand. "Yes, Tone?"

"Professor, there's a tale in our book called 'The Tale of Erik Spinning Sword.' He's supposedly the son of Jon Helgason, which means his name would be Erik Jon's son, or Erik Jonsson. Is he a relation to you?"

With an indulgent smile, he replied, "That would be nice. However, just because we have the same name doesn't mean we're related. While it would be flattering to be able to claim heritage, remember, though the actions of the sagas and tales are in the ninth and tenth centuries and earlier, the sagas and tales themselves weren't written down until sometimes two to three hundred years later. While there are kernels of truth in the tales, there are also bits of myth that sometimes makes it difficult to separate the two. Further, there could be many Erik Jon's sons who are not related as the names Erik and Jon are not uncommon."

"I know the syllabus says we're going to begin with 'Egil's Saga,' but could we start with Erik's Tale?" Tone asked. "I thought it was very interesting the way the author described the swords and how they whirled so fast."

Erik was momentarily caught off-guard. Tone was a very attractive petite blond, some would say 'stunning,' with large blue eyes that penetrated when she spoke. Her thick hair cascaded down her shoulders to the middle of her ample chest. His first thought was that she was subtly flirting with him. He quickly suppressed the idea as not only was she half his age, she was his student. He had always been careful not to let his imagination get carried away. Yet the way she looked at him gave him pause. He quickly glanced at the other five students to see if they perceived the same sensually charged aura, but their faces were either oblivious or marginally bored.

"I don't see why we couldn't," he said, recovering his composure. "Let's all turn to page 684 in the text. Who would like to read aloud?"

27

Tone's hands shot up. Receiving the 'go ahead' nod from Erik, she read in a clear strong voice.

The spinner of fate is cruel to me.
Hands bound, chained by the Pines
of the sea's golden moon,
on too many ships; the bringer of
battle is hard at work.

I have traveled on the sea-god's steed
a long and turbulent wave-path,
though none have I seen
like this Maker of War.
The soul-cleavers whirl in his two strong fists,
a thirst for bone and Odin's fury,
a god of the quick flying weapon
until he dealt out mortal wounds.

There thirteen men fell,
clad in a cloak of blood.

Stain wolf's teeth with blood

Wolf and eagle stalk,
Over the (dead)
in praise of the feeder of ravens.

While she read, Erik found himself distracted by the young attractive student. Every now and then she would look up and give a half-smile at him as she read. She was a senior and expecting to graduate next month. She was probably twenty-one or twenty-two years old... and also his best student. This wasn't the first class she had taken with him. He inwardly chuckled remembering that first class, almost two years ago, when she walked in the door. The course was early Anglo-Saxon history. There were ten students in the class. She was the last to enter. Taking a brisk look around the room, she had marched to a chair in the front row right in front of his desk. Taking off her backpack, she plopped down and pulled out her textbook, a pen and a pad of paper. He remembered thinking it odd that she handwrote her notes, eschewing the normal method of computer notepad.

The image of what she wore was etched in his memory – tan hiking shorts that revealed toned and beautiful legs that descended into a pair of ankle high hiking boots. Her top was a simple grey V-neck cotton t-shirt that displayed toned arms and emphasized her chest. As far as he could tell, she wore no makeup. She had a confident aura about her that said she didn't really care to fit into someone's preconceptions.

His first thought was that she was a granola-head, one of those crazy tree-hugging advocates always demonstrating against the evil of corporatism and pollution. Of course, on the face of it, he hated pollution just like any other sane individual did. That he didn't march and yell didn't mean he wasn't concerned.

As that was the first class, he knew none of the students and called out the roll. He paused when he came to her name: Tone Thorgilsdottir.

Pronouncing it 'TAW-nee', he called out "Tone Thorgilsdottir."

"My God," she exclaimed, "You're the first person who's ever pronounced it correctly."

"You have a most unusual name," he said with a smile, "one that fits in quite well with Old Norse history and literature."

"Both my parents are of Nordic heritage," she explained, "and I got stuck with their fascination of their past."

"Your father's name is Thorgil?"

"Yes."

"Most interesting. Good to have you in class."

That was three or four classes ago.

He chuckled to himself. Who was he fooling? He knew this was the eighth class she had with him and his pretend air of nonchalance poorly hid the fact that he looked forward to her presence. She had taken every class he taught. But, she had a boyfriend... at least she used to have a boyfriend, a handsome young man with chiseled face who dressed like an ad for a men's magazine. He would come by class to wait for her and together they would meander off in friendly discourse. But the young man hadn't appeared since this semester began.

Erik was pondering her love life when he felt his phone vibrate. Ignoring it, he listened as Tone read. The phone had barely stopped vibrating when it began all over again. Frowning with irritation, he carefully pulled it out to see who was bothering him during class. Whoever it was, was going to get a more than gentle reminder not to call during the day unless it was an emergency. Whoever it was should know better.

His frown deepened when he saw it was a text from Seth. Shaking his head, he replaced his phone and focused on Tone as she read. She was not more than half-way through the long tale when he realized class was just about over for the day.

He waited until she took a pause then interrupted. "That's enough for today. We'll continue with 'Erik's Tale' next class. Thank you, Tone. That was well read."

The other students had departed by the time Tone gathered her books, notes, and papers. Erik noticed her obvious dawdling but didn't want to press the issue. Once she had collected her things, she approached the desk.

"Professor Jonsson. Do you have a moment?"

"Of course," he replied, hoping to appear nonchalant.

"I've been thinking about what I want to do in the future and find that Old Norse literature is truly fascinating."

"You do?" he said, with surprise.

"Why does that shock you?" she said, smiling at him.

"Not many people find Old Norse very interesting," he lamely explained.

"I do. But that's my problem. I majored in history because I enjoy it, and now especially Old Norse history and culture, Vikings, and the settlement of Iceland in the ninth century. But what do I do with it? From what I can find out, I can either teach or work at some cultural site explaining the past to tourists."

Erik smiled at the description. "Unfortunately, yes. But I think the more important question is what is more important to you, making money or following your passion?"

"Money is over-rated," she answered.

"While I like your thinking, money does tend to make life easier."

"I'm not looking for an easy life," she said, staring at him with those penetrating eyes.

Erik held her gaze. "It looks to me like you've already decided what you want to do."

"I'll need to go to grad school."

"If you want to be competitive, yes, though if you haven't applied by now it's too late to apply for this fall. And of course, you'll have to attend another university somewhere else.

"I know. Thank God I'm graduating. I pity those poor souls who have to transfer to another college to continue their studies."

Nodding agreement, he said, "Grad school is expensive."

"I know. I'm going to take a year or so off to work and save money to pay for it."

"A good idea," he said, even more impressed with her pragmatic mind.

"I was wondering if you would write me a recommendation when the time comes."

"Of course. I'd be more than happy to."

Smiling her thanks, she remained by the desk.

"Something else?" he asked, doing his best to be the dutiful and caring professor.

"I was also wondering, since I'll be graduating in a few weeks and won't be a student here anymore, whether you would like to go out with me?"

Erik's heart quickened with nervous apprehension mixed with excitement. "I... I... don't you have a boyfriend?" he parried.

"No. If you're talking about the boy who used to hang around waiting for me after classes, he wasn't a boyfriend. I dated him twice. He was too immature and couldn't take the hint. I finally had to tell him outright that I wasn't interested."

"But Tone," he reasoned, "I'm twice your age."

"You're fifty?"

"No," he stiffened with indignation before understanding swept through him. "You're twenty-five?"

"Yes. I got a fulltime job right out of high school so I could pay for college."

Erik paused in thought, fascinated by this younger woman. His vanity liked her romantic interest, but his rational side argued against such a possibility. There was a seventeen year difference between them. He was nearly out of high school when she was born.

"Why me? There are plenty of men your age who would be thrilled to date you."

"Men my age are too childish and immature. Their priorities are screwed up. They want sex first and then they'll see if they actually like you enough to want to develop a relationship. No thanks." She stood there, books in her arms, gazing intently at him.

Erik smiled at the response. "I like the way you think."

"So? Does that mean you'll go out with me?"

His mind raced at the possible implications. Waiting until after she graduated meant she was no longer a student and therefore it would be permitted, but then the fact that she was a recent student would start the tongues wagging that they had been intimate all along and she had received special treatment and that could impact his position with the university... which was irrelevant now because when this semester was finished he no longer had a job at the university.

Tone watched him and was preparing herself for disappointment when he said, "Yes." Her face radiant, she said, "I graduate in three weeks. My folks will be here for graduation. I'd like for them to meet you, if you don't mind."

Erik grew suddenly nervous. Meet the parents?

Tone laughed when she saw his reaction. "It's not what you think. You're my favorite professor. I've mentioned you before to them and thought it would be nice for them to meet you."

Erik sheepishly grinned at his misunderstanding. "I would enjoy meeting your parents." His phone vibrated again and he let out a frustrated sigh. "This thing drives me crazy sometimes." He pulled it out and saw he had another text from Seth. Placing the phone on the desk, he gave his full attention to the beautiful woman standing before him, giving him an impish stare.

"My parents will come for graduation, but won't stay because they both work and have to get back home. Would this coming Sunday night work for you?"

"Yes," he smiled. "Sunday would be fine."

She handed him a slip of paper. "Here's my phone number. Call me anytime. I work an odd schedule so if I don't answer, just leave a message."

"Where do you work?" he asked, reading the number then placing the paper in his pocket.

"I work at a local attorney's office as a translator."

Erik blinked in surprise. "You speak another language?"

"A couple," she shrugged as if it was no big deal. "I suppose I'd better go. I've got to get to my next class."

"Of course," he said, wishing she didn't have to go. "See you Sunday."

Smiling at him, she started for the door then spun around. "You don't have to wait until Sunday to call me." Without waiting for an answer, she glided through the open door.

Erik remained rooted in mild astonishment. Not only was Tone more than attractive physically, she had a strength of personality that he found fascinating. And then there was her laugh... a disarming child-like joy that he found captivating.

The phone danced in vibration on the desk. Rolling his eyes as he uttered a loud grunt of impatience, he picked it up. It was another text from Seth. It said the same thing as the other three texts.

Did you check your lottery tickets? The drawing was last night and there were two winners.

As he punched in the response of *No, I left it at home*, he struggled to think where exactly at home it was. Then he remembered it was still in the top pocket of the shirt he wore after practice last night. Since he was finished for the day, he collected his books and papers, neatly arranging them in his briefcase, and headed out the door.

Halfway home, his phone rang. It was Seth. Ignoring the call, he let it go to voicemail. The phone rang again just as he walked in the house. It was Seth again and this time he pushed the button on the earpiece and answered it.

"No I haven't checked the numbers. I'll do it now." Closing the door, he walked through the hallway of the meticulously decorated home towards his study. Sliding open the door, he carefully placed his briefcase down by the antique oak desk. Walking past the bedroom where the bed was neatly made, he went to the laundry room and retrieved the shirt.

"OK," he said, pulling out the ticket. "I've got it."

"What are the letters?"

Erik looked down at the ticket. There was a letter of the alphabet in each of seven boxes. Looking at the letters, he sniffed a laugh at the absurdity. Twenty-six choices for each box made the chance of winning something like one in eight billion. And right now, what he wanted more than anything was just a little peace and quiet, time to ruminate on his future. But, Seth was not going to leave him alone unless he told him what was on the ticket.

"OK. Ready? Here's the first one: X-D-R-G-E-E-L."

"Nope. Not it.

"Here's the second one: K-Y-W-Q-M-Q-D.

"No," came the reply, tinged with disappointment then hope. "Next one?"

"OK. Here are the letters. U-A-L-F-R-E-D." There was a heavy pause as he frowned when he silently repeated the letters... Alfred?

"O my God!" Seth burst. "O my God. You've won. You've won." When he heard no reply he said it louder. "Did you hear me? You've won."

Erik blinked at the news, still marveling over the arrangement of the letters. "Are you sure?"

"Go online. Check it out yourself. O my God. I can't believe this. Wait 'til I tell Lisa."

Erik felt his pulse quicken, but then told himself to be calm. This was all a mistake or some sort of joke. Activating his monitor, he searched for the site page. When he found it, as he read each winning letter, his mouth slacked open wider and wider.

"I don't believe it," he mumbled.

"I told you I was lucky! Didn't I tell you I was lucky?"

"Yes you did," he replied without thinking. "It says here that there were two winners. How is that possible? There's not that many people on the planet."

"Most folks buy more than one ticket," Seth explained. "I got a cousin who buys ten."

"Ten? That's a lot of money," he frowned, calculating the cost at $5 per ticket.

"Yeah, well, he's got it so he can spend it."

Erik closed his mouth though still struggling to understand the fact that he had actually won something. Suddenly Tone's piercing eyes, angelic face, and dazzling body crystalized and he worried about their first date. Then the logical side took over and he relaxed as he realized he would be gone for a day or two at the most. No big deal. Lots of people had won the lottery and they all had a great time.

"How do I redeem this thing?"

"You gotta go down to the main lottery branch in town and they'll verify the winning number. Do it before you forget. And remember, you can take someone else with you. Think about it." He paused only a moment. "Didn't I tell you things were looking up for you?"

"Yes," he said, "you did. Thank you."

"Any time my friend. Gotta go. Gotta tell Lisa the great news."

Erik distractedly listened and then realized Seth had already ended the call. Folding the ticket, he stuffed it in his pocket then walked over to the TV screen, picking up the remote on the way. Despite the voice controls inherent within the TV, Erik preferred the old technology of a hand held remote to turn it on before flicking through the various screens until he came to the search screen. Yet he wasn't above voice commands when he was in a hurry.

"Voice recognition."

"Yes, Erik?" a sexy woman's voice answered.

"I want directions to Time Travel Incorporated in Corydon, Indiana."

"Yes, Erik. Here they are. Would you like me to print them for you or transfer them to your phone?"

"Not yet." He studied the map for a moment figuring the destination was a half mile or so away. "OK. You can send them to my phone."

"Yes, Erik. They are now on your phone. Is there anything else I can help you with?"

"No. Sleep."

The screen went blank and he punched the off button. Jabbing a hand into his pocket, he felt the ticket once more before heading out to claim his prize.

Chapter 2

July, Anno Domini Lord 793
Kaupang in Skiringssal

Having told my master of a desire to write my tale of woe, he laughed but indulged my need and allowed me use of ink and parchment for which I am eternally grateful, though my gratitude is poor barter for my freedom.

I write this in the Latin script so that I may give voice to my pain and at the same time prevent the heathens from knowing my words.

My name is Pearson. I have already recounted the causes for my present condition and see no need to relive that dreadful day a little more than a month past. Has it been only that long? It seems a lifetime ago that I lost my true and spiritual family. My sadness was then made greater when we arrived at this God-forsaken town and I was made to stand in public while strangers with no concern for human decency bid on the worth of my wretched life.

I watched in despair as my spiritual brothers were led away to their various fates. Brother Hugh, the most gifted of us in the knowledge of grains and seasons, commanded a large bid when it was learned that he had farming skills, though he was nearly not so fortunate as he did not understand the barbarian's tongue causing the savage to threaten to kill him. I know this only because the stranger who joined himself with these heathens speaks the tongue of the Holy Church, though he speaks it roughly.

Once Brother Hugh's fate was determined, bidding on the soul and flesh of man continued. Brother Nyle caused a flurry in bids when discovered he was an excellent cook. And in truth he was, for though I am well fed, no one cooks like he did. He was bought by the Ynglinga and now rules their kitchens.

Other Brothers were not so fortunate. Brother Wyne, whose skills as a scriptorium illuminator were without equal was sold off as a mere farm hand. I trembled thinking of those hands that once illuminated the words of God were now condemned to scraping away the thorns and thistles of Adam's sin. The few remaining Brothers were sold in quick succession to farms and houses days away in travel.

God gave me mercy when I was asked if I had any skills. I replied that I was just learning to farm and was a reasonably good cook, but that I could read and write in both Latin and my native tongue. Suddenly my worth as a slave declined for many grumbled I was too thin and lacked the muscle for hard work. Some ignored me as a waste of money.

My anxiety mounted as I knew slaves without value were disposed of. But by God's grace, Harek Halvarson, a wealthy trade merchant, took pity on me and bought me.

Since that time, I have done my best to earn his trust, remembering Joseph was a prisoner for thirteen years before God rescued him. I pray God delivers me far sooner than that.

Still, I praise God that He has put me with a man whose intelligence and business acumen is without equal in this brutish town. They call it the Kaupang in Skiringssal. Skiringssal is where the great hall lies, the home of the chieftain of the Ynglinga. His name is Halfdan. It is he who is responsible for my present circumstances.

There are over 200 residents in Kaupang, each engaged in some sort of trade like butchers or blacksmith or decorating metalwork or glass beads and more. Harek Halvarson, my master, is a glass bead crafter, a man of exceptional talent. His glass beads are in much demand for jewelry.

I am indebted to him for the relatively peaceful life I now experience. I serve as his secretary and bookkeeper, keeping track of his wealth and possessions, for he is a wealthy and meticulous man, which is so at odds with the rest of the barbarians here.

Though a slave, I am allowed free movement though I prefer to remain at the home, a large longhouse to the north of Kaupang, though not as grand as the hall at Skiringssal as he likes to remind me, but big enough for his family, slaves and animals.

I confess that after the serene silence of Lindisfarne, I cannot get used to the madness and noise of this house or these people. And privacy. It's as though these people thrive on living on top of each other. I miss the calmness, the time of meditation, the Breviary. I miss the holiness of our purpose, the daily joy of worshiping the one true God. These filthy pagans and their false gods are nothing more than children of Baal. I would escape if I could, but to where?

Still, today I make myself a promise. Should God grant me opportunity, I will escape this prison and return to the sanctity of the Mother Church.

It took several false starts before Erik finally decided to call Tone. He was thankful when he received her voice mail and chuckled when the recording telling him to leave a message was in Old Norse

"Hi Tone. This is…" He hesitated as he pondered what to call himself. Doctor Jonson sounded much too formal, especially if he was looking to go out with her. "Erik. I know you're busy. So when you get a chance, feel free to call me back."

He had no sooner disconnected when his phone rang.

"Hi Erik," Tone said. "I was wondering if you were ever going to call."

"I wasn't sure when a good time would be," he replied, wondering how unconvincing his excuse sounded.

"I was just getting ready to go out the door."

"Oh, sorry," he said.

"Don't be. I'm glad you called. When I hadn't heard from you for a couple of days, I thought maybe you had changed your mind."

Change my mind? You kidding me? Don't confuse ugly with stupid. "I, uh, had to get some last minutes things squared away," he lied. "If you need to go, I won't keep you."

"I do need to go, but I wanted to say why don't you come over to my place on Sunday and I'll fix us dinner."

"Are you sure? You're a college student making ends meet." He felt a twinge of guilt as soon as he said it. Here he was, an older college professor looking to date a young college student, the quintessential example of a manther... a male cougar.

"I'm not that poor," she laughed.

There it was again, that disarming laugh he found so appealing. "Then your place it is. What should I bring?"

"Some wine?"

"I can do that. Red or white?"

"Red, though I am partial to mead."

"Mead it is," he confidently replied, wondering where he was going to find it. He'd probably have to go into Louisville.

"See you Sunday then."

"Wait," he interrupted. "Where do you live?"

"245 Lemmon Street, apartment G."

"Got it."

"See you then," she said followed by the silence of disconnection.

Erik felt his heart skip and inhaled a slow calming breath before walking into the bedroom to stand before the full length mirror by his wardrobe cabinet. He stood studying himself, more critically this time. Sure he had spent time in front of the mirror ensuring he was properly dressed and checking himself out before he emerged into public. That's what most people do.

But now? Now he had a beautiful coed wanting to date him.

Staring at himself, he wondered what was so fascinating that would cause a very attractive woman seventeen years younger than he to want to spend time with him. He leaned forward to scrutinize his face. He wasn't what he considered handsome. He wasn't ugly, just average. His hair was thick and reddish blond, curling over his ears, ending above his shoulders.

He stood back to evaluate the rest of his body. He was taller than some and shorter than others, being a little over six feet tall, which again, to his mind, was average. However, there was one thing that he was proud of and that was his fitness. He exercised every day, if not at the Dojo then at the gym. He wasn't muscular in a body builder sort of way, but he was muscular with symmetry and balance, well defined and strong muscles. Further, he was confident in his ability to defend himself, especially after all the years of martial arts.

Stepping back, he gave one last look at himself and shook his head. "Who am I kidding? Wake up Erik. She's seventeen years younger than you. She's a babe. You know what's going to happen. Someone her age and better looking is going to come along and spoil all your fun, not to mention your vanity taking a huge hit when Mister Right snatches her

away.   Wake up and smell the coffee.   You're boring.
Remember?"

Heaving a wistful sigh, he headed to the living room and
picked up his guitar, playing diminished arpeggios and letting
his mood pour out into the music.

That was two days ago.   Last night, he was surprised
when she called.   They had talked for over an hour.   By the
time the conversation ended, Erik was more than captivated
by her.   Infatuation?   He chastised himself for acting like
some teenager in love.   Yet he couldn't deny his emotional
response to Tone, so different from Linda.

Linda was obsessed with two things: her career and her
looks.   When she wasn't home berating him for his dead end
job, she was either at the office or at the gym holding age at
bay so she could participate in the three P's, all the while
flaunting herself in the latest fashions.   He had to admit she
looked great for a 42 year old, better than most of the women
half her age.

But beauty had its limits.   While she was pleased that he
was physically fit, she didn't like his choice of clothes.
'Archaic Preppy' she called it.   For him, his clothes were
comfortable.   Style was over-rated.   Besides, given enough
time, his clothing would be back in style.

Yet her objection to his choice of clothing was merely a
manifestation of a deeper rooted problem.   She found
numerous other deficient areas in his life: his music, his
books, his career, his friends, the way he organized and
folded his socks, and what was so damned fascinating about
studying people who had been dead for over a thousand
years?   The most hurtful accusation was that he was boring,
usually said with a sneer.

Despite his best efforts, he finally accepted that it was
over, especially when she announced that she was leaving.
She was moving up the corporate ladder while he was

content where he was. They had parted without rancor, at least on his part. She moved out to an expensive high rise in Louisville. Last he heard, she had been promoted to some VP position.

So why was he so nervous now, standing outside the door to Tone's apartment?

Part of him wondered if he was setting himself up for failure. After all, his track record for relationships was rather dismal. But it wasn't all bad. Yes, he was divorced and just lost his job. Other than that, life was wonderful.

With a calming sigh, he pressed the door buzzer.

"You are so funny," Tone said, opening the door. She was dressed in tan hiking shorts, sandals, and a sleeveless brown button up blouse that fit snugly across her chest, not so subtly revealing that she wore nothing underneath. "I saw you on the vid screen in the kitchen. You stood there like you weren't sure you wanted to be here." She stepped aside to let him in.

"I'm feeling a little awkward," he admitted, stepping inside. Glancing around, he noticed the apartment was clean, tidy and organized.

"Why?"

"Still wondering why me?" he said, handing her two bottles of mead. "I had them in the frig so they'd be cold."

"Come into the kitchen while I get two glasses. I hope you like Chinese," she chuckled, "because I ordered delivery."

"Chinese is perfect," he replied, following her past the couch in the living room.

The apartment was small, a one-bedroom affair with a living room/dining room combination and a small kitchen. Yet the furnishings were not cheap.

She noticed him looking at the dining room table. "My folks are pretty well off. I brought some furniture from home. Though I won't accept any help with my education, I'm not above stealing some stuff from home." She flashed a smile and handed him the corkscrew. "Open the mead."

While Erik tore the foil from the bottle's neck, she said, "I told you before 'why you.' I was attracted to you from the first day of the first class. But you were married and so I just kept my interest to myself. Then when I heard you got divorced, I thought perhaps there might be a chance."

"But there are so many men your age –"

"Why do you keep saying that? I told you before, men my age are too immature. You make it sound like I'm still in high school."

"Now that would be weird," he grinned.

"Yes, it would," she agreed with a smile. "You're only seventeen years older than I am, which in the age of the universe is nothing."

"Yes," he said, "but in dog years, I'd be a whole lot older."

She laughed and he was smitten.

Midway through the meal, as he watched her select a piece of stir-fry chicken with her chopsticks, he wondered if anything more would happen between them, whether she too would get bored with him.

She noticed him staring at her. "What?"

"Just wondering," he answered.

"Wondering what?"

"Wondering why?"

"Are we back to that?" she said, narrowing her gaze at him.

"I can't help it. Look at you. You're gorgeous, you're smart, you've got a phenomenal personality. You're perfect. There has to be at least ten million guys fighting for your attention." He paused and leaned forward, staring intently at her. "You're not an axe murderer are you?"

"The axe is in the closet," she deadpanned. "Sharpened it just before you got here."

"Ah," he nodded, picking up an egg roll. There was that smile and giggle again.

"That was very sweet what you just said. I'm glad you feel that way, because I think the same about you."

"Now you're being silly," he replied. "That's like comparing beauty to the beast."

"Now who's being silly?" she challenged. "Why can't I feel the same about you?"

Because no one ever has… certainly not Linda. "It's something that I'm not used to hearing, especially from gorgeous coeds."

"Coed," she repeated. "There's a term you rarely ever hear."

"I know. I suppose it is a rather archaic term. It just seems to have more substance to it than 'female' student. 'Coed' implies a sort of vitality and youth to it, whereas 'female' is simply a gender." He was about to jab his chopstick into the egg roll when he said, "Oh, I just remembered something. I won the Time Travel lottery."

"You did?" she burst, her eyes wide. "Really?"

"Yes, really. My friend Seth bought me a ticket, knowing I'd never buy one myself," he explained. "Claimed I needed some excitement in my life. I thought it a kind, but silly idea, the odds of me or anyone else winning was right on up there with aliens showing up here and offering to make us dinner."

Cupping her ear, Tone leaned over to stare in surprise at the door. "Did you hear the doorbell? I told those aliens I was ordering take out."

Grinning, Erik shrugged. "Yeah, I know. So much for that theory."

Giving him that bewitching smile, she said, "That has to be so exciting. Where and when do you want to go and when do you take the trip?"

"That's just it," he answered. "I've never thought about it."

"Never?" she questioned in feigned surprise.

"OK, maybe once or twice," he admitted. "But only as a daydream. It's not like I thought the actuality."

"So? Where do you think you might like to go?"

"Though I was initially thinking of Iceland in the early days of the land-taking, the fact that there were no towns would make our arrival more than obvious. So I thought England had towns in the 9th century and it was a time of Danish strength. So, I figured around 893 when Alfred the Great was in his prime. You and I showing up in a town wouldn't be to out of the ordinary."

"That would be so –" she began until she realized what he said. "You and I?"

"Yes," he hesitantly answered. "I thought that… maybe you might like to go with me."

"My God. Are you serious?" She leaped up and darted around the table, clapped both hands on his face and planted a firm kiss that lingered far longer than a simple 'Thank you' brush of the lips.

He felt his knees begin to quiver as the strength of her kiss poured through him. Catching his breath as she broke the kiss, he stared up into her penetrating eyes that glowed mischief and passion, her face still inches from his.

Tone pushed his chair to the side then straddled his lap. Without a word, she pressed her lips to his as he wrapped his arms around her.

Erik didn't know how long they kissed, but it fleetingly reminded him that he couldn't remember the last time he felt like this. Then logic was vanquished by the passion of their embrace. By the time they paused to remember where they were, dinner was cold and the wine warm.

Erik reached up and gently ran a finger along her cheek. He gazed into her eyes that seemed to search inside him as though looking to find hidden secrets.

She sat back, her hands on his shoulders. "Part of me wants you to spend the night."

Erik did his best to remain noncommittal while the inside of him screamed *O Please*!

"Another part of me says that we don't know enough of each other yet. Would ennui settle if the bedroom was our first stop? What do you think?"

Erik chuckled. "Hmmm. That's sort of like asking an exhausted starving tiger if he wants antelope or a good nap. He's hungry now, but a nap will make him even more hungry? The question is, will the food taste better after the nap?"

"Depends how it's cooked," she replied with an impish grin. "And then there's the delivery. It's amazing how an average meal can be made to look better with a few garnishes."

"There is absolutely nothing 'average' about you," he said, his heart dancing. "The very first time I saw you come into class, I found you intriguing."

"Intriguing? Just intriguing?"

"It was more than that, but I can't think of the right word at the moment. You were just so self-assured, not in the arrogant way of folks who think more highly of themselves, but in a calm at-peace-with-myself sort of way. Your beauty added to your allure. I found myself thinking about you."

"Did you dream about me?" she teased.

"'Fantasize' would be the better word," he grinned. "And then when I read your first paper, it was so well written that I initially thought you had plagiarized some academic research paper. I confess that I submitted the paper to the Double Check site and it came back as all original with sources sited properly. I wasn't used to such scholarship. But then the more of your work I read and the more we interacted in our classes together, the more I realized you were not normal."

Tone laughed.

"In truth, I found you much too distracting," he continued, relishing the closeness of her delicious body, "especially as my own romantic life was spiraling out of control. I thought that it wouldn't be good to get entangled in something that had no likelihood of ever happening. So I tried to put up this wall to protect myself."

"Did it work?"

"Apparently not," he smiled and looked around the apartment. "Here I am."

"So," she slyly teased, "you did fantasize about me."

"More than is proper for me to admit."

"I dreamed about you too," she said, not as an admission, but as fact. "In fact, there were days after class, I would come home, take my clothes off and um... stretch out on the bed, pretending you were there with me. It got to where you were beginning to be a distraction, especially after I found out you were divorced."

The vision of Tone naked on the bed caused Erik to be even more aroused.

"I had no idea," he said, his voice thick.

"Of course not," she replied. "I wasn't sure you'd think I was all that interesting. I figured you'd have all these educated, single, good-looking faculty ladies throwing themselves at you." Her eyes slid away then came back to peer intently at him. "So one time I followed you."

"You did?"

"Yes," she sheepishly admitted. "I waited until you got home then followed you. You were carrying a bag and it wasn't until you went to your dojo that I realized you were into martial arts, and the bag had your uniform. I stood outside the dojo windows and watched you. My God you were amazing. Your strength and power, and the way you performed your routines were beautiful to watch. I found myself mesmerized. And then the one time when you broke all those boards with punches and kicks, twirling in the air like some kung fu god. There had to be something like a hundred boards you destroyed that night."

Erik's jaw dropped. "You saw me that night?"

"By the time I thought to get a video of it, you were finished. And then you stood there as though it was no big deal. You bowed to some older gentleman and took your place by his side."

"That's Sensei Yang Lei. He owns the dojo."

"He seems nice. After that time, I came back as often as I could. It reminded me of when I used to study Tae Kwon Do."

Erik's jaw slacked open in a combination of surprise and joy that they shared a common bond. "You did?"

"I started when I was in grade school and continued up until I graduated from high school. I was working on my third degree black belt when life interrupted."

Erik cocked his head to the side, his brow furrowed.

"Up through high school," Tone explained, "my parents paid for things like that. When I graduated, it was now up to me to bear the expense. When I decided to go to college, I had to make a choice, either Tae Kwon Do or school."

"And your parents wouldn't help?"

"They would have, but I couldn't ask them to do that. It was my life now and my responsibility. I had to figure out how to balance finances and the things I wanted. So school won out. I still practice though, mostly working through forms and such." She smiled. "So when I discovered where you went, I couldn't help but want to watch you. Perhaps I'd only watch for five or ten minutes before heading off to work. But the more I watched, the more I saw how you interacted with the other students. You are ever the teacher, patient and kind. Yet you are a natural leader and the students respect you."

She giggled. "You almost saw me one time. I noticed you looking out the window when I was standing there. The sensei gentleman caught your attention and I snuck away."

"So it *was* you," he grinned. "I thought I was going crazy. I don't know why I looked out there, but I swore I saw you. But when I looked again, you weren't there. I thought it was my imagination."

"It was me," she readily conceded.

Silence settled a moment before Erik said, "You know what's one thing I love about you?"

"What?"

"You're lack of show. No games. What you see is what you get. You say what you think. I noticed that in class. You never had a problem disagreeing with others, but you always did it in such a polite way that they were almost pleased that you didn't agree with them."

"That doesn't make any sense," she laughed.

"And the way you laugh," he continued. "I love the way you laugh."

"Now you're making me self-conscious," she blushed.

"No reason to be," he said, lightly tracing the flawless skin along her cheek. "I still don't understand why me, but I'm glad it is me. I just need you to make sure this is where *you* want to be."

"I have been obsessed with you since the first time I sat in your class," she said.

"Obsession is one thing; a relationship is quite another," he said, remembering his failed marriage.

"Have you been in many, relationships?" she asked.

"Serious ones? Just two," he half smiled. "My first girlfriend in high school and then my ex."

"Where did you meet your ex?" Tone said, standing. She picked up the two wine glasses and walked into the kitchen where she poured the contents into a mason jar, tightened a lid on it and stuck it in the frig.

Looking over her shoulder at Erik's smile, she explained, "I don't like warm mead. I'll open the other bottle. Where did you meet Linda?"

"You know her name?" he said, surprised.

"Yes, Doctor Jonsson," she replied, flicking her eyebrows. "I did a little research. But you were telling me about Linda."

"Not much to tell. We met in college. She was very pretty and I was surprised she might be interested in a quiet guy like me."

"Sounds familiar," she teased, pulling the cork out of the mead bottle. "Then what happened?"

"We dated," he shrugged, "and decided to get married after we graduated from college. While I went to grad school and then the PhD, she worked in the corporate world, moving up the proverbial ladder."

"When did things start to go wrong?" She handed him a glass of cold mead.

Erik tilted his head to gaze at her. "Why are you so interested in my past?"

"If we're going to have a meaningful relationship, I need to know all about you." She sipped her mead and sat down across from him.

"Well what about you? How many relationships have you had?"

53

"None," she sighed. "Most of the guys I dated were interested in one thing. Those who weren't were obsessed with role-playing games or virtual dating, which got kinkier than I was willing to accept."

"How can you virtually date?" he frowned.

"You'd be surprised." She shook her head and rolled her eyes. "I guess for some folks, it's more enjoyable to vicariously live out fantasies in the virtual world. For someone who is socially awkward or insecure about himself, the virtual world lets him venture out in ways he can't in real life."

"How can you have a meaningful relationship that's virtual? By definition it's not real."

"In many ways, it is," she countered. "They still talk in their virtual world. They develop friendships and relationships. They even have virtual sex."

Erik's jaw dropped. "How can you have virtual sex?"

"Some people like to watch," she pointed out.

"I suppose so," he said, unconvinced. "That's not what I prefer."

"Nor I," she agreed then changed the subject. "By the way, when is our trip?"

"Not for another couple of months."

"So," she smiled coyly at him. "We're going back to 893 to see King Alfred where?"

"Probably London. It's large enough that we shouldn't be noticed."

"Guess I better brush up on my Old English," she said then winked. "I'll probably need a tutor."

"I know someone who can help you."

"Is he available for two months?"

"I heard his schedule just got cleared for the foreseeable future."

Tone's lips tightened. "How can they just let you go like that? I thought when you had tenure you were protected from things like that."

"My choice of life pursuit is a small and dwindling interest. So few care about the past that even fewer know about it. My enrollment numbers dropped to where they said they couldn't justify my classes anymore. Logically I can see their point. It doesn't mean I have to like it."

"That's because the virtual world has taken over," she said. "Everyone is into role playing. Whole industries are devoted to role playing. No one lives in the real world anymore."

"Which sort of begs the question of what do we do when we get back?" he pointed out. "I'm going to have to look for a job. Sensei Lei has offered me a position at the dojo." He sighed and shook his head. "While the thought is nice, it seems such a waste of my education. All those years studying for the PhD so I can teach little kids how to kick and punch." He gazed affectionately at her. "And what about you? Do you really want to be a docent somewhere giving tours to a group of half-interested folks whose numbers decline to the point where they let you go so they can tear down the site to make way for a virtual building?"

"You sound so pessimistic," she remarked.

"More like realistic. Once we get back, real life intrudes and we'll need to find something meaningful to do."

"Who knows what the future holds," she offered, "but I like the way you say 'we,' as in being together."

"You may feel differently later," he warned. "Remember, my ex said I was boring."

"Did she ever watch you break a hundred boards with your hands and feet?"

"She never came to the dojo or watched my competitions," he answered.

"Never?"

"Never."

"Why not?"

"Didn't interest her. She said it was too... what was the word she used? Brutish, yes that's the word. Too brutish. All these people punching and kicking."

Tone stared at him and frowned. "It is obvious, to me at least, that she knew nothing about you. When I watched you, it was like you were in a ballet, so graceful."

Erik shrugged. "Somewhat moot now. Thankfully. She has her life and I have mine."

"Yes," she smiled. "And in two months, we're going to go back in time to London, England. Just imagine how jealous she'll be once she finds out."

"She won't be jealous at all... of where or when we're going. She'll say it was a dumb choice. But," he paused with a knowing grin, "she will be jealous when she sees the gorgeous cover-girl who's going with me."

Tone gave him a self-conscious smile. "You say the sweetest things." She sipped her mead then placed the glass on the table. "Actually, I do know what the future holds."

"You do?" he said, more than curious as she stood, came around the table and took his wine glass and placed it on the table.

Straddling his lap, she sat and rested her hands on his shoulders. "I predict a kiss is in our future." She leaned in and delivered a deep kiss, her tongue exploring his mouth.

Erik's knees again began to quiver.

After a long sensuous kiss, she pulled back and studied his face.

"I saw you staring at my chest this evening," she teased.

"Guilty as charged," he huskily replied. "How could I not? You're stunning."

"I now foresee," she said, taking his hands and placing them on her breasts, "that you will unbutton my blouse."

Sucking in a deep breath, he paused then withdrew his hands to slowly release the buttons, starting at the bottom. When the last button was free, he pulled the blouse open and pushed it off her shoulders.

His eyes lingered on her perfectly shaped firm breasts, the nipples like small cones. His hands went to where his eyes lingered.

Leaning forward, she whispered in his ear. "The future is in the bedroom."

Chapter 3

The man was young, late 30's, impeccably dressed in a three piece gray pin-striped suit with darker gray shirt and pink tie. He stood at the window, his arms folded as he stared out at the Louisville skyline. The day was a brilliant sunny spring day with a cloudless sky and he studied the way the buildings seemed cleaner, fresh.

Standing before his desk, a woman in a no nonsense business suit of dark blue offset with blue and white shoes with low practical heels, held a folder in her hands. She was an attractive 40-year old brunette and the suit was fashionably cut with wide lapels. The white button up blouse had a wide collar that draped over the lapels. Beside her, a man in a lab technician coat fiddled with cleaning his glasses, waiting for the man at the window to say something. In the silence, he distractedly focused on the name plate carved from cocobolo wood: Jakob Cooper.

Still gazing out the window, Cooper said, "Where does he want to go?"

"Ninth century England," the woman replied

"What's the problem, Meredith?"

"The earliest we've sent someone back in time was to the late 16th century," the technician interrupted, putting his glasses on.

"We've been lucky so far," Meredith said. "Everyone up to now, except for that one weirdo wanting to go back and watch the public executions during the French Revolution, has only wanted to go back a max of two hundred years.

"So I ask again, what's the problem?"

"The machine still has quirks that we're still working on," the technician explained. "In tests, we've been consistently accurate with both time and location back to the mid-1500s. Beyond that, we're running into problems with either the time or the location out of whack."

"By 'out of whack' you mean what?" Cooper asked, still gazing out the window.

The technician shot a glance at Meredith who gave him a quick tick of the head telling him to continue.

With a nervous breath, the technician said, "Say someone wants to go to Machu Picchu in the 14th century. Our capabilities so far will get him to Peru, but not necessarily the Cuzco Region or the 14th century."

Cooper lifted a hand to stroke the edges of his goatee, tilting his head as if staring at some distant object. "So you're telling me that this gentleman wants to go back even earlier."

"Yes, sir. Specifically, he wants to go to London in 893."

"London," Cooper repeated, twisting his head to look over his shoulder, "As in England in the 9th century. Why?"

"He wants to see King Alfred the Great."

"I see." Cooper turned back to gaze out the window. The sun warmed the room despite the shaded windows. "And you're telling me that we can't guarantee he will end up where he wants to go."

"Yes."

"Recommendation?"

"Obviously we can't let this get out," Meredith said, stating the obvious. "The damage would be catastrophic. Our ads tout 'When in Rome, do like the Romans do.' Fortunately no one wants to go back to Rome, especially after we inform them they need to speak Latin. But this case is different. The man's a medieval Norse and Anglo-Saxon expert and speaks the lingo."

Cooper turned around and his stare narrowed on the two standing on the other side of the desk. "We certainly can't tell him 'No' can we?"

"We've told others 'No,' before," Meredith pointed out.

"Why?" he asked, locking his dark brown eyes in an intense stare at her.

Meredith thought for a moment then said, "Usually because they wanted to witness a battle or other dangerous event, like the French Revolution weirdo."

"Bingo.   This man's request is neither of those. Besides," Cooper replied through tight lips as his anger mounted, "the whole world knows he won the lottery. They're waiting for his story. How do we tell them that we can't send him back 1000 years because you can't get that goddamned machine to work?"

"We're working on it," the technician whimpered.

"This is worse than a marketing nightmare," Cooper exploded. "This is a disaster."

Meredith mused, unaffected by the outburst. "Actually... if we do this right, we can use this to our advantage."

"How?"

"We simply tout the limitations of the machine at the moment. We pull the Roman ads and shift the campaigns to recent past travelers, pull up a few of the more memorable ones, expounding the adventure of their travels. Make it sensual and exiting. We emphasize the 'now' of their adventures. We run those for a couple of months then we subtly infuse the idea that one can only go so far back in time. Today it's 1600... With TTI, will tomorrow bring 1500 or 1400? With TTI the past is tomorrow."

Cooper's scowl softened. "That's not bad. I like it." He spread his hands like an advertising banner. "With TTI, the past is tomorrow. Excellent. Let's run with it."

"What about this Jonsson fellow," the technician interrupted.

Cooper shifted a glance at Meredith who paused for only a moment then smiled with evil intent.

"We go ahead and send him back like he wants."

"But there's a greater chance it won't work," the technician sputtered.

"That's fine," she said with cold determination. "If it works, great. If it doesn't, we leave him wherever he is and say he escaped and eluded our safety measures."

"But Mister Cooper, he could alter time," the technician nervously fretted.

"We prevent that by ensuring he doesn't have the opportunity," she asserted.

"How are we going to do that?" he complained.

"You let me worry about that," she coldly retorted. "You just make sure that machine works like it's supposed to."

"I don't like it," he said with nervous anxiety.

"You don't have to like it," she said. "Your job is to take care of the machine. I suggest you do so."

"But he's got a companion with him," he pointed out.

"So?" She cocked an eyebrow at him intimating the answer was obvious.

"But you can't —"

Still by the window, Cooper held up his hand and the technician stopped. "You've got your marching orders."

The technician scowled but kept his mouth shut. Obediently turning around, he headed for the door and was soon on his way back to the lab.

"What's your idea, Meredith?" Cooper said.

"Delayed explosion capsule," she said. "We tell them it's a tracking pill used as a precautionary measure. We make them swallow it before the trip, set it for the day after the trip ends. They don't return; it explodes; they're dead. Problem solved. They come back; we simply remotely deactivate the pills and no one is the wiser. The pill will eventually pass through their systems a day or two later.

The corners of his mouth curved into a smile. "I like your solution. Make it happen."

From the time of his first visit to her apartment, Erik and Tone spent all their free time together. Evenings were divided between his place and hers, eventually settling on his place as it was bigger and the bed larger.

Erik did his best to appear the impartial professor during the last few weeks of classes, but it was difficult when his attention was riveted on the divine goddess who sat in the front row reading Norse tales aloud while he remembered the previous evening's passionate lovemaking session.

He had never experienced it before. Yes, making love to Linda had been exciting… at first. Then it became routine then an obligation then not at all. Sad to say, he didn't miss the dwindling intimacy with her. What had once been intimate encounters became sessions for her ridicule and the listing of his faults.

Then came the news that she was seeing someone else. Was it a bombshell? Not really. Erik had long suspected she was dabbling outside the marriage. The funny thing was that it was a relief as it accelerated the divorce process. Even now he wondered why he had hung on for so long, sort of like standing on the bridge of the Titanic as she's nose diving into the frigid waters, proclaiming that it will all get better if we just give it some more time.

Then there was Tone.

He chuckled that it supposedly wasn't fair to compare, but how could he not? But, to be honest, it's not like he spent much time thinking about Linda. Except for the time he and Tone had gone to Louisville to buy mead. Of all the places to bump into the ex, the wine shop was the last place Erik expected to run into her.

Linda saw them first and made a beeline to intercept them as they ambled down the aisle.

"Well what a surprise," she said with a condescending smile. "Look who's here, and with the neighbor's daughter."

Initially caught by surprise, Tone frowned at her then turned to Erik, catching the flash of anger in his eyes.

Tone twisted her head to look at her and politely asked, "You are?"

"I had the misfortune of being married to him once," Linda said with biting arrogance.

Tone shifted around to Erik and in mock horror said, "This is *the* Linda? My God, you poor man. I thought you said she was your age." She turned back to Linda. "You may want to think about quitting drinking. Too much can really affect the way one looks, especially at your age. Did you not get any sleep last night?"

Startled, Linda scowled. "At least I'm not dating some high schooler."

"Thank you," Tone grinned. "I'm actually twenty-five, which still makes me less than half your age. You know, once you hit fifty, a woman's body really begins to change. When those once perky boobs start sagging it becomes painfully obvious that you're over the hill. And then the flabby arms… another sign of too much booze and partying, trying to act and look like she was my age." Tone smiled sweetly at her.

Linda's nostrils flared and she struggled with a retort when she heard Erik snort a laugh. "You think that's funny?"

Erik paused for just a beat. "Actually I do. And she's right. You may want to think about joining a fitness club or something."

"I'll have you know I've got a membership at the exclusive Imperial Gym," she retorted.

"You ought to start using the weights and treadmills instead of just watching," Tone suggested.

Linda's lips tightened and she half turned to walk away when she stopped. "I heard you won the Time Travel lottery."

"Yes, I did."

"Where are you going?"

"The year 893 CE," Tone answered for him, slipping an arm around his.

"What's so fascinating about 893?" Linda sniffed in disdain.

Tone gazed up at Erik and switched into Old Norse. "This woman's crazy."

Erik grinned, replying, "That she is. Just imagine being married to her."

"You poor man. This is fun. We can talk about her and she hasn't a clue about what we're saying. I can call her a fat cow and she'd never know."

"You can call her more than that," Erik readily agreed.

"Oh how cute," Linda sneered. "You have a private language."

"It's called Old Norse," Tone corrected her. "You were married to him once. I'm surprised you didn't know that. Apparently your job was more important than your marriage."

"It wasn't much of a marriage to begin with," Linda snipped.

"That's what he said," Tone nodded. "He told me that you were too busy working your way to the top to work on a marriage."

"There was nothing to work on," she shot back. "So I got rid of the useless baggage and worked hard to get where I am."

"I'm sure you've worked hard. It's obvious from the way you look that you didn't sleep your way to get where you are."

Linda stiffened, a snarl curling a corner of her lips.

Tugging Erik's arm, Tone gazed up at him. "Babe, let's go get our mead." As she led him away, she spoke loud enough for Linda to hear. "How could you stand being married to her? She's boring."

What Erik remembered most about the interaction was the look on Linda's face when they walked away. It was a look of defeat, of a sudden realization that her ex was far happier than she was.

"That was fun," Tone grinned, retrieving several bottles of mead.

Erik simply shook his head and smiled, once again wondering what she saw in him.

Later that evening, after the dinner dishes had been cleaned and put away, Erik serenaded her with his guitar as she sat enraptured listening to his expert renditions of compositions by Tárrega, Sor and Albéniz.

"You play so beautifully, with such soulful expression," she complimented him.

"It's easy to do when you have someone who appreciates good music."

"Unlike a certain person whose name won't be mentioned," she said with a smile as she stood. Gently taking the guitar from him, she placed it on the stand then straddled his lap. Tenderly placing both hands on his cheeks, she leaned in and kissed him, deeply. Then leaning back, she unbuttoned his shirt and tugged it off his shoulders and arms, dropping it to the floor. She then unbuttoned her blouse and let it drop on top of his shirt.

Letting his eyes devour her bare breasts for a lingering moment, she pressed her body against his, luxuriating in the sensation of flesh against flesh as she slowly gyrated against him. Feeling his arousal and surging desire, she pressed her lips against his, her hands roaming his head and back then down to the belt securing his pants.

For the next two hours, they made use of the dining table, the couch, the kitchen counter and the doorway to the bedroom. By the time their passion was spent, they snuggled in the middle of the living room on a thick Flokati rug that Erik had yanked out of the closet.

With exquisite contentment, Erik vacantly stared at the ceiling fan above them as the blades lazily spun, his mind reliving the past hours. Whatever stress there was in his life was forgotten in the warmth and softness of the stunning beauty curled against him.

"You are far and away the most exciting thing that has ever happened to me," he said. "Sometimes I need to pinch myself to make sure this isn't all a dream, a fantasy."

Tone snuggled closer, her arm draped over his chest. "I feel the same way."

"I know you don't like me saying it, but I still have to wonder why me?"

Tone raised her head to gaze affectionately into his eyes. "Listen Mister, I've dreamed about being with you from the moment I first sat in your Anglo-Saxon History class. I had lust-at-first-sight. You were so hot."

Erik smirked. "Not a word I would think of to describe me."

"And the way you moved around the front of the class, hopping down from the one-step platform then stepping back up, never looking where you were stepping. You were so confident, so self-assured."

Erik scooched over onto his side, using an elbow to help prop his head up. He traced the perfect skin of his lover across the shoulder then down to the full curves of her breasts then back up along her jaw and cheeks, an act of awe and worship.

"Speaking of hot," he grinned. "The moment you stepped into my class, I prayed I would see you again."

"And I ended up taking every class you taught," she laughed. "And you still had no clue that I was hot for you?"

"I just figured you were looking to major in Nordic studies, which quite naturally thrilled me. Never once did I expect to end up like this." His gaze traveled her naked body.

"I dreamed it would," she cooed. "Can you... will you be happy with me?"

"Good God," he answered. "How could I not?"

She tenderly placed a palm on his cheek and peered intently into his eyes. "I'm in love with you. I've never told that to anyone before... well, I have to my parents, but they don't count. I'm in love with you Professor Jonsson."

Erik's heart quickened and raw emotion surged within, causing a sudden fear. He was infatuated, but was that love? When he said the word, he wanted to mean it. He had used it before, with Linda, and the truth was that he had never *loved* her. Sure, they had told each other "I love you," but neither had truly understood the word, the depth of responsibility and commitment. Their marriage was more of a business arrangement, roommates with benefits. Once Linda's career took off, she no longer saw the benefit of the arrangement. He then saw the disappointment in Tone's eyes.

"What?"

"I told you that I love you. I was hoping you felt the same."

Erik paused before softly saying, "I'm afraid. I've used that word before, with Linda, and it's obvious that I didn't know what it meant."

"Or that you said it but really didn't mean it."

"That's just it," he agreed. "I vowed that the next time I used the word, I would know what it meant and mean it."

"Do you feel the same way about me that you did for Linda?"

"Good God not even close," he sniffed. "Yes, I was happy that I was going to be married. All my friends were doing it and so I would now fit in. But then life settled into an almost monotonous routine." He focused his gaze upon her. It was a look of wonder mixed with joy.

"But with you... I'm a man obsessed. You occupy my every thought. I live and breathe you. I ache when we're apart. I can't get enough of you. Something simple like watching you walk across the floor to get something from the fridge fills me with overwhelming pride and adoration. I'm more than infatuated. You possess me. You have become my soul."

A sly smile curled her lips. "That sounds like love to me."

Erik inhaled a slow breath and nodded. "It does to me too." Then in a release of epiphany, he accepted it. "It's true, Tone Thorgilsdottir. I am madly in love with you. I am head over heels in love with you. You are the woman I dreamed about, my perfect partner and lover. I just never thought Miss Perfect existed."

"And here I am," she laughed.

"Yes," he cooed, his fingers lightly caressing her cheek. "Here you are. If this is all a dream, may I never wake up."

When graduation arrived, Erik met her parents who either didn't notice the intimate relationship their daughter had with the older professor or chose to ignore it. True to Tone's word, they left shortly after the ceremonies, taking time to snap a few pics. Watching them get into the rental car and drive off, Erik turned to Tone, still dressed in her graduation robe.

"They didn't stay very long," he said, disappointed at her parents' cavalier attitude about her accomplishment.

"I've three older sisters, remember? They all graduated on time and they're working in viable fields. Two are in technology and one is in HR. Me? I majored in Old Norse. You can imagine their disappointment."

"You're still their daughter," he mumbled.

"That may be true, but they're busy in their own little worlds." She slipped an arm around his. "Let me change and then get something to eat. I'm starving."

"How about some pizza at Shirley's? If Lisa's working, Seth will probably be there."

"Pizza sounds wonderful."

As they ambled back to Erik's place, arm in arm, Tone noticed the overt grins of students and the frowns of disapproval from some of the faculty and administration. She was about to comment when Erik spoke.

"Screw 'em. They're just jealous because I'm with a goddess."

"There you go again," she said, hugging his arm tighter. "I need to send a thank-you card to Linda for giving you to me."

"I'll sign it," he chuckled.

She laughed and he couldn't help but feel joy in the sound of her voice, especially in laughter. More than once, he had to pinch himself at the change in his fortune. Perhaps Seth was right. Life was improving.

The time after graduation was even better, especially in the bedroom. Tone was almost insatiable and he found his long dormant passions finally given free rein. He chuckled thinking of some of the long nights of pleasure then to finally drift off to sleep as dawn emerged. They slept spooned together, waking in time for her to get ready for work while he prepared brunch and a snack for her to take to work.

What surprised, though pleased him was his continual distraction, obsession and infatuation with her. Nothing else was important, even that he had no job yet. The severance package would hold him until the end of the year, plenty of time to find something. In the meantime, Tone was his world.

What thrilled him was the reciprocal intensity of emotion, for Tone poured herself inside him. So unlike Linda who eschewed any public display of affection or association, Tone couldn't keep her hands off him, hugging an arm, or walking hand in hand, or arms around each other as she slipped a hand into his back pocket and squeezed his butt as they walked.

Even Sensei Lei noticed the difference.

"I see you have found peace with your situation," he said with a wise smile.

"I'm in love," Erik replied.

"Ah," Lei grinned. "Love has a tendency to overpower even the sanest man. Is that the young, ah... woman I've seen here a few times?"

"Yes," he said, making no effort to hide his joy.

Lei nodded, smiled and said nothing. Erik was happy and that was all that mattered.

On his last day at the university, while Tone was at work, Erik cleaned out his office, pausing one last time in the doorway. As he took in the clean desk, the empty bookshelves and the bare walls, he was surprised that he wasn't as wistful as he expected. The office held no special memories. Though the familiarity had bred comfort, many others had occupied it before he came along, and many more would sit behind the desk in the future, each claiming the space as his or her own for a time.

Time.

Time was the one great specter hovering over mankind's shoulder that few gave notice to, except for old people. They were keenly aware of time, but made little accommodation for it. Those healthy enough to postpone the inevitable usually spent their lives living vicariously through the daily lives of their grandchildren.

Time.

Now that he had Tone, time seemed to speed up. Their time together always went too quickly. Would it change when they had been together for years? Would she become bored with him? Erik vowed then that he would do everything in his power to please her.

He smiled at the memory of two nights ago. They were sitting on the couch munching on caramel popcorn, both of them cross-legged facing each other when she let slip the word 'married.' It had surprised him and he commented on it.

"You realize what you just said?"

"What?"

"You said 'after we're married.'"

Tone paused and peered intently at him. "Yes. I did. What do you think about it?"

"Is this a proposal?" he asked with a smile.

"I should be on my knees, shouldn't I?" she replied with mock worry.

"You can be on your knees later," he said with a wink.

"I look forward to it," she said with a leering grin then turned serious. "You haven't answered the question."

"What do I think?" Erik repeated. "I think I would be deliriously happy married to you. I told you I love you. You are Odin's Valkyrie who has given me life. I'm head over heels in love with you. There is no one on this earth I'd rather spend the rest of my life with. Does that answer your question?"

"I'll take that as a 'yes,'" she grinned. "Odin's Valkyrie... I like that."

"You are," he sighed meaningfully. "You have infused such a passion for life in me again. What was missing in my life was you... Odin's Valkyrie... the beautiful creature who has the power over life and death. In this case, you have given me life. The question is... now that you've given me life, are you sure I'm the one you want to spend the rest of your life with?"

"I was sure of that a long time ago," she answered. "When I discovered you had divorced and were free again, I vowed to make you mine."

"How could you be so sure?" he frowned

"I just was," she shrugged. Flicking a piece of popcorn at him, she said, "When?"

"How about as soon as we get back from the time travel trip?"

"How about now?"

"We leave for England in less than five days. There's no time to do a proper wedding unless you want to go to a JP."

"I'm OK with that."

Erik studied her expression to see if she was teasing. "You don't want a big fancy wedding with cake and decorations and people throwing rice at you?"

"Actually, no I don't. I detest weddings from the perspective of wastes of expense and time. And then there's the divorce rate that makes all that cost of grand weddings seem so absurd. People go from "I'll love you to the end of time' to 'You're dead to me.' I'd rather go to a JP and get it done. No muss no fuss."

"Speaking of divorce," he softly said.

"I'm sorry. I didn't mean to bring that up." She scooted closer so their knees touched then placed a hand on his cheek.

"It's not a touchy subject. It's just that I am divorced, so my record of successful marriage is zero and one."

"But we're different," she soothed. "I know in my heart we are. You just chose the wrong person the first time."

"You would have been eight years old the first time I got married. I think they have laws against that."

"You should have waited," she stated.

"I didn't know you existed until you showed up that first day of class."

"And it was love at first sight," she melodramatically sighed, folding her hands.

"I suppose it was, now that I think about it."

"So? JP?"

"Is that what you want?"

"Is that what *we* want," she corrected. "We're a team now. We do things together. We make decisions together. I'll do whatever you want to do."

"I feel the same way. A JP is fine with me."

"Now?"

Erik laughed and nodded. "Now would be wonderful."

While Tone changed, Erik used the TV to find the nearest Justice of the Peace only to discover the office was closed until Monday. Additionally they were required to both get blood tests.

"Blood test," Tone complained.

"That's to prove we're not related," he joked. "How about we wait until we get back? We can do all the preliminary work and as soon as we get back, we tie the knot."

"I suppose," she replied, disappointed before seeing the gleam in his eyes. "What?"

"How about we get married in England?"

"How?"

"We're there for a day, right?"

"Yes," she replied, eyes bright with excitement.

"We find a priest and we get married. By the time we get back, we'll have been married for over a thousand years."

Tone burst a laugh and threw her arms around him. "I love that idea. No one else can make the same claim."

"We'll still need to make it legal here," he reminded her.

"I'm OK with that," she agreed. "This will be fun."

"I know it will," he replied. "We're going to have the most amazing life together."

"What's today?" she asked.

"Friday the thirteenth, a very lucky day," he grinned.

She peered up at him, her eyes filled with devotion. "Today is a special day. Today is the day that we declared our eternal love for each other. We must always remember this day, June 13th, 2031."

That was two days ago. Now as he stood in the doorway of what was no longer his office, his heart thumped with joy. In a few days, he and Tone would be in England in the year 893 CE. He laughed at the thought of having King Alfred act as his best man.

Casting one last look at the empty room, he turned away to begin a new adventure with Tone.

Erik and Tone sat in the pre-Travel room waiting for someone to come brief them.

"Nervous?" she asked him.

"Yes and no," he answered. "Yes, because it's something so out there, and no, because I'm excited to see what life was like, and to see if all that studying I did was worth it. You?"

Clasping his hand, she squeezed it. "I'm excited and a little scared. Thankfully I'm with you."

He squeezed back. "This is going to be great."

"Just imagine," she said, eyes aglow, "getting married in England in medieval times. This is more than a girl could ever dream of."

"Getting married again was more than I dreamed off," he remarked, "especially to a goddess like you."

"I'm so lucky," she said.

"I'm luckier than you are," he answered.

"No you're not," she laughed, poking him.

He leaned over and gently placed a finger under her chin, drawing her closer and kissed her, feeling the electric pulse of touch and passion exploding within. He felt her hand on his head as she pressed her lips to his.

Tone was in the process of moving to sit on his lap when they were interrupted by a gentle cough, causing them to awkwardly pull apart, smirking at their unbridled desire.

"Sorry to intrude on your passionate display," the man said walking in. "You may want to think about getting a room when you get back, but we do have to get this show on the road. My name is Marcus Freytag. I'm the Travel Coordinator for Time Travel Incorporated." He was a lean man in his mid-40's, crisply dressed in a light grey three-piece suit. His hair was black, thick and wavy. He walked around them and leaned back against the table.

With him was a man in a lab technician's coat. He was slender and spare with the habit of pushing his glasses up the bridge of his nose with his middle finger. He looked to be ten years older than Freytag.

"I'm here to welcome you to your next adventure. You are Erik Jonsson and with you is Tone Thorgilsdottir. Is that correct?"

"It's pronounced Taw-nee," Tone corrected.

"My apologies, Tone." He dipped his head then continued. "Your wish is to go to back to London, England in the year 893 CE. Is that correct?"

"Yes," Erik answered for the both of them.

"Excellent. As you know, any time travel imposes certain restrictions and considerations. Obviously you cannot take anything with you that even remotely suggests that you do not belong there. Simple things like watches or toothbrushes or plastic combs. Even a wallet with your drivers ID is verboten. All your personal effects will be secured for you and returned to you upon your safe return to the present. Likewise, all clothing must be exact and you will not be allowed to wear any synthetic material or clothing that is not historically correct. Further, you will be attired as is customary to the time and location. Is that understood?"

Again they nodded.

"Because of the time and place you have selected, you forced our researchers to dig far deeper than they have ever done before. I know you'll be pleased to see what they've come up with. In addition to the correct period clothing you will wear, there was the issue of money. As you are going to London in the year 893, the coinage reflects the period, which is that of King Alfred. Each of you will be given a mix of gold and silver coins. Use them judiciously. And remember to not arouse outside interest with your wealth. If I remember my history, thieves and pickpockets abound in London."

He paused to ensure they both understood. "Now one more thing. Escorts. The escorts are there to protect you and to ensure you get safely home. Should any event or circumstance indicate any sort of danger, they will immediately get you back to the portal and bring you back home. They are not there to act as guides or explain what is happening. It is your responsibility to ensure you are intimately familiar with the environment in which you are inserted. They are there to protect, not act as tourist guides. Under no circumstances are you allowed to be separated from your guides, even if you have to use a bathroom somewhere. Further, they are charged with determining safety and security. If at any time they believe you are in danger or about to be compromised, they will escort you back. They have the final word. Is that understood?"

"Yes," they said in unison.

"Good. Doctor Lawrence here," he said, nodding dispassionately at the lab technician, "will assist you and answer any further questions you may have. I wish you a safe and wonderful journey."

Doctor Lawrence waited for Freytag to leave then explained, "As part of the safety of time travel, all participants are required to have a tracking device upon them. As we are sensitive to the anachronistic nature of time travel, tracking devices must be such that any compromise will have no effect. We accomplish this by the simple procedure of a small pill that you swallow. The pill will stay in the body during your travel experience. As it is non-digestible, it will easily pass through your body. You need not worry about retrieval of the pill as it is biodegradable. Questions?"

"Yes," Tone said. "I assume I must dress like the women of the time?"

"Of course," he said with a frown.

Squeezing Erik's hand, she said, "Too bad. I like the men's clothing better."

Uttering a long suffering sigh, Doctor Lawrence asked, "Are there any other questions?"

"Yes, one more question" Tone said. "I've always wondered how time travel works."

"You travel back in time," Lawrence said, raising an eye brow.

"No," she chuckled. "I mean the science part of it. How does it work?"

Lawrence regarded her with a look of surprise as no traveler had ever asked the question. Surprise morphed to erudite condescension as he now had a chance to display his superior intelligence.

"It's an interesting paradox," he explained, "for the problem on the face of it seems simple. We have always thought of time in three parts: past, present and future. The truth of it is that there is no future in time. Everything is either present or past with the present being a very tiny part of the time continuum. Each word that I speak, as soon as it is uttered, is now a part of the past. Yet you comprehend what I say and have said, your mind analyzing in the present, each part of the analysis shifting into the past as it formulates into a cogent thought. You might say that we, in effect, continually live in the past. You can go back in time, but you can never return to anything more than the present."

"But am I not returning to a future of sorts when I return to the present?" Tone said. "After all, when I go back in time, let's say I'm there for a day. When I return, to your present, it will be the future for me."

"Ah," his eyes brightened, "an excellent question. The problem is that while it might be the future for you, it will still always be the present on the time continuum, for while you are suspended into the past, time continues moving in the present."

"Suppose I was locked in the past for fifty years," Tone postulated, "and was brought back fifty years later. Am I not in the future?"

"Again, the future for you perhaps," he replied, using his fingers to make quotation marks at the word 'future.' "But it is not the future as far as time is concerned. It doesn't matter if we sent you or everyone in the world back in time fifty years or one hundred years. Once they returned fifty years later, it would be the present, because time moves forward regardless of where you are. It's a bit like the old supposed conundrum that if a tree falls in the forest and no one is there to hear it, does it make a sound? Of course it does. It's called sound waves. The fact that no one 'hears' it," he again make quotation marks with his finger, "does not mean that no sound was made."

"I don't understand," she said.

"The sound waves," he replied, staring at her as though the answer was obvious. "The sound waves continue regardless of human participation. It is the same for time. It moves forward, regardless of where we are."

"So how do we go back in time then," Erik asked, redirecting the conversation.

Lawrence blinked in momentary irritation to be diverted from his discourse but then realized they did have somewhere else to go. "It's a process based upon bending time. We can fold time backwards, but cannot fold it forwards beyond the present. So, we bend time to send you back, then bend it again to send you to the present."

The door opened and an attractive lab assistant poked her head in. "They're waiting," she reminded him.

Assuming a professorial air, Lawrence asked, "Any other questions?"

Receiving a shake of their heads in reply, he said, "Please wait here while I fetch your tracking pills."

Waiting until they were alone, Erik leaned over and said, "I don't do pills and I don't intend on taking it."

"They're not going to let you go unless you do," she reminded him, surprised at his adamancy. "What are you going to do?"

"I'll make them believe I swallowed the pill," he replied. "Besides, if we have escorts with us at all times, why do we need a tracking pill? Something just doesn't seem right about that."

Tone thought for a moment, trying to come up with a rational explanation.

"Have you heard of any other time traveler mention the tracking pill?" he said. "They talk about safety with the escorts in the ads, but they never mention a tracking pill."

"Huh," she said with a slow nod. "You're right."

"Usually am," he grinned.

Smiling back at him, she said, "So how do we make them believe we've swallowed the pill?"

"Palm it," he replied, "like this." He withdrew a dime from his pocket. Displaying it before her, he went to put it in his mouth then made an overt exaggeration of swallowing it. Licking his lips, he took a breath then held up the dime in his left hand.

"That was so believable," she gushed. "Here, let me try."

Imitating him, he was impressed with her skill. "Very convincing."

"What do we do with them?"

"Toss it in the trash as soon as you can. I seriously doubt they're really tracking pills."

"Then what are they?"

"I don't know," he shrugged, "and that's what concerns me."

They were interrupted when Doctor Lawrence returned with a lab assistant carrying a tray with two plastic cups of water and two small dishes with a pill on each one. Handing the water and pill to Erik then to Tone, the lab assistant waited while the two went through the motions of swallowing the pills.

"I don't like pills," Erik made a point of saying. "They always get stuck in my throat." He feigned swallowing. "Do you have more water?"

The lab assistant hurried out while Erik swallowed and rubbed his neck, coaxing the imaginary pill down his throat. When the lab assistant returned, Erik downed the entire contents then relaxed.

"That's better. Thanks."

Doctor Cooper looked inquisitively at Tone who said, "Pills don't bother me. I'm fine."

Satisfied, Doctor Cooper flipped a hand at the lab assistant, shooing him away.

'Time to get ready," he said, smiling with only his lips.

Letting him lead the way, they both slyly tossed their tracking pills into the trash can by the door.

Erik and Tone followed Doctor Lawrence towards the double doors of the Time Machine room. Tone was dressed in a sleeveless linen chemise, drawn loose at the neck by a ribbon. Over the chemise, she wore a hangerock, an apron-skirt secured in the front by two large turtle brooches. Handmade turnshoe-style shoes made of leather adorned her feet.   She scrunched her toes inside the woolen socks, thinking them quite uncomfortable.

Gazing over to Erik, she smiled. "You look handsome."

"I feel awkward," he admitted, "like I'm dressing up for Halloween only to discover that that I've worn the wrong costume."   He tugged at the collar of the darker blue overtunic. "The neck on this kyrtill is a bit tight."

"You won't have to wear it for long," she consoled. "What do you think of the woolen socks?"

"A bit hot in the summer, but probably warm in the winter," he answered, gazing down at his feet.

Lawrence opened the right side door and they came into a large windowless room with a thick glass partition that went from floor to ceiling, effectively dividing the room: one third for the control console and the other two thirds for the Time Machine. A doorway led from the control side to the machine side.

The control console, comprised of several flat screens, keyboards and switches, stretched about two meters wide, the numerous wires protruding out the back then inserted into a silver conduit that ran along the floor next to the glass partition before sharply ascending the side wall and into the ceiling. Other than two swivel chairs for the programmers, the only other furniture consisted of four plain maroon upholstered armchairs used for VIPs.

The Time Machine itself was in the shape of a cube, with one side open facing the control room. Inside the cube were four thickly padded chairs with arm rests, anchored to the floor. The front right chair had a red button covered by a plastic shell to be used by the escorts in case of an emergency. Tubes and heavy cables twisted up and out from the sides and top of the cube.

Doctor Lawrence noticed their fascination and proudly said, "It's quite simple, you know. All I have to do is enter the date, place name and geo location at this terminal." Withdrawing a slip of paper from his shirt pocket, he scanned the contents before leaning over the desk top and typed in 8-9-3-0-8-0-8 L-o-n-d-o-n 51.507351 - 0.127758. "There, the eighth day of August of the year 893, London, England. Then once you are settled in the Time Machine, I simply raise this cover." He lifted the hard plastic cover protecting the SEND button. "Then I press the button and you're off."

"What about getting back?" Tone asked.

"It's already been programmed into the Machine," he replied. "Your guides know how much time you have and will escort you back to the Machine when it's time to return." Ignoring them for a moment, he double checked the entry data.

The main door opened and a burly man and an athletically built woman entered, dressed much like Erik and Tone, both obviously not thrilled with the choice of clothing.

"Finally," Doctor Lawrence chastised, casting the two escorts an irritated stare. Turning his attention to Erik and Tone, he said, "These two are your escorts. Do exactly what they ask of you, and you will have a good trip. Any questions? No? Good. Go ahead and take the two seats to the rear. We'll begin as soon as everyone is settled."

Erik turned to introduce himself and Tone but the two escorts brushed past him and took their seats, stonily waiting for the two travelers to join them. The man sat in the chair with the emergency button.

"Good to meet you too," Erik deadpanned then turned to Tone. "Ready?"

"I'm more than ready. This is going to be a great adventure." She stood on her toes to kiss him and said, "One of many for us. Our future together is just beginning… in the 9th century," she added with a silly grin.

"C'mon," the man escort admonished. "Let's get this show on the road."

Erik and Tone walked into the cube and seated themselves. Doctor Lawrence's voice came out of several small speakers in the cube.

"Once the process starts, it will seem as though the room is spinning. That is natural. If you feel yourself getting dizzy, close your eyes. The spinning will stabilize followed by darkness. As you get closer to your time and destination, light will return as will colors. The spinning sensation will resume and will stop once you are there. Give yourselves a few minutes to adjust before exiting the machine. And last, but not least, listen to your escorts. Here we go."

The Machine started to hum and Erik watched as the room began to spin, going faster and faster until it was a blur, the humming growing louder. Just when the colors began to blend, it abruptly went dark and silent. He reached a hand over to Tone, feeling her squeeze it in return.

Then darkness began receding as strips of colors started streaking across their front. The spinning resumed, rapidly morphing to a blur.

As the spinning started to slow, the colors streaking across their front likewise slowed, the dominant color being green.

Finally the cube settled and the spinning stopped. His spirits euphoric, Erik inhaled deeply, smelling the bouquet of the sea. Grasping Tone's hand, he was out the front of the cube before the escorts had a chance to recover.

"Stay where you are," the male escort demanded. "Wait for us."

Erik and Tone stood gazing out at the endless ocean to their side. Erik worked to get his bearing as the wind whipped across the flat grassy land, flapping their clothing. Despite their clothing, it was chilly, especially with the thick overcast sky. The ground was wet from rain and the sky threatened more.

Turning around in a circle, he saw that they were surrounded by water. A narrow strip of land stretched before him. To his right, shallow water separated this part of the land from the mainland. Off in the distance across the stretch of water he saw what looked to be a large structure reminding him of a priory.

When the two escorts emerged, Erik turned to them and said, "I don't think we're in London."

"Where are we then?" the senior escort grumbled, his hair swirling in the wind.

"I don't know. It almost looks like we're on some sort of island, but I can't be sure until we start exploring. That," he said, pointing to the structure, "is where we're headed." He then looked each one in the eye. "Unless you're a linguist, I suggest we keep our mouths shut for the time being."

"A good idea," Tone smiled, slipping and arm around his.

"I'll lead the way," Erik said, asserting his authority as the scholar amongst them. Hearing no argument, he headed away from the Time Machine, the escorts falling in behind.

Though relatively flat, the going was slow due to their caution and the frequent stops Erik did to take stock of his surroundings. Yet they met no one until the narrow strip of land widened and they saw farm fields to their front.

Hugging the coast line, Erik led the way towards the building that he could now see was constructed of stone. It reminded him of a castle, yet it lacked the parapets and crenelated walls necessary for defense.

As they approached, he saw a man, dressed as a monk, standing outside the doors looking back at them. He expressed no alarm or concern as he waited for them. He was of average height

He greeted them with a friendly wave and spoke words that none of them immediately understood until Erik realized the man was speaking Old English. Deciding his Old English was far too rusty, Erik replied in Latin.

"Greetings, Brother. God bless you."

The monk eyed him with curiosity. "I see you are an educated man," he replied in Latin. "Your accent is a bit odd, but you speak with fluency. How did you come by your knowledge?"

"At the university," Erik said, immediately regretting this anachronistic admission.

"University?" the monk said with a frown. "What is that?"

"It's another name for a large school," he explained.

"Ah," the monk nodded in understanding. "And where was this school?"

Erik thought quickly. "It was in a city called Heidelberg, about two months travel by foot north of Rome," he lied.

"Rome," he responded, wide-eyed. "Have you been to Rome?"

Erik remembered his one vacation to Europe with his parents when he was in middle school. They had spent a day in Rome on their whirlwind excursion of visiting as many countries as possible in the two week vacation.

"Yes, I have," he admitted, "but I was very young then and do not remember much."

"Ah," he bobbed his head in commiseration. "I have not yet been to the Holy City."

"Where are you from, Brother?"

"I am from Alnwick, not too far from here."

Erik smiled politely, abruptly realizing not only were they not anywhere near London, they were not even close. "Tell me brother, does the wind whip across this island all the time?"

"All the time," he said, rolling his eyes. He then looked at the others who appeared trying not to be noticed. "Do you also speak Latin?" he asked.

"They don't," Erik answered for them. "We are all from the same village, but I was the only one sent to school. The two escorts act as guards to protect my wife and I while we travel."

The monk nodded in understanding then looked at their clothes. "How did you get here?"

"We walked."

"But the tide is in. How is it that you are not wet from the crossing?"

"We crossed when the tide was out," Erik said, "and set up camp to wait out the rain."

"Of course," the monk politely smiled. "Your camp is on the other side of the island?"

"Yes."

"Why did you not come here first?"

"I wished to take time for reflection and the spot we chose seemed to suit my needs."

"I understand completely," he said with a smile. "There are times being truly alone is best. But come, I have kept you too long. I expect you wish to see the Shrine of Saint Cuthbert."

"Yes, we do," Erik readily agreed, struggling to remember where and when he had encountered that name.

"Are you seeking a miracle?" the monk asked, leading them to the large central doors to the priory.

Erik leaned over and whispered, "My wife is barren."

The monk silently nodded in sympathy then said, "Let us pray that the Saint will answer your prayer."

"How long have you been here, Brother?"

Pausing in thought, he replied, "It's been six summers since I first came to the priory here on Lindisfarne. An especially propitious year as it was the centennial anniversary of the death of our patron Saint."

Lindisfarne! Erik's joy morphed to concern. "I should know, Brother," he politely said, "but what year did Saint Cuthbert die?"

The monk eyed him curiously. "It is but a simple mathematic problem. I am surprised that you speak Latin but lack the basic skills of mathematics."

"I do not lack the skills, good Brother, but we have been travelling for some time and I have been so preoccupied with my wife that I confess I do not even know the month we now share."

"It is the month of Iunius," the monk smiled, "and the day is the eighth."

Two months off, but at least they day right. Erik nodded with a thankful smile hoping the man would tell him the year. When no further explanation came, he asked, "But then, what was the year the Saint departed for the celestial presence. I ask because we have visited other priories to avail ourselves of the saint's miraculous powers only to discover that their method of dating was off by a year or two. You know how important it is to be accurate in the astrological signs."

"Ah yes," he bobbed his head in understanding. "Our Saint passed on to his heavenly glory the twentieth day of the month of Martius in the year 687. One hundred and six years later brings us to the year 793. We are very particular here, so you may rely on our accuracy."

"June eight, 793," Erik repeated when suddenly his eyes burst wide. "O my God." Whipping around to the others, he motioned with his hands as though pushing them away from the doors. "We have to go. Now."

"What's wrong?" Tone said, backing up.

"Lindisfarne, 793, Viking raid," he blurted, but too late.

Around the sides of priory, Viking raiders swarmed to the main doors.

"Head for the machine. Hurry," Erik cried out, falling back to let the escorts lead the way while he protected their rear. As they passed the far wall more Vikings rushed around the far corner.

"Run," Erik urged before spinning around to confront the threat.

Tone hesitated, fearful, as she watched Erik dodge the first sword thrust then leap in the air and kick the Viking in the head, detaching the man's helmet from his head. Dodging another man's sword, Erik dove and rolled, picking up the other man's sword then pressed the attack, forcing the man to stagger backwards under the onslaught.

As more Vikings swept around the sides of the priory, the senior escort forcibly grabbed Tone's elbow and commanded. "We got to move."

Yet still Tone hesitated until Erik saw her over his shoulder.

"Go," he yelled as more Vikings encircled him.

It was when four of the invaders broke off to give chase to the three time travelers that she jolted into action and fled.

The Vikings were fast, but fear fueled the legs of Tone and the escorts and they lengthened the distance between them. Cresting a low ridge, they saw the Machine off to their right and bolted for it, diving into their seats.

"Wait!" Tone exclaimed as the senior escort slammed the return button.

"We don't have time," he snapped. "He's as good as dead."

The Machine started to hum and then to spin, going faster and faster until it was a blur, the humming growing louder. Like before, the colors began to blend and then went dark and silent.

"No!" she called out, but it was too late.

As quickly as the darkness enveloped them, it began receding as strips of dull grey started zipping across their front. The spinning resumed, rapidly morphing to a blur then slowed, the streaking grey across their front likewise slowing until the cube settled and the spinning stopped.

They were back in the lab, much to the surprise of Doctor Lawrence and the other Machine operators.

Lawrence immediately saw they were missing a traveler.

"What happened?"

"We were attacked," the male escort replied, emerging from the Machine. "Vikings."

"Where's the man?"

"Left behind."

"Left behind?" Doctor Lawrence bellowed.

"We couldn't help it," the woman escort said, defending their actions. "It all happened so fast."

"They left him there," Tone interrupted. "They left him there to defend himself. We have to go back."

"It's not that simple," Lawrence replied.

"You sent us to the wrong place," she accused, "and the wrong time."

Instead of answering, Lawrence went to the main console and typed in a message. The response came an instant later. With a nervous frown, he glanced back at Tone and the escorts.

"Mister Cooper is on his way down."

"We have to go back," Tone repeated. "I know where and when to go back to."

"You do?" Lawrence said, surprised.

"Yes. Lindisfarne, June eighth, 793. You can determine the time of day from the time you sent us there. We have to go back, now," she urgently demanded.

"We'll wait until Mister Cooper arrives."

"But we're wasting time," she exploded. "I'm sure he's still alive. We have to go back." She headed to the console but was physically blocked by the escorts. Spinning around to confront Lawrence, she yelled, "You just can't leave him there."

"We'll wait for Mister Cooper," he stubbornly repeated, his arms crossed. Casting a sharp look at the escorts, he said, "Tell me what happened?"

Before he had chance to explain, Cooper burst in.

"What happened?" Cooper coldly demanded.

"We have to go back," Tone insisted.

"Let me first find out what's going on, madam," he said, his gaze boring into Doctor Lawrence.

"I was just getting to the bottom of it when you arrived," Lawrence meekly said.

Cooper turned to the lead escort. "Who are we missing?

"Erik Jonsson," Tone replied for him

"What happened?" Cooper asked, looking directly at the male escort.

"Everything was fine, Mister Cooper. We landed on an island and apparently it was not where we were supposed to be."

"It was the wrong place and the wrong time," Tone shot back.

"Where did you end up?"

The woman escort looked at Tone who said, "793, June the eighth at Lindisfarne, England."

"And where were you supposed to be?"

"London, England, one hundred years later."

"Interesting," Cooper mused. "Then what happened?"

"Like I said," the male escort continued. "We landed on the island. It was a small island and we could see some buildings not too far away. So we go to the buildings and there's a guy outside dressed like a monk. Jonsson talks with the man for a bit and the next thing we knew, Vikings come around the corner and start attacking everyone. We had barely enough time to escape."

"What about Jonsson?"

"He dropped back as a kind of rearguard while we led the way back to the Machine. By the time we arrived, he wasn't with us anymore. Since we were still being chased, I made the decision to get us out of there before were all dead."

"A good decision," Cooper nodded appreciatively. He then turned his attention to Tone. "I'm sorry to have to say this, but most likely, your friend is dead."

"You don't know that," she objected. "He could still be alive for all we know. Unless we go back, I'll make sure everyone knows what happened here, that you all screwed up and left a Time Traveler to die."

"Now, now, Miss Thorgilsdottir," Cooper calmly replied. "There's no need to get melodramatic. I'm sure we can find a suitable compensation for the inconvenience of this trip."

"Inconvenience?" she blurted, hardly believing her ears. "This isn't an inconvenience; this is murder."

Smiling with only his lips, Cooper looked at the woman escort. "Why don't you take Miss Thorgilsdottir to the After Travel Lounge. I'm sure something to eat and drink might help."

"I don't need to eat or drink," she exclaimed. "I want to go back. In fact, why can't you just redial this machine to yesterday? That way we can avoid this whole screw up."

"It doesn't work that way," Lawrence said, his frustration mounting.

"Why not? All you have to do is go back a day and everything will be fine."

"But it doesn't work that way –"

"You said that already," Tone asserted, cutting him off.

"It's like this," Lawrence explained. "Your boyfriend –"

"Fiancée," Tone sharply corrected.

"Fiancée," Lawrence repeated, calming himself. "Your Fiancée is spatially in another plane, a sort of another dimension. See, it's the law of physics... Pauli's exclusion principle. Two objects cannot occupy the same space at the same time. That applies when everything is in the present, the right now. But when you add the time factor, you create a sort of doppelgänger. The 'real,'" he said, making quote marks with his fingers, "Erik is back in time over a thousand years ago. That is where he is spatially located. You could go back a few days, but you would be interacting with the doppelgänger, the other Erik."

"You're not making any sense," Tone fumed.

"It's science, damn it," Lawrence snapped. "I can't help it if you can't understand."

"I understand plenty," she coldly replied. "I understand you and your machine here have totally obliterated my future, my happiness. I understand that you're also too incompetent to fix it."

Dismissing him as insignificant, she twisted to face Cooper, jabbing a finger at him. "Find someone who *can* fix this. I want my fiancée back before the end of this day."

"I'm afraid that's out of the question," he said with finality.

"You can't just leave him there."

"We will, for the time being," he replied. "Miss Thorgilsdottir, assuming your fiancée is still alive, we just can't go back there with guns blazing. We need a plan and accurate insertion data. We need to make sure we're not interfering with the time continuum, especially now that Mister Jonsson is stuck there. As you can imagine, not only is this unexpected, but fraught with unintended consequences. Despite your unfavorable view of Doctor

Lawrence, he happens to be one of the best in the field of time travel and you will find no one better. Now, please, go with the escort and give me a few moments to sort out just what needs to be done. Once I've determined a plan, I'll ask you to come back here. In the meantime, go to the Lounge and wait while I sort out the details."

He smiled serenely at her. *Besides, if he isn't already dead, he will be in two days.*

"Oh," Tone said, far from mollified. "Until you know for sure he's dead, you have to assume he's still alive. How long will it take?"

Cooper pursed his lips and leveled his gaze at her. "A lot longer the longer you stay here interrupting me."

"Fine," she huffed and stepped towards the door, the guard in tow.

"By the way, you need to stop by the tracking department on the way to the lounge," Lawrence said. "It appears the signal from your tracking pill wasn't working properly. They can determine the cause."

"I didn't swallow the pill," she sheepishly admitted.

"What?" He stiffened, jerking his head to see the look in Cooper's face, a look that said all hell was going to break loose once this foolish woman was out of the room.

"Neither of us did," she shrugged. "They're in the trash basket in the briefing room."

"Damn," Cooper snarled through tight lips. Twisting his head to look at the senior escort, he snapped, "Get someone up there ASAP. You," he said to the other escort. "Take Miss Thorgilsdottir to the After Travel Lounge."

Frowning, Tone asked, "What's wrong?"

"Proprietary technology," he tersely replied. "Now if you would please accompany the escort to the Lounge."

Waiting until the doors closed behind her, Cooper turned a cold glance at Lawrence who whined, "What are we going to do? There's no way I can guarantee we can get back to the right place or time."

"He could be dead for all we know," Cooper unconvincingly said.

"And he might still be alive," Lawrence countered, wringing his hands. The phone on the console beeped startling him.

"Pull yourself together, man," Cooper admonished then pressed the speaker button. "Yes?"

"It's gone, Mister Cooper."

"Gone? How is that possible? Trash is picked up after hours."

"I don't know what to tell you, sir, but it's not here."

"Find out where it is. Now."

"Yes, s –" he replied before Cooper cut him off.

Cooper twisted his head to stare at Lawrence. "How long before we can get back there?"

"It could take years," he whimpered. "We were lucky to get a one hundred year difference this time.   Each time adjustment takes verification. That takes more time the farther we go back. It's taken us almost two years to go back to the 16th century. We need to go back to the 8th century. That could take another sixteen years."

"You don't have sixteen years," he seethed. "You make it happen ASAP. I don't care if you don't sleep or eat, but I want it done now."

"I can't do it by myself," he whimpered. "I need more people, qualified people."

"Don't be a damned fool, man. This needs to be kept quiet. Do you understand?"

"Yes," Lawrence whimpered.

"I want around the clock operation, you understand?"

"Yes," he sighed, defeated.

Cooper leaned over the console desk and pressed the speaker button. "Jakob Cooper for Meredith Nelson."

A moment later her voice came over the speaker. "Yes sir?"

"My office. Five minutes."

"Yes, sir."

Cooper stood staring out the window then looked over his shoulder when the door opened and she walked in.

"We have a problem," he tersely said.

"Yes?"

"Erik Jonsson did not return with the group."

"Why?"   She walked over to where he stood, his arms folded.

"They were attacked and in their haste to beat a retreat, he was left behind."

Meredith shrugged. "So? The explosive capsules will fix that."

"They didn't swallow the pills," he informed her.

"They didn't?" she said, eyes popping wide.

"They pretended to swallow them and left them in the trash basket in the briefing room."

"Have we retrieved the capsules?"

"Not yet," he sighed with frustration. "Apparently someone has collected the trash already."

"But it's not even five o'clock," she frowned. "Trash isn't collected until after hours."

"Tell me something I don't know. I've got them looking for it. But we have a more significant problem. What do we do with our Time Traveler? She can't be allowed to talk."

Meredith mused for a moment then said, "Why not get her to help?"

"Help?" He warily regarded her. "How?"

"It's probably going to take a while to fix the problem. Let's train her for the environment on the condition she keeps her mouth shut."

"That could take a whole lot longer than we can afford," he sourly pointed out.

"So? We make her an employee of TTI, she signs the requisite security forms and she has to keep her mouth shut. While we're working on the problem, we send her to school to get her Masters, which if I remember is in the same ancient crap that Jonsson studied. If she finishes the Masters before we find the solution, we send her for more schooling. If we're still not ready, we bring her back here to act as a consultant. When we solve the problem, we send her and the escorts back to just before the attack, collect him up and bring him back."

Cooper shook his head, not convinced.

"It's the personal connection," Meredith explained. "We want her to be a devoted follower of TTI. The best way to do that is to make her an offer she can't refuse. We pay for schooling and provide a living expense under the condition that she must return to TTI when completed. That will be far less expensive than dealing with the negative publicity."

Cooper had a sudden inspiration and smiled. "Done right, we could exploit the romantic connection. See? They were engaged to be married but postponed it to go on their trip."

Meredith instantly understood and her smile widened. "This could be a marketing dream. We wait until we have the kinks worked out then do a marketing blitz." She spread her hands like an advertising banner. "Lover gets caught in time warp; she goes back to rescue him." She grinned at the inspiration of her own idea. "And we can say that she was so confident of our success that she became an employee of the company."

Cooper nodded, pleased with the plan. "I like it. Bring her up to my office and let's get this show on the road."

"Yes sir," she replied.

Tone stood in Cooper's expansive office that overlooked the Ohio River in downtown Louisville, irritated that he appeared far too calm for the calamity that had just happened. A woman she had not met before sat in a chair next to the desk, facing her.

"Here's the situation, Miss Thorgilsdottir –"

"Just call me Tone," she interrupted.

"Tone," he repeated. "After investigating the situation, I'm afraid it's going to be more difficult than we first expected."

Tone's nostrils flared and her lips tightened.

'Before you get upset," Cooper placated, hands up, "hear me out. Your boyfriend –"

"Fiancée," Tone objected. "We were supposed to be married in a few days, but you have managed to royally screw that up."

"Fiancée," Cooper corrected himself, ignoring her outburst. "Your fiancée, we have learned, is more than able to take care of himself and so there is a good chance he is still alive."

"I said that from the beginning," Tone huffed.

"Yes, I know. If you will allow me to finish?" He stared imperiously at her. Receiving a curt nod, he continued. "We proceed under the belief that your fiancée, Erik, is still alive. With that in mind, we need your help."

"My help?" She frowned in surprise.

"Yes," he serenely replied. "We believe you would be the best suited to lead the team when we send you back." He inwardly smiled at her subtle change of attitude. "Erik is a

Nordic expert and, I believe, you were likewise studying Norse history."

"I was."

"Excellent," he smiled. "Here is what we propose. While TTI remedies the time machine, you will continue your studies, paid for and supported by TTI."

Tone cocked an eyebrow. "You're going to pay for grad school?"

"Exactly," Meredith interrupted, "and any other expenses you need while earning that MA."

Tone slowly turned to look at her. "And who are you?"

"This is Meredith Allen," Cooper answered, "Director of Marketing and Vice-President of external affairs."

"Impressive title," Tone scoffed. "So you're willing to pay for my advanced schooling in exchange for what?"

"For returning and leading the expedition to find your lost fiancée," Meredith answered.

"He's not lost," Tone retorted.

"He's not here, is he?" Meredith sniffed, not liking her arrogant attitude.

"That's because you all screwed up," Tone snapped.

"Please, please," Cooper interrupted. "This gets us nowhere." Addressing Tone, he said, "We want to solve this problem as much as you do. In pragmatic terms, you've lost a future husband. For us, if word gets out, we stand to lose a fortune."

"What a pity," Tone sneered.

"Do you want to help or not?" Meredith snapped. "If not, then be on your way and let us handle things as we see fit. If so, then why not zip it and help?"

Folding her arms across her chest, Tone shot a cold glare at her. "Really? How are you going to explain his absence? Who pays his utility bills, his car insurance? What will you tell Master Lei when he doesn't show up to teach his martial arts classes? What will you tell his friends when he hasn't returned from his trip?"

"We were hoping you would help us there," Cooper soothed.

"Me?" Tone snorted a derisive laugh. "What you're telling me is that you want me to lie for you."

"We prefer to see it as temporarily manipulating the facts," Meredith said with a condescending smile.

Tone's brows furrowed as she shook her head. "You people are incredible. First, you totally screw up and dump my fiancée in the past, leaving him there with no clue as to how to rescue him. Now you want me to lie for you to cover *your* asses until you can figure out what to do."

"Do you want him back or not?" Meredith seethed.

Instead of answering, Tone turned to Cooper, jerking a thumb at Meredith. "If she's an example of the caliber of people you have working here, let me say right now that my faith in your success has dwindled down to zero."

"How dare you," Meredith snarled.

"You're marketing, right?" Tone said, knowing the answer while not giving Meredith a chance to reply. "You know nothing about how the machine works. Your job is to pimp this company. Stick to something you might have a clue about." She redirected her attention to Cooper. "I want to talk to the Time Machine people, someone who knows what's going on... that Lawrence fellow."

"I will arrange it," Cooper placated, inwardly chuckling at the verbal assault Meredith just suffered. "In the meantime, we really do need your help. Please understand that if word gets out that your fiancé was left behind, investigations will hinder any chance of rescue. The longer we have interference, the longer it will take to solve the problem."

"And the longer we take," Meredith tartly added, "the longer your fiancée will be in that environment. And who knows, he might even find himself another love interest."

Tone flashed a maternal glance at her. "It's obvious you know nothing about love. It's not like some blouse you bought, wore a while then decided you liked another one better."

"Alright, enough," Cooper interjected with authority. "Here's the situation. We all want to rescue your fiancé. To do that, we need time. At the same time, we need to create a cover story as to why he is not here. We want you to deal with his friends and family and anyone else close to him. As far as his daily bills and expenses are concerned, have them forwarded to TTI. We will pay them until he returns. If you are willing to help us, we can reunite you with your fiancé.

Tone glared at him then softened, knowing she had no other choice. "Fine. I'll play your game. But it better not take too long."

"Trust me," Cooper said, "we don't want it to take too long either."

"Grad school?" Meredith asked.

"Yes."

"Where?"

Tone thought a moment then smiled. "University of Oslo."

"Oslo?" Meredith said with a puzzled frown.

"Yes," Tone said, dripping condescension. "You know, like in Norway?"

"I know where Oslo is," Meredith bristled.

"Fine," Tone said. "Then I'll expect you to take care of my admission as well as tuition, books, lodgings, stipend, and any other expenses, including travel."

"Consider it done," Cooper buoyantly answered.

"You'll need to become an employee of TTI," Meredith pointed out.

"Why?" Tone asked, suddenly suspicious.

"Because we can write it all off in taxes," Meredith said rolling her eyes. "If we just give you the money, it's considered a gift and we don't get the tax break we would if you were an employee. Relax. Your job," she said, making quote marks with her fingers, "is as a student. Your responsibilities are to complete your studies as quickly as you can so that you are as qualified as possible to lead the mission."

It was then the ramifications of what might be happen if Erik was not on Lindisfarne swept through Tone. She would need to know far more than just the language. She would need to immerse herself completely in 8th and 9th century Scandinavia. And she also realized that these folks were buying time. They knew it would take more than a year to get the MA. At that moment, and epiphany emerged and she knew what she had to do.

Chapter 4

There were at least two dozen Vikings coming around the corners of the priory, two splitting off to take care of Erik while the others swung toward the open doors. Grinning wickedly, the first Viking raised his sword to attack only to be sent flying when Erik attacked first, delivering a spinning kick to the head.

"Erik," Tone called out as he parried a thrust.

"Run," he yelled over his shoulder. Marking his opponent, Erik feigned a high attack and instead delivered a bone crushing kick to the man's knee causing him to cry out in pain and drop to the ground. In one swift slicing motion, Erik arced a leg down on the man's neck, cracking the spine bones, causing the head to twist in a grotesque angle.

Grabbing the dead man's sword, he went over to the first Viking and stabbed him through the chest. By now, the ransacking of the priory was in full force with the slaughter of the helpless monks.

Jamming the sword tips in the ground, Erik hurriedly pulled off his outer tunic, allowing him more freedom of movement. Retrieving the swords, he hefted them in his hands, feeling the weight and balance and moved without thinking, the years of training taking over his emotions.

Several Vikings saw their compatriots on the ground and the victor moving towards them. With an urgent call, half a dozen Vikings emerged from the priory and headed towards Erik, swords at the ready.

Erik watched his opponents as they positioned themselves for the attack. They were soon joined by several more who circled their prey. Behind them, the pillaging continued as more monks staggered out the doors to fall spread-eagled on the ground. Those not dead were quickly dispatched with a thrust to the stomach.

Two attackers launched at him, their swords high to strike. Faster than they had ever encountered, Erik launched into the air, his swords crossed in front. Up over their shoulders he sped then swung down with both swords, catching the two warriors in the neck, nearly decapitating them.

As the two stumbled and fell into the dirt, the others drew back. One hefted and hurled a spear at Erik, but by the time it was launched, Erik had already moved out of the way and the spear impacted harmlessly behind him.

Marking the others, Erik slowly positioned to defend himself. More Vikings joined the circle until there were twenty or more surrounding him. He slowly turned around inside the circle, gauging and measuring, waiting for the next attack. One raised his bow and notched an arrow. As he raised it to aim, a deep voice spoke.

"Hold."

The man hesitated then lowered the bow.

A portion of the circle parted and a tall man, well-built and with a broad chest, entered. His copper blond hair was tied behind his head. A thick beard, cropped an inch below his jaw, covered most of his face, yet revealed a healed scar across his left cheek. His blue eyes bespoke one who measured his words. Taking a measure of him, Erik reasoned the man would be considered handsome, even with the scar.

"You fight well for a pilgrim," the Viking said, eyeing him favorably.

"I get by," Erik answered in Old Norse.

The Viking cocked an eyebrow. "You speak our language."

"Yes, but not as well as you."

The man grinned while others chuckled at the response. Behind them, the mayhem was settling and the last of the priory's treasures were being hauled off to the waiting ships.

"You also speak the language of these monks?"

"I speak some of their common tongue, though I do know the language of their religion."

The man frowned then asked, "Where did you learn our language?"

"It's a long story," Erik replied, cautiously marking the positions of those surrounding him.

"It's a long journey back home," he said. "What are you called?"

"I am called Erik, Erik Jon's-son."

"Ah," the man nodded with a satisfied smile. "A good Ost name."

"So I've been told."

"I can use a man like you," he said. "You're a fine warrior."

Erik looked back over his shoulder, realizing that Tone and the escorts were long gone. Once inside the Time Machine, the escort would have wasted no time and slapped that return button as hard as he could.

Then reality burst, and he suddenly realized there was more than a good chance he wouldn't be going back. Instead of seeing King Alfred in the 9th century, they were 100 years off. Something had gone terribly wrong with the time machine. Doubt abruptly invaded his thoughts as he remembered Dr. Lawrence's nervousness during the pre-travel briefing… and Cooper's smug arrogance when he wished them a happy journey. The man knew something was wrong, but figured there wouldn't be a problem like just happened. And then there was the fine print on the waiver stating that it was possible that they might be inserted outside the specified time and that TTI was not responsible, etc., etc.

But surely they would send someone back to retrieve him… assuming he wasn't already dead. *Damn them. Damn them all.* The epiphany hit along with frustration and anger. There was no way to pinpoint where he was. The time machine wasn't as accurate as they preached. *My guess is that they're hoping I'm already dead.*

He was stuck here... and there was nothing he could do about it.

What was worse was that Tone was gone… forever.

And there was nothing he could do about it.

Rage swelled inside him as he pondered a future without the woman he had given his heart to. There was no one like Tone… and there never would be.

Knowing his fate was here and now, Erik grit his teeth while offering up a silent prayer that somehow, somewhere he would see Tone again. Focusing on the man who was waiting for an answer, he said. "Yes, I will join you, but I do so as a free man."

The man held up both hands in acknowledgement. "I agree. I am called Halfdan."

Halfdan turned to one of the men to his right, a stout powerfully built man with a torque around his neck. "Bjorn here will help you get settled." Without waiting for a reply, he cast a quick glance around the devastation, calling out to those slowly working their way around the priory, finishing off wounded monks. "Anything left?"

Receiving grunts and head shakes, he turned to the assembled men. "Make ready to sail. Erik, you will sail with me."

Erik watched as the Vikings paid him no mind and disbursed to collect their booty. Two Vikings drew Halfdan aside and spoke in subdued tones, casting accusing glances at Erik. Halfdan nodded, flashed a quick wary look at Erik before returning to direct the departure.

"Come with me," Bjorn said without emotion, leading the way around to priory to the beach close by where three beached ships waited, their sails furled.

Bjorn headed towards a long-ship, its prow decorated with a dragon's head. Wading into the cold water, Bjorn hauled himself over the side, waiting for Erik to follow. With graceful ease, Erik catapulted over the side to land on the deck.

While other Vikings clambered aboard, Erik took in the long-ship. Oars, still in the oar holes, were pulled in onto the deck, resting close to each man's storage chest that doubled as a rowing seat. He quickly added up the rowing positions, twelve on each side for a total of 24. Counting the helm there were 25 Vikings on this ship.

With a quick glance at the other ship, Erik counted nearly 50 Vikings on this raid. He turned around to stare at the monastery. *50 Vikings against however many monks, priests and an abbot. Talk about overkill.*

"Stand back here," Bjorn ordered, directing Erik to the aft section of the ship.

Making his way past the loosely furled sail, ready to be raised when the winds were favorable, Eric noticed that a number of Vikings remained on shore, patiently waiting for the rest to board. Those on board went to the aft section, stuffing spoils into the seat chests then gripped their oars in the ready position.

While those on shore pushed, the rowers dipped their oars into the water and pulled, shaking the ship loose from the beaching. At the last moment, those on shore clambered on board as the ships maneuvered away from the shore and the carnage left behind. It was all done with such precision and quickness that Erik marveled at the speed of the entire raid.

Once far enough from shore and with a steady wind behind them, they hoisted the sail and hauled the oars in to rest on the loose decking. Bjorn handled the tiller, steering the ship towards home.

Satisfied all was in order, Halfdan sat on his sea chest positioned in front of Bjorn. Catching Erik's attention, he scooted to the side of his chest and said, "Come sit with me."

Obeying, Erik settled on the edge next to him, reminding himself that he needed to fit in, to not just pretend that this had been his whole world, his whole life, but to act like it and believe it. At that moment, he was thankful for all the years of study and teaching. He vowed there and then that no one would ever call him boring again.

"Where is home for you, Erik Jon's-son?"

Erik's mind churned as he thought of a suitable answer. The best one would be partly true. He was from far away. In this instance, it would be far enough away to prevent discovery.

"In truth, my home was taken from me when I was young. What I remember is a farm. Before I was sold into slavery, my mother told me to return to Hålogaland, to reclaim what was once mine."

Bjorn's face creased into a scowl. "Your parents?"

"My father was killed in the raid. My mother, being fair and comely, was taken… as was I. Deciding he did not want another man's whelp, I was sold."

Halfdan nodded in understanding. "Continue."

"I was sold to a trader who sold me to another trader. How many times I was sold I choose not to remember. What I do remember is learning early on to trust only in myself, to depend only on myself. If change was going to happen, I had to make it happen. I ended up on in the far south, across the seas here and into the kingdom of Charles the Great then finally to a mountainous city called Geneva, among a people whose language I did not understand. Though I learned their tongue, I vowed never to lose my own."

Erik paused, feeling the breeze and inhaling the bouquet of the ocean, pondering the breadth of his tale, all the while wondering if Tone was safe.

"For some reason, the fates were kind to me and I was sold to a bookseller."

"Books?" Bjorn repeated with a sneer. "What use are books? It is silver and gold that a man needs... and women... a man needs a woman."

Erik twisted his head to gaze at the man at the tiller. He was half-a-head shorter than Halfdan, with dark blond hair swirling in the wind around his head. His beard came down to the middle of his chest.

"Tell me, Bjorn," Erik politely inquired. "When Odin's Valkyries determine it is your time, how much gold and silver will you be taking with you?"

"None," Bjorn begrudgingly admitted.

"However, if I write your name into a book and perhaps tell a bit about you, your bravery, your exploits, a thousand years from now, you will be remembered. People reading the book will wonder, 'Who is this Bjorn and what was he like?' They will think to themselves, 'I wish I could have met him. He sounds like such a brave and interesting man.' Silver and gold are good for here and now. But your name in a book can make you immortal."

Bjorn frowned, though pleased with the accolades.

Halfdan barked a laugh. "He's right, though someone else will have to tell your tale. Otherwise who would believe it?" He turned back to Erik. "Continue, Master Story-teller. I'm enjoying your tale."

Erik cocked an eyebrow. "You don't believe me?"

"I didn't say that," Halfdan said, locking his gaze on him. "There is much to learn about my newest crewmember. Please continue."

"As you wish," Erik replied with a dip of his head. "Like I said, I was sold to a bookseller and taught the art of book making. Though interesting, I preferred the writing to the making."

"So you learned to read and write?" Bjorn interjected.

"Yes. The bookseller was a kindly man and when he discovered my talent for learning, he adopted me as his son and allowed me to attend the Academy of Rhetoric and Grammar in the city. I excelled among the students there, marred only by my penchant for getting into fights."

"Fights?" Bjorn said, leaning forward to hear more.

"Damn you man," Halfdan barked. "Pay attention and steer the ship. You can listen well enough where you are."

Bjorn straightened and shifted his gaze out to the endless ocean.

"Go on," Halfdan said.

"I got into fights because my accent was foreign. One can only be called filthy barbarian a certain number of times before the accusation needs to be answered. I got the worst of it in the beginning, but they knew I was not afraid and as time went on and I grew into a man's body, I'd been in enough fights so that by the time my schooling was at an end, my oppressors knew enough to leave me alone. Besides, I had excelled past their efforts both in academics and fighting and so could look down on them... even if they were born of higher station. When my reputation as a fighter reached the ears of the jarl, I was offered the opportunity to train as a soldier. Or rather, I should say I was strongly encouraged to pursue that line of work, if you know what I mean."

Halfdan laughed. "I understand."

"I learned to use all sorts of weapons as well as fighting without any. In this, I again excelled. I was sent to a special teacher, one who taught the craft and art of stealth war. I learned many things there. Unfortunately, the jarl was the jealous type and begrudged my success, especially with the fairer sex." He winked and grinned.

"Ah ha," Halfdan gleamed. "I bet I know what came next. He caught you with his wife."

"You are close to the mark," Erik replied with a sly grin, "though I would not be so dishonorable to do that. However, his wife, who was more than passing fair, making one wonder how she managed to share his bed... perhaps she feigned illness or the monthly time whenever he sought her pleasures... Still, I know he gave me opportunity and one does not lightly snub such bounty, but by the gods he was an ugly man."

"What happened with the wife?" Bjorn blurted.

"Ah yes," Erik said, enjoying the captive audience. "His wife was not so... um... how shall I say it? Discreet... yes, that's the word... she was bold enough to claim to his face, mind you, that she was going to bed me and make him watch."

"By the gods," Bjorn exclaimed. "She was going to cuckold him and force him to watch?"

"Well," Erik said with a shrug. "I don't know if she meant it or said it to spite him. If I was unfortunate enough to be married to a sow like him, I'd be looking elsewhere too. Either way, when word got to me that my benefactor was out to kill me, I knew it was time for us to part ways. So I quickly packed my gear and headed across the mountains, working my way north, deciding it was time to head back to my true home."

He paused again to look back. The island had merged into the coast of England, which was receding in the distance. Soon, only the North Sea would surround them.

"Where are we headed?" he asked, turning to look ahead out over the prow.

"To the Kaupang in Skiringssal," Halfdan replied. "We'll sell the slaves and trade for goods we need."

"Was the raid a success?" Erik asked.

Halfdan smirked. "Too easy."

"What happened between the time you left the jarl and now?" Bjorn asked, his curiosity unsated.

"I worked my way back through Charles' kingdom, finding work where I could." He barked a laugh. "At one point, when it was discovered that I spoke the language of the Christian Church, they did their utmost to try to get me to become a monk. Can you imagine? Me a monk? I laughed at them and continued on my journey."

Though enjoying the tail, Halfdan raised an eyebrow. "How did you end up on the island? Why didn't your trek take you to the country of the Danes?"

"Ah," Erik nodded with a wistful sigh. "It all happened when I was in a town called Paris, far larger than Geneva. It is a sprawling city of more than 20,000 people surrounding a river called the Seine that runs to ocean."

"By the gods," Bjorn intoned. "20,000... 20,000 people living in one place... Why would anyone want to live like that, piled on top of each other. A man can't breathe in a place like that."

"I agree," Erik replied with a smile. "However, there are benefits to places like that. First, there are untold riches in a city like that. Churches filled with gold and silver and precious stones... moneylenders and shops and livestock and rich people. If one could raid such a town, you would never have to raid again. You could retire rich as a king."

Erik chuckled at the look in Bjorn's face, his dreamy eyes imagining a life of ease.

"One can retire when one is old and no longer wants to go on raids," Halfdan dismissively said. "Until then, what joy is there in life unless one plunders?"

"And besides," Erik added, "One would need a large army to raid Paris and then have to fight against Charles' even larger army to escape."

Silence settled among them as they each became lost in his own thoughts until Halfdan turned an eye back to Erik. "You said something happened in the town called Paris."

"I did," Erik acknowledged. "I met a woman and lost all sense of direction."

Halfdan smiled knowingly. "Women have a way of doing that."

"Quite true, my friend," Erik chuckled. "I tumbled head over heels for her and I believe she felt the same way about me, for, in truth, she did say so. Her name is Tone, Tone Thorgilsdottir."

"Ah ha," Bjorn exclaimed, "A fine Ost name."

"It is," Erik readily agreed. "She is more than the fairest among women."

"That's what all men say in the beginning." Halfdan snorted a laugh. "Then married life settles in and they can't wait to get away from the nag."

Erik laughed. "So you don't believe in a happy marriage, that a husband a wife can be truly consumed with each other?"

"I suppose it can happen," Halfdan admitted. His gaze shifted to one of the crew near the prow, a young virile man in his prime, fresh faced and excited to be on this successful raid. "Halvar there is one of those, though he's only been married two years now, not long enough to count."

"And yourself? Are you married?"

"Twelve years."

"Children?"

"Two stout lads and two girls."

Erik turned to Bjorn. "Are you married?"

"Yes. Fifteen years now. I've three boys, the oldest to start raiding with us next year. But you've not finished your tale. You met this woman in that one town…"

"Paris," Erik said, helping him out.

"Yes, that one. What happened then?"

"I met Tone and like I said, I was smitten. I'd never met a woman like her before: beautiful, clever, and smarter than any man alive."

"She sounds dangerous," Halfdan opined.

"In some instances, I'd agree. What separates her is she has no guile. She says what she thinks –"

"Ach," Halfdan grunted a laugh. "Then she truly is dangerous. Who wants to hear the jabber of a woman who constantly speaks her mind?"

"Sounds like someone we know," Bjorn smirked.

"You just steer," he gruffly answered then ticked his head at Erik to continue.

Though puzzled at Bjorn's comment, Erik plodded on. "Tone was in Paris with her parents, wealthy wool merchants who owned flocks in Wessex and other places."

"Where's Wessex?" Bjorn asked.

"To the far south of that island we just left. That little island is part of a larger island separated from the main continent by a wide channel of water."

"We know that," Halfdan dismissively stated.

"You do?"

"Of course. We've been sailing these waters for years, even all the way to Ireland."

Erik blinked in surprise then realized he really shouldn't be all that surprised. Vikings were known for their seafaring journeys.

"Of course," he admitted then proceeded to weave his tale. "At first, her parents weren't keen on my attention to their daughter, especially as I appeared to be a man of no consequence. They wanted a far better match for their daughter."

"Don't we all," Halfdan muttered, thinking of his own daughters.

"However, when they discovered that I was a soldier and seeing that their daughter was determined to be with me, they agreed to let me accompany them back across the channel, me acting as a sort of personal escort. During the trip, they were surprised that I was a learned man and their dislike of me was somewhat softened. Once across the channel and back in Wessex, Tone convinced her parents that she make a pilgrimage to the shrine of Saint Cuthbert, the patron saint of the little island where you so recently paid a visit. I and several other guardians went along to ensure her safety."

Halfdan gravely nodded. "Several men said they saw a woman and two men with you who ran off. They gave chase for a bit but let them go, except for one who said he followed until he came upon a small building that vanished before his eyes."

Erik twisted his head to face him, cocking an eyebrow. "The only buildings I saw were those of the monastery."

"That may be," Halfdan acknowledged, "but what happened to the woman and the men?"

"No doubt hiding in some depression or other," Erik answered with a shrug. Turning to face the prow, he uttered a grunt of frustration as he leaned forward, resting his forearms on his thighs. "This will not go down well with her parents."

"But you stayed behind to defend her," Bjorn pointed out, "a very honorable thing to do."

"They won't see it that way. They were against my going from the start." He sat up straight and glanced back over his shoulder. "Her escorts will relay the tale in their favor." With a wistful sigh, he said, "I pray she does not forget me, as I can never forget her."

Turning to his benefactor, Erik said, "Tell me Halfdan, are you the chieftain of Skiringssal and does the Kaupang belong to you?"

A smile flicked across Halfdan's face. "How did you guess?"

"It wasn't hard," Erik grinned. "You own longships and all these men serve you. One has to be rich or a chieftain to own longships. In this case my guess is that you are both."

Halfdan barked a laugh, slapping Erik on the back. "Not only do you tell excellent stories, you are clever as well."

"How old are you Erik?" Bjorn asked.

"What does it matter?" Halfdan gruffly stated.

"It doesn't," Bjorn replied. "I was just wondering how he managed to fit in all the things he's done."

"Humpf," Halfdan grunted, having wondered the same thing.

"I am two and forty winters old," Erik answered.

"What?" Bjorn snorted in derision. "Impossible."

Erik shrugged. "It's true."

Halfdan cocked an eyebrow as he studied the man seated next to him. "How can that be? You look as young as Halvar."

Erik smiled and shook his head. "That is too much flattery. If only I was as young as Halvar but with the brains and experience of the years I have now."

"You are truly two and forty winters old?" Bjorn asked, not wanting to believe this man looked years younger than he who was nearly ten years his junior.

"Yes."

Halfdan's brow furrowed. "This Tone Thorgilsdottir, you said she still lived with her parents?"

Erik suddenly realized his mistake and thought quickly. "Yes."

Bjorn caught the implication and asked the question. "How old was she?"

"Five and twenty."

"An old maid," Bjorn exclaimed.

"How is it one so fair should be so old and not married?" Halfdan questioned.

Erik rolled his eyes. "No one was good enough for their daughter, even a king."

Halfdan sat back, shaking his head. "I find this tale hard to swallow. Why would sensible parents keep their daughter at home when they could make an excellent match for her, especially in a city so big?"

"A fair question," Erik agreed. "You have not met her parents. Their desire to position themselves within the court of Charles caused them to scheme and counter scheme. Imagine a mother and father scheming so much that one suitor after another rose and fell depending on whether the king blew hot or cold. One day you're encouraged to court their daughter. The next day they sense the king has grown bored with you, or you have fallen out of favor, or he has sent you on a mission elsewhere and your influence is not as potent, and another takes your place."

"By the gods," Bjorn scoffed, wagging his head. "Who could live with such parents?"

"And remember I told you that Tone was clever, smart, and speaks her mind," Erik added. "Very few men were up to the challenge of winning the heart of a woman who surpassed them in intelligence and diplomacy."

"Ach," Halfdan sighed. "She sounds like more trouble than worth."

"There you have hit the mark," Erik said. "After a while, despite all their scheming, the number of court suitors began to dwindle, replaced by rich merchants wanting to make a better match. These were all scorned as inferior, undesirable. They were going to wait for the right moment for the right match."

"But she's five and twenty," Bjorn pointed out. "She's near past childbearing age. Who wants a match like that?"

"I do," Erik solemnly said. "I would trade the world's fortune to have her as my bride."

Halfdan smirked. "You do have it bad."

Tone stood in the doorway of Erik's townhouse, staring into the living room. An oppressive sadness filled her. She pondered if she should go back to her own place, but knew his presence was there too. Besides, most of her things were here. Walking in, she closed the door behind her and remained standing in the entry way. Heaving an anguished sigh, she cursed the gods who had snatched her lover and whisked him away beyond her reach, who were now conspiring to ruin her life.

Gritting her teeth, she steeled herself against the swelling emotion of utter despair, choosing instead to focus on her future and her mission. Nothing else mattered. Her resolve hardening, she whirled around and marched back out the door, deciding that now was as good a time as any to start implementing her plan. Besides, she had nothing left but time.

Shading her eyes with her hand, Tone leaned close to the window of the dojo and stared at the empty training room. It was still an hour before the first class and the lights were off though the door was open and the light was on in Master Lei's office in the back. Pulling the door open, she walked in, noting the pair of shoes at the edge and off the padded mat. Remembering protocol, she slipped her shoes off and strode across the mat. Floor to ceiling mirrors lined the walls, reflecting her deliberate steps.

Lei looked up from behind the desk and smiled as she stood in the doorway.

"Good afternoon, Tone," he said with a familiar smile. "You are back from your trip. I trust it was an exciting time."

"It was," she said with a wistful smile. "That's why I'm here."

"Oh?" Sensing something was wrong, he motioned for her to sit.

"I don't know how else to explain this," she said, sitting, "so I'm just going to say it. Erik won't be coming back for a while."

Lei's face turned impassive. "Why?"

Tone exhaled a slow breath. "They told me to lie, but I feel you deserve the truth. He trusted you and I do too."

"Go on," he encouraged.

Tone paused for a few heartbeats. "Erik was left behind."

If Lei was surprised, it didn't show. "This is what happens when one thinks he can bend time to his will. I have warned many not to tempt time or fate."

"You have to promise not to tell anyone," she emphasized. "They made me promise and you must promise too."

121

Lei regarded her with a smile. "Your promise did not last long."

Tone ruefully smiled. "That is because they are not honorable." She then explained about their offer of grad school and her acceptance. "In the meantime, I want to begin training here, taking up where I left off."

"You have studied before?"

"I was a second-degree black belt in Tae Kwon Do before I went off to college. I had to stop because I couldn't afford both."

Lei nodded in understanding.

"Then when I go to Oslo, I want to continue training with someone you could recommend."

Lei chuckled. "I don't know anyone in Norway."

"But you could find out who would be best."

Seeing the determination in her eyes, he said, "Yes. I will do that for you. When do you leave for school?"

"Probably not until January."

"Then I will see you tomorrow for your first class."

"Thank you." She bowed like she had seen Erik do.

Lei returned the bow from his seat. As she turned to leave, he said, "Do not give up hope. You are meant to be together."

Tone gave him an appreciative smile then turned so he wouldn't see the tears welling up in her eyes.

Erik stood on the prow as the crew rowed into the shallow finger of water called Kaupangskilen. The market center of Skiringssal lay before them. It was small, tiny compared to modern standards. It stretched to perhaps 100 meters to the left and right of the short pier that jutted out into the water. The majority of the thatched single story buildings were trade and workshops with smoke from cooking fires or smelters curling out from the holes in the middle of the roofs.

Kaupang... Skiringssal... Halfdan...   For the past two days of the sea journey, Erik had searched his memory, putting dates and names and places together. Some of it was easy. Kaupang was a well-known archaeological site of a Viking trading center that existed from the 8th century up through the early 10th century. The trading center was controlled by those who lived in Skiringssal, the location of the great hall of the Ynglinga dynasty.

What was not so easy to remember was the dynastic individuals and their genealogy. With probing questions, Erik had been able to piece together that the Halfdan navigating back to Kaupang was Halfdan the Mild, son of Eystein Halfdanson. Halfdan's youngest son was named Gudrod, the future Gudrod the Hunter who would become the father of Halfdan the Black who then was the father of Harald Fairhair, the first king of a united Norway.

But that was all in the future and unknown to everyone except himself. Deciding his efforts could be put to better use in the present, he asked Halfdan, "How many people live here?"

"Eh, probably around 200 or so."

"Not counting slaves?"

"Of course not," Halfdan replied, the answer obvious.

It seemed as if most of the town had emerged and waited on the shore, many waving to friends or loved ones on the ships. Oblivious to many of the respectful greetings called out to him as Jarl, Halfdan shook his head and cocked an eyebrow.

"Look at them," he scoffed to Erik. "With the way they're carrying on, you'd think we'd been gone a month or more. They'll be a lot happier when they finally see what we brought back. But, first things first."

With the ships secured next to the pier, Halfdan inhaled a deep breath and grinned. "Come, let's get the ships unloaded and the slaves sold. Then you will come with me to my hall in Skiringssal."

Expecting Halfdan to move, Erik stuttered to a stop as Halfdan waited while his men unloaded their respective seat-chests, carrying the spoils of the raid on Lindisfarne, which would be taken to the great hall in Skiringssal and divided among the raiders, Halfdan receiving the jarl's share. When the last man had disembarked, Halfdan led the way down the gangplank and onto the thick wooden pier.

"Ready?" he said. "Let's see what price the slaves will fetch."

Halfdan passed though the throng of town folk who glad-handed him and joked and vied for his attention. Erik watched, impressed as Halfdan had a word of greeting or friendly recognition for just about everyone in the crowd.

Soon Erik stood in the central market space with a small low platform in the center. The pathetic monks, disheveled and terrified, huddled to the side of the platform, their hands bound. Halfdan mounted the platform, hands on his hips, and twisted his head back and forth on a slow regal sweep of those assembled, the bidders and the curious onlookers.

"Though they might look like a miserable lot," he said with a grin, "there's talent among them. Let's find out, shall we?"

The crowd roared its approval.

Halfdan pointed to a monk whose tan and trim build said he spent time outdoors. "You first."

Two Vikings manhandled the monk and thrust him up onto the stage.

"What skills do you have?" Halfdan demanded.

The monk stared quizzically at him for a few seconds before saying, "Tu non intellego."

Halfdan's gaze hardened for an instant before he slowly nodded in understanding. With a nonchalant grin he turned to find Erik.

"What did he say?"

"He said that he didn't understand you," Erik replied, seeing the man's eyes, wide in fear.

"Tell him I better understand him or he becomes our first sacrifice."

Erik addressed the monk, speaking in Latin. "I suggest you make a strong effort to answer his questions. Otherwise, you are a dead man."

"Please, sir," the monk begged. "I only understand a little of what he says. My mother tongue is from the Gaels. I've only spoken Latin for the past seven years."

"What are your skills?"

"I was in charge of the fields and grains."

"So, you are a farmer?"

"Yes, both in my former and present life."

"What is your name?

"Brother Hugh."

Erik turned to Halfdan. "His name is Hugh, and he was and still is a farmer. He was in charge of the monastery's fields and grains. He does not speak the language of the Norse, but he is smart enough to learn."

"I bid two tenths of a measure," a voice called out.

"Three tenths," another voice responded, raising the bid.

"Four tenths," the first voice answered.

The bidding slowed when the price for Hugh approached five measures of silver. When no one raised the bid beyond four and five tenths measures of silver, Halfdan flipped his hands up and announced, "Sold to Asmund."

Asmund, a wealthy local farmer, nodded happily as he approached the scales table, withdrawing a small bag and spilling out pieces of hack-silver into his hand. Waiting until the engraved lead weights were placed on the pan on the one side, he added his portion on the other pan until the scales balanced.

While Asmund paid for his newly acquired thrall, Halfdan continued the auction.

"Bring the next one up."

The next monk tended towards the plump side. When it was discovered that he was a cook, the bidding started fast until Halfdan decided he wanted the cook for himself and shut off the bidding.

There followed more sales of monks whose perceived worth was not what they themselves believed or assumed. Those whose prior life involved long hours in a scriptorium or producing vellum fetched lower prices, being sold off as farm workers.

The last was a slender young monk about seventeen or eighteen years old, with a mane of unruly red hair. He had the look of a man who had been woken from a nightmare only to discover the waking world was far worse than his dream.

"What is your name and what are your skills?" Erik asked.

"M... my name is Pearson," the man replied. "I... I'm... a, I mean I was still learning to farm and cook. The abbot used me to write and translate correspondence for him. I can read and write Latin and Anglian, and even Saxon."

When Erik translated, there was an audible groan of disinterest and many turned away, the spectacle over.

Seeing the crowd dispersing, Pearson swallowed hard, the specter of his possible fate rearing up like a terrible beast.

Halfdan was about to condemn him to his fate when a voice said, "One tenth measure."

Halfdan smirked as he looked over at a middle-aged man with thick auburn beard and hair, wearing homespun clothing of high-quality wool.   "Anyone else?"   When no one countered the bid, he announced, "Sold to Harek."

As Pearson was led away, Halfdan stepped down from the platform and over to the scales table where the assayer was putting away his scale and weights.

"How'd we do?"

"Thirty-four and five tenths measures," the man replied.

"Not bad," Halfdan nodded.   "This is Erik Jon's-son. We picked him up on the way back."

The man frowned in puzzlement as he contemplated how that was possible given there was only sea in between here and there.

Offering no explanation, Halfdan introduced the man to Erik. "This is Hjalmar... Niel's-son. He's a silversmith and has the fairest set of scales around here."

Hjalmar was a middle-aged man with scruffy beard and stubby hands. He peered up at Erik, his light blue eyes studying him with an intensity that initially made Erik uncomfortable.

It was then that Erik recognized there was something else that set him apart. He had sensed it on the voyage here but he hadn't put it together. With Hjalmar staring up at him, Erik realized that he was probably the tallest person in the area by a good three to four inches.

"Come Erik," Halfdan encouraged.   "Time to settle accounts. You will stay with me until you can find your own way."

Erik nodded an affable 'well-met' to Hjalmar and followed Halfdan through Kaupang, past pottery shops with clay bowls and loom weights and spindle-whorls, on past the houses where glass bead makers turned colored glass into beads, past the blacksmith stoking his forge then onto the well-worn cart path leading to Skiringssal.

Rocky outcroppings crested with thick forest growth interspersed among farm and grazing fields. Halfdan maintained a steady pace along the path until the path curved to the left and the forest separated to reveal an immense structure in the distance. Halfdan stopped and gave Erik an 'are-you-impressed' look, immediately satisfied when he saw Erik's awe.

"Skiringssal," Erik reverently murmured. "Always wondered what it looked like."

Halfdan flashed a puzzled glance at him. "You have heard of my hall?"

"Who hasn't?" Erik said, stoking Halfdan's pride.

Skiringssal stood high and set apart from the surrounding land, much like a medieval castle perched on a tall hill. The great hall was shaped like a long ship with massive curved boat-like wooden walls with thick supporting buttresses outside, bracing the arched roof. A massive door painted red stood in the middle. Cows, goats, pigs, and sheep roamed in several fields surrounding the hall, all attended by what Erik assumed to be slaves for though they were diligent in their work, now that the Jarl had returned, none of them seemed thrilled to be there. In the penned space next to the hall, chickens and ducks pecked the remains of food scattered from the morning.

Just outside the front door, two young Vikings stood guard over the pile of loot liberated from Lindisfarne. Halfdan's children stood near the pile, gawking at the bounty. Seeing their father, they dashed down the path, the youngest leaping into his arms.

"Did you get me anything," she said with an expectant smile.

"We'll see when everything is properly divided."

"Who's he?" the oldest boy asked.

"His name is Erik Jon's-son. He's going to stay with us for a little while. You all be good to him."

"Is he gonna take our bed?" the other boy complained.

"No, Gudrod," Halfdan answered, unloading the youngest from his arms. "You all go back and tell Mama that I'm back and brought company."

"She already knows you're back," the youngest unformed him.

"Fine," Halfdan smiled. "Do what I tell you. I'm sure you all have work to do."

The four children headed off while the oldest, a pretty girl of twelve winters, just beginning to blossom into womanhood, hung back, studying Erik with a bold smile.

"You too, Astrid. Go help your mother. Tell her I haven't had a decent meal since I left and I'm ready for some good food. While you're at it, you can fetch me and my friend a mug of mead."

"Yes, Papa," she demurely answered and languidly strolled away.

"You have your hands full with that one," Erik laughed.

Halfdan rolled his eyes in response.

"Have you found a match for her?"

"Why? You interested?" Halfdan teased.

"Not at all. I'm old enough to be her father."

"Grandfather perhaps," Halfdan chuckled.

"I would have been making babies at thirteen winters, to be her grandfather," Erik pointed out. "I may be older than usual, but I can still fight with the best of them."

"So I saw," Halfdan said with a healthy respect. "I'm still sorting out what I'm going to say to the widows and their families. Word will get out of your involvement."

"It was self-defense," Erik objected.

"Yes, I know," Halfdan agreed. "Perhaps a man-price will be sufficient. We will see what the families demand."

"I'll point out right now that I don't have a lot of money with me," Erik said, suddenly remembering the coins he had were from the wrong century. "Tone's guards paid for everything."

"An interesting arrangement," Halfdan observed.

Erik sheepishly smiled. "They were afraid we would run off together."

Halfdan smirked while he scanned the pile of booty. His gaze paused when he spotted some books. Frowning, he pointed at the books, each with wooden book covers, the interior vellum pages link-stitched. "Why did someone think these were worth anything?"

Erik picked one up and opened the oak cover, a cross artfully carved in the center. It was the Gospel of Mark, heavily illuminated with Celtic designs and the letters written with a firm hand in tight angular letters, reminding Erik of the pages from the Lindisfarne Gospels. Blinking at the realization, he quickly scanned the rest of the pile and found two wooden book covers that had been torn from a book, both studded with precious stones.

Chuckling, he wagged his head. *Wonder what the British Library would pay me for the original covers to the Lindisfarne Gospels?*

"You may want to keep these," he said, nodding at the books. "While they might not have value to you, the Christian church will pay handsomely for them."

"Really?" Halfdan said, suddenly pleased.

"Yes. These take a long time to make and are very expensive to replace. You find a large church and instead of pillaging it, you trade for these. I have no doubt that they will pay well for them. You make a handsome profit with no effort."

Pleased with the news, Halfdan studied the rest of the loot as Astrid walked up with two mugs of mead, handing one to her father and deliberately handing the other to Erik.

"Thank you," Erik said, giving her a salute with his mug.

Halfdan raised his mug, took a satisfied sip then leaned over to whisper in his daughter's ear.

Nodding with a smile and a more than passing interest at the newcomer, she dashed off, returning moments later and handed her father a silver arm ring.

"Here." Halfdan handed the arm ring to Erik. "This is for you."

"For me?" Erik asked, startled at the gift. "Why?"

"Because you are now one of us."

"But I haven't done anything worthy of this magnificent gift," Erik replied, gazing at the craftsmanship of twisted silver with a wolf's head at each end.

"You will," Halfdan said with a satisfied grin.

"You can take time to give presents to total strangers but you can't take the time to greet your own wife?" a voice teased.

Erik looked over to where an attractive strawberry blond stood in the doorway, her hands on her hips. She was a shapely woman, which surprised Erik considering she had birthed at least five children, not counting other possible births of children who did not survive.

"Hullo Liv, my pet," Halfdan grinned then introduced her to Erik. "My wife, Liv Dagsdottir."

"A pleasure, m'Lady," Erik said, respectfully dipping his head. "I am Erik Jon's-son."

Liv cocked her head back and gave him the once over. "Where'd he find you?" Before Erik could answer, she turned her gaze to Halfdan. "He's not like the other louts you bring home. This one has manners. What a refreshing change."

"Pay her no mind," Halfdan confided with a smile.

Liv's attention shifted to down the road where half a dozen men and women marched purposefully towards the long house.

"That looks like Oluf and his brother's wife," she said. "They don't appear to be too happy. What happened?"

"Erik killed Gosta," Halfdan explained.

"It was self-defense," Erik quickly pointed out.

Seeing Liv's questioning stare, Halfdan said, "I'll explain later. Right now, why don't you take Erik in the house. I'll be in in a bit."

Immediately understanding, Liv motioned for Erik to follow her.

"Perhaps you can tell me what happened," she said, entering the house.

"I'd be happy to, m'Lady," Erik answered.

Liv abruptly stopped and faced him. "I appreciate you being polite, but my name is Liv and you are welcome to call me that. Everyone else does."

"But you are the Jarl's wife," Erik countered, "though if I remember right, you have your own pedigree as being the daughter of King Dag of the Vestmar."

Liv stared intently at him. "What has he told you?"

"Only that you were the fairest creature he has ever seen," Erik flattered. "And now I see the good cause for his doe-eyes every time he talks about you."

Liv laughed. "You have a smooth tongue in that head of yours. I think I may like you."

Stepping into the home, Erik's first impression was the reconstructed longhouse of the Lofotr Viking Museum in Lofoten.

The house was divided into four parts: living quarters, a banquet hall, a workshop/storage room, and a stable for farm animals at the end. Ornately carved beams supported a roof that he guessed rose ten meters above their heads. Second story lofts ran the length of both sides of the house, leaving the center open. He was surprised that instead of a hard-packed dirt floor, smooth level paving stones covered the ground. Further, instead of one central fire pit for cooking and heating, two fire pits divided the house in thirds, providing more heat. One pit was used exclusively for cooking and heating while the other was used for heating and smithy work. Slaves busily attended the fires, or cleaned, or cared for livestock. The atmosphere was one of nonstop work.

"So what happened that caused you to kill Gosta?" Liv asked, leading the way to the seating area of the banquet hall.

"He attacked me," he said, taking a seat opposite her, "and since I didn't appreciate that, I returned the favor, much to his dissatisfaction."

Liv smirked and nodded. By now, the children had gathered near her, the youngest crawling up on her lap. Astrid stood to the side, boldly appraising the stranger.

The door opened and Halfdan walked in, his face a study in frustration. Crossing over to where Liv and Erik sat, he plopped down next to his wife and exhaled an irritated sigh.

"As I expected, families of two of the men have demanded restitution, despite my warning. Like all the men in their families, the brothers are headstrong and have demanded a holmgang."

"A blood challenge?" Erik replied, surprised.

"Yes," Halfdan replied, shaking his head. "They are within their rights. Still, I don't have a good feeling about this."

"I can take care of myself," Erik asserted.

"It's not you I'm worried about."

Erik nodded in understanding. "I'll try not to kill them. When does the challenge occur?"

"As soon as possible."

"Then I ask for time to allow me to gain a weapon of my choice."

Halfdan nodded agreement. "That is allowed. In the meantime, you will stay here. You can help me divide up our things from the raid."

"I would be honored to assist you," Erik replied, "and I am further honored by your kindness to me."

Liv leaned into her husband. "I like him. He has manners. And speaking of manners," she locked her eyes on her husband, "we need to invite your sister to a meal... very soon."

Halfdan's puzzled frown vanished in understanding. "Yes, you're right. It's been too long since we've seen her."

Tone struggled to keep herself occupied, but there was only so much one could do with all the free time she now had. TTI was more than generous in providing for her needs, so much so that there was no need for her to work. In fact, TTI insisted that since she was now an employee of TTI, she was not authorized or allowed to work for another company. She knew it had more to do with their fear that she might slip and reveal the glaring defect in TTI's armor. Of course, that defect was already known to some outside TTI. She remembered Seth's reaction when she told him what happened.

"Those bastards," he snapped. "And they were gonna just leave him there, hoping it would all just fade away."

They were sitting at the small dining room table in Lisa's apartment.

"What are you gonna do?" Lisa asked, her hand over the top of the coffee mug, feeling the moist warmth.

"I'm going back to get him," Tone asserted. "That's all there is to it."

"How?" Seth frowned.

"I don't know yet, but I'm gonna get him back one way or another."

Lisa gazed at Seth. "Sort of makes you rethink this whole time travel thing."

"Yeah," he sighed, rolling his eyes.

That was two days ago. Since then it was the same routine. Still, one can only clean house so much, straighten clothes, and organize. She had moved out of her apartment and settled permanently in Erik's place, which really didn't require much effort as most of her things were already there.

Yet, except for her martial arts training, she had little to occupy her time or look forward to. Days were spent meandering the hiking trails of the Hoosier National Forest or long runs on the back roads south of Corydon. Evenings found her at the dojo, studying the martial arts even when she didn't have class. Master Lei noted her presence and offered her individual attention.

Back home, she devoted time to studying 8th century Scandinavia or Old Norse, learning more vocabulary, all the while praying that TTI would solve the time problem before she left for grad school. Late night meals were simple affairs with a preponderance of Chinese take-out. Yet she could not ease the ache in her heart as she sat at the table envisioning her love sitting across from her as she remembered the ecstasy of life with Erik. What little sleep she did get was spent on his side of the bed, snuggling with his pillow.

Yet it had not even been a week since Erik was left behind and already she was more than wanderlost. Little things that once brought a smile had lost their allure or became a nuisance, a reminder of what was missing in her life, like seeing lovers, arm in arm, walking in the park, entwined around each other, a union of souls.

She found herself resenting others' happiness. Her own pain was almost more than she could bear, especially when once again, she bumped into the ex at the wine shop.

"Well look who's here," Linda sneered, gazing past Tone. "Where's Mister Manther? I figured you two were joined at the hip. Of course, when you get to be his age, anything in a skirt that says more than 'Hi' sends him off into fantasyland."

"Apparently something you never did," Tone shot back.

Linda stiffened, frustrated that this, this… girl… wouldn't be intimidated or put in her place. "So how was the trip to… um, where was it? Some silly place in some long-forgotten century?"

"It was London in 893 AD," Tone calmly answered before slowly cocking her head and peering intently at her. "I'm still trying to understand how you two were ever married. You might have been attractive when you were younger, but the shrew factor had to have outweighed that."

Linda's face froze in anger. "Listen you little trollop –"

"Trollop?" Tone interrupted. "That's a good word for what you are. I'm surprised you know what it means. Now if you don't mind, I'd rather not have to spend any more time talking with you. It's sort of like wrestling with a pig. It doesn't matter if you win, you'll still get dirty."

Without waiting for a response, Tone marched past her to the checkout counter. Though the sparring had felt good, it did more than remind her that she was alone. She could handle 'alone.' It was without him that made it unbearable.

Once back home, she stuck the two bottles of mead behind the half-filled bottle of cold mead in the frig. A glass of mead sounded good at the moment and she poured a full glass before walking to stand in the living room. Gazing around the tidy room, her eyes rested on Erik's guitar and an image coalesced of him bent over the instrument as his hands danced upon the strings, performing a composition he had written. She had called him a 'True Renaissance Man.'

She lifted the glass to her lips and took a deep swallow. The sweet honeyed wine felt good for it suddenly reminded her of the first time with Erik at her house. He had been almost shy, yet strong. That first kiss, right after he had told her he wanted to go back in time with her, had been electric. The long pent up emotions, the patient waiting for the school year to end before asking him for a date, the thrill of when he said 'Yes,' followed by the excitement of him coming to her apartment had created such anticipation that the proverbial emotional floodgates had exploded.

From that moment on, she was caught up in a whirlwind of joy and passion, knowing without a doubt that she had found fairytale happiness. Yes... she had found true love alright... that's why she was standing here, alone, in his apartment, in what should have been *their* apartment.

Her reflections were interrupted when her phone rang. Hope burst within when the screen said 'Meredith – TTI.'

"Hullo?"

"Tone?"

"Yes."

"This is Meredith from TTI."

"Yes. I know. Have you found a solution for the machine?"

"Uh... no, not yet, but we're making progress."

"How much is progress?" Tone interrupted.

"I don't know," Meredith snapped, her frustration evident. "The reason I called is that the university accepted your application and classes begin in three weeks. We've already made travel and lodging arrangements as well as the visa and residence permit. All you need to do is show up."

Tone heard the smug satisfaction in the woman's voice.
"When do I leave?"

"Next week. You'll need time to get settled and get familiar with the city. I'll email you the particulars. I assume you have an up-to-date passport."

"Of course."

"Fine. I've assigned Lisa Bright to be your point of contact. If you have any problems or need assistance or have any questions, just contact her. Her contact info will be in the email. Good luck with your studies."

Tone listened as Meredith ended the phone call without so much as a goodbye. It was as though she couldn't wait to get off the phone.

Tone once again glanced around the living room at the signs of a man's presence, a man whose love of things past was evident. Yes, there were the requisite contemporary items like the TV above the fireplace and the couch and chair. But one could not help but feel the man was a sort of anachronism, living in the wrong place and time. The walls were adorned with framed vellum pages of Gregorian chants, antiphonies, and illuminated Bible pages, each one over 1000 years old. The large display cabinet against the wall contained Viking jewelry, medieval cross pendants, coinage, and even a well-preserved sword with the rare Ulfberht mark.

Tone chuckled. She was living in a museum.

Yet she appreciated that with all the artifacts and other mementos, Erik was somewhat of a neat-freak. While some people might call it anal retentive, for him it was just business as usual. The place was clean and tidy. Even the items in the frig were arranged.

The funny thing was that she was the same way. She liked order. Not that she wasn't a free-spirit, but one can't live for the moment without some sort of plan. *Who am I kidding?* She chuckled. *I'm the poster child for anal retentive, especially the hard to please part. Just ask any of the guys I've dated... which is all moot because I've finally found the one knight in shining armor... although 'found' may be stretching it as I have no clue where he is at the moment. All I know is that wherever he is, I should be there... I* will *be there.*

Erik was up early the next morning, heading down to Kaupang before breakfast.

"You've not eaten," Liv chided, wrapped in a bear fur overcoat.

"I'm not hungry at the moment," he replied, guessing she was naked beneath the coat. "I'll get something when I come back."

"Where are you off to?" Halfdan frowned as he sat up in bed, revealing a bare chest leading Erik to assume he too was naked.

Erik shot a quick glance behind him at the children still asleep on their respective beds, though Astrid stirred at the sound of adult voices. Two slaves attending the fires did their best to appear focused on their work.

"I'm going to the smithy," Erik answered. "I need some weapons."

"I've got a sword or axe or anything else you need," Halfdan reminded him.

"I've got something special in mind," Erik cryptically replied. "I won't be long."

Once outside, Erik inhaled a slow deep breath, savoring the clean air and the bouquet of farms and trees, and radiance of a sun-filled day. It was the kind of day where one would have to work at being unhappy, though in this moment of time, his life was incomplete because she was not here. He thought yet again that his life would never be complete without her.   And once more he prayed that somehow she would find a way to come back to him.

Heading down the road to Kaupang, he ruminated his circumstances.   Here he was living in the very world he studied and dreamed about.   The question was whether he would be allowed to remain here, which begged the question of whether TTI would send someone to fetch him back to the present.   Logically, TTI would have to send someone back, if nothing else to see if he was still alive, which was complicated because they hadn't a clue where he was, which meant that Tone likewise had no clue where to look for him.

What he needed to do was to somehow provide her a clue, something that only she would understand.   An idea coalesced and he smiled at the possibility.   He would need the perfect spot and someone who knew something about carving stones.

Kaupang was already busy with merchants and food vendors preparing for the day.   A little ways into the town, Erik found the man he needed and approached the smithy, giving him a winning smile.

"I understand you are the best weapon forger in all the Ost."

"I have that reputation," the man stated without conceit, "because I am good at what I do and I value my name."

"A wise perspective," Erik said.   "I have a special weapon I'd like for you to make."

"Ah," the smithy nodded.   "A sword or axe?"

"Neither," Erik answered.   "What I have in mind is like nothing you have ever seen.   I want two metal bars connected by a chain.   The length of each bar is from my elbow to the wrist.   The length of the chain connecting the two bars is half the length of a single bar.   I want the bars smooth and round, the diameter of each bar to be two fingers in width."   He then went on to describe the chain and the design. "Lastly, I want two of these weapons made."

The smithy rewarded him with a curious frown. "This is a weapon?"

"You'll see," Erik replied with a smile. "How long will it take to make them?"

"It should not take long," the smithy answered. "Come back day after tomorrow."

"There is one more item I would like," Erik said, "a small two pronged utensil I can use for eating."

The smithy raised an eyebrow. "What's wrong with the knife?"

"I prefer to use what is called a fork."

"A fork?" the smithy repeated.

"Yes, like a fork in the road where it splits in two. The fork will have two pointed tongs connected to a handle."

"And you will eat with this?"

"Yes." Erik laughed at the man's incredulous stare. "I would like it made of silver."

"To eat with?" The smithy's expression said Erik was more than crazy.

"Yes."

The smithy shook his head. "While I can make something like you suggest, it would be better for a silver smithy to do what you ask."

"And if I want you to make one of steel? How long would that take?"

"It will be ready day after tomorrow."

Chapter 5

Halfdan cocked an eyebrow when Erik showed him his new weapons. "You will fight with these?" He reached for one and held it in his hand, dangling a bar from the chain.

"Yes," Erik nonchalantly replied. "These are my spinning swords."

"Swords?" Halfdan scoffed. "You have no blades. How do you intend to win this fight without a proper weapon? Oluf and Tue are strong and good fighters, especially Oluf. They will use sharp battle axes. These," he held up the nunchuk, "will be of no use."

Erik grinned with self-confidence. "You'll see. Where do I go?"

"There is a field across the water from Kaupang." Halfdan shook his head. "Are you sure about this?" He handed the nunchuk back to Erik. "I have plenty of good weapons, axes and bucklers that would be far better suited. Leave these toys here."

"Trust me," Erik replied, unabashed. "It will be fine. When do we fight?"

Halfdan glanced back at Liv whose countenance said she too thought Erik's choice of weapons was more than foolish. With a sigh and a helpless shrug, he turned back to Erik. "I will send word. Their farms are less than half a day's travel. So I expect them to be here tomorrow."

The holmgang field was on the finger of land across the water close to the mouth of the Kaupangskilen. Erik smiled for it seemed that most of the town was there to watch the spectacle. He noted that even the smithy was there, his face a mask of overt curiosity wondering just how Erik would employ these strange weapons.

Halfdan stood in the center of the clearing, Erik to his left and Oluf to his right. He addressed both of them.

"You know the law. Let this matter be settled now and forever." He stepped away to the side where Tue and his relatives stood.

Erik faced his first opponent, a stout man of twenty-three winters and two raiding campaigns with Halfdan. He carried a battle ax in his right hand and a buckler in his left. He glared contemptuously at Erik, his eyes mocking the strange bars in his hands.

"Are you ready, stranger?" Oluf said, oozing confidence, noting the strange contraptions Erik held in his hands.

"Sure," Erik casually replied. "But I do have to ask, are you sure you want to this? When we're finished there will be one less to go raiding. Pity it would have to be you."

There was a scattering of tittering mixed with grunts of disdain for this man's arrogance.

"Brave words for an old man," Oluf sneered.

"I suppose they are," Erik shrugged. "Well then, are we going to talk each other to death or do we fight?"

"We fight." Oluf raised his sword.

Nodding, Erik slowly began spinning his nunchuks by his sides. The murmuring and noise of the crowd silenced broken by the occasional cry of the gulls.

Gauging the spinning bars, Oluf sniffed in scorn and took the first step to press the attack only to find the bars spinning at Erik's side were now crisscrossing in front of him like a windmill. Brought up short in his attack, Oluf feinted left then attacked to his right.

Though Oluf's speed impressed Erik, it did not impress him enough to stop him from launching his own attack. With his left hand, Erik flicked a nunchuk at the man's head, causing him to instinctively raise the buckler in defense. At the same time, Erik's right hand twirled a hard whack against the man's side, impacting in the middle of the ribcage, resulting in an audible grunt of pain.

Erik pressed the attack, his nunchuks whirling faster and faster in so many directions that Oluf staggered back, vainly struggling to find an advantage.

In a twirling leap, Erik smashed one nunchuk against Oluf's buckler causing him to stumble to his right. Erik followed with a low swept swing, banging a nunchuk bar against Oluf's knee and dropping him like a toppled monument, clutching his knee and writhing in excruciating pain, his face scrunched in agony from a dislocated knee and cracked ribs.

Towering over him, Erik stepped on the man's ax, pinning it to the earth, his nunchuks spinning at his side. "Do you yield or shall I kill you?"

"I yield, I yield," Oluf groaned through gritted teeth.

Erik walked to stand before Halfdan, one bar of each nunchuk tucked under his armpits. "I am ready for the second blood challenge."

Suppressing a shocked grin, especially with how quickly Erik had dispatched Oluf, Halfdan turned to Tue who stood to the side, his face a mix of shock, fear, regret and awe. "Are you ready?"

Tue swallowed hard, his eyes flicking between the relaxed man with the strange weapons and Oluf, curled on the ground, groaning in misery as several men bent down over him trying to coax him onto a makeshift stretcher.

"Uh," Tue squeaked then cleared his throat. Never thinking he'd actually have to fight, especially with Oluf's reputation as a fighter, Tue rapidly reassessed his chances for success. "Uh, perhaps I was too quick. I think a weregild would satisfy everyone."

"No," Erik flatly stated.

"No?" Tue's eyes burst wide.

"No?" Halfdan said with a frown. "He has offered to accept a man-price instead. Why not accept?"

Erik twisted his head to give Tue a hard stare. "He issued a holmgang challenge to me, which I accepted. He figured that Oluf would either defeat me and he would not have to fight, or Oluf would so wear me out that he would have an easy victory. Now that he realized his chances of winning are zero, he wants to back out. The challenge stands."

"Erik," Halfdan said, lowering his voice. "This challenge does no one any good. You've already eliminated one man from most likely ever being a useful fighter. You go on like this and I won't have anyone left to go on raids with me. For my sake, accept his weregild and be done with it. I will pay the price."

Erik focused his gaze on the Viking Jarl. "Because you ask it, I will do as you wish, but the weregild is my responsibility. I cannot ask for such favor from you when you have already done so much for me." Seeing the pleased reaction in Halfdan's eyes, Erik knew he had hit the mark.

Turning to Tue, Erik said, "Our Jarl has asked that I reconsider. Thus, I will accept the offer of weregild. However, I will only pay half per the laws of holmgang absolving me of any wrong."

There was an overwhelming murmur of respect and approval for Erik's response. Recognizing he had been outmaneuvered, though thankful he did not have to fight, Tue nodded agreement and stuck out his sword hand. Erik clasped the extended hand and the agreement sealed.

Tone sat at a conspicuous table in the TTI employees' cafeteria pretending to read a book. The lunchtime crowd was just starting and she surreptitiously lifted her eyes each time the cafeteria door opened. As the crowds grew, many employees loaded up their biodegradable containers and headed back to their offices to eat while they worked, while the rest chose to enjoy their half-hour for lunch and stayed in the cafeteria, chatting with friends and coworkers.

As the crowds grew, seating space became a premium and she found herself more than once asked to share a table. Seeing the attractive woman alone at the table, no wedding ring on her finger, a number of men made a beeline to occupy the three vacant spaces, each time receiving a warm smile and a "Please sit," before she resumed reading.

Though a few were polite and let her read, the others wanted to engage her in conversation, the usual icebreaker being "That's a large book you're reading."

Tone would nod and smile and allow the conversation to continue as she subtly asked seemingly innocent questions, essentially determining where they worked and in what capacity and just how useful they might be in the future.

After two days of listening to their puffed up visions of themselves, she was beginning to wonder if her plan was such a good idea. After all, one can only drink so much coffee and put up with the idle chitchat while delicately fending off unwanted advances.

Nearing one o'clock, with the lunch crowds slowing down and spaces freeing up, she wondered if it was time to call it a day when she saw Brent walk in. She remembered him from yesterday. It was a pleasant conversation made easier because he was also attractive.

Working his way down the serving line, he paused at the cashier, paid for his lunch then lifted his tray and scanned the dining hall. Seeing Tone, he smiled a greeting, lifting his tray slightly, asking to join her. Receiving a nod, he happily made his way to her table.

"You haven't finished the book yet?" he teased, sitting.

"Not yet." Though smiling at his jest, she silently chuckled that she's been reading the same page for the past two days.

Before he had a chance to continue, a man walked up, lunch tray in his hands.

"So this is why you went to lunch late."

As Tone looked up, she saw the fleeting look of irritation in Brent's eyes.

"Mind if I join you?"

"Not at all," Tone answered, much to Brent's disappointment.

"My name's Gene, Gene Milligan." Sitting, he unfolded his napkin, placing it on his lap. "I wondered why Mister Routine here suddenly changed his dining hour," he teased, giving Brent a knowing look. "Quite unusual. Now I see the reason why."

Tone smiled as she studied the man. He reminded her of many men she had met before, a hail-well-met sort of guy who put on a good show, but you didn't want to turn your back on them. In his favor, Gene was a tall handsome man with the chiseled looks and body of a model, complete with wavy blond hair and perfect teeth.

"My name is Ingrid," she lied with a winning smile, noting the casual way he looked at her eyes, all the while the peripheral vision was checking out her body. She inwardly chuckled, pleased that her choice of clothing was working. Though dressed business, her suit emphasized her assets.

Gene glanced down at the book. "Icelandic sagas. Some light reading I see."

"They're actually quite enjoyable," she said.

"And you read that for fun?"

"Yes and no. Do you two work together?"

"No," Brent quickly answered. "He works down in the mushroom hole."

"The mushroom hole?" Tone repeated with a grin.

"He's jealous because I work in the Time Machine department, the core and soul and the very reason this company exists. While Mister Routine here lives it up in Research, I'm working my ass off keeping everything straight with the machine."

"Is there a problem with it?" Tone innocently asked, struggling to remember if she had met him before, though thrilled that all the time sitting in the cafeteria was finally paying off.

"Naw, not really. For some reason Corporate has come down on us like a ton of bricks. We're now bustin' our asses to program the machine to operate farther back in time."

"I thought it could do that already," Tone said, her brows knitted as though puzzled.

"Naw," Gene said, shaking his head. "It's never been programed to go farther back than four to five hundred years." He took a bite of his sliced turkey.

"So why are they pushing to make it go back farther?" she asked. "It seems to me that the further back you go, the more difficulty you'd have, not with the machine, but with people fitting in. It's not like you can send just anyone back during the Roman times. Not only would they have to speak Latin, they'd need to know something of the historical setting."

"Exactly," Gene complimented. "Take Brent here. He's a wiz at research, the best in the business. But how many languages does he speak?" He twisted his head and stared at Brent.

"I don't speak any," Brent huffed. "I don't need to. Besides, there are superb language translator apps out there that can handle what I need."

"But that's my point," Gene said, returning his attention to Tone. "Brent here is an example of the limitations of the Time Machine. Sure, we can punch you back in time, but if you can't fit in, what does it matter? Pretty much everyone we've sent back was sent back to a time where they still talked the same language. How many people today can talk like Shakespeare talked and that was what... something like only four hundred years ago?"

"So if that's the case," Tone said, "why the big rush to go back farther in time?"

Gene shot a quick glance around the dining room then leaned in and lowered his voice. "What I tell you stays right here." Waiting until they both nodded, he said, "From what I can discover, someone wanted to go back farther in time and there was a screw up."

"What happened?" Tone asked, her eyes bright like she was sharing an intimate secret.

"I don't know the whole story, but from what I can piece together, the guy ended up in the wrong place and the wrong time."

When he didn't continue, Tone frowned. "That's it? That's the reason for Corporate to get their panties in a wad?"

Gene snorted a laugh. "My, my, such language."

"Sorry," she sheepishly replied.

"Nothing to be sorry for," Gene reassured her. "So where do you work? I haven't seen you before."

"She's a new hire," Brent answered for her, wanting to show that he already knew more about her than Gene.

"I've only been here a couple of days," she explained.

"What department?" Gene asked.

"That's just it. I don't have one yet."

Gene blinked in confusion. "No department? They hired you without a position? How is that possible? What do you do all day?"

"I study," she said, holding up the book.

"Icelandic sagas? No offense, but how does that fit in with TTI?"

"Actually," Tone said, "they're sending me to grad school."

"They are?" Gene's eyes popped wide, a mixture of surprise and jealousy. "For what?"

"Nordic studies."

Gene's mouth slacked open then shut. "How did you manage that?"

"I graduated summa cum laude in Nordic studies and they offered me a job. I was just as surprised as you are now," she said with a shrug, which technically was the truth.

"Nordic studies..." Gene repeated. "I assume you speak some ancient language with that?"

"Yes. I speak Norse."

"Do you speak any other languages?" Brent asked, worming his way into the conversation.

"Yes. I speak Old Norse, Norwegian, Danish, Swedish, German, Icelandic, and Spanish."

"My God," Gene blurted, impressed. "Where are you going to grad school?"

"University of Oslo," she said. "Part of the studies will also be in Iceland."

"How long will it take you?" Brent asked, likewise impressed.

"The program is for two years." She grinned and whispered, "I'm looking to figure out how I can get them to spring for a Ph.D."

Gene laughed and took a sip of his drink. "When do you start school?"

"I leave next week," she replied. "Part of me wishes the school was closer because I've really enjoyed the people in the company here. Another part says it will be fun being in a new environment."

"What about your parents or your boyfriend?" Gene asked, fishing.

"I stopped living with my parents when I was eighteen," she answered. "And I don't have a boyfriend." Which was also technically true because Erik wasn't a 'boy-friend'; he was her fiancé.

The men's faces lit up at the news and the plotting began in earnest, especially with her departure next week. Gene was the first to pounce.

"A bunch of us are going to Frisco's for drinks after work," he said with a winning smile. "Why don't you come too?"

"Sounds interesting," Tone answered. "Is that a bar or a restaurant?"

"It's both," Brent interjected. "We usually go to the bar and order munchies."

For some reason, Erik's ex, Linda, came to mind and her obsession with working her way up the corporate ladder. Though Tone knew Gene's invitation had more to do with getting her in bed than working his way up the ladder, she still felt the tinge of ennui that people like Gene and Linda must experience as they tried to give meaning to their pointless lives.

"You bringing your girlfriend?" Brent asked, trying to make it appear an innocent question.

Heaving a dramatic sigh, Gene hung his head in defeat. "We broke up."

"That's too bad," Brent commiserated with a forced smile.

Yet Tone knew the truth. She had met a few Gene's in her life.

He was the kind of man who could weave a convincing story and charm any listener. Invariably, no one would ever see or meet any of Gene's supposed girlfriends as his tale of woe would repeat with each new conquest. But the pain of a broken heart would work on some unsuspecting victim of his charm.

It usually started with drinks at some bar after work as he poured out his story to the attentive and interested dupe. But he was both clever and patient. Nothing would happen that first time other than him relating his tale and her compassionate empathy.

He would call her the next day and apologize for unloading all his troubles on her, but that she was just so easy to talk to and "Thank you for listening to me. That's all I wanted to say. Just thanks. Hope you have a great rest of the day."

"Wait," the woman would hurriedly reply. "If you're not doing anything tonight, would you like to go for a drink again?"

"I... I mean..." Gene replied, doing his best to appear hesitant yet interested. "I don't want to bore you. If we do, I want to hear all about you."

That was all it took. The fish had swallowed the hook, sinker, line, and the fishing pole.

By the third rendezvous after work Gene was sharing her bed and making her breakfast the next morning.

After a month or two of lovemaking sessions, always at her house, and the excitement of the chase had worn off and the routine of a relationship reared its proverbial ugly head, Gene would adroitly ease himself out and begin the quest for new game. Yet he was clever in his method. The fault was all his... the woman was the perfect partner... she was not to blame… he just had too much baggage… he just needed time to sort himself out… once he did, he would be back.

His victims were only too willing to wait.

How did Tone know all this? One of the victims at a previous company decided not to wait and discovered Gene giving his attention to another woman. They say jealousy is an ugly thing. The catfight between the two women vying for Gene's attention made the gossip rounds in the company. While it tarnished both of their reputations, somehow Gene came out unscathed.

But Tone was no fool. Besides, she had a purpose, a mission, and the Gene sitting here was merely a means to an end.

"Sure," she said with a smile. "I could use a little diversion. Where is it and what time?"

"Around six," Gene answered followed by directions.

"Good. It'll give me a chance to go home and change into something more comfortable."

Tone arrived fashionably late, dressed in heels, tan slacks that hugged her legs and hips, and a white short-sleeve silk blouse that accentuated her chest. She stood in the arched entrance to the bar area and was surprised that it was larger than she expected, with the requisite TVs above the bar adding to the cacophony. The whole ambiance reminded her once again why she avoided places like this. One invariably had to shout to be heard, even to the person sitting next to you.

Glancing around the bar, she didn't recognize anyone and began to wonder if she was at the wrong place. Working her way past seated patrons on barstools at the bar or seated and standing around high tables with tall chairs, she was halfway through the room when she realized that the bar had an outside patio overlooking the Ohio River. Seated around two tables pushed together were Gene, Brent, two men and three women, and an empty chair between Gene and Brent.

"I was wondering if you got lost," Gene joked when he saw her pushing open the door.

"Only once or twice," she replied with a smile, coming around the table to the empty spot.

Gene made the introductions and did his best to act the charming host.

Tone ordered a glass of white wine, chuckling to herself as she watched each of the table's occupants checking her out, especially the women as though she were a threat, their smiles artificial until they learned she was leaving next week. She understood their irritation, especially when it seemed that Gene was being overly solicitous towards her. One woman sitting across from her named Janice, a pleasant brunette trending towards pudgy with cheerful eyes and a killer smile, did her best to appear happy to see her, though Tone recognized the desire, the quest in Janice's body language. Tone gave her a sympathetic smile. No doubt there was someone who would love Janice for who she was. Unfortunately that someone was not Gene.

Once the initial superficial 'get-to-know-you' questions were answered, conversations returned to somewhat normal with Tone joining in with questions of her own, discovering Janice worked in wardrobe while the others worked in other departments of not enough interest to warrant Tone's attention.

"So how did you get hired on in wardrobe," Tone asked Janice.

"I like to sew," she replied. "I also belong to SCA, the Society for Creative Anachronism."

"I've heard of them," Tone nodded. "Do you have a favorite period?"

Janice blushed, expecting teasing. "I like the Viking period the best."

Before Tone could respond, Gene piped in, hooking a thumb at Tone. "You two ought to get along great then. She's going to grad school for Nordic languages or something like that."

"Nordic studies," Tone gently corrected before turning her full attention to Janice whose face looked like she had just found a long lost puppy. "Have you had the chance to make any Viking clothing for TTI?"

"No," she sighed, "not yet. The closest I got to making clothing from that period was for a man and woman who went back to England in the late 9th century."

Momentarily startled, Tone quickly recovered, trying to remember if she had met Janice before. "9th century England? Why would they want to go there and then?"

"I don't know," Janice shrugged. "I just make the clothes."

"So you didn't meet them?" Tone pretended to be disappointed.

"I never meet the travelers."

"Then how do you know if the clothes will fit?"

"We have a tailor who specializes in that. He's quite good and knows exactly how to measure and cut."

Tone remembered the slender fastidious man whose unsmiling no-nonsense approach made her wonder if he enjoyed his job.

"So once he measures, you make the clothing. How do you know what materials to use?"

"We have a research section within the department who does that and then goes out and buys the fabric or has it made to order."

"Then you put it all together?"

"Yes."

Tone nodded appreciatively. "I imagine you being a member of SCA has helped. How long does it take to make an outfit... like the ones for those people who went to England?"

"It depends on the outfit, depending on whether I have to hand stitch or can use a machine. Older costumes like the one worn going to England took me a couple of days because I had to hand stitch those."

"So if I wanted a Viking shield-maiden outfit, how long would that take?"

Janice's jaw dropped as she exclaimed, "That's what I am... in the SCA."

"Then you know exactly what I want," Tone complimented.

"You want to be a Viking?" Gene interrupted with a laugh. "A little late for that, isn't it?"

"It's never too late to be a Viking," Tone replied, causing him to laugh. Turning back to Janice, she repeated, "How long would it take to make?"

"I'd have to do it at home," Janice answered, "for obvious reasons."

"Of course," Tone said, understanding. "I'm not in a rush. I'll be back for Christmas break."

"I can definitely have it by then," Janice eagerly replied.

As the evening progressed and more appetizers ordered and devoured along with numerous bottles of beer and wine, Tone nursed her wine and nibbled on nachos and chicken wings. Eventually one of the women said her goodbyes and headed on home, soon followed by several others so that only Gene, Tone, and Janice remained. Realizing Janice was going to stay to the end, Tone decided she was ready to go home.

"It's been fun," she said with a smile. "Pity I'm leaving next week. I really enjoyed myself."

"I'll walk you to your car," Gene offered.

"Might as well call it a night myself," Janice said, either ignoring or not noticing frustration flicker across Gene's face.

Thwarted at getting Tone alone, Gene escorted the two ladies to their cars, disappointed when Tone got in her car first and waved before driving off.

Every workday over the next week, Tone had lunch again with Gene in the TTI cafeteria, finally culminating with a dinner date two nights before she departed. While not leading him on in the strictest sense, she also did nothing to hinder his attentions. The 'hard-to-get' aura simply inflamed Gene's quest.

"So what *exactly* is it that you do?" Tone said, sitting across the table from Gene, waiting for the server to bring their appetizers.

"I've already told you," he replied, pleased that he was making progress, simultaneously praying that he would get lucky and they would end up back at her place for a bed romp.

"What you told me was that you work in the Time Machine department," she chided him. "Whenever I ask for more specifics, you suddenly change the subject. Is what you do so secret that you can't tell anyone?" She smiled impishly at him. "Or is it because you're just the janitor and you don't want me to find out."

"I'm not the janitor," he laughed. "Those of us who actually work with the machine aren't supposed to talk about what we do, especially in public, because you never know who's listening. You already know that TTI has exclusive rights to time travel and though a private company, we're heavily regulated and have to maintain all sorts of security procedures."

"There you go again," she teased. "I ask what you do and you give me a dissertation on TTI's security. I'm beginning to think you don't even work down there. I suppose I'm going to have to ask Brent. Hmmm... wonder what he's doing tomorrow night."

"OK, OK, you win," Gene grinned. Leaning forward, he whispered, "I work in programming and time control."

"Specifically?"

"I develop parameters synchronizing spatial mass and placement."

"I won't pretend to understand what that means," she coyly giggled. "But see? Was that so hard? You act like you're some international spy. So where did you do you studies?"

"MIT."

Tone nodded with respect. "Are you one of those wunderkinds?"

"If you mean was I ahead of my peers, then yes." He sipped his wine. "They wanted to hire me before I even graduated."

"Impressive," she said. "Maybe you can answer a question for me."

"OK?"

"Suppose I go back in time, say to the year 1600 in London, England. I'm walking around there with my TTI escorts and we get separated. In fact, when the time comes to return, they can't find me and they go back and I'm stuck in 1600 London, England. Why don't they just redial the time machine to when we first landed? Wouldn't I be there?"

"That's a question we get asked a lot," Gene acknowledged, pleased with the opportunity to display how smart he was. "What people don't fully comprehend is that time does not stand still. While we could redial the machine, like you said, back to when you first landed, you wouldn't be there. Let's say it takes twenty minutes for the escorts to get back, explain what happened and then redial the machine to the exact time and place of your initial insertion. When they arrive, you'd already be somewhere in London, England twenty minutes beyond when they landed."

"What about the doppelgänger?" Tone asked, puzzled. "I forgot who it was who told me that instead of the real you there, it would be your doppelgänger."

Gene shook his head in disdain. "That's old school. We've got some of those dinosaurs still working there. It's myth based upon Pauli's exclusion principle. It assumes that time has no impact of your mass in the sense that you have to be at a certain location at a certain point in time. But it completely neglects the fact that the mass, your body, has already advanced in time and cannot go back once it is placed at a point in time. The doppelgänger schtick is pure myth." He shook his head in mild frustration. "We got a few of those relics who refuse to accept science. Sadly, they're in charge."

The epiphany burst within her. "So what you're saying is that in order for you to find me in London, England, you'd have to calculate the exact duration of time between my initial departure and your reinsertion. If you were a minute off either way, you'd either always be a minute behind me or a minute ahead of me."

"Exactly," he exclaimed. "Why is it that it is so obvious to you who are not a scientist, yet these morons in TTI can't grasp a simple concept."

"I should think that it would be near impossible to rescue me then," she said, hiding her fear.

"Not at all," he said, flipping a hand. "The machine can do it all. All we have to do is punch in the initial departure time and the machine factors in the rest based upon present time."

"Suppose it was days or even months?" she asked, hope rising. "Suppose I went back to Roman times. If I correctly remember what you told me, the machine is good only so far back."

"Careful," Gene warned. "Let's stop right there. I understand your question and the answer is that it doesn't matter how long it was between the time you left and the time I arrived to rescue you, be it a day, month, or five years or a hundred years. Of course," he grinned, "if it was a hundred years, you'd probably be dead. But the real concern is; *where* are you? While I could get back in your exact time, the longer the gap, the less likelihood I'll ever find you."

"I could leave clues," she said with a smile.

Gene laughed. "I suppose you could, though you'd have to be careful in that any permanent type clues would end up on the real present."

"What do you mean?"

"Suppose you carved your message in a rock. 'Gene. I'm at such-and-such Baker Street in London.' As soon as you engrave the stone, it becomes a part of history. The theory is that the stone would then appear somewhere in the present, provided nothing had happened to it along the way."

Tone smiled impishly. "Just imagine all the mischief I could do. I could leave all sorts of messages and drive future historians crazy."

"And that's exactly why we can't leave anyone in the past," Gene pointed out.

"Makes sense," she agreed. "Oh, I have another question."

"Yes?" Gene chuckled, shaking his head when the server approached with the dessert menu.

"OK. Suppose a person went to Waterloo in 1815, right in the middle of the battle, and he and the escorts were all killed. Is the time machine then stuck in the past?"

"Another excellent question," he said, wanting the meal to end so he could maneuver her back to her place. "There is a fail-safe built into the machine. The machine is programmed to be at a certain location for a certain amount of time. Once the time has expired, whether anyone is on board or not, it returns to the present."

"Suppose," she said, eyes bright, "Napoleon stumbled aboard just as the machine returned to the present?"

"Then he would be brought back."

"Sort of like *Bill and Ted's Excellent Adventure*," she laughed.

Gene joined her laughter.

"How about we get a cup of coffee somewhere else?" she offered.

"I like that," he quickly agreed, expecting her to ask him back to her apartment.

Catching the server's attention, he paid the bill and they were soon outside.

"Follow me," she commanded and headed to her car.

Gene raced to his and tucked in behind her as she headed down 3rd Street into old town, turning right on West Ormsby then parking in front of Annie's Diner.

Masking his disappointment, Gene followed her into the quaint 1950's themed restaurant with the wait staff dressed in period clothes.

An hour and a half later, after several cups of coffee and a piece of raspberry ripple cake large enough to feed six people, Tone decided she was ready to go home and motioned for the check.

Escorting her to her car, Gene stood close enough to be respectful, yet indicating he'd like more.

"Thank you for a lovely evening," she said. "Perhaps, if you're still available, we can continue this when I come back for Christmas vacation. I know it's asking a lot, but I don't date much and so I like to get to know someone before it goes too far. I will understand if you'd rather not."

"I would like that," he gushed, "very much."

"Good," she smiled at him as though relieved, knowing full well he would be enjoying the intimate affections of other women in the interim.

"Tomorrow night?"

"I'm afraid I need to finish packing for the trip. In the meantime, my email address is Ingrid25 at Friends-dot-com." Placing her hands on her hips, she regally stated, "I expect an email before I land in Oslo."

"Done," he answered, dipping his head.

"Then I better go."

She closed the gap between them and pressed herself against him, delivering a deep kiss, her tongue exploring his mouth, her hands sliding down to his hips and tauntingly close to his butt.

Completely caught off guard, he felt the explosion of sensual desire as he felt her firm breasts pressed against his chest, her tongue in his mouth and her hands sliding down to rest on his hips like they were about to slide back and squeeze his butt.

Before his brain had a chance to comprehend what was happening, she pulled back and tweaked his nose.

"Bye."

By the time Gene caught his breath, she was in her car, waving a hand out the window as she drove away.

Erik walked about the various shops in Kaupang, idly chatting with the owners and complimenting them on their wares. Pausing to admire the numerous intricately designed glass-beads in one shop, he wondered what Tone would look like wearing a necklace of these beautiful beads.

"See anything you like?" the owner asked. He was a jovial middle-aged man with thick auburn beard and hair, wearing homespun clothing of high quality wool.

"I remember you," Erik said. "You are Harek… Harek… Halvarson. You bought that one young fellow on the cheap."

"That I did," Harek grinned, pleased to be remembered.

"How's he working out?"

"Smart lad, dutiful, does what I ask." He leaned in a little bit to share some wisdom. "I find these Church fellows to be good slaves. They'll work hard for you, but they do tend to wear their melancholy like a wet woolen robe. Even this Pearson lad I have here. I told him to work hard and I might consider freeing him after a few years. You'd think the lad would leap for joy. Him? He acted like I was exiling him." He looked up when the young man in question walked in. "Well look who's here. We were just talking about you."

"Yes Harek," Pearson obediently replied. He had the look of a man whose glass was perpetually half empty.

"I was commenting to Erik that you've fit in very well here, that you're quickly learning our language."

"Yes Harek."

"Don't be so dour lad," Harek teased. "Tell the man how good you have it since I bought you."

Pearson mechanically turned to Erik. "He treats me well."

Erik switched to Latin. "Have faith son. Harek is a good man and will do as he says. You need patience. Endear yourself to him so that he comes to think of you as a son."

Hearing the language of the Church, Pearson's face brightened. "Please, Sir. Can you help me?"

"I heard my name," Harek said.

"I told him to be thankful he in in your house. I also told him that you are an honorable man and always do what you say you will do."

Harek dipped his head in appreciation, immediately liking the stranger. "I see you speak his tongue. Where did you learn it?"

"I lived for a time in a kingdom ruled by a man called Charles, across the sea. The church of the Christians is strong there."

"Does everyone speak that tongue?"

"No," Erik replied. "There were many peoples and many languages. The language of the rulers is called Franconian, but the language used for laws and administration is the language of the Church, called Latin."

"You are an educated man?"

"Yes."

Harek slowly nodded, impressed. "Perhaps you and the lad here can talk in his language for a bit while he's here." A customer entered and his attention diverted to displaying the latest glass beads.

Pearson watched Harek move away to talk with the customer then addressed Erik. "Please sir. You speak the Holy tongue. Are you a Christian?"

Erik thought about it. He had been raised a Southern Baptist, but hadn't been to church in years. Still, that didn't mean he had abandoned his faith.

"Yes," he answered.

"O my God, my prayers have been answered," Pearson gushed.

"Not so fast," Erik cautioned. "Just what do you think I can do for you?"

Pearson shot a quick glance at Harek, even though the merchant didn't understand a word the young monk said. "I need you to help me escape."

"Escape?" Erik cocked an eyebrow and stared at him. "And just where would you escape to?"

"I... I don't know. You'll think of something," he pleaded.

"Because I speak your tongue you think that justifies me jeopardizing my position here? You think I'm going to go around and liberate slaves because I'm a Christian. What does it say in one of Saint Paul's letters? Slaves are to obey their masters and do so with an honest and sincere heart, not toadying or pretending to please. If you do this, you will be blessed."

Pearson's countenance fell.

Erik narrowed his gaze at him. "You're not thinking straight. You're letting your emotions rule you. Has he beat you or abused you?"

"No."

"Look at the clothes you wear. They're not slave clothes nor are they common folk clothes. My guess is that they're a lot nicer than the robes you used to wear."

"But the robes are to remind us of our sinful nature," Pearson argued.

"Oh puh-lease," Erik said, flipping a hand. "You're telling me that a loving God wants you to suffer by making you wear itchy robes?"

"We suffer because of sin," Pearson self-righteously stated.

Erik leaned forward. "And what sin in your life led you here?"

Startled, Pearson's mouth gaped open as he tried to think of an answer.

"Remember Joseph?" Erik challenged.

"Yes."

"What sin did he commit to land him in prison?"

Again Pearson stared dumbly at him.

"Further, he was sold as a slave, unjustly accused then spent the next thirteen years in prison. What happened after that?"

"He was made second to the pharaoh."

"Why?"

"Because he interpreted dreams."

"That's it?"

"Uh… "

"Because he trusted God and was honest and dependable in all his time in prison," Erik said, relishing the role of the teacher again. "If you remember, Joseph was such a model prisoner, that the jailer put him in charge of all the other prisoners. Now consider yourself. Your master here said that if you work hard, he'd probably free you in a couple of years. That's a whole lot less than thirteen."

Pearson frowned in thought as he puzzled out Erik's counselling.

"Look at it this way. Does your master have any children?"

"Two daughters, but one's married."

It was the way he said 'two daughters' that caused Erik to inwardly smile, for Pearson could not hide the look that flickered across his face, a subtle indication that the unmarried daughter had caught his attention.

Erik shook his head. "You're so concerned about getting out of here that you don't see what's in front of you." He paused, hoping Pearson would catch on. When the young man continued his dumbfounded stare, Erik said, "Every father wants a son to carry on the family business. That could be you."

"But I'm not his son," Pearson said, stating the obvious.

"I know that," Erik said, exasperated at the man's obtuseness. "Ever hear of adoption?"

"But I don't want to be a merchant," he stubbornly replied.

"Who says you have to be a merchant your whole life? Remember Joseph? He probably thought he'd take over Jacob's role. Instead he was sold into slavery and it wasn't until he was thirty winters old that another opportunity presented itself, an opportunity far greater than the one he had envisioned. How old are you?"

"Eighteen."

"You could be a merchant for ten years and still be younger than Joseph when you go back to the church. For good measure, how old was Moses when God said he was ready?"

"Uh... I don't remember."

"He was eighty. Eighty," Erik emphasized, "before he was ready for God to use. You're eighteen. You're just a child. Use your situation to your advantage. Your master is an honest man. Become the son he always wanted and pretty soon you could be wealthy enough to build your own church."

Erik saw the epiphany burst in Pearson's eyes, knowing again he had hit the mark. Man's vanity was the key to success.

"Thank you," Pearson said with heartfelt gratitude. "I shall do as you suggest." Just as abruptly, he furrowed his brow. "How is it that you know the Scriptures so well?"

"I can read." Erik almost added 'just like everyone else,' but thought better of it when he remembered the when and where of his present circumstances.

"Can you write?"

"Of course. But you waste your time learning about me. If you want your future to change, you need to please him." He hooked a thumb at Harek,

Pearson bobbed his head and smiled, making peace with his circumstances.

As he bustled out, Harek came over. "I sense a change in the young man. What did you tell him?"

"I told him the truth. Aside from the unlikely chance of him being made Jarl, he was in the best place to be here in Kaupang. You were more than a master; you were a kind of father to him, that he needed to learn from you as you had so much you could teach him."

"That I do," Harek said, liking this stranger even more. "He's a fine lad and useful to me."

"He's smart and I believe he'll be better than a slave."

"Ach," Harek said, shaking his head. "I know it's not normal, but I don't like slavery. I find an honest man will do an honest day's work better if he's a free man. When I saw nobody bid on the lad, I felt I had to so that his short life wasn't take from him."

Erik clapped him on the shoulder. "You're a good man, Harek. I have a feeling he's going to surprise you."

"And what about you?" Harek asked with a sly grin. "Surely there is a wife or lady friend that could use some adornment."

"There is," Erik sighed, suddenly feeling the ache of Tone's absence. "Unfortunately she is far away."

"Ah," Harek nodded in sympathy. "Your wife?"

"Not yet."

Harek grinned in understanding, assuming Erik was raiding in order to accumulate enough wealth to make himself a worthy suitor.

One of Halfdan's slaves, a young man with red hair, entered the shop and spotted Erik.

"Master," the slave said with respect, "the Jarl wishes your presence."

Giving the man a brisk nod, Erik turned to Harek. "Another time then, Master Harek."

"Another time," he replied with a dip of the head and a smile. "Your lady… she is fair?"

Erik slowly shook his head. "Beyond description."

"Perhaps one day you will bring her here and let her choose," Harek encouraged.

"I would love nothing better," Erik replied.

"Master," the slave interrupted. "The Jarl waits."

"Coming."

When Erik entered the longhouse at Skiringssal, Halfdan sat at a table with Bjorn and Ingvar, also known as Ingvar the Short, sitting across from him. Erik remembered him as helming the other longship on the way back from Lindisfarne. The man had to stand on a sea-chest to gaze over the prow. Yet his strength and determination more than made up for his stature.

"Ah, Sword-spinner," Halfdan greeted him as Erik approached the table. "Glad you're here. I can use your input. Ingvar here says the men are ready to sail again."

"The last raid was too easy and too short," Ingvar stated, causing Bjorn to smirk. Ignoring him, Ingvar continued, "It's only the beginning of Hayannir. We've got time to do another raid and still be back in time for harvest."

Erik did a quick calculation for Hayannir and the Gregorian calendar and realized he'd been here for over a month, living in Halfdan's home, adjusting to life as a Viking, or 'Ostman' as they called themselves. He was surprised at how quickly the time had passed, though his ache for Tone remained the same. He wondered what she was doing at this very moment.

At the same time, he had wrestled with his conscience. He had never before killed a man except in defense. He found it strange that killing the men while defending Tone had no effect upon him. Their deaths were a result of them attacking him. It was necessary. The same applied to Olaf, though he didn't actually kill him. Yet he would have if necessary. But the thought of raiding and killing for the sake of stealing another person's property seemed nothing more than murder and robbery. Yet this seemed to be accepted as normal.

"What do you think, Sword-spinner?" Halfdan asked, interrupting Erik's musings.

Erik looked at Halfdan who grinned at him then at the other two. "I think the decision has already been made."

Halfdan barked a laugh and slapped the bench seat next to him. "Sit. Bjorn here," he explained, "wants to hit somewhere safe. Ingvar wants to find a big prize and pluck it. What do you think?"

"I think," Erik said, sitting next to Halfdan, "it depends. Lindisfarne was easy because the monks were not only unprepared, they never suspected such a thing could ever occur. Likewise, the place was a treasure trove of plunder, in addition to all the slaves you brought back. I guess my question is; what's the objective? I mean other than gaining wealth. Do you wish to lose some men in the process, or do you wish it to be another Lindisfarne?"

"Another Lindisfarne," Bjorn exclaimed with a laugh.

"I agree," Ingvar said, "though it doesn't help our fighting skills much. Still, if we can walk away with as much as we did in this last place, then I'm all for it."

Halfdan turned to Erik. "Suggestions?"

Thankfully, during the past month, Erik had given some thought to his future, especially concerning participation in raids.

"If you want it to be easy, I suggest repeating what you did on Lindisfarne."

"We already determined that," Ingvar sourly pointed out.

"What I mean is," Erik replied, ignoring Ingvar's interruption, "that there are other monasteries and priories up and down the same coast down from Lindisfarne. I can think of a couple that should be suitable. Since it's only been a month since the last raid, they'll not have had time to build any defenses, especially those placed on islands. Though I imagine word has spread and they'll be far more watchful."

Halfdan half-smiled as he studied Erik. "You have adapted rather well to life here in the Vestfold."

Erik shrugged. "It's in my blood though I have been gone for so long."

"True," Halfdan grinned with a quick dip of his head. "Then it's settled. We find another place where the Christians have placed one of their holy sites. You have a place in mind?"

"I was thinking of Tynemouth Priory," Erik replied.

"Where is it?" Bjorn asked.

"South of Lindisfarne."

"How far south?" Ingvar queried.

"I don't know how to measure it in sailing time," Erik replied, shaking his head. "It's probably three to four days walking south of Lindisfarne."

"It's not on an island?" Ingvar frowned.

"No. It's on a little promontory on the north side of a good sized river, wide enough for all your longships to navigate."

"How do you know all this?" Ingvar said, an eyebrow raised in suspicion.

Erik was half-tempted to say he had been there once as a student on vacation far in the future, but remembered he had a tale that needed to be consistent.

"I walked through there less than two months ago, escorting a young woman to the holy shrine on Lindisfarne."

Ingvar shot a doubting glance at Halfdan who simply nodded with calm reassurance.

"Did you visit the Christian place?" Bjorn asked.

"Briefly," Erik honestly answered though all that remained when he visited were ruins and a graveyard.

"Did you see anything worth taking?"

"I really didn't pay attention. I had a mission to get her to Lindisfarne and any side trips were a distraction and interference to me."

"Spoken like a man with a purpose," Halfdan chuckled then shifted is gaze to Bjorn. "Send out a scouting ship. No raiding. Remind them. Get out and back as quickly as possible."

Bjorn nodded then grinned at Erik. "Want to go on a scouting trip?"

"I want him to remain here," Halfdan interjected.

Bjorn frowned momentarily then understood. "Maybe next time, Sword-spinner."

Halfdan shifted his attention to the bustle inside the longhouse. Preparations for a feast were in progress with various game and farm animals roasting over the open fires, tables tugged into place, along with cleaning the inside of the large home.

"I look forward to tonight's feast," Ingvar said with much appreciation, noting that unlike other Jarls, Halfdan was not quite as forthcoming with food and ale for his loyal followers, though he more than made up for it with gifts and raid allocations. Still, his 'feasts' were more intimate affairs usually a dozen or so in attendance. Those fortunate enough to be invited dined on the best food and mead in the Vestfold.

"Is Kolga coming?" Bjorn asked.

"Yes."

Bjorn turned a playful gaze at Erik. "I know your heart is supposedly claimed by another, but you will forget all about her when you meet Kolga. Except for the lovely Liv," he diplomatically said, winking at Halfdan, "there is none fairer in all the Vestfold or the Vestmar or anywhere else for that matter." With a gleam in his eye, he leaned forward to emphasize, "And she's rich."

"I look forward to it," Erik replied, wondering who Kolga was and whether her wealth was the reason for her invitation.

A raised voice by the cooking fires diverted their attention.

"You made me the cook," the man snapped. "Now leave me alone and let me do my job."

Erik lifted his head to see the former Brother Nyle, a plump still-tonsured man in his mid-30s, fussing at Liv.

Halfdan half rose out of his seat to deliver a strong rebuke when he caught Liv's eye that told him she could handle it.

"We don't cook goat that way," Liv sternly replied.

"Of course not. You're heathens and wouldn't know a decent meal if it bit you on the ass. You use way too much salt and cook the meat too fast. You've got to cook it slowly, and baste it more. Your meal ought to be an experience, something to indulge in, to look forward to with anticipation of all the culinary delights known to man... not some sort of barbaric activity to merely feed a man's stomach."

Instead of taking offense, Liv snorted a laugh and waved her hands in defeat, having already taken a shine to the finicky man.

Erik watched the exchange, thankful that Nyle was here, for he was a superb cook. Liv knew that too. Erik had been very careful in his dealings with Nyle for the monk had not forgotten Erik spoke Latin and on several occasions tried to engage him in conversation. Always replying in Old Norse,

Erik reminded Nyle that he would have no part in any schemes or plots.

"It's a good thing the man can cook," Halfdan growled, "or he'd be the next sacrifice."

"Liv seems to like him," Erik pointed out.

"Lucky for him," Ingvar commented.

Chapter 6

Suddenly my status as a slave is not as perilous as I once thought and I have reminded myself that Joseph served the jailer so well that he was put in charge of all the other prisoners. Yet he was still a prisoner, a slave. Since my capture, I have thought long about Joseph and his transition from favorite son to slave to prisoner to ruler. I remember asking Brother Nyle a question about Joseph when I was at Lindisfarne. I posed it like this: Joseph was a slave in Potiphar's house. Though he gained favor, he was still a slave who was then falsely accused and instead of killing him as would be expected, he was thrown in prison. Why? Brother Nyle answered that it was God's will. God was caring for Joseph even when everything seemed against him. The answer seemed good to me then and it does so now.

I confess that it was not like that when I first arrived here at Kaupang. But God has placed me with a kindly man who treats me more like a son than a slave. And then the stranger called Erik visited today and told me again about Joseph. I see it as a sign. God sent Erik to remind me to be faithful and patient. Like Joseph, I too will rise above where I am.

Harek let me watch the fight today. He called it a holmgang, which means some sort of blood feud. What I learned was that Erik killed a man and the brother wanted satisfaction. It is a barbaric way to settle accounts, but I remind myself that despite Harek, I am among ignorant savages, pagans who worship false gods.

Erik fought with the strangest of weapons: two equally sized bars held together by a length of chain, something like a flail, yet without the spiked ball at the end. The bars were perhaps the length of a man's forearm. Erik had two such weapons and spun them so fast and furious that his opponent had no chance to properly defend himself. The fight was over in less time than it takes to boil an egg, if even that long, much to everyone's shock, expect Erik.

I shall now write about Erik. He is a comely man, quite tall for he stands a hand's width above everyone in Kaupang. He has confidence and the appearance of a traveled man. Though his Latin is coarse at times, he speaks it well enough to indicate he is educated. He speaks the savages' language quite well, though there is an accent. I myself, gifted in languages, for I could speak and write the Church's tongue when I was but nine years old, am learning the savages' tongue well enough.

Unlike the savages, Erik shaves his face. We will see if he continues that practice when winter smothers us with its bitter cold. Yet there is a difference in Erik not found in the savages, for he treats both free and slave the same. I have seen him stop and help a slave overburdened with firewood, carrying the wood himself while offering encouragement. I have seen him give a kind smile to other slaves.

I am convinced that God put Erik here to help me. Today he placed in my mind the reason why God put me here. I am to build a church, here among the pagans. I am to rescue these pitiful savages from their idolatry.

Twenty guests showed up for dinner, including Bjorn and Ingvar and their wives. The remaining guests were a mix of wealthy merchants and loyal retainers. Halfdan's table was centered and elevated on a platform with Halfdan seated in the middle, Liv to his right and an empty seat to his left. Erik sat next to the empty spot with Bjorn's wife, a pleasant woman with blond hair on his left, and Ingvar to her left. On the other side of the table, Bjorn sat next to Liv with Ingvar's wife on his right, and a retainer named Felman, a stout full-bearded man, to her right, thus ensuring no ladies were at the ends of the table.

Slaves began placing food platters on the tables when the main door opened and a woman walked in. Erik knew at once it was Kolga.

Kolga was a strikingly handsome woman with strawberry blond hair and eyes the color of reflected sunlight upon lush meadow grass. Her skin was smooth and blemish-free like new porcelain. Slender and graceful, she moved as one comfortable with her position and place as a wealthy and much desired mate. Her eyes roved and took in who was there.

She wore an ankle-length cream colored linen shift with an ornate silver brooch at the neck. Over the shift, she wore a light green hangerock, a shorter length woolen dress held up by shoulder straps fastened with brooches similar to the one at her neck. A finely woven belt cinched the dress tight against her slim stomach, emphasizing her ample bosom and svelte hips. The cut and weave of her clothing along with the superior workmanship of her brooches advertised that she was a wealthy woman. Seeing Halfdan, she smiled and made her way towards him.

Halfdan leaned into Erik and lowered his voice. "Is she not as Bjorn described?"

Erik couldn't help but nod.

"Kolga," Halfdan said with a grand flair. "I'm glad I could entice you away from that farm of yours. It's been too long since we've seen you."

"When my brother the Jarl sends a man to request my presence, who am I to turn down such an offer." She smiled sweetly at him though her eyes flickered to take in the tall man sitting to his left.

Her brother? Erik smiled to himself as he realized the reason Bjorn was so deferential in describing her. Though in truth, she was a beauty.

"This is Erik," Halfdan said by way of introduction, "my newest retainer. He's quite the fearsome and brave fighter."

"So I've heard," she agreed, narrowing her gaze at him.

"Lady Kolga," Erik said, standing up and giving her a polite bow. It was then the disparity of height became obvious for Kolga, standing straight, came no higher than below his chin.

Kolga craned her head back to look up at him. "A mannered man as well. How did you end up with this ruffian?"

"He was passing by the same neighborhood I was visiting," he replied with understated amusement.

Halfdan barked a laughed and slapped the table. "Come then Kolga; sit at my table next to our newest friend."

Acknowledging with a nod, Kolga came around and sat down next to Erik as a trencher of beaten copper containing stewed goat was placed in front of her. Withdrawing her personal knife, she pondered which morsel to stab when she glanced over at Erik as he jabbed a piece of meat with his fork and used the knife to separate it from the bone.

Kolga's head and eyes followed the piece of meat's journey from the trencher to Erik's mouth. "What is that?"

"It's called a fork," Halfdan answered for him.

Kolga's head twisted to look at her brother. "You don't use one?"

"I can eat with a knife just fine," he replied, plopping a bit of goat into his mouth.

Kolga turned back to Erik, fascinated. "Wherever did you find that?"

"I had it made," he answered, pausing to show her the utensil.

"How marvelous," she said. "I must get me one. Who made it for you?"

"The silversmith in Kaupang, the man named Stian." Erik paused and deliberately wiped the fork clean on his hand cloth used as a napkin. "Here. If it is not too presumptuous of me, take mine with my compliments."

Surprised, though obviously pleased, Kolga accepted the fork, both she and Erik missing Halfdan's smug satisfied grin.

"Thank you," she said with earnest appreciation. Imitating Erik, she stabbed a piece of meat, sliced it free and triumphantly placed it into her mouth. "Is this an invention of your own?"

"No, m'Lady," Erik suavely replied. "I saw its use during my travels."

"You have traveled much then?" she said, giving him her full attention.

Over a thousand years, he thought with a wry smile before relating the same story he told Halfdan and Bjorn on the ship, though skipping over his infatuation with Tone, a subtle fact that did not go unnoticed by Halfdan.

"But tell me, m'Lady," Erik began before Kolga cut him off.

"Please. I am merely the Jarl's sister. I would like it if you called me Kolga."

"Kolga," Erik repeated with a slight dip of his head. "I am told that you are unmarried. I find that difficult to understand."

"Why is that?" she said, cocking an eyebrow.

"My lady Kolga," Erik said. "You are one of the fairest women I have ever seen. There must be thousands upon thousands of men seeking your attention."

Kolga blushed slightly, her eyes peering intently at him. "That was very sweet of you. But the truth of the matter is that I was married once."

Immediately understanding, Erik placed a gentle hand on her arm. "I am so sorry. That was unkind of me and I apologize."

"You have nothing to apologize for," she answered, once again surprised by this man's behavior, liking his gentle touch on her arm, an act both sympathetic and intimate. "My husband, Egill, was killed several years ago."

"Again, I am sorry," Erik said, withdrawing his hand.

"Don't be," Kolga said with a shrug. "He was a good man and is in Valhalla now. Yet I can ask the same question of you. You are not married?"

"No."

"And you have never been married?"

"No," Erik answered, having already worked through the point that his real past would only encourage more questions. Far better to condemn Linda to oblivion than having to create a story of where they met, what happened to her, and all the other nuances of overlapping real life on top of the 8th century.

"And no one has caught your interest?"

"You need more mead," Halfdan interrupted, flipping a hand at a slave. "More mead over here." Leaning around his sister, he looked at her then Erik and back to her. "You should have seen him fight Oluf. It wasn't even close. By the gods," he slapped the table, "I wish I had a dozen more like you."

"But you do," Erik replied, "men like Bjorn and Ingvar, both fearsome fighters."

"Spoken like a diplomat," Halfdan laughed.

"You could use someone like him," Kolga observed with a hint of admiration, "especially dealing with Thorsten."

Staring at Erik, Halfdan cocked his head to the side, his brows furrowed as an idea germinated. "Once again, sister, you have keen insight."

"Who is Thorsten?" Erik asked with the uneasy feeling Halfdan's studious musings involved him.

"He's the king of Haddingjadalr," Kolga answered.

"More of that later," Halfdan said with a smile though shaking his head in subtle warning at his sister. "We need to enjoy ourselves here and now." He lifted up his mead cup in salute. "I'm glad I found you, Sword-spinner."

"Why do they call you sword-spinner," Kolga asked with an interested smile.

"His swords are like nothing you've ever seen," Halfdan answered for him. "Tell her."

Erik smiled self-consciously. "It has to do with my choice of weapons. Unlike the normal swords that Halfdan and the others so skillfully use, I have a weapon that I learned to use during my travels." He then explained the design of the nunchuk.

"And you spin these around and they can actually kill a man?"

"Yes," Halfdan again answered for him before Liv yanked on his arm, giving him the 'leave-them-alone' glare.

Halfdan sheepishly turned back to focus on the festivities, all the while hoping that Kolga would capture Erik's interest.

It was early in the morning when the feast ended and guests either wandered on back to their own homes or settled down on one of the beds converted from dining tables. Standing next to his bed, Halfdan had watched with satisfaction as Kolga and Erik, who had spent the evening focused on each other, now said their 'goodnights' and went to their separate sleeping pallets.

"She may seem interested," Liv whispered, "but she's also pragmatic. Erik has no wealth. There is nothing to interest her other than the man himself. And remember, he's two and forty winters old."

"Do you not find him attractive?"

"Yes, he's a handsome man," Liv muttered in exasperation, "but he's also two and forty. Kolga will want a man who can grow old with her. You know how she is."

"That I do," Halfdan nodded with an impish grin.

Liv noted the look. "What are you planning?"

"You'll see. Now go to sleep."

"Where are you going?"

"I'm just going to the privy."

Erik had barely settled when he felt a jab on his shoulder. Gazing up, he saw Bjorn towering over him.

"I need to talk to you," Bjorn whispered.

"Now?" Erik raised his head to look around to see if anyone else was up. In the dim light of the two cooking fires, now rippling embers, there was little movement and the annoying guttural snore the only sound.

"Yes, now." Bjorn motioned for Erik to follow him.

Flipping the thin blanket off, Erik stood and slipped on his shoes.

Once outside, Bjorn led the way to a far corner of the longhouse, the moonlit morning illuminating his body.

"What's going on?" Erik asked.

Bjorn leaned back and cast a quick look around, ensuring they were alone. "Some of the men and I were talking and we think it's time to make a change."

"A change of what?"

"Not so loud," Bjorn warned. "Keep your voice down."

"Fine," Erik said, his voice softer. "What kind of change?"

Bjorn peered intently at on him. "We've followed Halfdan for too long. We do all the raiding, take all the risks and all he does is sit back, out of danger and then takes what he wants, which is always more than his fair share."

"He's the Jarl," Erik pointed out, not liking where this was headed. "He's the one who plans and organizes the raids."

"Someone else can plan and organize the raid."

"They're his longships," Erik pointed out.

"There are other longships."

Erik stared intently at him. "So what are you saying?"

Bjorn paused before answering. "I'm saying that a number of us have decided to make a change."

"You said that already."

"We're going out on our own," Bjorn stated.

"So go ahead. No one is stopping you. If you've got a longship, you're free to raid on your own. You don't need his permission." Erik said, frowning.

"Yes. But we need a man who can lead us, someone we can trust to treat us fairly, someone who can plan strategy and pull off successful raids."

"And you're telling me this because?"

"We want you to be that man."

"Me?" Erik sputtered.

"Yes," Bjorn nodded. "We're all agreed. You're a born leader. You're smart, you know how to plan attacks and you're lucky."

Erik snorted a laugh. "You'd be foolish to follow a man who seems lucky because sooner or later his luck will run out."

Bjorn smiled in acknowledgment. "True. But you're a natural born fighter and leader. The men are looking for someone to follow. I can guarantee that at least half the men following Halfdan will desert him if a real leader were to emerge. And once the other half sees what's happening, they'll desert him too. All you have to do is give the word and we can get rid of him and you can take over as Jarl."

Erik's face hardened. "You want to kill Halfdan and make me Jarl."

"Yes."

"You're serious."

"Deadly."

"Deadly is right," Erik scoffed. "What about his brothers, Sigfrig and Eystein? You do know that once they hear about this, they'll join forces and march down here and kill everyone involved."

"We can handle them," Bjorn said with confidence.

Erik narrowed his gaze and focused on the man. "You do realize that what you're saying is treason. I'm surprised that you would even think about such things. I thought you were loyal to Halfdan."

"I'm loyal to a point. There comes a time when it's in my best interest to move on," he coolly replied. "And now is that time, now that you're here."

"Why me? If so many are dissatisfied, why not take charge yourself and become Jarl?"

"Jealousies," Bjorn replied. "There's too many others wanting the same thing. And besides, we know each other too well. With you, you're new, and you've impressed everyone with your fairness and fighting."

"You're serious about this?"

"I wouldn't be here if I wasn't."

Erik shook his head in disbelief. "This doesn't make any sense. Why would you knowingly compromise yourself and those who you say follow you?"

"Like I said. We're all ready for a change."

"The change you speak of is treachery. But I will answer your question. If you choose this path, you will need to find someone else. Under no circumstances will I compromise my loyalty to Halfdan and I will fight by his side against you."

"Even to be Jarl?"

"Especially to be Jarl. I have absolutely no desire to be Jarl. Not only that, I consider Halfdan to be my friend. He has done more for me than I deserve. To pay him back in such fashion says that not only was his trust misplaced, it says that I am not a man deserving such honor, either as his friend or Jarl. Further, why would I want the headache of being Jarl and deal with all the whining, complaints, and threats to my position by men like yourself? I am perfectly happy where I am."

"But think of the riches and glory you could achieve as Jarl," Bjorn tempted.

"What glory is there in treachery? What honor is there in stabbing a friend in the back? And riches? You and I will gain, lose, and gain riches again and again. But honor? Honor is permanent and we can forever tarnish it if we compromise ourselves, even one time. I urge you to reconsider your purpose."

"And I suggest you reconsider my offer."

"What offer? I've already told you I will have no part of it."

Accepting he could make no further progress, Bjorn glanced around and lowered his voice. "I trust you will keep this to yourself."

Before he could continue, Erik held up a hand. "I cannot. How can I say I am loyal and then keep secret such threats to him?"

"You would tell him?" Bjorn was aghast.

"I must. I have no other choice." Erik affirmed.

Bjorn's look of shock and dismay morphed to calm humor as Halfdan emerged from the side of the longhouse.

"Halfdan?" Erik sputtered, as the Jarl clapped Bjorn on the back.

"Thank you, friend Bjorn," Halfdan said with a satisfied grin. "That was fine performance."

Erik looked at Halfdan then at Bjorn's grinning face then back to Halfdan before understanding pulsed within. "Very funny. There's no plot. This was all a joke."

"You are right that there is no plot to get rid of me," Halfdan said, his smile reflecting a deep appreciation for Erik. "But it was not a joke. I must know who I can trust. And you, my friend, have surpassed my expectations."

"You should have seen his face when he thought I wanted to kill you," Bjorn chortled.

"A face can reveal much about a man," Halfdan said with a slow nod, "which makes my decision all the easier."

Erik said nothing, waiting for Halfdan to answer his curiosity.

"I need someone I can trust in Hringariki."

"Hringariki?" Erik said, furrowing his brow.

"It's like this," Halfdan explained. "You remember Kolga mentioning Thorsten, the king of Haddingjadalr?"

"Yes."

"Thorsten and I have an uneasy truce in Hringariki. He sticks to his half and I stick to mine... for the time being. Kolga's farm lies on the jut of land between the Steinsfjorden and the Tyrifjorden."

"In Hringariki?" Erik interrupted.

Halfdan rolled his eyes. "Yes. Egill, the man she married, had a good sized farm there already."

"To whom did he belong?" Erik asked.

"He was Thorsten's man, but not a blood relative. Though she did not consult me, I felt it a good match as it would join me to Thorsten, no matter how slim the connection, so I did not object."

"But now that Egill is dead," Bjorn said, "Thorsten is growing bolder in his demands."

"Especially the inheritance demands," Halfdan added. "He claims there is a blood relative who is entitled to the man's portion."

"Which is two-thirds of the farm," Erik said with a nod of understanding.

"Exactly," Halfdan said, folding his arms.

Erik mused silently for a moment then asked, "What is it that you wish me to do?"

"I own the other jut of land to the west of her. It is very good farm land. I am giving you this farm as a present."

Startled, Erik started to respond but Halfdan cut him off.

"Don't think I'm doing this because I want you out of my hair," he said with a laugh. "The children and Liv have grown very fond of you."

"The feeling is mutual."

"Especially Astrid," Bjorn smirked.

"Don't even go there," Erik chided.

"I will explain more in the morning, but the essence is this. Thorsten must use the Snarumselva to get his boats and trade goods down to where it intersects with the Drammenselva. Your farm is positioned to influence that traffic."

"You wish to antagonize him?"

"Eventually, yes. I will explain more in the morning. In the meantime, I suggest you get some sleep. I need to talk to Bjorn a moment."

"As you wish." Erik gave them both a respectful nod and headed back to the front door.

"What do you think?" Halfdan asked as the door closed behind Erik.

"He's a strange one. Who doesn't want to be Jarl?"

"Perhaps he has a firmer grasp on his abilities," Halfdan replied, shifting a glance at Bjorn.

"I got enough trouble at home with the wife," Bjorn joked, lifting his hands in mock defense.

Halfdan turned back to stare at the door. "Think Kolga will make him forget about that other woman?"

"If she can't," Bjorn intoned, "no one can."

Tone stood on the balcony of her apartment in Oslo, thankful she wasn't paying the rent. Oslo was expensive. Still, the view from the top floor balcony, though only three stories up, provided a nice vista of the courtyard, trees and homes behind the apartment complex on Josefines Gate street. Though a bit farther away for the university than she liked, a bus and transit stop were a block away. Besides, after four years of college and struggling to make ends meet, it was nice to have someone else foot the bills. For the first time in her life since leaving home at eighteen, she didn't have to worry about expenses.

As expected, Gene's email was in her in-box when she arrived, along with emails from Brent and Janice. Gene's email was short, essentially saying that he was still recovering from the kiss and hoped it would happen again and more frequently when she returned for Christmas break.

Though not as overt as Gene, Brent's email was friendly and newsy with the latest at TTI, ending with the hope that he might have the opportunity to spend some time with her. Tone read it with bemusement. She knew his frustration with playing second fiddle to Gene.

Janice's email was encouraging, especially regarding the creation of the Viking shield maiden outfit. Tone knew she had to tread lightly as she didn't want to alienate Janice before she completed the clothing.

The one area she still had to develop was money, specifically gold and hack-silver. She would need to be frugal in these next few months to balance the accumulation of Viking currency.

Not only did Halfdan give Eric a farm, he also provided him with a fine horse and other gifts. The journey to the farm was made all the better as he rode along with Kolga and her retinue, the two of them spending the following four days riding side-by-side. Eric found his talent for creating fabrication stretched almost to a breaking point. Thankful neither she nor anyone else in the group had ever traveled much farther south than Kaupang, he was careful in reconstructing his past, making the most of the conjured time on the continent.

They were a day into the trip back when Erik, beginning to wonder if he was going to last four days in the saddle, fidgeted once again only to notice Kolga's bemused smile.

"I'm not used to riding," he sheepishly admitted.

"Then how did you travel?"

"I walked," he replied with a shrug. "I'm surprised you didn't take a ship here. It would have been quicker."

"I came to feast with Halfdan. Using a ship would have been a waste of a ship needed for something more important, like raiding or moving goods. Besides," she explained, "if I took a ship, they would see me far enough away when I returned that they would have time react. This way, they won't know I'm back until I suddenly appear."

"You have problems with your workers?"

"A couple, which is one reason why I'm glad my brother placed you here. I have been managing the two farms ever since my brother acquired the rest of the land between the Steinsfjorden and the Storelva. As a widowed woman with no children..." she paused when she saw his frown of puzzlement.

"I have had four children," she solemnly stated, her eyes moist. "Two died shortly after birth, one died before his first year, the last, a daughter, was born deformed."

Erik didn't have to ask what happened to her. "I'm sorry."

"Don't be," she said, exhaling a full breath and wiping her eyes. "The greater loss was my husband."

"What happened?"

"He left on a raid shortly after our last daughter was born and never came back."

"He was killed in the raid?" Erik delicately asked.

"No," she said, shaking her head as though still trying to understand. "A storm came up and two of the longships floundered and sank, taking all aboard to the bottom. My grief was shared by far too many."

"How long ago was that?"

"Three years."

"You were sixteen when you married Egill?"

Kolga titled her head to gaze at him. "Yes. How did you know?"

"Simple math," he said with a smile. Knowing that those wives who lost husbands had most likely remarried, he said, "You have not remarried. Is it because you are the Jarl's sister?"

"You are being polite," she remarked. "That is merely the excuse some will use. I have lost four children and a husband. I am unlucky and who wants to wed an unlucky woman... even if she is the Jarl's sister."

"I don't believe in luck," Erik calmly stated. "Things happen for a reason. There is a logical explanation for most things."

"You don't believe the gods interfere in our lives?" she asked, surprised.

Erik leaned forward and lowered his voice. "The gods are far too human for my tastes."

Kolga stared at him for a moment. "I have heard of some who worship a man called Christus. We have slaves taken from their abbeys. Some of the bolder slaves have even tried preaching this religion. Those who refuse to be silent are threatened with death and seem to welcome it instead of obeying, so we oblige them. Are you also a follower of this Christus?"

"I am," Erik acknowledged.

"He can't be much of a god," she dismissively stated, "if he allows his followers to be captured so easily."

"You mean like three longships of successful raiders halfway home when a storm comes and their ships flounder and sink and they all drown despite begging Odin to save them?" Seeing her blanch, he was contrite. "My apologies. That was unkind."

"But true, nonetheless," she acknowledged and pondered a moment. "You do not preach at us like they do."

"I am not a monk," Erik answered, "but a simple man trying to survive in this life."

Kolga smiled. "There is nothing simple about you."

Tone's heart quickened as she reread Gene's email for the third time.

Hey Beautiful.

Not meaning to brag, but I figured out the spatial location glitch in the machine. As an added bonus, we're able to program accurately back to 1000 CE with pinpoint accuracy. We had some dude who wanted to meet Genghis

193

Khan, LOL. Obviously we weren't going to accommodate him - the dude didn't even speak Chinese or Mongolian or whatever. Anyway, we chose some safer spot and since the guy did speak French, we decided to send him back to Paris. Everything worked out perfectly. Needless to say the big guy was thrilled and I got a promotion, much to the irritation of some of the older slugs. So now I'm the Director of Time Management. I even got my own office and a nice bump in the $$.

Speaking of bumps... I'm still reliving that beautiful "bump" you gave me (two of them, in fact ... wink, wink ;) when you kissed me. And am counting down the days for your return for X-mas vacation.

In the meantime, let's play a little game – where are some of the weirdest, odd, not normal, unusual places you've had sex? What made the place fun? If you could choose a place wherever you wanted to have sex, where would it be?

Tone skimmed the rest of the email, which tended to be more of the same, wondering how she should answer it without triggering alarms. She had been the one who had first broached the subject of sex with an "innocent" comment about how sensual kissing could be and how a good kisser was essential to what followed. She then boldly stated that he was a good kisser. Apparently that was all the nudging he needed.

Yet something nagged at her. Why hadn't TTI notified her that they were making progress? Perhaps they wanted to make sure before notifying her. Still, they'd had enough time, especially since the trial was a success.

With a sigh, Tone pushed away from the table and checked the clock. It was time to get ready for her martial arts class. Master Li had found a school for her conveniently located one bus stop north on Bogstadveien. And added bonus was the number of instructors in MMA, which she found particularly enjoyable as it allowed her to give vent to some of her frustration.

It's going to be a nice day, Tone mused as she headed up Josefines gate to catch the tram at Bislett Station. Once on the tram, she sat next to the window to gaze out at the passing shops and restaurants and occasional graffiti. She smiled at those sitting at the outside tables of the various restaurants, chatting with friends or reading newspapers or books, sipping coffee and simply enjoying the ambiance of a warm early fall day. She felt a wistful melancholy, wondering what it would be like with Erik, sitting outside on a morning like this, together, watching the tram go by as they ate their breakfast rolls and sipped their coffee.

Too soon her reverie was interrupted as the tram pulled into the Universitetet Blindern stop across the street from the Henrik Wergelands building, a twelve-story affair with lesser wings that housed the Humanities department and classrooms. An impish voice inside her whispered to skip class and enjoy the day outside.

Ignoring nature's siren call, she shouldered her backpack and headed to the elevator, pressing the third floor button, immediately holding the door when she saw Elsa, a petite blond with striking blue eyes and a voluptuous body, hustling to catch the elevator.

Elsa smiled when she saw Tone. "Good morning."

"Good morning," Tone cheerily replied. She liked Elsa for her buoyant personality and her sometimes acid tongue when she shot down guys whose rude behavior deserved more than a tongue lashing. Elsa had made it an art form. More than once Tone had witnessed Elsa's skillful delivery, like a fencer slicing bits of clothing away until the opponent was totally exposed for the fool he was.

"You ready for another two hours of Johans Kallevig's Old Norse language and texts class?" Elsa said, flicking her eyebrows.

Tone laughed, for she understood Elsa's not so subtle intimation about Professor Kallevig who was ruggedly handsome in an Olympic alpine skier sort of way – trim and fit with wavy blond hair. He had his bevy of undergrad coeds, and not a few grad students, who collected at the doorway to his office or classroom. It was obvious that he relished the attention and rumors abounded that more than one fair damsel was getting extra credit.

"It's going to be a tough one today as I'd rather be outside."

"Me too," Elsa sighed. "Don't know how many more days like this we'll have before the cold really hits. At least we have some eye-candy to look at." She winked.

Walking into the classroom, Tone went to her usual spot right up front. Elsa sat in the chair next to her. By the time Professor Kallevig walked in, fifteen students were scattered around the room.

"Good morning," he said with a smile then switched to Old Norse. "I hope everyone enjoyed the assignment for today."

What followed was an oppressive awkward silence until Tone responded in Old Norse.

"Yes, as a matter of fact, I did enjoy the assignment, though to be honest, I'd read that part of the saga before. In fact, I had translated the entire saga during my undergraduate studies."

As soon as Tone began her reply, Kallevig's smug condescension evaporated as his mouth gaped wider and wider.

"You speak Old Norse?" he said, shocked.

"Fluently," she replied, suddenly regretting her reply when she saw the fleeting self-conscious look and realized she probably spoke it better than he did.

"How... where did you learn it?"

"My parents spoke it at home –"

"Your parents spoke Old Norse?" he blurted.

"Not all the time, but enough to make sure we were conversant."

"Why?"   He closed his mouth and frowned in bewilderment.

Tone shrugged.   "They were very much into their Scandinavian heritage and felt we needed to be rooted." She was going to say that she and Erik used to chat for hours in Old Norse, but decided it might be TMI... too much information.

Suddenly realizing that no one in the class understood the conversation, he switched back to English.

"It appears that this class is well below Miss Thorgilsdottir's skills." Turning his attention back to Tone, he said, "I know it is a requisite class, but I don't see how it is going to improve your already remarkable linguistic skills. Do you speak any other languages?"

"Yes," she replied, felling a little bit self-conscious now that everyone was looking at her with either admiration or jealousy.

"What other languages do you speak?" he encouraged, impressed but intimidated at the same time.

"I also speak Norwegian, Danish, Swedish, German, Icelandic, and Spanish."

Amidst the stunned "O my Gods" and groans of perceived unfair competition, Elsa leaned over and place a hand on Tone's arm, giving it a gentle squeeze. "You rock."

Patting her hand, Tone mouthed 'Thank you' and looked back to the Professor.

"This class is a waste of your time," he said. "Unfortunately, you are still required to take it. That said, I will excuse you from attendance with the caveat that you assist the other students on an as needed basis."

Tone knew what he was doing. Her presence in class would undermine his expertise.

Addressing the rest of the class, he said, "Miss Thorgilsdottir will be available at her convenience for a total of four hours each week. If you require help and I am unavailable, she will assist you." He turned back to Tone. "This way you are still part of the class, but are not required to be here. Is that acceptable?"

"Yes. Thank you."

"Good." He smiled and flicked his hands at her. "Now shoo. Off with you while I teach these dullards a thing or two about Old Norse. Please stop by my office later and we'll further discuss."

"Yes, sir," she said, catching Elsa's smirk and wink. Collecting her things, she leaned over to whisper to Elsa, "I'll be at the café."

Once outside, Tone inhaled a deep peaceful breath, thankful to be free of sitting in the classroom then headed down the street to the traffic circle where the Café Istanbul occupied the end of a shared building with a small grocery store, a florist and a nondenominational church.

Seated outside with her coffee, she did a slow gaze around before settling on an older couple across the street as they shuffled to the pharmacy. He held the door open for her, giving her a loving pat on the shoulder. Tone smiled at the gesture, a simple act that expressed a lifetime of love.

Pulling out her text for her other course in Runology, she turned to the 'Categories' chapter and began studying the various categories of Rune Stones, beginning with the RAK style. Slowly perusing the numerous pictures, she took her time when she came to the profile styles, especially the early Ringerike and Urnes style. So engrossed in reading about the locations, styles, and inscriptions, she didn't realize Elsa was there until she scooted a chair out.

"Talk about oblivious," Elsa chuckled as she sat and leaned forward to see what Tone was reading. "What's so fascinating?"

"Runology," Tone said, holding up the book.

"I take that next semester. You can give me all your notes and test answers when you're done."

Tone laughed. "How was class?"

"I think you spooked ol' Kallevig," Elsa said. "Took him a couple of minutes to get himself together. But, he's easy on the eyes and so I didn't mind. Other than that, we did the usual noun-verb agreement and then went over the saga for today. Pretty straight-forward. I don't envy you the life-sucking demands from the other students in the class. I have a feeling there are a couple who will pester you until you end up doing their homework. How's the coffee?"

"Usual."

"I'll be back."

A few moments later, Elsa returned with her coffee in a biodegradable cup. "I'd watch yourself when you go visit brother Johans today. He's good looking and he knows it."

"Yes, mother," Tone replied with mock sincerity.

Elsa patted Tone's hand. "I know you're a big girl, but Mama's just trying to take care of you."

"I appreciate it. Speaking of which," she said, checking the time on her phone, "I'd better head on back to catch him before his next class."

"You up for dinner tonight?"

"Yeah," Tone replied, collecting her books, "anything but pizza."

Johans Kallevig stood behind his desk pretending to leaf though student papers when Tone poked her head in.

"Is now a good time?" she asked.

"Yes. Come in." He motioned to a seat on the other side of the desk.

Glancing around the office, Tone saw the usual academic degrees hung on the side wall along with pictures of him cycling in what looked to be some sort of semi-professional uniform. Though the office was not large, it was neatly arranged, making the most of the space. The single window provided a view of the parking lot between the two academic buildings though if one stood closer, one could see the outskirts of Oslo.

"I was impressed with your linguistic skills. Can't say that I've ever known a grad student who spoke as many languages as you do, even if some of them are related." He abruptly glanced down at his phone and frowned. "Now what?" Tone watched as he tapped the answer button and listened to the one way conversation. "Yes, Heidi? Now? But I'm with a student. Couldn't it wait? Fine. I'll be there in a couple of minutes."

Pressing the 'disconnect' icon, he gave Tone an apologetic look. "Sorry, but I need to go to the dean's office. I'm not sure how long this will take and I don't want to waste your time. We could talk expectations after my last class this afternoon, if you're free."

"That would be fine," Tone readily agreed. "Where shall I meet you?"

"You like Indian food?"

"Love it."

"How about Diamond India?"

"Perfect. That's just a couple of metro strops up from where I live. What time?"

"I should be there around six-thirty."

"See you then." Tone was halfway out the door when she heard his phone ring and knew that no one had called before. It was all a charade to get her to dinner.

Back in her apartment, Tone logged into her laptop and sure enough, Gene had responded. She scanned through the opening paragraph of the usual mundane details of what was going on at work, smiling that Gene was doing his best to say something other than what he really wanted to talk about, which came in the second paragraph.

I really liked your response ref the various places you've enjoyed yourself. I also noted there seems to be a theme here – in the office. What is it about the office that turns you on? My guess is the possibility of getting caught. And then there's the thought of coming to work the next day and the office somehow has a different aura to it, knowing that the day before it was a rendezvous for sex. Hmmm... sounds very appealing.

She skimmed the rest of the email, noting that he said little of the actual places he had sex, but rather talked about places where he would like to have sex. It was obvious he was attempting to portray himself as having little experience. Still, she had planted the seed and that was enough. Now all she had to do was add to the scenario while getting him to think it was his idea.

"How is it that you have never married?" Kolga asked as they rode along after they had ferried across the Drammenselva at Stromso.

Skirting the mountains to the west, they entered a wide fertile valley dotted with farms close to the Lierelva that snaked its way up towards the Tyrifjorden and their final destination.

"Never had the opportunity," he replied, inhaling the morning air, clean and fresh with hints of pine and spruce. The mountains on both sides of the valley were carpeted with spruce, birch, pine, yew and other trees, the birches already starting to turn yellow.

"You mean to say that in all your travels there was no one who caught your passion?" She gave him a look of doubt.

Erik pondered a bit debating whether to tell her about Tone... or rather *how* to tell her about Tone. He had wrestled with the question ever since he boarded Halfdan's ship to Kaupang. The tale he told Halfdan and Bjorn was good enough for them, but would not work with Kolga. With a woman's intuition and skillful manipulation, she would ask probing and thoughtful questions, eventually discerning the truth... which would not be to Erik's advantage, especially as Tone was still in the future.

Though the explanation Halfdan gave concerning Erik's newly acquired farm made sense, especially regarding future actions against Thorsten, that it was next to Kolga's farm was just too convenient.

"Is the question too difficult to answer?" Kolga peered intently at him, a curious smile curling the corners of her lips.

Erik returned the look. Kolga was indeed a beautiful woman and at times reminded him of Tone for she had that same self-assurance, the same what-you-see-is-what-you-get personality.

"Yes," he said, "there was one." If Kolga was disappointed, it didn't show.

"What happened?"

"It didn't work out," he replied, which was technically true as he was here and Tone was across an ocean of space and time.

Kolga nodded in understanding. "What was she like?"

"A lot like you," he replied without thinking, turning to glance around, Tone's image suddenly filling his memory.

"How so?"

"She too is incredibly beautiful," he said, gazing down the cart path yet noticing nothing, his mind filled with visions and memories of Tone. Still distracted, he didn't see Kolga's momentary blush.

"What else?" Kolga studied him, wondering if he realized what he had said. Seeing Erik's puzzled look, she knew he hadn't a clue what he said, which made the compliment all the more satisfying.

"What else?" he frowned.

"Yes. You said she was a lot like me."

"Yes," he replied vaguely remembering the direction of the discussion. "You're both confident and self-assured, but not in a superior way. You say what you think, but do it in such a manner that people respect and listen to you. You're smart and clever and your smile is worth the price of precious gems."

Kolga laughed. "Now you're being sarcastic."

"Not at all," Erik smiled. "I'm just taking a little poetic liberty."

Though smiling, Kolga narrowed her focus on him. "Is it true that you are two and forty winters?"

"Yes," he nodded. "Does that surprise you?"

"You look at least ten winters younger."

"Now who's being sarcastic?" he said with a chuckle.

"I'm serious," she firmly stated.

"Then I accept your compliment." He dipped his head deferentially. "The problem with being two and forty winters is that just about every father views me as far too old to be a match for his daughter, which I fully understand. I too would be hesitant to seek such an arrangement were I a father."

"You have no wish to be a father?"

"That's not what I said," he replied, though kindly. "Yet think about it from my perspective. First, I'd have to find someone that I love deeply enough to want to spend the rest of my life with."

"Is love necessary?" she teased.

"Absolutely, otherwise why bother? Yes, I know all about arranging matches to improve one's position and the hope the two will eventually love each other. But the matches that work are the ones where the two were already interested in each other."

"So what's the next problem?"

"Say I find this wonderful woman. There's at least another nine moon cycles before a child is born, provided the woman conceives as soon as we're married. By the time the child is old enough to marry, I'd be at least seven and fifty winters old. And suppose she conceives two winters later or even five or more? I would be a grandfather raising a child."

"All valid points," Kolga agreed, "though it seems a pity that, to me at least, you have resigned yourself to a life of solitude."

"How so?"

"If a woman finds you desirable and is still of child-bearing age, what should it matter how old *you* are? You will have children who will be proud to bear the name of Eriksson whether you are there to see it or not. It is the same if an Ostman is killed while on a raid. His wife is left a widow with their children. Should the two never have married because he might get killed?"

Erik knitted his brows, wondering if he had missed something. "I never said I didn't want to get married."

204

"You just don't want children," she harrumphed.

Recognizing he had struck a chord, Erik said, "That's not what I said."

"What you said –"

"Let me finish," Erik interrupted. "What I said was that I understood fathers not wanting me as their son-in-law, especially since I'd probably be older than the father. I provided a logical reason as it relates to the age disparity. Essentially, I would be a grandfather raising children. You took that to mean I didn't want children. Let's put it in your perspective: how would you feel if your daughter-in-law was older than you?"

Kolga blinked in reflection. "That would be a bit awkward."

"Then you understand my dilemma. It's not a question of resigning myself to a life of solitude. It's a question of whether I could ever find the right woman." Erik inhaled a slow breath, a tinge of melancholy settling within. *I found the perfect woman and lost her. Am I condemned to never see her again? Surely TTI will send someone to get me. But how will they know where I am? How will* she *know where I am?* An idea blossomed and his melancholy faded, replaced by a purpose.

Chapter 7

I confess that I have lost track of time, though to be honest, I do not miss the daily Matins and Laud prayers. Early morning was always a struggle for me, though looking back I can remember I was not alone in my drowsy prayers. Thankfully I am still able to perform a private Compline each evening before I sleep.

What I find curious of late is the contrast of my sleep from when I first arrived. Unlike then, I now sleep soundly – even though I am still a slave. Yet when I compare my present circumstances against the other brothers brought here with me, I am most fortunate for Harek is not like these other barbarians. There is goodness in him and I am determined that he will be my first convert.

Yet each day I struggle against temptation.

Harek has a daughter, yet unmarried, two years younger than I am. Her name is Alvi. She is the gentlest and fairest of women with hair the color of strawberries and skin the color of cream, with a sprinkling of freckles upon her cheeks. Chaste and virtuous, she is the desire of many men who press their crude suits as though they were bartering for a milch cow. Yet she rebuffs them all with gentle words, which only increases their passions for her. Her father, though worried she will age into spinsterhood, is unwilling to arrange a marriage to which she is not fully committed.

She calls me 'Slave boy,' but it is the way she says it... not mean-spirited or with spite or haughty, but warm and tender. I cannot fully explain it. When I told her my name was Pearson, she said, "I know." I didn't know what to make of it until I realized she called all the other slaves by their names, all expect me.

I find myself distracted by her smile, her eyes the color of a young fir, her smooth effortless walk, the delicate way she eats. She invades my every thought, even during my attempts at Compline prayer.

I have prayed and prayed to purify my thoughts, but Satan has placed her here as a stumbling block. I know this in my mind, but my heart flutters every time I see her. I am weak. I wish Erik was here. He would know what I should do.

In the late afternoon, Tone sat inside the Café Istanbul helping Simon with Old Norse verb tense agreement. In his early 20's, Simon was attractive in a geeky college-guy sort of way. Yet when it came to languages, the man was a dullard and after the third time of explaining, "Strong verbs replace the root vowel. It's called 'ablaut.' Remember I used the example in English of the strong verb 'sing.' You have sing, sang, and sung," she was ready for him to pester someone else. The fact that he was attracted to her did not go unnoticed, which made the tutoring session all the more painful.

Finally, after the fourth time correcting him, she picked up her phone. "Oh look. Time's up. We can continue this session another day."

Simon scrunched his face and checked his phone. "But I've still got another hour."

"Wrong," she emphasized. "The rules are that I am available, at my convenience, for four hours a week. And right now, 'my convenience' is finished. You need to study verbs more. Memorize them. Then come back to me."

Simon was about to argue when Elsa came in and marched up to the table.

"You still here?" she said to Simon.

"He was just leaving," Tone answered for him.

"Good," Elsa said, "because it's my turn now."

"I'm sorry," Simon said, scooting back from the table. "I didn't know."

"Well you've had her long enough," Elsa chastised. "Time to share."

"I'm going."

Once Simon had collected his books and pushed out the door into the overcast day, Elsa took his seat and leaned forward, her eyes mischievous.

"So? It's one thing getting stood up for dinner. It's another thing not sharing what happened."

"Meh," Tone said with a smile. "There's not much to tell. On the plus side, he paid for dinner. On the negative side, it was obvious he was on a fishing expedition. My God, if compliments were clothing I'd have a store. The man gushed on and on. You can imagine his shock at the end of the evening when instead of a kiss, I stuck out my hand for a handshake."

Elsa burst out laughing.

"I give him credit though," Tone continued. "He was polite and shook my hand, though he did hold on to it for longer than normal."

"What're you going to do if he asks you out?"

"He already did," Tone replied.

"My God," Elsa sputtered. "What if the university finds out?"

"Well," Tone explained, "it wasn't quite an asking me for a date. He wanted to go over some Old Norse grammar with me."

"In his office, right?"

"After tonight's evening class."

Elsa sat back. "Are you sure you want to play this game?"

"He's the one who has the most to lose. Beside," she fluttered her eyelids and pouted, "I'm just a naïve little grad student."

Kolga stood next to Erik as they stood on the hilltop in front of the longhouse and surveyed what was now his farm. She followed his gaze as it settled on the three beached longships and two knorrs tethered at wooden tie-off pilings in the shallow bay to his left.

"Yes," she affirmed, "those are yours."

"He gave me a farm with five ships?" Erik was still in shock at the vastness of his holdings which included all the land south of the Storelva and west of Kolga's holdings where a thick strip of forest separated the two farms and ended 300 meters from the shore where several of her own longships were beached.

"Actually you have six ships. One of your knorrs hasn't returned yet. It should be back in the next few weeks."

"How many people are on this farm?" he asked, still staring at the ships.

"Come," she said with a smile, recognizing the look of a man overwhelmed. "Let's take a walk and I'll explain all." She stopped when she saw a man approaching. He was a short stout man with a full russet-colored beard. He walked as a man of authority.

"This is one of the ones I was telling you about," she whispered as he came up, "Kjell the Short."

"My Lady," Kjell said with exaggerated deference, "why didn't you let me know of your arrival. I would have had everyone here to welcome you."

Though Kjell spoke to Kolga, Erik noted the man's not so subtle attention on him.

"You know that would be unnecessary," she reproved him. Motioning to the tall man beside her, she said, "This is Erik. My brother has giving him this farm."

Kjell's ingratiating smile wavered and the light in his eyes dimmed, like a man who suddenly discovered his full glass was now half empty.

"Welcome my Lord," he said, smiling with only his lips.

"You are the foreman of this farm?" Erik asked.

"Yes my Lord."

"Good," Erik replied with a disarming smile. "I will return at midday. I want a report on how many individuals work here; who are thralls and who are freemen; how long have they been here; who does what; how much livestock is here; when is the next harvest scheduled; what are the conditions of the houses and outbuildings; and much more. Is that understood?"

Kjell's eyes grew wider with each additional task. "Yes, my Lord."

"Good. In the meantime, Lady Kolga and I will walk around a bit. Do not bother us unless it is an emergency. Lady Kolga will stay for the midday meal. Be sure it is worthy of her."

"Yes, m'Lord,' he answered, bobbing his head.

Waiting until he bustled off, Erik turned to Kolga. "I know I should have you asked first, but I hope you don't mind the impromptu invitation."

"Not at all," she grinned. "That was well done. I'm impressed."

"Don't be," Erik said with a chuckle. "I may be a thorn in your side for a while until I get my land legs here."

"I doubt you could ever be a thorn in someone's side," she said, "and I fully intend to enjoy having a man around who is obviously educated. You will let me return the favor and you will dine with me tomorrow night."

"I look forward to it, m'Lady," he replied with a gallant bow.

It was late afternoon when Erik departed from Kolga's longhouse, lazily guiding his horse back along the road between the two farms. These past several days riding beside the captivating woman had been more than enjoyable. She was intelligent and witty, not to mention beautiful. More than once he had been mesmerized by her charm and had to remind himself that he was spoken for... at least he was when he left however many days or weeks... or was it months ago?

Though he believed TTI would want to send someone for him, his faith in seeing anyone from the future weakened with each succeeding day. Suppose they did send someone back to the exact time when he and Tone arrived on Lindisfarne? Wouldn't he have to go back in time in order to be there when they arrived? How could he be here and there at the same time? That whole doppelganger thing seemed more smoke and mirrors for saying "We don't have a clue."

And suppose they got back just as he and Halfdan were sailing away? They'd have no idea where to look for him. And then, if TTI couldn't locate him, how was Tone supposed to find him? The idea he had on the ride up from Skiringssal seemed like a longshot, especially if no one ever found the message. Still, it was better than nothing.

His musings turned back to his farm. He understood what Kolga meant when she said to be wary of Kjell and Sture, the freeman, or 'karl', responsible for the cattle. Sture was a slender man whose impatient demands had the others, especially the slaves, or 'thralls', in a constant jittery state. Erik had said nothing when he saw Sture cuff a thrall lad who had failed to adequately please the man, deciding then was not the time for corrective action. He would have to assert his presence and position.

During Kjell's briefing, Erik discovered he owned eighteen thralls, six of whom were very attractive young women who worked in the longhouse. The way they looked at him gave him pause, for two of them looked at him with overt sexual desire while the others with a sort of relief. He guessed that Kjell had been enjoying himself at their expense.

Yet his musings meandered back to Kolga. How long could he or should he wait for Tone? Were his hopes delusion? He knew if he pressed it, he could win Kolga. Was that what he wanted? Suppose he did win her and just when they consummated their marriage Tone showed up? Was this like the old 'if-you-were-on-a desert-island' question? How long would you wait for your true love to show up? Forever seemed like a long time.

Yet deep in his heart he knew Kolga was not Tone. He had spent years getting to know bits of Tone during the time she attended his classes. Then the revelation at the end of her senior year sent his soul soring. He finally gave vent to the pent up emotions, giving voice and action to the fantasies. There was only one Tone and she would find him. He would just have to help her.

Tone sat inside Kallevig's office while he finished teaching his class, leafing through one of the books she had pulled out of the bookcase, wryly noting a significant portion relating to nude photography, especially by David Hamilton. Tone instead chose a book on Skaldic Poetry.

Hearing his footsteps echoing outside in the hallway, she pretended to be engrossed in the book when he entered.

"Good evening," he suavely said as he glided in to stand next to her. "I'm so glad you're here. What are you reading?"

"One of your books on Skaldic Poetry," she said, standing and replacing the book back on the shelf. "I noticed you have a lot of photography books."

"I enjoy photography. Are you familiar with David Hamilton's work?"

"Yes," she replied, "but I prefer my models to have at least reached puberty."

"I take it you're not a fan of his work," he said with a smile, easing himself around the desk and sitting.

"He was the master of soft focus, if I remember correctly. But, like I said, if I'm going to look at photographs of nude people, I'd like for them to be old enough to understand what they're doing and the extended consequences of their choices. Somehow I don't think thirteen year old girls fit that category."

"It wasn't uncommon for thirteen year old girls to marry in Norse times," he countered, "especially when the life expectancy was around 20 years. By the time a boy reached sixteen years old, he was expected to assume the roles of an adult male. In fact, to be a judge at an Althing, a boy could be as young as twelve years old."

"All true," she acknowledged. "But how many thirteen year old girls would pose nude in Norse times?"

"Different value systems. Do you not like nude photography?" he challenged with an innocent smile.

"Depends how it's done," she answered. "The human body can be beautiful and a tasteful photo of a nude is fine. What passes for tasteful these days is questionable. So to answer your question, yes, I do like nude photography. But I qualify that with *good* nude photography."

"Any particular photographer that you like?"

"None that I can think of. It's not something I go out of my way to find. But am I here to discuss nude photography or Old Norse grammar?"

"Why not both?" He locked his gaze on her

"I fail to see the connection." Tone challenged, enjoying the repartee. She had an idea of where the discussion was headed and wanted to see how he maneuvered it there.

"Who said there had to be a connection? You commented on my photography books, an interest of mine. This is merely more of us getting to know each other. I like nude photography and we were simply discussing a hobby of mine."

Deciding to force the game, she said, "Fair enough. So are you a nude photographer?"

"Yes, I am." He leaned back in his chair.

"So how do you go about finding someone willing to pose for you?"

"There are websites with women available to model," he said with a nonchalant shrug.

"You sound like those don't interest you."

"While the women are all beautiful, they do it for a living. They lack innocence. It's artificial. They've done a particular pose a hundred times, all with the same artificial face. You can't fake innocence. You can tell the difference in a photograph."

"Then how do you find suitable models?"

"I look for someone I think would be a good model and then I ask."

"That's it? 'Hi. I'm Professor Kallevig. How would you like to take your clothes off for me so I can take pictures?'"

Kallevig laughed. "Not quite, but something like that. I explain that I am a photographer looking for nude models. I will pay them –"

"How much?"

"Depends on the session, which usually takes a couple of hours. But my base offer is $200 per hour."

"What about rights to the photos?"

Kallevig dipped his head, impressed. "Most models don't even ask until after the shoot. But I approach it as a joint venture. My policy is that the photos are private until such time as I determine a book could be viable. At that time, all models have to agree to be in the book. I retain 50% of the profits with the other 50% divided among the models."

"Have you published a book?"

"I have one out," he said, standing and retrieving a book from amongst the photography books and handing it to her.

"Eros by K," she read aloud the title. "Interesting." Opening the book, she flipped through the pages filled with beautiful women in various poses, all sensual and tastefully done, many of them taken outside. "I see hints of David Hamilton in some of the soft focus shots."

"Thank you. I take that as a compliment."

She was about to close the book when she saw a model who looked vaguely familiar, long straight blond hair, smooth flawless milk-white skin and well endowed. Pausing, she studied the woman only to realize the photo was of a woman who sat next to her in Runology class. Her name was Siv.

Deciding to keep that tidbit of information to herself, she handed the book back to him. "These are all good photos, well arranged and tastefully done. You have a good eye."

"Thank you."

Locking her gaze on him, she said, "Do I assume part of the reason for me being here is that you would like me to pose for you?"

"The thought had crossed my mind," he said with a hopeful smile.

216

Tone stroked her chin. "It's something I'll have to think about. How much have you made from the book?"

"It's in its third printing," he said with pride. "I noticed you paused at the layout of one model. While I will not divulge anything else about her, I can tell you that she has made enough to pay for college and live comfortably while doing it."

Tone raised her eyebrows in surprise. "That much? I didn't realize that coffee table books were still in such a demand."

"Depends what you're selling," he said with a knowing smile, "and how good your work is. My photographs are only available via the book. The photos are all copyrighted and unavailable online. I have a friend who is a lawyer so that any pirated material is effectively dealt with."

"Have to you had to use him?"

"Once," he grinned. "We both made a tidy sum."

"Interesting," she mused.

"So you see," he encouraged, "I'm very protective of both the model and my work. Nothing happens without your approval."

Tone slowly nodded. "Give me a couple of days to think about it. It sounds interesting."

"Take all the time you need," he solicitously said.

Tone sat next to the window as the #17 metro train slowed to a stop at Bislett Stadion. She had declined Kallevig's offer of a ride home, preferring to have time alone to ponder his proposition.

Disembarking the train, she headed towards the traffic circle where six streets converged, making her way past the sports stadium, crossing two more streets to get to Josefines gate to walk down the leaf laden sidewalk. It seemed the trees were shedding their leaves faster than the residents could pick them up. It reminded her of fall in Corydon, Indiana.

Her loneliness ached within and she heaved a cheerless sigh, surprised that she would even consider posing nude for someone who was almost a stranger. Pity it wasn't Erik. If he were the photographer, it would be more than fun. And afterwards they would make passionate love. But Kallevig? Taking her clothes off for him would be like going to the doctor for a physical. Yeah, she could pretend to enjoy it, but in the end, all she would be doing is satisfying his penchant for naked women and then getting paid for it.

All this waiting was beginning to make her edgy. Something had to give real soon or she was going to go postal on someone. Thank God she had her martial arts to vent her frustrations.

Once back in her apartment she sat down at the dining table and flipped open her laptop. She groaned when she saw another email form Gene. The guy was beginning to be like gum on her shoe.

Initially bypassing his email, she read everything else, immediately deleting all the spam, wondering how so much of it made it past her spam filters. Finally, when Gene's email was the last one unopened, she opened it then went to pour a glass of mead, noting with bemusement that a glass of mead could almost make anything more bearable.

Sitting back down, she nearly choked on her wine.

Hey Doll,

We did it. Or rather I should say I did it. I discovered another glitch in the system and realized we had left out a tiny bit of the destination equation, which affected the time probability factor. We can now go back to the Romans! Although before I get too full of myself, I might add that the destination factor is still squirrely, which means that we can get you back to the exact time and day... It's just that you might be 100 kilometers from where you expected to be once you go back beyond 1000 CE. But hey, it's a step in the right direction and the high and mighty are again stumbling over themselves with praise for my work. I got my performance review today – by the VP of Travel! – and you'd think I invented the wheel!

She skimmed the rest, which had the usual comments about sex. An idea popped into her mind and she sat back to think about it before beginning her reply. Starting off with the usual "I'm very impressed with your genius for machines and math and yada yada," she settled down to the next paragraph, which she knew would get his attention.

I've been approached by a photographer to do some nude shots. I'm seriously thinking about it. I've seen some of his work and it's very good, all done very tastefully. What do you think? Should I or shouldn't I?

She sat back and smirked. That should get his mind working overtime.

Kjell was not pleased at all when told he would have to find other accommodations.

"This is my house," Erik sternly affirmed. "You may stay tonight. Come tomorrow morning, I expect you to find other lodging. I'm sure with your reputation you will have no problem. If you wish, you can stay with the other bachelor freemen."

"But... but, m'Lord," Kjell sputtered. "Am I not your foreman?"

219

"Yes, but you are not kin. You've been a guest in my house for long enough. Time to find a place of your own."

"But, m'Lord. Where will I go?"

"Like I said, I'm sure you've endeared yourself to everyone on the farm. Someone is bound to give you a place until I can build a place for you."

"You will build me a home?" Kjell said, surprised.

"Of course," Erik said, as though the answer obvious. "A foreman deserves his own place."

"Thank you m'Lord," Kjell obsequiously replied, relieved. "I'm sure I can find a place in the meantime."

"Good. And think of someone to replace Sture."

"You want to replace Store, m'Lord? He one of the best farmers in these parts, most knowledgeable."

"I'm sure he is. The problem is no one likes him. I want this farm's production to increase and it won't if people hate it here." It seemed a logical conclusion despite Erik having no clue on how to farm. "I'm not satisfied with the way he treats my thralls. Give me a recommendation tomorrow evening."

"He will not be happy, m'Lord," Kjell said.

"Do you think he can change?"

"May I work with him?"

"Yes. How much time do you want?"

"A month, m'Lord?"

"A month it is." Erik pointed his finger at him. "Warn him. Tell him I will not tolerate abuse. Punish a thrall if he or she deserves it. But I will not tolerate abuse."

"Yes, m'Lord."

"One more thing. Is there a stone carver around here?"

"There is one in Hønefoss, north of here.

"I remember," Erik nodded, "though we were about three kilometers south of it."

Kjell's look of confusion was followed by, "Kilometers, m'Lord? What are those?"

Erik silently chastised himself for slipping into modern measurements. "It's a unit of distance measurement I learned about during my travels. You were telling me about Hønefoss."

"Yes, m'Lord. You can be there and back in less than a day."

Erik wasted no time in saddling up and riding north. After two hours of passing numerous small farms, the road curved and the tiny trading settlement lay ahead.

Hønefoss was strategically located at the bend in the river just south of where the Randselva and the Adalselva joined to form the Storelva. To call it a trading center was to give it far more status than the seven clustered homes deserved. Still, these seven houses were home to seven extended families with a population of almost 100 individuals.

The word spread when a young man working a farm field saw Erik approach. By the time Erik guided his horse into the middle of the town, a half dozen men waited for him.

"I am Erik," he announced, dismounting. "I own the farm next to Kolga."

"Yes, we know," a weathered man with graying hair replied. "Welcome to Hønefoss."

"Thank you. I understand there is a stone carver here."

"I am the stone carver," another man spoke up. He was a trim man who looked to be in his late 40s but was probably in his 30s. He scratched his cheek through the thick auburn beard. "I am called Sioni."

Erik dipped his head in acknowledgment. "I wish to raise a rune stone. How long would it take?"

"Depends," Sioni said, "on how much is desired on the stone."

"Nothing elaborate… about fifteen words or so."

"If it's just writing, it shouldn't take long at all," he deferentially replied. "Weather permitting, perhaps a week or two."

"Perfect," Erik said, pleased. "When can you start?"

"Let me attend to the needs of my farm first. I can be there later today."

"I look forward to it."

By the time Erik returned home, he sensed a subtle energy among his farm workers as though anticipating some sort of surprise. Kjell stood at the doorway of Erik's longhouse, trying not to appear too smug.

"Welcome back, m'Lord. There is a man from Thorsten here to see you."

"What does he want," Erik said, dismounting and giving the reins to a thrall.

"He's inside."

"You left him alone inside my house?" Erik frowned in irritation.

"Of course. He's not going to do anything."

Heaving a sigh of frustration, Erik opened the door to find a well-muscled man sitting at one of the tables, drinking a mug of mead. The man turned when he heard the door open. Seeing Erik, he rose and walked towards him, measuring him as he approached.

"I am Ingvald. I am here to challenge you."

Ingvald was about three inches shorter than Erik, with close cropped hair and a thick rust colored beard. He wore silver arm rings and a torque.

"Challenge me to what?"

"To fight."

Erik let out a slow breath. "Are you sure you really want to do that?"

Ingvald sniffed in disdain, choosing to keep silent about Thorsten's offer of half of Erik's farm for killing Erik. "Do you accept?"

Studying the man, it dawned on Erik that Ingvald would be the first of many of Thorsten's men to come here and challenge him. It was then Erik understood why Halfdan sent him here. Was the farm really Halfdan's to begin with? Erik had a passing thought that the farm was an in-your-face act by Halfdan.

"Yes," Erik replied, "I accept. Let me get my weapons." Turning to Kjell whose arrogance had returned, he commanded, "Take him to the level spot beside the sheep pasture."

There was no 'Yes, m'Lord' in Kjell's reply. Instead, the man merely ticked his head at him and motioned for Ingvald to follow. Erik watched them leave, silently musing that Kjell expected Erik to lose, which caused him to wonder whose side was Kjell on.

Collecting his nunchuks, Erik arrived at the challenge site, a grassy level area by the wattle fence that kept the sheep away from the grain fields. Ingvald had his sword already drawn, waiting, a confident smile curling the corners of his lips.

As he turned to Kjell, Erik noted the gathering of a number of the farmhands. "Hold these," he said, handing his nunchuks to Kjell whose puzzled frown revealed that he didn't think the fight was going to last very long if Erik was going to use these strange weapons.

Erik walked over to stand in front of Ingvald. "You have issued a challenge. I have accepted. What are the terms?"

"We fight to the death or you yield."

"This is my home, my farm," Erik calmly answered.

"Then we fight to the death," Ingvald said with arrogant disdain.

"So be it. You know what I'm going to do first?"

Ingvald's brows furrowed then an eyebrow raised. "What?"

Pointing at the man's head, Erik said, "I'm going to place my right foot on the left side of your head.   And you know what?"

"What?" Ingvald stared at him as if he had lost his mind.

"There's nothing you can do about it."

"Wha –"

In a whirl faster than lightening, Erik swung an inside crescent kick to Ingvald's head sending him reeling to the ground then calmly walked back to Kjell to collect his nunchuks. Languidly moving to the center of the clearing he waited as Ingvald, now on his hands and knees, shook his head, trying to figure out what had just happened.

Reaching for his sword, Ingvald pushed himself to standing, his face flushed with anger and doubt, especially when his opponent began spinning those metal bars in his hands. Crouching in a defensive position, sword and buckler ready, he carefully measured Erik's body, focusing on his hands and the spinning bars.

Erik watched his opponent, instinctively noting the balance and position of both hands and feet, the angle of his body and especially his eyes, for the eyes usually revealed intent. The nunchuks were now crisscrossing in front of him like twin buzz saws and he inched forward as Ingvald backed away vainly searching for an opening.

Deciding to use the same tactics he employed with Oluf, Erik flicked a nunchuk at Ingvald's head, causing him to over react and lean backwards out of the way. In that instant, Erik attacked, leaping and spinning midair as the other nunchuk whirled in a wide powerful sweep and embedded with a crack on his ribcage.

Ingvald reeled backwards, his breathing suddenly exploding pain, and his strength compromised. He weakly lifted his buckler too late as the metal bar smashed into his head and the world turned black as he crumpled to the ground.

Erik stood over the prostrate body, staring at the indentation in the man's skull. He was still alive though unresponsive, blood seeping from his nose and ear. Erik bent down to retrieve the sword, noting the faint engraved 'Ulfberht' on the blade near the hilt.

As he turned to speak with Kjell, he saw the astonished faces of his farm workers who had expected to watch a lengthy slugfest and instead witnessed a battle so lopsided that they barely had time to comprehend what had just happened.

"Bring his horse," Erik commanded. A teenager ran off to fetch the animal.

Directing his attention to Kjell, he said, "You will take him back to Thorsten."

At that moment, Kolga came cantering up. Dismounting, she handed the reins to a man close by and strode over towards Erik, appraising the scene as she approached. Stopping, she focused her attention on the limp man on the ground.

"I don't recognize him."

"He's one of Thorsten's men," Erik answered, "sent here to challenge me for the farm."

Shaking her head, she pursed her lips. "I had a feeling this would happen."

"Care to explain?" Erik said, raising an eyebrow. "Just a moment," he added, holding finger up to stop her before turning to Kjell. "You better start moving. I want you to tell

Thorsten that I send back what he sent to me. Take Sture with you."

Erik's glare told Kjell that he would brook no discussion and the foreman glanced quickly around at the other men. "Help me get him up on his horse."

While the men muscled the battered man to drape over the horse, Erik turned back to Kolga. "You were saying."

Kolga gave him a nod of approval. "Egill and I gained this farm as a gift from Thorsten when we were married. Not to be outdone, Halfdan gave us the farm where I now live. Obviously the two farms were more than we could manage, especially with no kin to help us, but we managed. When Egill was killed, Thorsten tried to assert his claim to the farm. Halfdan countered with a claim of his own. As a compromise, Thorsten sent Kjell to help me. Halfdan agreed under the condition that the farm still belonged to me."

"If the farm is yours, why did Halfdan give it to me?"

"I had asked my brother to find someone suitable to take over the farm, someone we both could trust. Like I said, two large farms were more than I could handle. I was wearing myself out trying to keep up with everything."

Erik frowned when a thought abruptly emerged. "How did Thorsten know I was here?"

Kolga smiled. "He has spies here just like we have spies there."

Still frowning, Erik wondered, "How did you know what was going on here?"

Kolga laughed and pointed across the water to her longhouse on the hill. "Just as you can see me from here, I can see you too. When I saw the men gathering at this spot, I decided to come see what was going on."

"I'm glad you're here," he said, giving her a warm smile. By now, the men had gone back to work, the tale of Erik's victory beginning to gain mythic proportions. "I can use your wisdom."

"Let's talk about it over the evening meal," she said, "at my home. You can escort me back."

"It would be an honor and a pleasure," he suavely replied with a bow. "I'll be right back."

Watching him head back to the longhouse to inform the household that he would be gone for the evening, Kolga mused that she more than liked what she saw. Not only was he tall and handsome, there was something about him that she found appealing. Actually, if she were honest, there was more than just some *thing*. The man was obviously educated, far more educated than anyone she'd ever known. Yet he never lorded it over others. He was kind and considerate… and had manners. All the days traveling together, the more time she spent with him the more time she wanted to be with him. He seemed fascinated with everything she said, asking far more questions than she could answer, like some child in innocent wonder. It was as though his life was an adventure to be experienced and shared… something she was missing ever since Egill left.

She reminded herself to thank Halfdan for sending him here. Not only did he make her feel safe, he was a joy to be with. And the fact that he was handsome added to the pleasure of his presence.

She smiled at him as he approached. Life had definitely gotten better.

Tone was early for class and was surprised to see Siv seated in the back, studying. Siv looked up and gave her a friendly smile.

"You're here early," Tone said, weaving around the desks to plop down next to her.

"Just wanted to find a quiet place to relax and figured no one would be here."

"Oh, sorry. I'll leave you alone." Tone started to get up when Siv stopped her.

"You're fine. I like you," she said with a smile. "Some of the others in class are just a little... ah, too intense, too 'O my God, rune writing, let's spell my name in runes, I'm gonna write my cat's name in runes, my emoji is going to be a rune symbol,' and on and on. Makes me want to hurl."

Tone laughed. "I know what you mean. They've learned the alphabet but they still can't translate."

"Right?" Siv exclaimed. "And these are grad students. Sort of makes you wonder how they managed to graduate in the first place."

"I know," Tone agreed.

Siv suddenly felt self-conscious as Tone visually undressed her. "Uh..."

"I'm picturing you naked," Tone admitted.

Siv half-smiled and frowned at the same time, leaning away slightly. "O... K?"

"I saw you in Professor's Kallevig's book," Tone explained.

"Ah," she chuckled and relaxed. "What did you think?"

"They were well done. You're beautiful."

Siv blushed. "Thank you. I bet he's asked you to pose, hasn't he. You are too gorgeous not to want to see naked."

Tone smirked. "Wonder what someone would think if they only heard part of our conversation. 'You're too gorgeous not to want to see naked.'"

Siv snickered and nodded.

"Do you have any of the pictures?" Tone asked.

"Yes, but with a stipulation. I'm not allowed to sell or distribute them without prior authorization." She shook her

228

head and sniffed, "Like I'm going to stand on the corner and try to sell nude pics of myself."

"So what made you do it?" Tone asked.

"A couple reasons," Siv shrugged. "First, I'm not ashamed of my body. I take care of it. I exercise, eat right and all the other things to look good. I figured I'd like to have some pics of me so when I'm old and time and gravity have taken advantage of me, I can look back and see what I once was. Sort of like the glory days our male counterparts so often reminisce about."

"And the other reasons?"

Siv leaned closer. "The money was *real* good. Kallevig's a superb photographer. It wouldn't surprise me if he decided to do that full time."

"So he pays you a lot for the sessions?"

"While the sessions are good for the time invested, it's the book sales afterwards. He's got a following and he restricts sales so that he creates a demand. And the books are not cheap. I was hesitant at first because I wondered how much a coffee table book would sell, especially with all the online access to porn and stuff."

"But this isn't porn," Tone pointed out.

"Exactly. You'd be surprised at the competition out there for well-done nude photography. Lots of folks say they do it, but very few are really good at it."

"Does it bother you when someone recognizes you?"

"Surprisingly," Siv said with a wry smile, "you're the first."

"What? Really? I'd have figured word would be out by now, not just for you, but for all the others before you."

"Like I said, he has a clientele list that he restricts, so the only time you see his work is if you buy the book from him. He doesn't publicly advertise. I don't know how he does it, but he is making a killing."

"Wonder why he still teaches?" Tone said.

"Great place to find models," Siv said and winked. "Look at us…"

"Touché."

"So? You going to do it?"

"I'm not sure. I wanted to talk to you and get your perspective. What was he like?"

"Eh… there were times I felt he was coming on a little too strong."

"Did you two ever do anything?"

Siv paused then sheepishly admitted, "Yeah, a couple of times. He's good looking and I figured, why not?"

"And?" Tone pressed.

"It was good. He's an excellent lover."

"But?"

"But nothing more. It became obvious that he wasn't interested in a long term relationship. It wasn't like we parted on bad terms. Not at all. We're still friends. I suppose he'd still be amenable to having sex with me again, but from my perspective, what's the point other than sexual gratification? I want something more, something lasting, something permanent. I want to find my dream man, my knight in shining armor. You know what I mean?"

Tone slowly nodded. "Yes I do."

"You ever have one of those in your life?" Siv wistfully asked. "What am I saying? You're here. If you did, you wouldn't be here or he'd be here with you. No offense."

"None taken," Tone quietly answered, as she internally debated whether to tell Siv the truth. An idea began to coalesce, but she needed to work it through first. Instead she replied, "One of these days."

Tone had two emails amidst all the junk flooding her in-box waiting for her when she returned back to her apartment, the expected one from Gene and one from Kallevig. She decided to read Kallevig's first.

Tone. Just a note to let you know that your tutoring has been most beneficial to your fellow students. Keep up the excellent work. Also, have you had a chance to consider my proposal concerning the other matter we discussed? Looking forward to your input.

Johans

It was innocuous enough. She'd string him along for a little while longer as she still hadn't made up her mind. Why was she still debating? Part of her thought it a wild and fun idea while another part fretted about what Erik would say if he were here? Yet another voice said, 'What would it matter if your plan fails and you never see him again?' And still another voice said, 'It's your life. Do what you want to do.' If Erik were here, he would be the one taking the pics. But he wasn't here, and she had no clue as to when or even *if* she'd ever see him again. As it stood right this second, she didn't even know if he was still alive. Yet she knew she could not give up that easily, especially if there was even the remotest chance that he was still alive. As to her posing nude, there was no doubt her parents would not be very happy...

That caused her to chuckle. But how would they know? If Kallevig had to have her permission to use her pics... and if she wasn't around to give that permission... they'd never get published. But what was she going to do with the pictures? She certainly couldn't take them with her... Maybe she'd ask Siv to pose with her. That way Siv would have the pics and the memories and Kallevig would still be unable to publish them. But she'd have to tell Siv what her plans were.

Thinking of her plans, she opened Gene's email which was short and to the point.

Nude pics?   O god yes!!   And I want copies.   Please, please, I'm on my knees begging you.

He enclosed a pic of a bedraggled starving man on his knees in the desert, his hands clutched, pleading, which caused her to laugh.

With a devilish grin, she replied:

I have a friend here who is absolutely gorgeous and has posed nude for this same photographer.   I was thinking of maybe asking her to do a photoshoot with the two of us together.   Do you think I should?

She burst a laugh as she hit 'send.'

Chapter 8

Satan wars against me. Despite my every effort to fight temptation, I find myself growing weaker and weaker. Yet I cannot reconcile Alvi with the evil Jezebel. Unlike Jezebel, Alvi is pure of spirit and chaste. She has no guile or deception. She is so unlike the other barbarian women that I am convinced she secretly is a Christian.

Why do I say this? While she knows of all the false gods these savages worship, she pays them only lip service. I have overheard her challenging her father about their power and presence. If only I was able to talk with her and explain my Faith, I am convinced she would worship the true God.

But I am like a fumbling oaf around her for she dazzles me. Yet she treats me with kindness and gentleness, even while she calls me 'Slave boy.' I see it in her eyes, her smile for me. They say so much more than her words.

And I find myself obsessed, consumed. My waking thoughts are of her and she invades even my Compline prayers. It has become an effort to focus and I am constantly asking forgiveness for my distractions. But it is my dreams where she resides most, happy dreams that give me joy and rest.

I do my best to hide my infatuation, but even Harek has seen my attention drift. It happened once when I was pumping the billows to the furnace and she walked by.

"Wake up, Pearson!"

Startled, I realized I had stopped pumping. I immediately starting pumping again, embarrassed. But when I looked up, he merely shook his head and smiled. I suddenly realized that he had called me by my name. I had always been just 'You' before.

Ever since then, Harek has called me by my name, singling me out and teaching and encouraging me. He even let me craft some beads. Not wanting to disappoint, I focused all my attention on making beads I thought would please him.

His praise was wonderful. He said my beads equaled any of the other masters of the craft. I said I was merely doing what he had taught me, trying to come close to the beauty of his work, for there is no other bead maker his equal.

He was pleased with my words. What followed sent a thrill down my spine for he told me that Alvi was taking some necklaces and bracelets to Skiringssal and that I was to accompany her to help answer any questions.

Beside myself with joy, I walked beside her all the way to Skiringssal and back. We talked and talked about all sorts of things. She asked about my past and when she discovered how educated I was, she was very impressed. She told me that she already knew I was smart. And instead of calling me 'Slave-boy,' she called me Pearson. The way she said it nearly took my breath away.

When we arrived at Skiringssal, Jarl Halfdan wasn't there, but his wife and children were. His wife's name is Liv. She is a very beautiful woman, almost as beautiful as Alvi. Alvi showed her the necklaces and bracelets. Liv was so impressed she wanted all of them, especially after Alvi told her the price.

"You're not charging enough," Liv said.

Alvi explained that this was a special price her father gave only to Halfdan. Liv smiled and sent the oldest daughter to fetch the payment, which consisted of Roman silver coins.

We took our time on the way back because the day was warm and the skies bright blue with a gentle wind coming off the sea. We talked and laughed and I don't remember a happier time in my life. Just to be with her was more than I ever expected. All her attention was on me. Me! Just me.

Then, where the road bent and the trees blocked the view between Skiringssal and Kaupang, she abruptly stopped and quickly looked all around before stepping close to me and kissing me – on the lips!!

I nearly fainted on the spot.

"Don't tell my father," she warned me.

Why did she kiss me? She said that I was different from the other men she'd met. All they wanted to do was marry her and make babies. She said I was different because I talked to her like she was intelligent. Intelligent?! She is the smartest woman I've ever met.

Is what she said true? I don't know or care because I don't think my feet touched the ground the rest of the way back.

Now every time I see her, I feel her lips on mine. I feel the overwhelming surge of love and devotion.

But at the same time I am terrified. What would happen if Harek found out? And suppose he approved and in some crazy world said I could marry her? What do I do when the time comes to perform the act of husband and wife? I've never been with a woman before.

I wish Erik were here. He would know what to do.

For the next two weeks, Tone danced the edges of commitment with Kallevig while simultaneously getting to know Siv better. She liked her studious demeanor and no nonsense approach to things. And she had a quick sense of humor and Tone enjoyed spending time with her, especially as Elsa had found a young man who had captivated her attention.

Gene's emails got more graphic and gushing and Tone realized she had opened Gene's Pandora's Box. To slow him down while keeping his interest up, she wrote back a couple of what she called 'camp letters,' those 'life is wonderful here at camp' screeds that counsellors made their campers write. Gene got the hint and toned down his panting, which Tone swore she could hear in the emails.

One morning as Tone and Siv walked into the classroom, sitting in their usual seats up front, Siv leaned over to whisper to Tone.

"I've got a surprise for you."

"I was wondering why you've been so antsy this morning," Tone chuckled. "What is it?"

"Patience," Siv replied with an impish smile. "I think you'll like it."

"You are so evil," Tone pretended to pout.

As soon as the bell rang to begin class, Siv's hand shot up.

"Professor?"

"Yes, Siv?"

"I think I may have found a new rune stone."

"Really?" He ticked an eyebrow up in curiosity. "Where?"

"Just outside of Royse."

"Royse?"

"It's on the Tyrifjorden peninsula, south of Hønefoss. My aunt and uncle have a farm there."

"Why do think there's a rune stone there?"

"I saw it."

"Impossible," he gently corrected her. "Every rune stone in all of Scandinavia has been identified and catalogued, and either left in situ or moved to a protected location."

"I thought so too," she replied. "I was down there this past weekend and one of the farmers, a Mister Osberg, said he noticed a stone in the field by the bus stop. He said it wasn't there before. He showed it to me and, at least to me, it looks like it's been there a while. I copied down the runes and translated part of it." She turned to Tone and with a triumphant grin said, "What's odd is that it mentions your name."

"Me?" Tone sputtered.

Slipping a copy of the notes to Tone, she stood up and handed the notes to the professor who studied the paper, silently translating the runes.

The furrow of his brows deepened in puzzlement. "Interesting. It's in the transition Furthark where the Younger is beginning to take over. It says 'Erik raised this stone in honor of Tone Thorgilsdottir, Odin's Valkyrie who gave him life.'"

"O my God," Tone burst. "He's alive."

"Pardon?" the professor said, giving her a quizzical frown.

Tone cleared her throat to cover her outburst. "Sorry. I was thinking of something else." She smiled, her heart still pounding. "I'm sure I'm not the only Tone Thorgilsdottir in history."

Giving her a patient smile, he gazed back down at the paper. "And these markings that appear to be Roman numerals?"

"Those were on the stone as well, at the bottom of the inscription," Siv said. "It didn't make any sense to me as, like you said, they're Roman numerals, which is inconsistent with the Nordic runes."

The professor peered intently at her. "Where did you say this stone was?"

"South of Royse."

"Yes, I know. Where in Royse?"

"Just up from the bus stop at Dakotaveien," Siv replied. "There's a tree or a bush next to a telephone pole and the stone is next to the bush."

The professor checked his watch. "My first inclination is that this has to be some sort of forgery. That said, it might be interesting for the entire class to see. Though I doubt its authenticity, it might prove a learning experience. Thus, I believe we can take a field trip. We will continue the remaining discussion of the RIK stone style later. Collect your things and meet me down in the faculty parking lot. My vehicle is large enough for the six of us."

On the drive up, Tone sat next to Siv who had still another set of her handwritten notes with the runes, translation and the Roman numerals, pointing to a set of Runes.

"See? There you are, 'Tone Thorgilsdottir.'"

"What are the odds?" Tone chuckled then glanced down at the Roman numerals arranged in columns.

VIII	XIII
VI	VI
VII	XX
IX	XXXI
III	

"They make no sense to me," Siv said as Tone silently read *eight, thirteen, six, six, seven, twenty, nine, thirty-one, three.* She then read them in columns: *eight, six, seven, nine, three... thirteen, six, twenty, thirty-one.*

It was when she paused after the five and read twenty thirty-one together that a nervous realization grew: 2031... the real present year at this very moment. Thirteen wasn't a month so it had to be a day... the 13th of the six month, which is June... *O my God.*   Her heart raced at the epiphany... June 13th, 2031... *Our special day.*

She reread the first column then forcibly controlled her excitement, staring out the window a moment before saying, "Professor. While the second column of Roman numerals is odd, the first column is interesting: eight, six, seven, nine, three. One could look at it as a date, the 8th of June 793, the day Vikings sacked Lindisfarne."

"An interesting supposition," he replied as they crossed the bridge over the Sandvikselva. "The problem with that is that 793 would be written DCCXCIII."

"Yes, I know," Tone replied.   "I just thought it interesting." *But I know the truth. Erik left this for me. He's telling me he's alive and probably somewhere near here, apparently doing well enough to be able to raise a stone.*

Peering silently out the window, she gazed out at the passing homes, businesses and landscape then at the finger of the Tyrifjorden as it gradually widened until it filled the vista. *I wonder where he is now.*

She felt Siv lean into her and turned to gaze into questioning eyes. "There's something you're not telling me," Siv whispered.

"I will," Tone whispered back, deciding there and then to tell Siv the whole story.

The rune stone lay flat near the tall bush like Siv said. It wasn't a grand stone like some that Tone had seen, set in the middle of a field like some resplendent obelisk. This stone nestled in the tall grass between the bush and the telephone pole, barely rising above it as though peering out over the edges, wanting to be noticed but afraid to poke its head too high.

The face of the stone was smooth, the letters deeply engraved in orderly lines across the face. While the professor kneeled down to study the positioning, Tone lightly ran her fingers in the runes of her name, imagining what was happening when Erik had this made. *At least he's alive.* She raised her gaze to stare out over the fields then across the water to the forested hills in the far distance. *My God, how long will it be before I find you?*

Straightening to standing, the professor shook his head in puzzlement. "From what I can tell, it appears this stone has been here a while. Everything about it seems authentic... which makes no sense. How could we have missed this in all the hundreds of years we've studied this area? My first inclination is that this has to be a forgery, someone playing an absurd joke. But the size of the stone and the positioning would require some sort of earth moving machine that would have left telltale signs in the farm field leading up to this cropping."

"Something the farmer or neighbors surely would have noticed," Siv added.

"Correct," the professor said with a nod. "Until I can get this analyzed, I suggest that we refrain from sharing this news until we can discover the truth." He turned to Siv. "Well done. If this is authentic, you have discovered an important find."

Pleased with the possible recognition Siv watched Tone tenderly fingering the engraved letters of her name.

Tone? She already knew the stone was authentic. Notoriety because her name was in the stone? What did it matter when the author of the stone was 1000 years behind her? At least now she knew where he might be.

The professor dropped the students off back at the Humanities building, reminding them to keep quiet about the find. Siv hung back with Tone as the other students headed off in numerous directions.

"You were awfully quiet on the ride back," Siv commented. 'Mind telling me what's going on, especially when you said, 'My God, he's alive.'"

"Walk with me," Tone said as she headed down Niels Henrik Abels vei towards the café.

Once on the sidewalk, Tone relayed the story of her and Erik and their consuming passion for each other. She then told of Erik winning the time travel lottery and the catastrophic consequences.

"O my God," Siv interrupted. "He's still there and you think he had this stone made to let you know he was still alive."

"That's what I'm hoping," Tone sighed. "Besides, how else do you explain the sudden appearance of a new rune stone?"

"And the Roman numerals?" Siv asked then suddenly understood. "Eight, six, seven, ninety-three... the 8th of June 793, just like you said about the attack on Lindisfarne and the exact day that he was left behind. So thirteen, six, twenty thirty one is the 13th of June 2031. That's only a couple of months ago."

"Almost four months ago," Tone said, her face tight. "Our special day, the day that we declared our eternal love for each other..."

"And the time travel people were just going to leave him there?" Siv said, shaking her head in disbelief.

"They were until I raised a stink," Tone said, her disdain obvious. "They're supposedly working on it, though it does seem they're making progress."

"How?"

Tone explained the improvements to the time machine's accuracy.

"How do you know that?" Siv questioned, surprised at Tone's inside knowledge.

Tone gave her an impish grin. "There's this guy named Gene." She then told her how she had been leading him on and then revealed her final plan.

Siv's laughter at the Gene story then slammed to a halt as she realized, "You're going back?"

"Yes," Tone emphatically stated, "and Gene is the key to getting me back. Why do you think I've been playing him like this? The man's a philanderer. Even if Erik were not in my life, there is no way that I would even remotely consider Gene as suitable for anything let alone have sex with him."

"Tell me how you really feel," Siv deadpanned.

Tone smiled despite herself. That was one of the many things she liked about Siv. She could diffuse even the most tragic scenarios.

"So you're here because?" Siv asked.

"Because TTI wants me out of the way and far enough away to leave them alone."

Epiphany hit Siv and she marveled, "TTI is paying for your grad school."

"Yes, plus a salary as I'm officially an employee of TTI."

"Must be nice," Siv said, a fleeting jealousy replaced by a subtle happiness for another person's bounty. After all, with the income she'd earned from posing for Kallevig, she had more than enough to pay for grad school and a Ph.D. if she wanted.

"To a point," Tone replied. "It's allowed me to improve my Old Norse and my martial arts skills, but I feel like I'm treading water. The longer I stay here, the farther away from shore I get."

"But how are you going to go back?"

"Like I said, Gene is the key."

"Once you find him, are you coming back?"

Tone liked Siv's assurance... *once you find him.* She gazed at Siv with intense eyes. "What's to come back to?"

"You're going to stay there, in the past?" Siv was so startled that she abruptly stopped in the middle of the sidewalk, causing Tone to stop.

"Yes," Tone said with determination. "Look around you. What's to come back to? After you get your grad degree, what are you going to do with it? Teach? Be a docent at some historical site that eventually is bulldozed for some garish apartment building? Who knows, you might even end up working at TTI, stuck away at some remote desk, filing reports until they realize that no one needs Old Norse speakers anymore and they give you the pink slip."

"I ... I hadn't really thought about it," Siv lamely replied then heaved an exasperated sigh. "That's not true. I have thought about it. I haven't a clue what I'm going to do. I'm in the Viking and Medieval Norse studies because that's what I enjoy. But when I graduate?" She shook her head and shrugged. "Guess I'll cross that bridge when I get there."

"The way I see it, I'm going to live the dream," Tone replied. "I've spent years studying Vikings and such. If I can actually live there and then, I'd be crazy not to take the opportunity. And more importantly, the man I love is there and life is meaningless without him."

It was midnight when her phone's incessant ringing invaded her sleep. Scrunching her face and blinking to wake up, Tone rolled onto her side, her hand flopping on the nightstand, searching for the phone. The noise stopped just as she lifted the phone to eye level. It started ringing again, the screen highlighting the caller's name: Siv.

"Hey," Tone groggily answered. "What's up?

"I want to come," Siv blurted.

"What?"

243

"I want to come with you."

Tone sat up in bed, rubbing her eyes with the heels of her palms. "Are you sure?"

"Yes. It's like you said... what is there here for us. Our future is in the past. Maybe I might even meet a handsome Viking of my own."

Tone laughed. "I suppose that's possible."

"Will you let me come with you?"

"Yes," Tone said without thinking.

"Good. Now go back to sleep and we can talk about it in the morning."

Siv disconnected, leaving Tone wondering just how she was going to make this all work. Placing the phone on the night table, Tone curled the covers over her shoulders and snuggled back to sleep, her dreams filled with the quest to find Erik.

"So what's the plan?" Siv asked sitting across the small table inside the coffee shop on the corner of Josefines gate and Hegdehaugsveien. Outside, the weather was windy, chilly and raining while inside the shop, the aroma and warmth of hot coffee infused an ambiance of comfort and unhurried time.

"My plan was to go back during Christmas break," Tone explained, sipping her coffee, her hands wrapped around the sides of the cup for warmth. "I've been setting up a tryst with Gene in the time travel room. He believes he's going to get a big surprise." She snickered. "And it's going to be one he'll never forget."

"What about me?"

"I've been thinking about it and I've got a couple of ideas. The first is to introduce you into the equation with him."

"How?"

"The man reads like a cheap novel where you know the ending before you're a quarter of the way into the book. Right now, I've convinced him that he and I are going to have sex in the time travel room. His sole reason for living at the moment is his anticipation of that glorious event."

"You're not going to are you?" Siv asked, an eyebrow raised.

"Good God no," Tone said, flipping a hand and rolling her eyes. "Even if he were the last man on earth, I'd go to a nunnery before I had sex with him."

"There you go sugar-coating again," Siv said with mock seriousness. "You need to learn to say what you think."

"I'll work on that," Tone said with a grin. "My point is that the man is more than preoccupied with the event. It's all he thinks about or talks about. Now... if I were to add another beautiful woman into the equation..."

"Like a threesome?" Siv responded with a sly grin.

"You know where I'm going."

"The poor man," Siv laughed. "All the anticipation only to have it vanish."

"I'll start by mentioning that you're going to come back with me for Christmas. Then I'll start sending him pictures of us together... nothing overt or brazen. Subtle so that his imagination goes into overload."

"Like what?" Siv asked, curious.

"Like here for example," Tone said. "We get someone to take a picture of us enjoying our coffee. However, instead of sitting across from each other, we sit next to each other, our shoulders touching, smiling mischievously like we're hiding some secret. Though nothing is going on, his imagination will suspect something is. We build on that."

"I love it," Siv grinned.

"We'll need to get you appropriate clothing," Tone said. "I'll ask Janice to make you an outfit."

245

"Who's she?"

"She works at TTI in the wardrobe department. She's also into role playing and creating authentic costumes. I'm going as a shield maiden, but unless you have martial arts training, I suggest you go as a freeborn lady."

"That's fine with me."

"How good is your Old Norse?"

"Not as good as yours, from what I hear," she complimented, "but enough to get by. I can always claim I'm from another country."

"What other languages do you speak?"

"English and German," she answered, "neither of which are applicable. However, give me enough time and I'll speak like a native."

Tone nodded then narrowed her gaze at her. "Are you *sure* you want to go through with this?"

Siv inhaled a slow breath. "My parents told me they thought I was born at the wrong time. While other kids were engrossed in gaming, I was either reading or building forts outside and pretending to be a Roman general or a Viking queen. All the technology in the world does little for me. You see how it is. People are so engrossed in their cell phones that they miss the entire world around them, like the guy who was hit by the tram last week. Can you imagine? So focused on a piece of technology that he walked out right in front of it. He's lucky to still be alive, though I doubt he'll ever be the same. But he's the norm nowadays. People worship the god of technology, except me... and you. I'd rather live than be stuck going through the motions."

"I'll take that as a 'yes,'" Tone said with a smile. "There's no one or opportunity you're going to miss?"

"Sure," Siv answered. "There are lots of people I'll miss, like my parents and family. But it's like anything else: time moves on and I have my own life to live."

"And there is that handsome Viking waiting for you," Tone said.

Siv smiled. "Yes, there is. The sooner I find him, the happier I'll be."

"So what do you think I should do about Kallevig?"

"What's your reason for wanting to pose nude in the first place?" Siv queried. "It's not like you need the money."

"I don't know," Tone shrugged. "Maybe it's the illicit aura attached to it, though in today's world it doesn't seem to be that big a deal anymore. Maybe it's the wanting to have something to look back on and prove that I was once young and desirable."

"You plan on taking the pictures with you to the past?" Siv pointed out.

"No, and that's just it. I can't take them with me. Maybe it's the excitement of being nude, like at a nude beach, though now that I say it, being at a nude beach loses its allure rather quickly. After all, if everyone's naked, what's the big deal."

"And then there's no restrictions on who's at the nude beach," Siv added. "You get the good, the bad... and the really ugly, as well as the weird and creepy. You do know that Kallevig is going to want to have sex with you."

"That ain't gonna happen," Tone flatly affirmed.

"You and I know that. Are you willing to put yourself in the position to tell him 'Not only no, but hell no,' knowing that you will have to take another class with him? And then are you willing for him to have pictures of you nude?"

Tone gazed back at Siv with affection and appreciation. "Thank you for setting me straight."

"Anytime," Siv said with a professional air. "I make house calls too."

Back in her apartment, Tone sat at the computer and pulled up Gene's email. Reading it just once, she could feel the man drooling as he typed it. Talk about easy. Replying, she typed:

I talked with my friend, her name is Siv, and she was totally on board with doing a nude photoshoot with me. While I think about it, I've asked Siv to come back home with me for Christmas. I've told her all about you and she definitely wants to meet you. While I haven't said anything to her quite yet, my imagination went crazy with the three of us "exploring" in the time machine room.

Tone paused as her laughter made it hard to type. Enclosing the café pic of her and Siv, she pressed 'send.'

In the early afternoon, Erik stood in the doorway of his longhouse staring out over the empty fields, across the water to Kolga's longhouse, debating whether to ride over uninvited. Kolga had more than intimated that he was welcomed... no that wasn't the right word... expected, yes... expected... anytime.

Images of last night flooded his memory and guilt spilled into the memory. Immediately he sought to justify his actions, his lapse, his false words. Tone's vision had filled his dreams and instead of pointing at him and crying out "J'accuse," she was defeated, crushed with disappointment.

All because he had kissed Kolga last night.

It wasn't a kiss between friends. It was a release of pent up emotion, desire, and overwhelming frustration. It was a kiss that said his faith was wavering, that logic was hammering his conviction, that he hadn't a clue what the future held. And how long was long enough? Up until that kiss, he had been living his life as though Tone was going to show up at any moment. What had changed?

What changed was his belief that she would be thwarted in her efforts to find him, that the failures of the time machine would be too great to overcome, and the fear that by the time the machine was fixed she would have moved on with her life. So why did he raise the stone? He knew the answer.

He was unwilling to accept that they would never be together.

Erik tightened his cloak around him as the leaden skies promised rain and the wind coming off the water gave the air a damp chill. The days were beginning to grow shorter, and he chuckled thinking that a thousand plus years from now one day in October or November the world would reset their clocks back for daylight savings time. No one gave that any thought here, which made so much sense. The people lived according to the seasons. The harvest was finishing up and the hay for the farm animals stored in the grain shed. He'd decide which cattle to slaughter for meat throughout the winter, though fishing still provided plenty of food.

In the three weeks since he sent back the mangled Ingvald to Thorsten, three more champions had showed up, two at the same time, two brothers. The first man was dispatched with the same speed as Ingvald and sent back the same way, draped over his horse. The two brothers were more interesting in that the first one decided he wanted to fight Erik without weapons, which was fine with Erik as it allowed him to demonstrate his physical speed and skills. The poor man didn't know what hit him as Erik's blinding chops, punches, and kicks left the man sprawled on the ground and quite unconscious. The other brother, seeing the end state of his sibling, decided that he would save his challenge for another day, scooped up the battered brother and galloped away.

Erik hoped the onset of winter would dissuade others from showing up. Kolga, demanding that she be notified anytime one of Thorsten's champions showed up, had witnessed the three fights. The first time her apprehension before the fight was undisguised, especially as the opponent was a noted berserker. Her apprehension quickly vanished with Erik's overt domination. By the end, she was by his side, gently attending to nonexistent bruises, asserting her place.

With the second fight, her nervousness had lessened, but her post-fight attentions bordered on the fussy possessiveness of a girlfriend or wife. Thus, it was with some alarm when she learned about the stone Erik had raised, kicking herself for not knowing the stone carver was there. She had made it a point of him spending time at her house, a place where she had control. It wasn't until the carver had already been working for a week that she discovered his presence. Not wanting to appear too inquisitive, she had dropped subtle hints all of which Erik either ignored or chose not to answer.

When she learned the stone carver had finished and departed, she waited a day before sneaking over to see it for herself. In the dim morning light, she read the lines deeply engraved in the stone: 'Erik raised this stone in honor of Tone Thorgilsdottir, Odin's Valkyrie who gave him life.'

Her brows furrowed as she tried to make sense of the message, she pondered who Tone was and why was she a Valkyrie? As far as Kolga remembered, there were no Valkyries who had human fathers let alone one named Thorgil. But what did Erik mean by Tone giving him life? Did she save his life after a battle? And what about the strange numerals at the bottom, the kind that the Romans from long ago used? Nothing made sense. Deciding she would just ask him, she made her way back home and waited.

Folding his arms, Erik focused on the longhouse of the Jarl's sister. Last night had been an interesting experience. He had arrived, prompt as usual, expecting the usual banter and enjoyable evening, though lately he had noticed the not so subtle intimacy developing, at least on her part. Though to be truthful, he enjoyed her presence and looked forward to spending time with her.

Midway through the meal, she asked her question. "I heard you raised a stone. What does the message mean?"

Though momentarily caught off guard, Erik had prepared himself for the eventual need of an explanation. "It is to honor a woman who holds a special place in my heart."

Kolga's heart skipped a beat. "Did you love her?"

"Yes." Erik noted she used the past tense.

"Do you love her still?"

"How can one say he or she loves another then say he no longer does? Did you love Egill?"

"Yes."

"Have you stopped loving him because he is no longer with you?"

Kolga uttered a melancholy sigh. She hadn't thought about Egill ever since Erik showed up and reawakened her desires. But it didn't mean she didn't still love him. It's just that he was gone and he wasn't coming back. She had to move on with her life.

"What happened to her?"

"We were attacked," he truthfully answered then said nothing else.

Assuming that Tone had been killed and he had been unable to defend her, Kolga decided it was best to change the subject, though reflecting it was probably one of the reasons he fought so well. He was trying to atone for her death. For some reason, it made him all the more appealing to her. It was time to make a change in both their lives.

During all the time they had been together, she had never had to reprove him for unwanted advances. In fact, he hadn't made any advances at all. Yet she could tell that he was attracted to her and she liked the way he was always very respectful, almost maddeningly so. There were a couple of times very recently that it seemed he was going to kiss her goodnight, but he always stopped and very gallantly bid his farewells.

That was going to have to change.

When it came time for him to leave, she had pressed herself against him, pulling his head to hers, pressing her lips against his. The slight tremor of hesitation faded and she felt passion in his kiss, in the way his strong arms folded her against him. She felt the arousal in his body and hid her disappointment when he pulled away and gazed softly into her eyes.

"Thank you for a wonderful evening," he said, catching his breath. "I'd better head on back." He was about to say 'before I do something I may regret.' Instead, he added, "while I can still find my way home."

Half tempted to stand in the doorway and block him from leaving while telling the servants and thralls to find another place to spend the night, she decided there was a better time and place and the next time would be to her advantage.

"You be careful going back home," she said, tenderly stroking his cheek.

That was last night and the guilt was still there this afternoon. How could he claim to be eternally in love with Tone and kiss another woman, especially the way he did last night? He was a betrothed man, a man pledged to another.

In fact, if he and Tone had had their way, they'd have been married before the trip back in time.

But they weren't and for all he knew, they never would be. The obstacles appeared too insurmountable. He pursed his lips in frustration. How many times had he listed the reasons why he would never see her again? How many times had he argued the logic that he was stuck here... and she there... for the rest of their lives? Sure, he had raised a stone to her, but that assumed nothing would happen to it in the next 1200 years. It also assumed that somehow she would see the stone or at least the message. But that assumed far too much that was beyond mere coincidence. It also assumed that she was as willing to wait as he was.

It was then the doubts invaded like a swarm of evil bats. Tone was young and beautiful. He was seventeen years older than her. Yes, they had pledged their eternal love for each other, but was that merely the heat of the moment? Now that he was gone, had she settled into looking for another, someone closer to her age? Had she accepted the reality that she would never see him again?

He uttered an exasperated breath. What was his problem? Kolga found him attractive and she was the same age as Tone... though in this environment, he was old enough to be Kolga's father....which meant that he was also old enough to be Tone's father.

"Damn it all," he barked, angry at himself. "Just stop."

His outburst caused the thrall sent to check on him to pop back inside, like a prairie dog ducking back into his hole for protection.

Ignoring him, Erik continued his frustrated deliberations. What was his problem? Why was it so difficult to accept that some women found him attractive? Had Linda burned him that bad? But then, did it really matter what Linda said or did. That was in the past or in this case still in the future.

He smiled at the memory of when Tone and he had bumped into Linda in the wine store. Linda's initial expression was priceless for despite her best effort, she couldn't hide her jealousy and insecurity. He was with a babe, a stunning beauty whose appearance was everything Linda wanted. And then when Linda's true nature came out and her acerbic tongue tried to inflict pain, Tone's deft repartee left Linda in shambles. It was a memory he would always enjoy.

And then there was Kolga, so like Tone in many ways yet still different. She too was strikingly beautiful. Yet Kolga seemed older than Tone. Perhaps because she had been married and already lost a husband and was now making her mark on her own. Maybe it was because she had to grow up sooner than 21st century children do. Or perhaps it was because she was expected to marry as soon as she reached puberty. Maybe it was the overwhelming specter of mortality, that only half the children born lived beyond their seventh year, that she had already cheated death and was living on borrowed time.

Despite all the heartaches in Kolga's life, she was a strong and caring woman. Any man would be proud to be married to her. That she was interested in him surprised him, yet flattered him.

So why did he feel so guilty?

The guilt was there because he was still madly in love with Tone. The guilt was there because he wasn't ready to give up.

Tone found it curious she received emails from both Brent and Janice within minutes of each other. She opened Brent's email first.

Dear Ingrid,

Usually I let bragging pass by unnoticed because I consider bragging as a sign of insecurity. In this instance, I feel a need to say something in order to protect a person. In doing so, I hope you don't think I am trying to bad mouth someone just to get an advantage. Yes, I do wish to spend time with you – dating. However, if that is not to be, I would hope that we would become close friends.

As a friend, I have to tell you that Gene has been less than subtle in what he expects to happen when you come back for Christmas vacation. In fact, I consider his comments quite inappropriate, especially as he is dating a lady named Joanna. Of course there's the whole "man's code" of admiring a man playing the field and normally I might have gone along. But this time it concerns you. Gene is not to be trusted, especially when it comes to bragging about his conquests. If you value your reputation, please be very careful. I know you're a big girl and can handle yourself, but I thought you might like to know.

Tone breezed through the rest of the email, not really reading it as her mind played out the scenario. Her initial worry about Gene's indiscretion actually played out in her favor. The momentary concern faded and she smiled. *This could work out better than I first thought.*

Opening Janice's email, she nodded with satisfaction that Janice was more than willing to make Siv's outfit then shook her head at the poor girl's unrequited love.

I need your help. You never have any problems getting a man's attention. Guys trip all over themselves to get you to notice them. There's this guy I like but he only looks at me like a sort of sister or maybe not even that, more like a coworker. What can I do/should I do to make him notice me?

Deciding to reply to Janice first, she felt a little bit like Dear Abby.

Janice – If you want a particular guy to notice you, pay attention to the women he does notice. What is it about them that causes him to give them attention? Are they physically beautiful, have great personalities, or financially independent, or whatever? The point here is that you will have to mold yourself to what he desires.

But you need to ask yourself – is that what you really want? To change who you are to satisfy someone else? I'm sure there are plenty of men out there who would be happy with you just the way you are. And again, ask yourself, is this guy worth it if you have to change who you are to keep him?

If I were you, I'd be looking for someone who would love me for who I am and not for what he thinks I should be.

Pressing 'send' Tone sat back and worked through how to tell Kallevig that she wasn't interested. Pity that Erik wasn't here. A nude photo shoot with him would be an experience.

She smiled at the memories of their times together, especially back at his apartment though she thought of it as *their* apartment. She wondered what he was doing at the very moment. Was he safe?

Pulling up a satellite map of Norway, she zoomed in to Royce on the peninsula jutting out in the Tyrifjorden. Working the keyboard and mouse, she angled the imagery to study the land, noting the peninsula was mostly farm fields.

A wide shallow area to the east of Royce looked to be an ideal place for longships to pull up.

Tone zoomed out just far enough to see the distance between Kaupang and Royce, then remembered that the time machine worked on geocoordinates. Zooming back in, she clicked on the spot where she estimated the rune stone lay, writing down the coordinates: 60.072455, 10.197717.

Sitting back, she smiled a contented smile, imagining his surprise when she suddenly appeared. Of course, that assumed he was still there.

To say that Kallevig was disappointed would be an understatement. The man was crestfallen. His anticipation shattered, he tried to bribe his way to success.

"I'll double the posing fee," he pleaded.

"How much is that?" Tone replied, inwardly chuckling at the man's groveling.

"I currently pay $200 an hour. I'll pay you $400."

"You'll pay me $400 an hour to pose nude for you," she repeated as though having second thoughts.

"Yes," he brightened, latching onto any sign of weakening.

"And the royalty split?"

The question caught him off guard and he hesitated, quickly calculating the anticipated sales. That was the bonus of restricting sales and limited editions; he could charge more. Tone had that rare photogenic combination of sensual temptress and innocent girl-next-door, qualities he could photographically exploit, and hopefully enjoy off camera. She would be the centerfold model, the main attraction. Even giving her half the sales, he would still make a substantial amount and his reputation as a nude photographer would increase even more.

"I'll split sales with you," he finally said, "50:50."

"And how much would that be?"

"My last book netted over seven figures," he answered.

Tone gave him a curious look. "If you're doing so well, why are you teaching?"

"Where else can I find young and beautiful women all in one place?" he replied with a smile.

She nodded in understanding. "And the university doesn't mind you doing this?"

"There's nothing the university can do about it," he dismissively said. "Photo sessions and subsequent photographic representations are contractual agreements between consenting adults. The high court so ruled in 2023. While the university can establish standards as they apply to university specific activities, they cannot enforce those standards on activities not university related, unless of course those activities are illegal, which mine are not." He smiled at her. "We do things a little differently here in Norway than you do in the US."

"So," Tone said, "$400 per hour and 50:50 split on sales."

"Yes."

Tone furrowed her brows as though in pensive thought. "Make it $500 per hour and I'll reconsider thinking about it."

"Done," he said without hesitation. *I'd go $1000 an hour if you wanted it. That's nothing. I'll make that back with the sales of the first fifty books.*

Tone said nothing, her head tilted slightly as she pretended to reconsider. "Can you give me an estimated income from posing and sales?"

"Millions," he said with a confident smile.

Tone blinked in surprise. "You're serious?"

"Very," he said, his hope growing. "Some of my models have made more than enough to pay for schooling, a place to live, clothes, restaurants, and all sorts of fun activities. They won't have to worry about finances for a while."

"All that from one book?"

"Yes," he smiled with assurance, "all that from one book."

"How can you guarantee that the sales will be the same for book two?"

"Because I already have preorders for over half of the previous buyers, plus a wait list for any spots that open up."

"Huh," she said, impressed. The man obviously had business sense. "Where would the session take place?"

"My studio, which is not far from the Holmenkollbakken, down by the lake."

"The ski jump site?"

"Yes."

Tone was even more impressed for west Oslo was where the rich lived, especially a place by the water.

"You've given me cause for second thoughts. Let me think on it a bit more. How long would it take for the book to get published?"

"Not long at all," he assured her. "Besides, since I already have preorders, you would be paid your portion of the preorder amount, which at a 50:50 split would put your income at a little over $2 million."

Tone gulped, her eyes popping wide. "Just for posing nude?"

"Yes," Kallevig suavely answered, "just for posing nude."

Inhaling a deep breath, she said, "I'll let you know tomorrow. I want a day to think this over, but I think I may have changed my mind from what I first said. Tomorrow. OK?"

"Absolutely," Kallevig triumphantly agreed.

Siv sat on the couch in Tone's living room, sipping a cold glass of mead. "So you're having second thoughts?"

"I know, I know," Tone sighed with frustration. "Here's my reason. I'll need money when we go back in time, lots of money."

"How are you going to carry it?" Siv pointed out. "A million euros in gold is probably around twenty pounds of gold American. How are you going to hide that? Is it going to be coin or hack gold? Will you bring silver too, which will require more space and weight?"

Tone pursed her lips and shook her head. "There has to be a way of transporting enough with us so we don't have to rely on anyone or have to find employment while we're looking." An idea bubbled up and she grinned mischievously at Siv. "Why not buy our own ships and start our own business?"

"How?" Siv asked, knitting her brows.

"Kaupang isn't far from where Erik raised the stone. Why not just make some offers that can't be refused? And if we both carry gold, we should have more than enough to go around."

Siv took another sip. "It sounds crazy... but I suppose it's better than some of the other options. How are we going to get it into the building at TTI?"

"I haven't thought that far," Tone said, taking a deep swallow.

Siv peered intently at her. "So you're going to pose for him?"

"Why not? If it gets me the money I need to buy gold, it's a small price to pay."

"What about Erik?" Siv quietly asked.

Tone paused to soberly reflect. "I think he would understand."

"Will you tell him?"

"I'll have to," she said, "eventually."

"What if he asks me?"

"Tell him the truth. It's easier to remember."

"You really think he's going to be OK with your pictures in a book that thousands of men will drool over?"

"What will it matter?" Tone answered. "My pictures will be here, but I won't. And I won't know and won't care what goes on back here."

"Suppose they send someone back to get you and make you come back?"

"I'm not coming back," Tone fiercely replied.

"You still haven't answered the question," Siv said, leaning forward to pour more mead into her glass. "Your pictures will be here, forever immortalized in a book and wherever else he has the images stored. Are you sure Erik's gonna be OK with that? You know when we show up with all sorts of ships and merchandise, he's gonna ask how we got all that stuff."

"I'll tell him the truth," she said, not so assured as before.

"OK, I'll accept that. By the way," Siv adjusted to get comfortable, "we're arriving in the dead of winter and there's a good probability that nothing much is going on because everyone is hunkered down for the winter. Let's say we find and buy our ships, then what?"

"I don't know," Tone replied, "but all the more reason why we need money. Our first mission is to find Erik. I figure we'll play it by ear along the way."

Siv laughed. "Sounds like a plan."

Kallevig was elated when Tone informed him that she had reconsidered. "Wonderful. When is a good time for you?"

"Whenever you want," she said, wanting to get this over with as soon as possible so that the money would be transferred to her bank in the US. It amazed her that even with the advances in technology and security, banks still exploited customers, hanging on to funds sometimes for weeks. With less than two months to go before Christmas vacation, she didn't want any problems.

"How about this weekend? Saturday?" Kallevig suggested.

"That's fine. What time?"

"Are you a morning or afternoon person?"

"It doesn't matter," she said.

"Then let's do afternoon, say... one o'clock. That way we still have daylight to work with." He handed her a slip of paper with his address on it. "I can either pick you up or meet you at the Bogstad badeplass. The 41 bus goes through there."

"How about you pick me up here at your office?"

"Perfect. I'll meet you at one o'clock."

His arms folded, Erik stood before the boat sheds, studying the sturdiness of the construction as well as the size, large enough to accommodate all of his longships. Sensing movement to his left, he looked up to see Kolga riding towards him.

"You've been avoiding me," she chastised, dismounting.

"My apologies, my Lady," he answered with a polite smile. "I have been preoccupied"

"So now we're back to calling me 'my Lady,'" she snipped.

"You are the Jarl's sister," he said. "I am but a mere farmer, a bad one at that."

"What's wrong?" This time there was more compassion in her response.

Erik gazed at the beautiful woman standing before him, feeling his defenses weakening. Shifting focus, he replied, "Your brother sent me here for a number of reasons, among them was to protect what is his property." He turned and spread an arm at the farm behind him. "But how do I do that? I have slaves and servants. I have longships and trading ships, but I have no real assembly of men, no hirdmen to fight when the time comes."

"You have several men here who can fight as well as men up in Hønefoss who will raid and fight with you," she countered.

"Kolga –"

"Good," she interrupted, "we're back to using my name."

Smiling, Erik continued. "Kolga, what good are the men two hours away up in Hønefoss when Thorsten decides to attack me here? And yes, I have several men who are excellent fighters, but, again, what good will five or ten men be against thirty or fifty? Thorsten has sent men here to test me, to see just how good a fighter I am. At the same time, he has to know that there is only one of me, that should he want to assert claim to this farm, to your farm, all he has to do is arrive here by boat or land and take it. There is nothing we can do to stop him."

"If he were to attack," Kolga said, believing she understood Erik's recent aloofness, "he would wait out the winter and attack in the spring."

"If I were he," Erik said, shaking his head, "I wouldn't wait. These two farms are fertile and produce enough to trade. He would be a fool not to want them. Not to mention that these farms represent Halfdan's presence in an area Thorsten probably views as belonging to him. If I were Thorsten, I would attack in the deepest cold of winter and assert my position before Halfdan could do anything about it."

"He wouldn't dare do that," Kolga fiercely stated. "Not while I am here."

"Yes he *would* do that," Erik gently corrected. "You would be the pawn in the game. In this instance you would be Thorsten's permanent *guest*, a sort of bargaining chip. He wouldn't' call you a hostage, but Halfdan would clearly understand your position. I'm surprised he hasn't already tried that, knowing that Halfdan probably doesn't want a war, at least not yet."

Kolga's eyes widened as she realized her position wasn't quite as secure as she had always believed. "Why would he do that? It gains him little but the anger of my brother."

"So?" Erik shrugged. "Halfdan would have to assemble an army, most likely calling on his brothers to help. At the same time, he has to defend what he already has, so his army can't be too big. Thorsten has access through Hordaland to the sea and can probably gain allies along the way who want to see your brother's kingdom reduced."

Kolga looked at him with newfound respect. "How do you know all this?"

"I don't, but it is something that has occupied my thoughts since my arrival.

"I will send word to my brother," she said, assuming a no-nonsense approach.

"And what will he do?" Erik asked. "He knows his position is weak here. I believe he sent me here to warn Thorsten that it would be a mistake to try to reclaim these lands. But Thorsten has to realize that I am nothing more than a bluff, especially after the reports sent back with the defeated men."

Kolga's uneasiness grew. "What do we do?"

"I don't know... yet.   We need some sort of early warning system, something more than dogs barking."

Instead of answering, Kolga looked past Erik's shoulder, knitting her brows as she focused on a man walking down the pathway from Erik's longhouse.

Noticing her stare, Erik turned to see what caught her attention. As the man approached, Erik noted he wasn't a farmer by the way he moved, like one ready for a tussle. The closer he came, the greater scrutiny Erik gave him.

He was a well built handsome man with broad shoulders, muscular arms and a narrow waist. Long and curly thick dark blond hair tumbled down to his shoulders. Unlike other Ost men, while his beard was thick, it was cropped to two fingers' width. It was when he stopped two paces away that Erik noted the eyes the color of Robin's eggs... and the size of the battle ax in his right hand.

"You are Erik Sword Spinner?" the man asked, his voice deep.

"I am," Erik answered, immediately on guard.

The man nodded, studying Erik.   "I am Magnus... Magnus Armundsen, sometimes called Magnus the Silent."

"I know you," Kolga blurted. "You're one of my brother Eystein's men."

"I am," he agreed.

"You're a long way from Hedemark," she commented.

"Yes, I am."

When he didn't elaborate, she said, "Why are you here?"

Locking his gaze on Erik, he said, "I have come to be Erik Sword Spinner's man, if he will have me."

"Did something happen between you and my brother?" Kolga demanded.

"No," he replied.   "When I heard about Erik Sword Spinner, I asked to be released."

"Why?" she asked, suspicious.

"I have my reasons," he said with direct firmness. Then ignoring her, he addressed Erik. "Will you have me?"

"Can you fight?" Erik asked, knowing the answer.

"I can answer that for him," Kolga interrupted, now remembering who he was though flashing Magus a cold glance. "He is or was Eystein's champion. Why he is here has me more than curious."

"Eystein's champion?" Erik repeated, both pleased and surprised.

"Yes," Magnus said.

"And Eystein willingly let you go?" Kolga demanded.

Magnus slowly turned his head to give Kolga a stern stare. "I am not a thrall to be told what to do, where to go, what to eat, or who to follow. I am a free man and choose my own path." Returning back to Erik, he repeated his petition. "Will you have me?"

"Absolutely," Erik said with a broad smile, sticking out his hand and feeling the firm handshake in return.

Magnus visibly relaxed. "It is good then. Where may I place my things?"

"In the longhouse with me. Tell them to set up a place for you on the other side of the center fire pit."

Magnus placed a hand to his chest and dipped his head. "Thank you, Erik Sword Spinner."

"Just 'Erik' would be fine, Magnus," Erik said, pleased with the new addition to his household.

When Magnus was out of earshot, Kolga turned to Erik, shaking her head. "I don't have a good feeling about this."

"Why?"

"You now have a man pledged to you, much like a Jarl does. If I know anything about my brothers, they are jealous of their positions."

"One man?" Erik scoffed. "If Halfdan is jealous because one man came here, then he isn't the Jarl I believe him to be.

He knows that he has my undying loyalty. Were it not for your two brothers, Halfdan would be king. For me, he is my king and I will treat him as such."

"That may all be well and good," she said, "but we're also talking about Eystein. Why would my brother willingly let his champion depart?"

"Perhaps you should ask?" Erik said with a wry smile.

"I think I will," she said, returning his smile. "Will you dine with me tonight?"

"Not tonight, fair lady," Erik gallantly replied. "It would be rude to my guest."

"Bring him along," she said, frustrated that there was now someone else to distract Erik's attention. She grumbled to herself wondering why it was so hard to keep Erik's interest. She never had that problem before and didn't understand why now? Ever since that kiss, which was charged like lightning, he had stayed away. Had she frightened him away? Perhaps he didn't realize the depths of his emotions and needed time to come to terms with them. What she did know was that a bedroom experience would be all that she needed to capture his devotion. That would take some planning, but it was going to happen.

"Not tonight, Kolga. I'd like time to learn more about him. How about tomorrow night?"

"Fine," she said with a resigned sigh.

Tone glanced around Kallevig's studio, which was much larger than she expected with ceiling track lights, umbrella lights, reflectors, numerous backdrop screens, couches, chairs, and various decorations like plants on narrow pedestals. She turned when she heard the door open and he walked in, waving the contract in one hand, his book in the other.

"Let's go through the legal stuff first," he said, scooting a chair back from a small round glass lunch table. He slid a copy of the contract across the table to Tone who had pulled out the other chair opposite and sat.

"It's pretty straight forward," he continued. "However, please note paragraph five about the copyright ownership and transfer of rights. You are allowed use rights as you see fit, but are not allowed to use the photographs to make money. I retain copyright and all proceeds from sales, which are exclusively limited to the publication of book two of my work."

Tone nodded, and read through the several pages of contract duration, payment schedule, model release statement, liability limitations and so on. She lingered over the payment schedule paragraph.

"It says here that once today's photo session is complete, one half of the agreed upon funds will be paid."

"That's in case I can't use any of today's shots and I need to reshoot," he explained. "I'll look at the shots while you're here and I can make a decision if we need a reshoot."

"I don't see how many reshoots are allowed," she said, reading the contract again.

"It doesn't limit the number," Kallevig quickly replied. "That's to protect both of us. It's to prevent either one of us from delaying the contract."

"But you're much too good a photographer for that to happen," Tone said, gazing intently into his eyes.

"Let's hope so," he chuckled.

Redirecting her attention to the contract, Tone read again the amount: $2,343,767, with half payable at the end of today's session. This was by far the easiest money she would ever earn. *Wonder why I didn't think of this sooner?*

"One point I'd like to add," she said, "concerning reshoots."

"Oh?"

"Suppose I don't like any of the pictures from today? I'd like an addendum saying that I also need to approve of the photos used."

Kallevig was about to object when he realized it would necessitate additional photo shoots, which meant he would have even more pics of this gorgeous woman. "Agreed. I'll just write that in here on both copies and we both initial the change."

Waiting for Kallevig to make the change, Tone signed each of the several pages of both copies.

"So how do we start?" Tone asked.

"I brought the book so you can get an idea of the poses and arrangements." He twisted the book around and opened it. "Each model has a 25 page spread. Five models equals 125 pages of photos."

Tone turned the pages, noting the poses and the facial expressions. "I still don't understand how you're able to command such a high price for a print book when the internet provides pretty much the same thing for free."

"You're talking about porn," he said, curling a lip. "Have you ever seen what's online?"

"Some," she answered.

"What did you think of it?"

"Somewhat crude from what I remember."

"Exactly," he said. "It's tasteless, done solely for the uncouth of mankind. Even the supposedly sensual scenes are done with pros who pretend they're enjoying themselves. It's not honest. At least with the amateurs you get honesty, but no talent as far as what the camera sees. Fortunately there are still people in this world who appreciate the glorious and sensual beauty of the female body. That is what I provide."

"At a price," she said with a smile.

"Why not," he smiled back. "I view myself as an artist and an artist, a good artist, ought to be paid for his work."

"I agree," she said, dipping her head.

"Well then," he said, standing. "Ready?"

"I think so."

"Let's see what clothing you brought with you," Kallevig said, maintaining an air of relaxed professionalism as he walked over to the blouses and pants hanging on a clothing rack. Stiletto heeled shoes, knee high boots, and sandals were neatly arranged on the floor below the clothes.

Kallevig's eyes immediately settled on a sheer long-sleeved blouse with ruffled collar and cuffs. "Let's start with this. The slacks you have on now will work with this. Are you wearing undergarments?"

"No," she replied. "You said not to because they would leave lines."

"Perfect." He handed her the blouse. "Go ahead and put this on while I get the lighting arranged. We'll start by the window so we can use the natural light while it's still light outside."

Pretending to look at the remaining clothes, his focus shifted to watch Tone unbutton her blouse and slip it off her shoulders.

Aware that the room had suddenly grown quiet, she looked up to see him staring at her... well, actually at her chest. Twisting slightly to give him a full view, she smiled with saucy aplomb as she slipped on the sheer blouse.

Chapter 9

Today was a day of shock and surprise. I walk around like a man drunk on too much wine. Harek called me to the dinner table today after the plates had been cleared from the evening meal. His wife Drofn was there as was Alvi. He said that he had a proposition for me. This is what was said to the best of my memory.

"I have watched you ever since you came here. Though you were upset at the beginning, you adapted and have had a much better attitude. Not only that, I have seen the way you work, the way you attend to the billows when we heat up the furnace. I watched the way you handled the mandrels and worked the glass. You have the gift of an artisan, for the times I let you create some beads, they were examples of fine workmanship. You have great talent. You are also good with numbers and I had you help me with my ledgers and accounts. In all instances you have been honest and diligent. I have talked it over with Drofn. We have decided to make you a free man under the following conditions.

"First, you will pay us back for your slave price. Second, you will apprentice here with me until such time as you are ready to help me expand the business by establishing another shop, one that you will run on your own. Third, you must stay here in Kaupang or another trading town that I decide conducting our business for a period of ten winters, after which you are free to go where you will.

"Do you accept?"

"Accept?" I said. "With my whole heart!"

My mind raced with the possibilities until I realized he had not adopted me. At first I was disappointed, almost angry until it dawned on me that he had acted purposely, probably seeing my affection for Alvi. Now that I am soon to be a free man, I can act like one.

What hinders me is my vows to the church. Yet Erik's words continue to sound in my mind: *You're so concerned about getting out of here that you don't see what's in front of you. It wasn't until Joseph was thirty winters old that another opportunity presented itself, an opportunity far greater than the one he had envisioned... an opportunity far greater than the one he had envisioned.*

I now know that God put me here to do his work. Yet I am torn between my vow to the Church and my desire to do what I believe God has set before me. I know that not everyone is cut out to be a monk or priest. It takes one who is committed and dedicated. I have seen many who came to Lindisfarne only to later renounce the Cloth and return to the ways of mammon.

Am I like they are? Am I renouncing the Cloth for my own selfishness? But there is a difference between them and me. They were not captured and made slaves. They had free choice to go where they wanted to do what they wanted. Like Joseph, I was sold into slavery. And like Joseph I was given freedom and position. Why?

The answer now is obvious. Like Joseph, I am here to do God's greater glory. Just like Joseph was not meant to be a slave or a son of a wealthy man, I was not meant to be a slave or a monk, but a merchant, a powerful tool for God.

I will stay here and build His Temple.

And God willing, Alvi will be by my side.

"So how did it go?" Siv asked, taking off her coat and placing it over the back of the chair in Tone's dining room.

"Pretty much what you told me to expect," Tone replied, pouring a second glass of mead and handing it to Siv. "He was professional, though I could tell he wanted more."

"Did he ask you out?" Siv pulled out a chair and sat, crossing one leg over the other.

"I didn't give him a chance," Tone chuckled. "When he finished taking the pictures, we reviewed them together."

"Really?" Siv said, surprised. "Didn't that seem weird, you standing or sitting next to him looking at pictures of you naked?"

"At first," Tone said with a smile, "but then I figured he'd already seen me in the flesh, these were just pictures."

"Were they good?"

Tone rolled her eyes. "They were great. I have to admit, he's a superb photographer. Made me look far better than I am in real life."

"I doubt that's possible," Siv said with mock seriousness.

"I thought so too," Tone said with equal gravitas causing Siv to laugh.

"So how many is he going to use?"

"None."

"None?" Siv stared at her, waiting for the punchline.

"I had an addendum written into my contract that I had to agree to which pictures would be published. If none were to my liking, we'd have to reshoot until I was satisfied."

Siv's mouth slacked open. "That means you'll have to do this again."

"I know," Tone nodded. "But it's like this; we're less than a month to Christmas vacation. He's deposited the agreed amount into my bank accounts back home. I know, because I watched him. We'll do another reshoot or two before vacation. I won't like any of those pics either."

"O my God," Siv brightened. "That's brilliant. He won't be able to publish any of your pictures because we'll be gone." She started laughing. "I wish I could see the look on his face when he discovers you didn't come back."

"And he's out quite a bit of money," Tone said with a sly grin.

"But what's to stop him from publishing your pictures anyway?" Siv said, rethinking the whole affair. "It's not like you'll be around to stop him."

"I know," Tone agreed. "That's why I have a lawyer friend involved."

Siv furrowed her brows and gazed at Tone. "Does your friend know what you intend to do?"

"Yes. He's also bound under lawyer-client privilege to keep quiet about it."

Siv sat back, slowly shaking her head. "You think of everything."

"I don't know about that," Tone said, "especially what we're going to encounter when we do go back. But one thing I do know for sure; I won't rest until I find Erik."

Siv sipped her mead, peering at Tone over the rim of the glass. "Suppose he's moved on, believing that he'll never see you again?"

"You mean another woman?"

Siv nodded.

Tone let out a slow sigh. "I've often thought of that. It's been almost half a year that he's been gone… half a year without him. I wonder what he's doing at this very moment, if he's come to believe that we will never see each other again. Part of me says he would never give up, while another part says how long would he wait before finally accepting that it was impossible for me to find him. Let's be realistic. The only way anything is going to happen is if I make it happen. There's nothing he can do except hope."

"But he's smart and resourceful," Siv pointed out. "You said so yourself."

"He is," Tone readily agreed. "If anyone can survive, he can."

"And don't forget your rune stone," she reminded her. "I doubt he's a stone carver, so he had to pay someone to do it, which means he had to have money, which means, again, that he's probably not doing too badly. And then there is the age factor. In Viking terms, he's already an old man. No offense."

"He may be forty two, but he easily looks ten years younger. But you do make a good point," she said, her hopes rising. "How many fathers would want to marry their daughters to a man in his forties? And widows would be looking to remarry as soon as possible."

"That's right," Siv said, rising to support. "He's probably positioning himself to have a comfortable life, waiting for you to show up."

Tone gave Siv an affectionate squeeze on her arm. "Thank you."

"In the meantime," Siv winked, "you've got a professor wanting to take more nude pictures of you."

Tone tiled her head to stare at her. "So how long did it take before he asked you out and how was he in bed?"

"My God, you're not rethinking –"

"Of course not, especially with him. He's good looking and all, but he's not my type. I was just curious. That's all."

"Good," Siv said, relieved. Standing, she crossed to the kitchen and opened the frig to pull out the mead bottle, holding it up to Tone. "More?"

"Yes," Tone said, holding up her glass.

"He actually asked me out the very first time we did pictures," Siv said, pouring the mead. "After a couple of evenings of delightful dinners we went back to his place. He's an excellent lover, attentive and gentle. We had sex a couple of times after that, but he had already moved on to his next conquest and I realized I was only fooling myself thinking that he was actually interested."

"Well, it's his loss."

"That's what I find so amusing with you and him. You're toying with him like he does with other women and he doesn't even know it."

Tone grinned and flicked her eyebrows. "He will soon enough."

"Just like Gene?"

Tone barked a laugh. "O my God, don't get me started."

"Is he always like that? I mean, once he had it in his mind that we were going to have a threesome, he's like a one song radio station… with no commercials."

"We need him, so feed his lust," Tone said, "which reminds me that we need to talk about how we're going to do that. Janice is making our clothes and I've got money deposited. Once I can verify it's all there, we buy gold. I'll have my lawyer friend act as intermediary."

"For a price."

"Of course. But at least I know it'll be done right. What did you find out about how Vikings carried stuff?"

"There's not a lot to go on. There's the Gokstad backpack, but that's based solely on the two oval oak panels found in the Gokstad ship. What it looked like is purely conjecture. My thought is instead to have a leather pack made, with straps. It would be easier to carry. We can get that done here in Norway. I've already located someone who can do it. It'll be expensive, but I think it's best. I'll pay for it."

"We have plenty of money," Tone said, "so don't feel you have to spend your own."

"The money *we* have is because of you. I want to contribute as much as I can."

"Contribute as much as you want," Tone said with appreciation. "Besides, it's not like we're coming back."

"So what about Gene?"

Grinning wickedly, Tone said, "Here's my plan."

The wind whipped off the water adding a bitter chill to the air as Kolga guided her horse along the path towards Erik's longhouse. The winter's first snow had mixed with freezing rain the night before and the fields were crusted in dull white caps. Overhead, the leaden sky threatened more rain. Kolga adjusted the hood and tightened the cloak around her neck.

Ahead, she saw the newest addition to Erik's farm, a rectangular building with a tall sloping roof and two fire pits. Not as large as the longhouse, it was where Erik did his training with his strange weapons as well as his other strange movements, what he called 'forms.' To her, it looked like some sort of mixture of dancing and fighting.

The fact that she was going to see him frustrated her. Ever since Magnus arrived unannounced, Erik had been reclusive, preferring to spend time on his own farm with the growing number of hirdmen.

Kolga's lips pursed as she added up the number of men Erik was collecting around him. The number now stood at 12, all willingly staying on a promise of future earnings from raids. Yet she noted a difference between the men surrounding Erik and the men at her brother's longhouse in Skiringssal. Halfdan's men were a rowdy bunch who liked to drink and fight. Erik's men were far more subdued as though following Erik's lead for the man was never drunk nor did he eat too much or speak too loud or even womanize... at least as far as she could tell and she knew just about everything that happened on his farm.

The man was too perfect, she thought with a smile.

And then there was Torben, one of the newest of Erik's hirdmen. Already he had been over to her place offering to assist in any way he could. It was obvious his intent. Though he was an attractive man, she had no intention of marrying him, a mere hirdman. There was only one man for her and she knew he had feelings for her. All she needed to do was convince him to give his feelings full rein.

Tying her horse up to the fence near the new building, she poked her head in, surprised to find it empty. Retracing her steps, she entered the longhouse where Erik sat in his high seat, his hirdmen to his left and right, forming a semicircle. In the middle stood a man she recognized. Erik looked up when the door opened, rewarding her with a warm smile.

"You're just in time, Lady Kolga. Kjell here has come with a message from Thorsten concerning our farms. Go ahead Kjell, explain to her what you just told me."

Assuming an air of indifferent condescension, Kjell turned to face Kolga. "It is good that you are here. King Thorsten has chosen to exercise relative rights concerning the farms you and Egill owned. Is it not true that you and Egill were married for more than twelve months?"

Kolga's face hardened, knowing where this was headed. "Yes. But as you know, Egill had no siblings. This farm belongs to me. Thorsten himself acted as witness."

"That may be true," Kjell loftily said, "but there is a male relative who has made his claim to what he is entitled to."

"And what is he entitled to?" Erik demanded.

"Two thirds of Kolga's farm and all of this farm."

Instead of getting angry, Erik laughed. Leaning forward, he rested an arm across a thigh and narrowed a cold stare at Kjell. "Here is my answer to your king. If he wants these farms, he will have to come and take them."

Kjell's confidence wavered. "You can't do that. It's the law." He pointed at Kolga. "She knows that and if you're who you claim you are, you know it too."

"What I know," Erik stonily replied, "is that your life is forfeit if I ever see you within an hour's walk from my farm. You tell Thorsten that my farm is a gift from Halfdan. If he wishes a fight, all he has to do is show up."

"But... but," Kjell whined. "You can't just outlaw me like that."

"Put him on his horse and get him out of here."

Two hirdmen grabbed Kjell and forcibly tossed him out into the rain.

"Make sure he doesn't bother anyone."

Nodding in understanding, the two men slipped out to 'help' Kjell find his way home.

"Thorsten can't be that stupid to want to get in a protracted fight with my brother." Kolga walked up to the empty chair next to Erik that Magnus had vacated when she entered the house.

Erik motioned for her to sit.

"Whether he is or not, there was a reason he sent Kjell here."

"Probably to spy on how many men we have," Magnus said, standing to the side.

"I agree, my friend." Erik nodded thoughtfully, "which means we need to be prepared." He addressed the group. "If you were going to attack, how would you do it and when would you do it?"

Though pleased to be part of the decision making process, the hirdmen paused to reflect. Magnus broke the silence.

"I would attack when you least expect it. Kjell knows the land and the spots to beach ships. If I was Thorsten, I would wait a month, two months when the days are cold and the earth is hard, and the rivers freeze. A man can't be on watch forever. At some point his attention will wander."

"Exactly," Erik agreed.

"But again," Kolga interrupted, shaking her head. "Why would Thorsten want to get into a fight with Halfdan and possibly my two brothers-in-law?"

"Perhaps he believes he can win," Magnus pointed out.

"He can't win against my brother," Kolga dismissively replied.

"He can if he has allies," Erik said.

Kolga's mouth gaped open. "Who?"

"Who did you tell me ruled in Pelamork?"

"Brynjulf Bearclaw," she answered, shaking her head before epiphany hit. "By the gods. His kingdom extends beyond Halfdan's southern borders. Halfdan would have to defend Vestmar and Vestfold. But... why would he do that when he has free sailing rights through Vestmar? We even have trading agreements."

Erik shrugged. "I merely point out the possibilities. Either way, I do not see Halfdan thinning his borders to assert a claim here. It will be up to us to defend our farms."

"How?"

"Obviously, unless they can fly," Erik chuckled, "there are only two ways they can approach, by sea or land. If by land, they will have to come from the north through Hønefoss. If by sea, they will have to come up the Bergsjøen. What we need is an early warning system at both places."

"Like what?" Kolga frowned.

"I don't know," he admitted. "I'm open to suggestions." He studied the men surrounding him, realizing they were fighters not strategists. Only Magnus had the true grasp of what was necessary. "I don't need answers right this moment. Think about it and let's talk more tomorrow."

Torben eased his way over towards Kolga, only to be disappointed when she turned her head to speak with Erik. However, Erik noticed his movement and caught his eye and smiled.

"You have something to add, Torben?"

"I was thinking about the beaches where they could land ships." Though answering the question, his attention was divided between Erik and Kolga.

Suppressing her irritation at the interruption, Kolga patiently smiled at the man. Torben was tall for an Ost man, nearly as tall as Erik, with long blond hair held back with a leather braid, and eyes the blue of a summer sky. Physically strong and a proven fighter, he had the annoying habit of challenging any and all to Idrótter, whether running, climbing, arrow shooting and even chess. His need to prove himself better than everyone else got old two days after he showed up. That he was two winters younger than she was another reason to put a halt to his attentions. She preferred older, more mature men.

"We could rig up some sort of spikes in the water to prevent the ships from getting close enough."

"What about the merchant ships?" Kolga pointed out.

"We attach ropes to the spikes so they can be lowered."

Erik's eyes brightened, immediately liking the proposal. "Well done Torben. That's a clever idea."

"How will you keep the spikes in place," Kolga asked, "especially in stormy weather?"

"I don't know yet." He gamely shrugged with a disarming smile.

Knowing Kolga was here to see Erik, Magnus interjected himself into the discussion. "Take some men and see what you can come up with."

"Yes, Magnus," Torben said, pleased with the attention.

Once Torben was out the door, Kolga turned to Magnus. "Think it will work?"

"Who knows? But he's happy to have something to do."

"Speaking of something to do," Kolga said, ticking her head at Erik though gazing at Magnus. "He has time to set up a rune stone to another woman who no one has ever seen or met, yet can't find the time to visit me and I live next door. Why is he avoiding me?"

"I'm not avoiding you," Erik blurted.

"I'm talking to him," Kolga airily teased, giving him a patronizing look before turning back to Magnus. "I'm beginning to think he doesn't like me."

"Oh, he definitely likes you," Magnus said with a smile as though sharing a secret.

"Really? So what's his excuse for not visiting me?" She folded her arms, pretending to be cross.

"I'm afraid the hirdmen have occupied much of his time," Magnus apologized, "and now with the threat of Thorsten... I'm sure you can understand."

"No I don't understand." She assumed a feigned pout. "You tell him I expect to see him tonight."

"I'm sitting right here," Erik smirked.

Kolga flipped a hand at him. "Hush. No one is talking to you." Turning back to Magnus, she pointed a finger of warning at him. "You tell him. I won't take no for an answer. And remind him, he's to come alone."

Magnus flashed a smile before resuming his polite demeanor. "I will tell him."

Satisfied, she gave Magnus a crisp nod. "Good. Well then, I've no more to do here. Always good seeing you Magnus."

Ignoring Erik as if he wasn't there, she pushed out of the chair and headed for the door, feeling two sets of eyes on her as she stepped into the drizzly day.

Wondering why Erik was so hesitant, Magnus' gaze followed the beautiful woman until the door closed behind her. "Short of ripping your clothes off right here, I'm not sure how much more obvious she could be." He swiveled his head towards Erik. "What is it about her that you don't like?"

"It's not a question of not liking her. She beautiful, smart and rich. What's not to like."

"So what's your problem?"

"My heart is not over a certain lady."

"Tone?"

"Yes."

Magnus silently mused Erik's reply before asking, "Where is she now?"

"Far far away," Erik said with a resigned sigh.

"Why didn't you bring her here with you?"

"It's complicated." He then explained about the attack on Lindisfarne and his presence here while Tone was 'whisked' away back to her parents on the continent.

"You think she believes you dead?"

"What would you think?"

Magnus nodded in understanding. "Why not go back and get her?"

"Again, it's not that easy. Halfdan has honored me beyond my comprehension. Why? I haven't the faintest idea. But I know I cannot simply pull up stakes and say, 'Thanks, but no thanks.' I am his loyal man and I will not jeopardize that."

Magnus looked him straight in the eye. "Even for true love?"

Erik's shoulders slumped and he didn't answer.

"Why not send a message to her, letting her know you are alive and safe?"

"I have thought of that," he said. "My fear is that her parents will intercept it and tell her a different tale, one that has me dead."

"Are they that controlling?" Magnus frowned.

"Yes. And there is also the possibility that she has found someone else." Though he said it, he didn't want to believe it. But what was the chance of him ever seeing her again? Was he a fool for refusing to accept reality?

Magnus was about to say 'So soon?' but knew that widows remarried quickly as a safety net, especially if she believed Erik was dead and even if she wasn't a widow yet.

"You will have to make a choice," Magnus wisely spoke, "very soon, or you will have lost both."

"Yes," Erik acknowledged with a sigh, "I know you are right, my friend."

Tone rolled her eyes as she read Gene's latest email, which repeated his desire to face chat. She had purposely avoided using the app as she had no desire to get entangled with the expected requests to display more of her body than she wanted to show, or the not so subtle hints of wanting to see her and Siv kissing, among other things.

It was times like this where she began to have second thoughts about the wisdom of her plan. Ever since she had intimated the likelihood of a threesome, Gene was a man obsessed. Sure, he still did the usual chit-chat, but as Christmas vacation got closer, the chit-chat portions of his emails diminished in proportion to the increase of his sexual imagination. At one point he had attached a story he had written about the three of them that was supposed to be erotic but was little more than graphic porn.

But he was the key and she would do what was necessary, short of compromising herself. Therein lay the question. Just how much was she willing to actually offer and would it be enough? With D-Day approaching, she sent a response.

Gene – just a quick note to let you know that Siv and I will be arriving on Friday. Give us a day to get adjusted to the time change. We'll meet you for dinner at 6 on Saturday. You pick the place. Be sure to get plenty of sleep the night before as it's going to be a 'busy' Saturday evening. ;)

She attached a picture of her and Siv standing before the Karl Johan monument outside the Royal Palace. The day is bright and sunny though cold. She and Siv have on winter coats and hats. An arm wrapped around each other, they look at the camera with impish mischief. It's a picture of two friends though laden with sexual overtones.

Hitting 'send,' Tone next sent an email to Janice.

Siv and I will be arriving Friday morning. We'd like to swing by on Friday sometime to pick up the outfits. I want to thank you once again for doing this for us. I will be sure to tell everyone who sees us about you.

The next email was from her lawyer.

Tone,

Per your instructions, $1.5 million was converted into gold bullion, the remainder of $500,000 set aside as retainer for my services concerning any and all legal matters during your and Siv Dahlberg's extended absence. In order to represent her, I will need to meet with her to sign necessary documentation and will be available at her convenience when you arrive in town on Friday December 19th.

The bullion is presently stored at the Union National Bank in Louisville and will be available during the normal banking hours on Friday or Saturday.

I trust this meets with your satisfaction.

Sitting back, she glanced around the apartment, wistfulness edging the corners of her emotions. She had enjoyed the time here. The only thing missing was Erik. With the money she made from the photoshoots they could live comfortably for a while. Of course, that assumed Erik wouldn't mind another man taking pictures of her naked. But she knew he would like Siv and who knows, maybe even the University would tap him for his Old Norse knowledge.

Yet she knew all this was temporary, even if Erik was here. She would have to finish her formal education at some time and get a job. *Or maybe not*, she chuckled. *Maybe I could be a perpetual student.*

Looking at the time on her laptop, she had another hour before her martial arts class. Since her arrival here, she had trained at least three days a week and was finally satisfied that she had recovered her previous form. Hopefully it would be enough when they landed in Kaupang.

Erik sat across from Kolga, enjoying the meal, which consisted of a meat stew of venison and rabbit mixed with onions and cabbage, along with warm fresh bread made from stone ground wheat, barley and oat flours mixed with whey, honey and walnuts. A drinking horn filled with cold mead perched to the side of his bowl.

"This is delicious," he complimented.

"It's good to see a strong man eat so well." Kolga smiled sweetly at him.

Erik was about to tease that she was fattening him up for the kill, but decided the joke might not go over too well.

Besides, what man in his right mind wouldn't want to be where he was? Kolga was beautiful, young, smart, and the object of many men's desire. So what was his problem? Why not sit back and enjoy it? As long as he didn't get her pregnant, they could maintain an illicit affair, though he doubted that was what she had in mind.

But did he want that? While he was enamored with her, he wasn't in love with her, certainly not like he was with Tone. It was that difference that held him back. Until he was sure... absolutely sure that he would never see Tone again, he could not give his heart to another.

How could he tell Kolga this? She already knew just enough about Tone to keep her curiosity at bay. But the longer he remained unattached, the longer Tone didn't appear, the weaker his excuses for not consummating a relationship. If only there was another woman around to act as competition. That way he could play them against each other.

Who am I kidding? I'm an old man, the age of a grandfather. I'm lucky this woman is even interested in me.

He surreptitiously studied her as he ate. Her hair was loose and the strawberry blond curls cascaded down her shoulders. Every time she looked at him, her green eyes sparkled with interest as though everything he said was important. She wore a shift made of silk that hugged her body, unusual in design for it had a keyhole neckline secured by three buttons that plunged down below her breasts, which pressed against the fabric. The hangerock worn over the shift was likewise unusual in that it was tighter, without brooches, the thin shoulder straps meeting the front of the dress at the point where her breasts pushed out the farthest. When she moved to eat or drink, the hangerock would occasionally slip and a nipple would press the silk shift, reminding Erik that she wore nothing beneath. The visible cleavage beneath the shift's keyhole added to the sensual allure and he found his desire stirring. If she was trying to seduce him, it was working.

Kolga picked up Erik's mead horn. "You need a refill."

"Thank you."

Instead of having a servant refill the horn, Kolga stood and walked over to the pitcher positioned on a shelf by the door. Erik watched her graceful movement, the hangerock and shift snug against her body, the belt tight enough to emphasize her narrow waist and hips.

Erik's mind wandered to what she might be like in bed and immediately chastised himself for such thoughts, yet the longer he stared at her, the more his imagination filled with her luscious body. He shook his head to distract his reverie.

She turned to face him, noting with satisfaction that his gaze was more than mere admiration. Locking his eyes with hers, she paused to slowly slide her hand down the left hangerock strap as though adjusting it to cover her breast. Yet she lingered long enough for the hard nipple to protrude and the smooth of the silk to curve with the fullness of her breast before sliding the hangerock back in place. She smiled when she saw his eyes shift from her face down to her breast before flickering back up to see her watching him. He blushed as though caught in some indiscretion.

"I'm curious," Erik fumbled, trying to cool the passion that refused to go away. "Why is it that you have never remarried? There certainly had to have been thousands upon thousands of men waiting to assume the role of your husband."

Kolga laughed as she returned to the table to stand next to him, handing him the drinking horn. "You say the sweetest things. Thousands upon thousands, eh? I doubt there are that many single men in all of Halfdan's kingdom even adding the ones his brothers rule." She gently touched his smooth cheek. Despite the season and weather, he still shaved his face. And from what she learned, he bathed more than the normal one day a week. In fact, she discovered that he bathed nearly every day, which pleased her for she shared the same behavior, believing it contributed to looking younger.

Erik delighted in the woman's touch and was half tempted to reach up and kiss her, but he held back and instead relished the sensation of her smooth hand. His eyes closed as his body relaxed to her caress.

Pleased with his response, she toyed with taking him there and then but decided to let dinner settle first. His eyes opened when he felt her touch disappear. The look he gave her seemed to be one of disappointment, which pleased her for she knew he would be hers this night.

Taking a seat again across from him, she said, "You asked why I hadn't remarried. The answer is simple enough. I haven't found anyone who has captured my interest." She almost added 'Until now,' but chose to leave well enough alone for the moment.

"I understand. I imagine it's hard to find another man like Egill."

"Egill was one of a kind, special in so many ways," she agreed. Her eyes narrowed as she emphasized, "But he is not here, nor will he ever be. I cannot change what has happened. I can only live for today, in the here and now. I have worked through my sadness and know that it is time to move on with my life, because I will not get another chance to live again."

"So there is no one who can take his place?"

"No one can ever take his place, and it is foolish to think it possible." She sipped her mead and studied him. He was tall and handsome, confident and strong, intelligent, and so many other virtues. Yet there were flashes of vulnerability that he revealed on rare instances, as though his heart had been hurt before. She understood the emotion, remembering the dagger of pain that exploded in her own heart when told that Egill was dead. For months afterward she refused to be consoled until Halfdan showed up one day. Instead of telling her to pull her head out of the place she uses to sit, he wrapped her in his arms and told her it was time to let go. Drying her tears, she once again recognized why he was her favorite brother.

"We are all different," Kolga continued. "It is foolish to expect someone to be someone else, though I know some who have tried. It never works. I accept that I will never have another Egill. It doesn't mean that I can't be as happy as I was with him when I find another."

Erik blinked at the wisdom of her words. He was head-over-heels in love with Tone. Though she wasn't dead, she might as well be considering the circumstances. Here he was, stuck in the 8th century because of a glitch in the Time Machine. There she was, stuck in the 21st century and because of a glitch in the Time Machine, the likelihood of him ever seeing her again was pretty much nil.

Still, could she somehow manage to go back in time? Would the Time Machine folks allow her to go back? If so, where and when would she go? Did time move at the same speed in the past as in the present? In other words, did time move parallel in the two periods. But that didn't make sense because they could send someone back in time to a specific and different day. But, he argued with himself, the time of day was always the same as it was in the present. Erik sighed a soft breath for he had gone over these arguments so often that he ended up more frustrated than convinced.

Was it time to accept that Tone was forever lost to him? Was it time to move on? Kolga's gentle smile distracted his musings.

"You were lost to me for a few moments,"

"Sorry," he sheepishly replied. "I was just thinking about what you said. There's a lot of wisdom in what you say. It seems to me that with all the time you spend with me, you are hindering your search for the right man."

Kolga shook her head at him. "All the men my age seem too young, immature."

Erik startled for Tone had said the same thing. "But I'm old enough to be your father."

"You certainly don't look it," she complimented. "You look to be my age."

Erik chuckled. "Now you're being silly. What you need is someone your age who can grow old with you."

"It's not your place to tell me what I need," she gently chided. "Besides, I bet you will live longer than any of the men or women on our farms, let alone Halfdan's kingdom."

"That may be, but wouldn't you want someone closer to you own age?"

"I've already answered that question." She focused a hard stare at him. "Perhaps you ought to answer the question of what do you want? Are you looking for a woman your own age?"

Erik smiled knowing that a woman his age would already be an old maid. "I suppose not."

"So you want a younger woman." She smiled mischievously at him.

Erik laughed. "I suppose I do."

"Someone who can keep up with you. Someone who can challenge you and make you want to come home, never raid again because you have everything you need right here on the farms."

Kolga's eyes swept the room, settling on the servants near the fireplace. Catching the eye of a woman not yet in middle age, she ticked her head towards the door.

Immediately understanding, the woman gathered up the rest of the servants. Erik watched them silently put on their outer cloaks and head out the door, wondering where they would go in this cold night.

"They'll be fine," Kolga reassured him. Standing, she gracefully moved to the fire pit and added several logs to the fire. Instead of returning to her seat, she stepped over to stand before him as he swiveled around on the bench seat.

Their eyes met and she bent down and kissed him on the lips. It was a brief kiss, an exploratory kiss. Liking his response, she took a half step back, their eyes still locked.

A thick carnal silence swirled around the room.

Kolga reached up and slowly slipped a finger under the left strap of the hangerock, pushing it off her shoulder. She did the same for the right strap, letting the apron-skirt fall to the floor around her ankles. Stepping out of the crumpled garment, she approached him, unbuttoning the shift. Hiking up the silk shift, she straddled him, pulling the shift off her shoulders and baring her firm large breasts. Pushing it off her arms, she reached up with both hands and pulled his head to hers, her mouth devouring his. She felt his strong arms wrap around her pressing her bare flesh against him as their mouths and tongues ravaged each other.

Then just as suddenly, like a sail luffing in the wind, the bursting passion suddenly cooled and she sensed his desire pulling away.

She pushed back from him, her face creased with a frown. "What's wrong?"

Erik slowly shook his head. "You are stunningly beautiful. I...I'm..."

Kolga's lips pursed and she pushed away to standing, the shift falling to the floor, leaving her completely naked. She spread her arms. "Am I not good enough?"

"That's not it at all," Erik asserted.

"Then what?" She jammed her hands on her hips.

Erik took in her perfect body, the porcelain smooth skin, the tight tummy despite giving birth to four children who didn't survive. The woman had had more than her share of misfortune and grief.

"I'm just not ready yet," he blurted. "I need time."

"Tone?" she accused.

"Yes."

"Still?" She bent down and pulled up her shift, leaving the buttons undone.

Erik fixed her with a compassionate look. "How long was it after Egill died that you decided it was time to let go? A month, two months, six months?"

Kolga's anger softened and while she understood, she didn't have to like it. "How long has it been?"

"Six months."

"You loved her that much?"

"How much did you love Egill?" he countered.

"A fair point," she admitted, remembering it had been almost a year before she was willing to even talk about her future.

"All I'm asking for is a little more time."

Kolga picked up the hangerock and slipped it over her head. Returning to sit across from him, she buttoned the shift. "She is still alive?"

"Yes."

"Why is she not here with you?"

"We were attacked. She managed to escape while I stayed behind to give them time."

"Them?"

"Her other escorts."

"She was wealthy then?" Kolga didn't like what she was hearing.

"Her parents were."

"How old is she?"

"Your age."

Kolga eyes widened. "And she still lived with her parents? Why hadn't she been married?"

"It's like I told your brother. No one was good enough. Her parents spent so much time trying to arrange the perfect match to improve their position that they ruined her life."

"You two should have run off together," Kolga observed.

"We had that in mind when we were attacked."

Epiphany hit and Kolga looked at him with sympathy. "Halfdan?"

"Yes. But I do not blame him. He didn't know. Besides, he has honored me far more than I deserve."

"Spoke like a loyal hirdman," she scoffed. "So why don't you go and find her?"

"It's not that easy. First, she probably thinks I'm dead. Second, learning how we feel about each other, her parents probably have already arranged a marriage. The last thing they'd want is for their daughter to run off with a poor man and ruin their chances to move up in society."

"You're not poor now," she pointed out.

"Doesn't matter," he said. "I'm not rich where they are and that's all that counts."

Kolga nodded, her hopes rising again. "Do you think you'll ever see her again?"

Erik inhaled a deep breath and let out a slow sigh. "I don't think so."

Satisfied, Kolga got back up and came around the table, and sat next to him. Taking his hand in hers, she squeezed it. Placing a tender hand on his cheek, she kissed him.

"I understand. I can wait."

Chapter 10

December 19, 2031
Corydon, Indiana

Tone unlocked the door to Erik's townhouse, immediately heading to the thermostat.

"It's cold in here," Siv complained, dropping her bags in the middle of the floor then closing the door.

"No wonder, it's set at 50." Increasing the temp to 72, she turned to take in the home she and Erik once shared. Everything was in its place as though she had simply gone out for groceries and just now returned. A thin layer of dust had settled in her absence and her first inclination was to start cleaning.

Siv walked into the kitchen and opened the door to the fridge. "Two bottles of mead and not much else," she chuckled. "At least you have your priorities right."

Tone checked the clock in the kitchen. "We need to get our stuff before we do anything else."

"I'm starting to get nervous now," Siv said with excitement. "Just think. In two days we'll be gone forever."

"A new adventure," Tone said, eyes bright. "C'mon. Let's go get our stuff."

It was midafternoon before they arrived back at the house, both tired from jetlag. Tone dropped the backpack containing the gold in the middle of the living room floor then went back to help Siv with the bags of clothing.

"I'm beat," Siv said.

"Me too," Tone readily agreed. "There's only one bedroom, but the bed's big enough for two. If you don't think it's too weird, we can share the bed. Otherwise the couch is available."

Siv looked at the couch and then at the bed through the bedroom door. "You promise not to take advantage of me?"

"I'll do my best," Tone smirked. "We'll need to make sure Gene knows we slept together. That ought to get him going." She glanced down at her phone. "I suppose I ought to turn this on." Gene had left two messages to call him when they arrived. "He can wait. I need sleep."

Crossing over to the front door, Tone locked and bolted it before shoving a chair against it.

Leaving the clothing bags in the living room, Siv picked up the backpack and carried it into the bedroom. "This is heavy. You sure you're going to be able to haul it around?"

"It'll get lighter as time goes on," Tone replied, checking windows and the front door again. "My main concern is making sure no one knows what we have in there when we get there."

Half-listening, Siv stripped off her clothes. "Which side do you want?"

"I normally take the left side."

"Facing the bed or in the bed?"

"In the bed."

Siv pulled back the covers, uttering a soft contented moan as she settled. "G'night."

Gene met them at the front door to the restaurant, an Italian place not far from TTI. "I finally get to meet Siv in real life. You're far more beautiful than the pictures reveal."

"And you are just as handsome as I expected," she parried.

"Now that the introductions are out of the way," Tone teased, "let's eat. I'm starving. And then after dinner, we'll see what mischief we can get into."

"I am yours to command," Gene said with a gallant bow.

Gene played the charming host and ordered for the three of them, adding a bottle of a superb Chianti to go with the meal. The Chianti was brought out first and Gene acted the connoisseur, examining the cork then swirling the wine in the glass and inhaling the bouquet before pronouncing, "Yes, this will do nicely."

By the time the meal was brought, they were on their second bottle of Chianti. Gene did his best dividing his attention between the two women whose sly grins and giggles overtly suggested they had been intimate before they came back to the States, causing Gene's imagination to fill in the blanks.

When the check was finally paid, courtesy of Gene, they bundled into his car and headed to TTI.

"You sure we'll be able to get in?" Tone asked.

"Not a problem," Gene confidently answered, parking in the Visitor Parking spot near the front doors. "Ready?"

"We're yours to command," Siv smiled, repeating his words earlier.

Inside, the after-hours lights dimly illuminated the receptionist desk where a single night watchman sat watching a college basketball game on his laptop.

The security guard looked up when Gene pressed the intercom.

"Yes?"

"Open the door Harry," Gene said. "It's cold out here."

"That you Mister Milligan?" Harry replied, buzzing the unlock.

Strolling in, Tone and Siv in tow, Gen crossed over to the desk. "I told you to call me Gene, Harry. When you say 'Mister Milligan,' it makes me sound like my dad."

Harry laughed, though pleased with the familiarity. "And who do we have here tonight?"

"Two friends," Gene replied, giving Harry the eye as a warning not to mention the other 'friends' he had also brought to work late on a Saturday night. "Ingrid here is actually an employee."

"I'm not going to be on your roster," Tone said when Harry pulled up the employee listing. "I'm sort of a special case… on an academic sabbatical."

"What's that?" Harry said with a frown.

"TTI is paying for her grad school," Gene explained. "She's an employee, but not official. It's confusing."

"I asked the same thing to HR," Tone added. "They gave me some lame answer that it had to do with taxes and employees versus contractors and other stuff that made no sense to me. But then, I find all that corporate tax accountability stuff painfully boring. I know some people just about orgasm over it, but for me, if I can't sleep, just start talking taxes to me."

Harry burst a laugh and nodded in understanding. "Whatcha got in the bags and backpack?"

Tone opened up the top to her large bag. "Janice asked if I wouldn't mind dropping some stuff off for her. She works in the wardrobe department. This is all period clothing." She smiled at him. "You wanna try some of it on?"

Shaking his head, Harry gave it a passing glance and winked at Gene, impressed that Gene had the moxie to bring two women here at the same time. "Enjoy yourselves," he said, returning to his basketball game. He would wait until they got onto the elevator then adjust the cameras to watch. The last time Gene brought a woman here, either he forgot that there were cameras in every office and corridor, or he chose to ignore the fact that he was providing Harry with a show.   Either way, Harry dutifully recorded over the frolicking with a splice from another office that looked the same.

"You want to drop that stuff off first?" Gene asked, pressing the elevator button.

"Janice can wait," Tone said with a knowing grin.

"That's what I hoped you'd say," Gene said with barely suppressed anticipation.

Noting the plethora of security cameras, Siv commented, "Are we going to be on camera the entire time?"

"No," Gene quickly reassured her.   "I can cloak the cameras in the Time Travel room so that no one will see what's going on."

Siv gently leaned against him as they stepped into the elevator and batted her eyes, innocently asking, "What might be going on in a little bit?"

Gene caught his breath as he felt her breasts pushing against him.   Unable to think of something clever, he simply smiled.

Beside the normal floor buttons was an alphanumeric keypad.   Instead of pressing the button for a particular floor, Gene tapped at least a dozen numbers, letters, and symbols on the keypad.   When he entered the last letter, the elevator began its descent.

As the elevator descended, Tone commented, "I'm surprised that there's only one security guard, especially with the Time Machine here.   Seems to me that just anyone could break in here and create havoc with the machine."

"There's too much technology for that to happen," Gene said with calm assurance.   "First, the only reason we got in here was that Harry knows me.   Normal protocol is that no one gets in afterhours unless they are an employee.   Second, if an employee has someone else with them who doesn't work here, Harry initiates a security sequence before he allows them inside the building."

"Like what?" Siv asked.

Gene shook his head with a smile.   "That's not something that is publicly shared."

Nodding in understanding, she said, "What next?"

"You'll notice I used the keypad to work the elevator. Within the sequence I entered is a code telling the elevator that all is normal. So, for instance, if someone got in here and tried to get me to enter the code, I would enter the false code and the doors would lock shut, a stun gas would be emitted and by the time the doors opened, we'd be lying on the floor, knocked out."

"Is there more?" Tone said, impressed.

"Lots more," he chuckled. "But I can tell you all that another time."

The elevator settled and the doors opened to the long corridor that Tone remembered she and Erik had traversed half a year ago.

The ceiling lights burst on the moment they stepped into the hallway, illuminating the doors to offices and research rooms. At the end were the double doors to the Time Machine room.

Tone and Siv walked close to Gene, a closeness that spoke a subtle intimacy. Siv couldn't help but notice his raptured look of anticipation.

"What's else is in the bags?" he asked, his imagination rampant.

"You'll see," she replied with sensual intimation.

Gene's smile widened as their footsteps echoed in the otherwise silent hallway. "I've been looking forward to this," he said, his voice husky.

"Me too," Tone said. "We're going to make sure this is a day you will never forget."

Gene caught his breath, shooting an overt glance at the beautiful woman walking next to him, imagining her naked.

Entering a code on the keypad next to the doors, Gene opened the one door and flicked on the lights, locking the doors behind them.

Tone stared through the glass partition separating the Time Machine from the controls, remembering that day when she sat next to Erik in that very machine. Reminding herself she had a purpose, she focused on the present.

"So how does this all work?" she asked, walking up to the control panel.

"Wouldn't you rather talk about something else?" Gene said, reaching for her hand.

"Patience Grasshopper," she coyly smiled, squeezing his hand. "I assure you, you will never forget this day. Remember, anticipation is half the fun."

"You two are driving me crazy," he gushed.

"And that's not all we're going to drive you," she said with a devilish smile and flicking her eyebrows. "Now, before you tell us about the machine, will you turn off the cameras here or are we going to give Harry a show?"

Gene walked over the computer, typed in a sequence on the keyboard, clicked a few icons on the computer screen, waited a few seconds then turned to them in triumph. "Voila. I wrote a program that inserts a stock image into the camera feed that allows us to proceed uninterrupted."

"So you've used it before?" Siv said with a sly smile.

"Only once," Gene lied, "before I met Ingrid."

"And Harry or someone else is not going to come barging in here?" Tone asked, knowing full well Gene was lying.

"Harry can't leave his station unless he has to go to the bathroom. As far as someone else coming in here, I just locked the doors to the room here from the computer. We do that normally as a precaution when the machine is activated."

"So how does it all work?" Tone asked.

With a sigh of resignation that patience was a virtue in this instance, he said, "It's really quite simple. All the programmer has to do is type in the location and date in year, month, and day format, wait for everyone to get settled then press this button." He pointed to a red button covered by a hard plastic cover.

"What about time of day?"

"That's already programmed into the machine based upon the event desired."

"Suppose someone was going way back in time and the time is somewhat unspecific?" Siv asked.

"What do you mean?"

"Like that one guy this past summer," Tone nonchalantly interrupted. "I saw him on TV. He was going to England in the tenth century or something like that. Whatever happened to him? How come we haven't seen his story on the show?"

Gene frowned at her before answering, "I don't know. I have nothing to do with the TV show."

"Sorry. I didn't mean it like that. Forget him," she said, flipping a hand. "Suppose I had no specific time of day. What then?"

"Then we just program you to the morning."

"OK," she said with an impish grin. "Suppose a traveler goes back 500 years to Mexico City right in the middle of a blood sacrifice. In their rush to escape, an escort trips and gets captured. Obviously you have to rescue him, but how do you know *when* to rescue him if they've hustled him off to the sacrificial holding room, especially, as you said, there is no doppelganger as time has already moved on?"

"Doppelganger?" Siv said, raising an eyebrow. "This sounds intriguing."

"It has to do with time and spatial presence or something like that," Tone said, hooking a thumb at Gene. "He can explain it better."

"It has to do with mass and time," Gen said, pleased to display his knowledge. "The old idea was that you had a doppelganger who would always be at the point of insertion while your real body moved forward with time. It's a silly notion that assumes that time has no impact on your mass in the sense that you have to be at a certain location at a certain point in time. But it completely neglects the fact that the mass, your body, has already advanced in time and cannot go back once it is placed at a point in time.

Siv held up her hands in defeat. "Sorry I asked. But to get back to... uh, Ingrid's question, if someone is stuck in the past, how do you know when to rescue him?"

Gene pointed to another section of the control panel. "This section here maintains a current time relationship to the past. Let's say it takes us two days to get escorts ready to send back. All I have to do is hit the sync button, scroll through the list of travelers and hit 'enter.' The computer links the two locations and syncs the time to the Time Machine so that they go back to get the guy about to be sacrificed, they'll be in the exact same time as the escort."

"Suppose it takes months to put together a team, assuming the escort hasn't been sacrificed? And suppose you had to send another traveler to the past in the meantime?"

"It doesn't matter," Gene confidently replied. "We maintain a data listing of all the travelers, so it could be one or a dozen travelers in between. It doesn't matter."

"OK," Tone grinned. "One more question. Suppose I'm sitting in the machine and I realize I've dropped something on the floor in between the time machine and the door. I suddenly get up and step off the machine. Half my body is on the machine and the other half is off just as you push the button. Will half of me be sent back?"

Gene laughed and shook his head. "You come up with some of the oddest questions, especially now."

Tone locked his eyes with hers. "It's called anticipation." Reaching into the bag, she withdrew a sheer blouse and held it up. "Know what I mean?"

"O my," Gene blurted.

Winking at him, she said, "Now answer the question so we can get to the business at hand."

"What was the question?" Gene asked, his brain momentarily fuzzed.

"Whether half of me would be sent back."

"Oh, right. The seats in the machine are pressure sensitive. If no one is sitting in a programmed seat, the machine waits ten seconds. If no pressure is applied, the machine shuts down."

"So you have to program the number of travelers."

"Yes, the minimum number is two: one traveler and one escort."

Tone stood at the console, nonchalantly scanning the layout and memorizing the appropriate sequence, at the same time figuring out how to apply weight to a traveler chair.

"Anymore questions?" Gene asked, ready to get on with the real reason for being here.

"Actually, yes," Siv smiled. "Suppose we all went back in time and something terrible happened that caused us all to be killed or captured. With no one to work the machine, would it just stay there in the past?"

"No," Gene said, ready to get on with the fun. "Once sent back in time, the machine is preprogrammed to activate a safety mechanism that returns it back to the present."

"Can you imagine if someone from the past was on the machine when it happened?" Tone laughed.

"Like a cave man or someone like that," Siv added.

"Didn't they make a movie about that?" Tone said.

"Any other questions?" Gene interrupted, his anticipation bursting within.

Tone tilted her head and gave him a carnal smile. Looking at Siv who smiled and nodded, she selected one of the VIP armchairs, she scooted it away from the wall. "I think we're ready. You sit here."

Needing no urging, Gene flopped down, his eyes glowing with desire.

"Get comfortable and put your arms on the armrests," she commanded.

Gene obeyed as he watched Tone withdraw two lengths of rope from her bag.

"Comfy?" she inquired with an innocent grin.

"Yes."

"Good."

Wrapping the ropes around his arms, she secured them to the armrests, neatly tying a bow on top.

"They're not too tight are they?"

Gene tested the restraints. While tight, they did not hurt though he was quite unable to free himself.

"I'm good," he replied

"Let's hope so," she teased.

Scooting another chair close to him, she folded the blouse against the backrest then placed the bag next to the chair. Reaching into the bag, she pulled out a small pillow then pried his knees farther apart and placed the pillow on the floor between his legs.

Gene sucked in his breath as she reached down and unbuckled his belt and slid it out from the belt loops.

"We don't want the buckle to get in the way," she said, curling it up and placing it on the adjacent chair.

Stepping back, she faced him and started unbuttoning her blouse, abruptly stopping halfway down.

"What are you stopping for?" Gene said, anxious with anticipation.

"I forgot something."

Stepping around to the bag, she bent over, giving Gene a glimpse of her breasts as she reached in the bag and pulled out a black silk scarf.

"The effect is better if you see the finished product instead of watching me change." She pointed to the blouse.

"At least let me see them before you put the blindfold on," he pleaded, staring at her chest.

"Hmmm," she pretended to muse. "It won't be the same."

"Please," he implored.

Tone stood back and unbuttoned the remaining buttons. In one smooth quick motion, she flashed him, rapidly overlapping the shirt across her breasts before he had a chance to register what he had seen.

"That's all you get for now," she said with a professorial air. Walking behind him, she wrapped the silk scarf over his eyes. "Can you see anything?"

"No," he said with a disappointed sigh.

"Good. Have patience, Grasshopper. All will be revealed in just a little bit." She bent down and kissed him fully.

As soon as Tone had placed the scarf around Gene's eyes, Siv kicked into high gear and changed into her traveling clothes, assuming the role of a wealthy Viking woman: an ankle length linen shift beneath a hangerock, a shorter length woolen dress suspended by shoulder straps fastened by silver brooches; woolen socks, and finely crafted thick leather ankle-high shoes.

With the scarf now covering Gene's eyes, Tone hurriedly changed into her traveling clothes, assuming the role of a Viking shield maiden: woolen breeches with leg wrappings that started below the knee and ended at her toes, woolen socks, leather turnshoe style shoes, linen undershirt, and woolen kyrtill.

"I'm almost ready," Siv said, keeping Gene's attention.

"What about Tone?" Gene asked, his voice throaty.

"I'm almost ready," Tone cooed with a grin, nodding to Siv that it was time for her to gain Gene's undivided attention while she focused on the Time Machine control board.

Siv took the blouse off the chair and folded it across his thighs before dumping all the remaining clothing out of the bag and onto the floor. Listening to the activity, Gene assumed the best and was particularly pleased when he felt the blouse lifted off his thighs.

"Almost ready," she cooed.

Resting her hands on Gene's legs, Siv dropped to her knees onto the cushion and slowly slid her hands forward, up his thighs to undo the hook securing the fly before slowing pulling the zipper down and opening up the pants, noting his overt arousal pressing up through his underwear.

"My my," she said, silently smirking. "I think we're all going to enjoy this."

Her hands on his thighs, she listened to his labored breathing as she turned her head to watch Tone at the programming console. Tone ticked her head towards the door separating the time machine from the control room. Siv immediately understood and pushed herself to standing.

"Where are you going?" Gene whined.

"Just repositioning myself," she replied, stealthily propping open the door to the time machine.

At the same time, Tone hefted up the leather backpack and purse and deposited them next to the chairs on the machine.

"What are you doing?" Gene asked, hearing noises that didn't sound like they were next to him. A sudden fear emerged only to be halted when he felt her lips on his.

"I'm giving us romping space," Siv whispered in his ear before gently biting the earlobe. "In a few moments, everything will be perfect and then I can settle down to business. Can you wait a little longer?" She reached down between his legs.

"O God," he quivered.

Tone made a bee line to the console and flicked on the power.

"What the hell?" Gene exclaimed, hearing the hum of machines. "What's going on? What are you doing?"

Ignoring him, Tone scrolled the travelers list. Erik and she were the eighth ones down. The two escorts were likewise listed. Highlighting the two names, she synced the present date and time with their insertion date then typed in 'K-a-u-p-a-n-g' in the destination box followed by the geo coordinates 59.035250 10.105940. A prompt asked for the traveler's name and she typed in 'I-n-g-r-i-d D-a-h-l-b-e-r-g.' The screen changed and a prompt asked for the escort's name. Typing in the man's name, she pressed 'Enter.'

The screen changed to another prompt that said, 'Please verify the travelers, escorts, destination and time are correct. Hit 'OK' when ready.

"What are you doing?" Gene again asked, nervousness invading his lust.

"Just a little ambiance," Tone chuckled.

Double checking everything was as Gene explained, Tone raised the plastic cover. Walking over to where Siv stood next to Gene, she whispered in Siv's ear, "Back chair left," then held her finger up indicating she wanted Siv to wait.

Tone dropped to her knees and placed her hands on his thighs.

"Everything is ready," she cooed. "Are you ready?"

"Yes," he answered, "but… but what's all the noise? It sounds like you've turned on the time machine."

"I did," she readily answered. "The thought that you and I could pick a place and jump back in time for sex makes me hot. I hope you don't mind."

"I don't mind," he said in a rush, "as long as you don't touch anything else."

"You don't want me to touch anything else?" she pretended to pout, slowly sliding her hands up his thighs.

"That's not what I mean," he said, his voice almost a moan.

Tone leaned back to untie his shoes, slipping them off his feet. "Lift your butt up," she ordered as she and Siv reached up and yanked his pants and underwear down to his ankles, leaving his erection fully exposed.

Tone stood and paused as she gazed down at him, impressed, smirked and crossed over to the console, flicking a finger at Siv.

Siv nodded and hustled to sit in the second row chair in the time machine.

Casting one last look at Gene all trussed up and exposed, she smiled and pressed the 'Send' button before racing to her seat in the machine.

Panic gripped Gene when he heard the Time Machine's activation. "O my God. Nooooo."

Once Gene and his two lovely guests had entered the elevator, Frank adjusted the camera feed into the computer screens, allowing him to follow them as they made their way down the hall towards the Time Machine room, tripping relays so that he always had a full frontal view. His focus narrowed on the women and he was rewarded when the one called Siv removed her coat and he let out a low whistle.

"Nice rack. Now you Ingrid."

As though she had heard him, Tone paused in the hallway, placing the bags on the floor as she slid off her coat.

"Oh yeah," he crooned, staring at her chest. "Gene... you are one lucky man."

His voyeurism rewarded, he watched as Tone handed her coat to Gene then retrieved her bags. Once they were through the door to the Time Machine room, Frank readjusted the monitors to all the cameras in the room.

Crossing his fingers in hopes that Gene would forget that he was watching, he let out a sigh of frustration when Gene crossed over to the control panel, hovered a finger over the 'enter' key then looked up at a camera and smiled.

"Damn," Harry grunted as the screens went blank. Momentarily cast adrift, he let out a slow breath and readjusted the monitors to the cameras in the hallways, leaving one camera in the Time Machine room just in case.

An hour later, his imagination, tinged with jealousy, played havoc with his concentration. After two hours, his imagination, tinged with admiration, created all sorts of vivid positions, including the two women together. After three hours, he wondered if they had fallen asleep.

His nervousness grew with each hour past midnight. Gene had brought women here before, but they were always gone well before midnight. By two o'clock, he knew he had to check.

Keying in the code to lock all outside entrances, Harry scooted back and headed to the elevator, punching in his access code. When the doors opened to the Time Machine

Hall, he bustled down the hall, pausing before the main doors to the Room.

Gingerly trying the handle, he was surprised the door was locked. Knocking gently at first, he leaned close to the door, listening. Believing he heard movement, he knocked again, louder.

"Gene? Hello? Open the door."

Pressing his ear against the door, he heard silence. Knowing damn well someone was in there, his knocking became loud and insistent.

"Open the door."

After repeated loud demands, Harry's frustration had enough. Fear gripped him as he realized he was going to have to do a manual override to the room security. That would require approval at a level high enough to make Harry believe he was going to be looking for another job. Indecision assailed him as he silently prayed that someone would open the damn door.

Bustling back down the hallway and up the elevator, he raced to his guard desk in the foyer and pulled up the Procedures folder, scrolling to the Emergency Procedures. Flipping down the Time Machine Room folder, he opened the file. One sentence was highlighted and bold:

Before activating a Security override, at least one of the following individuals MUST be notified for approval: TTI CEO, TTI Head of Security, TTI Director of Operations.

Deciding the Head of Security was the one person most likely to give him some support, he paused when he glanced at the time. It was nearly three o'clock in the morning... on a Sunday. Figuring it was easier to ask forgiveness than permission, he read further down in the instructions to the access sequence, writing down the code on a piece of scrap paper, reminding himself that he would need to shred the paper when finished.

Returning to the Time Machine Room, Harry punched in the override sequence, hearing an audible click. Testing the door handle, he opened the door to the brightly lit room. There close to the control board, a blindfolded Gene sat with his wrists tied to the arms of a chair and his pants down around his ankles.

Harry turned to gape at the empty room where the actual machine usually resided.

"O my God."

It was pitch dark when the spinning sensation finally stopped, immediately replaced by a bone chilling wind that swirled in through the open front of the Time Machine. Shivering, the two women unbuckled and huddled in behind the front row chairs.

Siv peered out into the darkness, her teeth chattering. "I'd say let's build a fire, but we probably don't want to draw undue attention to ourselves."

Clutching the backpack with one gloved hand, Tone squeezed the hood of her cloak tighter around her head. "We're going to have to make the best of it until daylight."

"You don't think we ought to see if there's a town close by?"

Tone shook her head. "We can't leave the machine alone here. We'll send it back when it starts getting lighter. Until then, snuggle close so we don't freeze."

As they wrapped themselves around each other, Tone once again thanked Janice for the forethought of winter clothing.

Dawn was still an hour away when Gene and Harry stood in front of Jakob Cooper's desk. Art Hegan, the Director of Security, stood to Cooper's right. Cooper, his face a mask of smoldering anger, glared at the two men rigidly standing before him.

Controlling the urge to reach across the desk and throttle them one at a time, Cooper flopped down into his chair. "Tell me again what happened."

"I'm totally responsible," Gene volunteered.

"Damned right you are," Cooper snapped. "But I'll deal with that in a minute. You brought two women into the Time Machine room for the sole purpose of sexual relations."

Gene swallowed. "Yes, sir."

Cooper's head jerked to the left to stare at Harry. "And you let him?"

"Yes, sir."

"Is this the first time?"

There was a thick awkward silence as both Gene and Harry suddenly found the floor fascinating. Finally Gene spoke up. "No."

"No?" Cooper's voice ricocheted in the room.

"No," Gene repeated.

Cooper's head slumped backwards and he stared at the ceiling. "Someone please tell me this is a dream."

"How did the women get control of the Time Machine if you were there?" Art Hegan queried.

"I... uh... was tied up."

"Doing what?" Hegan frowned.

"No, I mean, I was literally tied up."

"This is getting better by the minute," Cooper groaned.

The door flung open and Meredith burst in, looking half asleep, her brunette hair tied in a ponytail.

"What's going on?"

Cooper jerked a thumb at Gene. "Lothario here has managed to lose our Time Machine. I'll let him explain it."

"O my God." She swiveled mid-stride to confront Gene. "How?"

Gene shifted a quick glance at the others before explaining what happened.

"Are you really that stupid?" Meredith eyed him with overt disgust.

Gene chose not to answer.

"The two women," Cooper interrupted. "You said this Ingrid is an employee?"

"Yes sir."

"I've already checked," Hegan said. "There's no Ingrid who works here."

Cooper's eyes burned fire beneath his furrowed brow. "The other woman was a friend of hers?"

"Yes."

"Where did you meet them?"

"I met Ingrid down in the cafeteria. Siv was a friend of hers from the University."

"Here in Louisville?"

"No. In Oslo, like in Norway."

"O my God," Meredith erupted, storming around the office. "It's that Tone Thorgils-whatever. She's gone back to get him."

Epiphany swept through Cooper and he shook his head. "I'll give her credit. The woman's persistent." He turned to Gene. "Where did they go?"

"Kaupang, 793 CE," Gene answered. "Who's Tawny?"

"You know her as Ingrid."

Gene blinked at the revelation, the epiphany that he had been played beginning to piss him off. "We do have a problem."

"What?"

"While the Time function on the machine has drastically improved, the geocoordinates function still has hiccups."

"Where's Kaupang?" Meredith asked.

"I have no clue," Gene answered.

An oppressive silence filled the room until Gene pointed out, "After two days, the Machine will return on its own."

"That is small comfort," Meredith sneered, "to the fact that we now have three people back in the past. If the media gets ahold of this it will be a tsunami on top of all hell breaking loose, not to mention the likelihood of the government shutting us down." She scowled at Gene. "You've destroyed an entire corporation for a piece of ass."

"Three?" Gene sputtered. "There are only two."

"There's another one back there, Tone's fiancé."

"She's engaged?" he burst.

Meredith shot him a look that said he was a pathetic loser. "You got played like some pimple faced junior high school nerd. You've got 'sucker' engraved all over you."

"This gets us nowhere," Hegan huffed. "We need to come up with a plan of action."

Deciding he had nothing to lose and a job to save, Gene rose to the challenge. "Like I said, the machine will be back in two days, Monday midnight at the latest. In the meantime, we lock the room for Machine Maintenance to keep everyone out until then."

"That only solves part of the problem," Meredith grumbled.

"But it does solve the most pressing issue," Cooper acknowledged with a slow nod.

"What about the three people back in time?" Meredith countered, staring at Gene. "We can't leave them there. The two women are young enough to have babies, which means all sorts of possible variations in the time continuum."

"Yes it does," Gene agreed, "but we do have time. It's not like they're going to get pregnant in the next month or two."

"You don't know that," Meredith shot back.

Gene rolled his eyes. "Even if they did, it's still nine months before one of them delivers. I've been busting my butt to sync the machine back as far as possible and I've made incredible progress, especially compared to where we were not even a year ago."

Cooper half-smiled, recognizing the man was working hard to save his job. But he did have a point. Up until Gene arrived, progress had been painfully slow. Hiring him from MIT had been a coup, despite his coworkers here thinking him insufferable and arrogant.

"What do you propose?"

"First we find out where Kaupang is. Once we know the location, we get people who are knowledgeable about it. Select one or two of the best along with... ah, *appropriate* escorts to either retrieve them or... eliminate them."

"Bravely spoken," Hegan sniffed.

"She was studying some Norse thing," Meredith said.

Cooper flipped open his laptop. "How do you spell it?"

"K-a-u-p-a-n-g," Gene enunciated.

Cooper typed in the name. "It's south of Oslo." He sat back and cocked his head. "Why would she go there?" He shifted a glance at Meredith. "I thought her lover was on an island off the coast of England."

"Lindisfarne," Meredith elaborated, "under attack by Vikings."

Copper narrowed his focus on her. "She knows something... something that caused her to go to Oslo. Find out." Redirecting his gaze to Gene, his eyes hardened. "And you... I don't care what you do on your off hours, but while you're an employee here, you'll keep it in your pants. If I even suspect you screwing around here, I will castrate you. Understand."

"Yes, sir."

"Second," Copper continued. "Once the machine is back, you got 30 days to fix it. If I can't send a team back to where Tone went, you will wish you were never born. Now get out of here and take this idiot of a security guard with you."

Gene needed no additional urging and escaped out the door, Harry on his heels. Once outside the office, Gene was contrite.

"I am so sorry, Harry. I never meant to get you in trouble."

"I know," Harry replied, seemingly unaffected. "I already squared it away with Hegan. He's got my back."

"Really?"

"Yeah. Besides, what're they gonna do to me? They fire me and I'll inadvertently blab something to the papers. They know that. They can't do anything to me other than write me up. And even that is questionable. So I'm OK. It's you that's gotta worry. Cooper plays nice when things go his way. When they don't… watch out."

They were in the elevator when Harry winked at Gene. "You get any?"

Gene pressed the button for the main floor. "I got screwed, but not in a good way."

Dawn rimmed the morning sky when Tone stepped off the machine, her legs stiff, her body cold. Siv awkwardly descended to stand in the snow next to her.

"We should probably send it back," Tone mused as she looked down at her feet in the ankle deep snow.

"Why? Gene said it would go back on its own."

"Suppose someone comes by and ends up getting sent to the present?"

"That would be funny," Siv chuckled. "But that's their problem. Right now I need a fire and a cup of hot coffee."

"They don't have coffee here, remember?" Tone said with a sigh.

"O my God. No coffee?" Siv wailed with feigned distress. "We gotta go back."

"Too late," Tone said with a nonchalant shrug. "C'mon. Let's see if we can find something to eat."

"What about the machine?"

"You're right. It's their problem." Tone stepped away from the machine to scan the surrounding terrain, which was mostly a forest of leafless trees. "I say we head east, towards the sun. We should hit a road or something…or even the coast."

"Lead on Macduff," Siv said with a shivering smile.

Tone worked her way through the trees, coming to a halt a few minutes later when the forest abruptly ended and the land spread before them, wide and flat, dotted with clumps of bare trees and the occasional farmer's cottage, smoke curling out from the middle of the roofs. In the distance looked to be a sort of wall on a berm. The scent of the sea filled the air.

Puzzled, Tone looked at Siv. "I don't remember Kaupang ever having a wall around it."

"Maybe it's not Kaupang," Siv muttered.

Her heart sinking, Tone pressed on. They soon came to a rutted road dusted with snow that went north and south. Following the road north, they came to an intersection that went east towards the berm. The closer they came to the berm, the more distinct it became until they saw that it was a palisade rampart with a thick timber front with a gate across the road.

They were seen well before they arrived at the gate.

Standing above them behind the palisade, the guard frowned at them before scanning the land behind them.

"Who are you?"

"We are cold and weary travelers," Tone replied, in Old Norse. "Is there some place within the walls that will offer us food and warmth?"

His frown deepened. "You're alone?"

"Yes. We were waylaid by thieves who managed to make off with our wagon and goods."

The guard cocked an eyebrow. "You fought them off by yourselves?"

"Yes," Siv boldly stated, striding up to the gate, forcing the man to bend his head to stare down at her. "My friend here is a shield maiden."

"I knew that by the way she's dressed," he retorted. "Not many women dress up in men's clothes."

"Then you know she is a skilled fighter. Once again, is there food and drink available?"

The guard warily regarded them. "Where were you headed?"

"Why do you persist in asking foolish questions," Siv demanded.

"Because we like to know who we let in. Now answer the question."

"We are headed to Kaupang –"

"Kaupang?" the guard snorted a laugh. "Woman, you aren't even close."

"Where are we then?"

"You don't know?" he mocked.

"Like I said," Siv answered, assuming a condescending attitude, "we were attacked."

"What about your guards?"

"They were part of the thieves' gang."

The guard sniffed in disbelief. "You expect me to believe that?"

"Enough," Tone exploded. "Are you going to open this damned gate or am I going to have to climb up there and rip your heart out?"

Startled, the guard sized her up, unimpressed with her size, but unsure of the threat. "Now just hold on there –"

"Hold on?" Tone snapped. "You see two women out here with no one else around and you're asking a lot of stupid questions. You're either an idiot or a fool. Which is it?"

His lips pursed, the guard descended and opened the gate.

"Thank you," Tone tartly said. "Now where are we?"

"Hedeby," the guard answered, shaking his head.

"Hedeby?" Tone exclaimed.

"Excellent," Siv interrupted, grabbing Tone's arm. "This is where we were headed to begin with. We're right where we wanted to be. What luck."

"Yes," Tone flatly responded, giving Siv a quizzical glance, "what luck."

"Come then," Siv urged. "I'm hungry."

Leaving the flustered guard to close the gate, Siv headed towards the small trading village of Hedeby, which was just beginning to flourish.

"We're not even close to Kaupang," Tone bemoaned, walking beside her. "My God, I'm not even sure we're at the right time."

"We've got a day or two before the machine goes back. Let's find out for sure before we abort this adventure. We can handle the wrong place at the right time."

"You're right," Tone said, her confidence returning.

The gap between the wall and Hedeby consisted of fallow fields covered in snow. Hedeby itself was a collection of single story thatched-roof buildings crowded close to the shore where several piers jutted out into the water. Activity by the piers indicated the town was awake and doing business, despite the time of the year.

As they passed by a house, a woman opened the door, a breakfast scrap bowl in hand. Seeing the two women, she paused and stared at them.

"Pardon, my lady," Siv said, "but is there a place close by for food and warmth?"

"Two houses down on the left," she stonily replied, tossing the scrapes into the yard.

Siv started to say, "Thank you," but the woman disappeared back inside.

"Downright friendly," Tone chuckled.

Two houses down was an ale house. Conversations stopped when the two women entered. Ignoring the overt stares and ogling, Tone quickly scanned the half-filled room, finding an empty table close to the far wall.

The aroma of stew covered the odor of unwashed bodies. The proprietor, a stout man with auburn hair held back in a ponytail and an unkempt full beard, bustled over and placed two bowls of stew on the table, along with a half loaf of day old bread and a slab of cheese.

"What would you like to drink?" His gaze had a subtle lasciviousness to it.

"What are the choices?" Tone asked.

"Milk, buttermilk or ale."

Unsure of the sanitary status of the milk, Tone shot a glance at Siv before answering, "Ale."

"Me too," Siv said.

As the proprietor ambled away, a man at an adjacent table tapped his table mate on the arm and leaned back to give Tone an unfriendly stare. He was a palm's width taller than Tone, with a wiry frame of one used to labor.

"Why are you dressed like a man?"

Tone returned the stare and without missing a beat said, "Why are *you* dressed like a man?"

The titters at the surrounding tables caused the man the man to bow up.

"Because I *am* a man."

Tone rolled her eyes and sighed loudly, playing to the audience before directing her attention to the man. "How often have I heard that only to discover he needed two hands to find it."

The room erupted in laughter as the man shot up out of his seat.

Amidst the catcalls and jeering, the proprietor strode over to confront the man. "Sit down Dag. I'll not have you chasing my customers away." Turning to Tone and Siv, he placed the mugs of ale on the table. "Ignore him. Where are you from?"

"Ulleval," Tone replied.

The man blinked in ignorance. "Never heard of it."

"It's in Vingulmork, north across the sea from here."

"What are you doing here?"

"We are returning from a journey in the south."

When she didn't explain more, he asked, "Where are your guards, your escort?"

"Our guards turned out to be thieves," Siv chimed in. "We had hired them in Hanover, on the recommendation of a man we trusted. Little did we know that we would be robbed and nearly killed."

"Don't worry," Tone reassured him when she saw his expression turn cold, "we can pay for our meal."

The man relaxed. "You are heading back home?"

"Yes."

The proprietor looked at Tone and half-smiled. "I must ask, but why *are* you dressed as a man?"

"I am a shield-maiden," Tone said with a frustrated shake if her head. "I am here to protect my friend."

"A shield-maiden?" Dag sneered. "I bet I could take you with one hand."

"I accept." Tone leveled a hard stare at him.

"Huh?"

"I said I accept your wager."

"But… but…"

Tone addressed those in the room. "You heard him. He bet that he could beat me with one hand." She shifted her attention to Dag. "How much are you willing to wager?"

"I… but…"

"I heard him," a voice jested. Others joined in calling for Dag to make good on his bet.

"To be fair," Tone said, still looking at Dag, "I'll make it easier for you. You can use two hands. I'll wager our meal. Well?"

Dag thrust back from the table and stood. "Alright. You want to play games. I'm your man. Choose your weapon."

"No weapons," Tone coolly said. "Just hands and feet and hips and whatever else you want to use that is a part of your body."

"You're serious?" Dag chortled. "Then I accept."

"Not in here," the proprietor exclaimed. "Take it outside."

As the patrons rose en masse and pushed through the door to watch, Siv leaned over to Tone and whispered in English, "You sure about this?"

"Let's hope," Tone grinned.

Once outside, the patrons formed a large circle in the middle of the main street. Dag stood in the center, his outer cloak held by another. Tone entered the ring, handing her outer cloak and backpack to Siv.

"Guard it with your life," she warned, reminding Siv of the wealth in the pack.

Siv slipped it over her shoulders, feeling the weight of all the coins.

A low murmur of humor and expectation settled on the crowd as more town folk and others joined in to see what was happening.

Tone and Dag faced one another about four paces apart, carefully measuring each other. Dag moved first, feinting left then right, moving in closer. He was in the act of closing the gap when Tone spun around, leaping into the air with a spinning hook kick to the head that sent him crashing to the hard cold ground.

The good natured murmuring stilled as the shock of her speed and delivery caught the crowd by surprise, though not nearly the surprise that Dag had experienced. Still seeing stars, he wobbly forced himself to standing to confront his opponent. Though momentarily shaken, he knew he was stronger than her and figured if he could grab hold of her, his strength would overpower her.

Raising his hands to grab her, he misjudged the gap and her speed as she delivered a jumping double roundhouse kick to his head causing a minor whiplash that left him momentarily standing before collapsing in place. As Dag's friend bent down to check on him, Tone located the proprietor who had left the warmth of the alehouse to not miss the excitement.

She hooked a thumb to the fallen Dag. "Our meal is on him."

"Someone help me drag him inside," the friend said, shaking his head. Two patrons bent down to help lift the limp Dag and carried him inside the alehouse, dumping him back into his chair

When Tone and Siv returned to their table, the other patrons regarded them with newfound respect and awe.

A man scooted a chair out and sat down at Dag's table though his attention was on Tone. He was an attractive man with a chiseled face partially hidden beneath a rust colored beard. "You fight like nothing I've ever seen."

"Thank you." She gave him a friendly nod and resumed eating. Pausing, spoon in hand, she knitted her brow at him. "With all the confusion these past several days, we've sort of lost track of time. Is today laugardagr or sunnudagr?"

"Sunnudagr."

"The seventh day of Mörsugur?"

The man cocked an eyebrow. "Yes. How long have you been traveling?"

Tone rolled her eyes. "A very long time. After a while the days run into each other. We're both ready to get back home."

The man smiled. "I understand." His attention was diverted when a friend scooted a chair out to sit next to him.

Her face awash with relief, Tone leaned in to Siv and whispered, "We're good. Today's Sunday, December 21st. Let's pray the time is also right."

When the man turned back to Tone, she couldn't help but notice his attention diverted to the backpack before resuming his friendly conversation.

"I heard you say you were from across the sea."

"That's correct."

"Surely you know there is no one here who will brave the winter seas for little or no profit."

"We know," Siv nodded, wondering why this man was so interested. "Once we are fed and warmed, we will need to find a place to stay."

"You will stay over the winter?" He seemed surprised.

"What else do you suggest?"

"If you had your own ship and crew..." he let the sentence hang.

Tone snorted a laugh. "First, *if* we had our own ship and crew we wouldn't be here. Second, since we *are* here it's obvious we can't afford a ship and crew. Third, like you said, only fools try to brave the winter seas."

Unaffected by her brusque response, he smiled. "Yet there are occasional fools who *do* brave the winter seas... for the right price."

Tone studied the man, wondering what his game was. She became keenly aware of the backpack and his attention to it. The scenario suddenly crystalized. The man would offer to sail them across the sea for a price. They wouldn't be more than an hour's sail into the journey when she and Siv would be tossed overboard or killed.

"I suppose you know such a fool?" Tone said with a chuckle.

"I might."

"You might or you do?" she challenged. "If you don't, then don't waste our time with empty promises."

Her assertiveness startled the man, but he quickly regained his composure. "I do."

"Am I talking to the owner or merely a crew member?"

"The owner."

"Does the owner have a name?"

"I am called Steiner. And you?"

"I am Tone and this is Siv. How soon can you be ready to sail?"

Steiner laughed. "A day or two. I've got to collect men who are willing to risk the sea."

"Tell them they will be well rewarded, which reminds me, we have not talked price. Why are you so willing to take the risk?"

Steiner did his best to keep his eyes off the backpack, having already surmised it contained things of great value, especially with the way the one called Tone guarded it.

"Ten gold a piece."

Siv's eyes shot wide. "Ten gold. For ten gold a piece we can comfortably wait out the winter and in the meantime find someone far less expensive."

Tone leaned forward, locking her gaze upon him. "I see the way you stare at my pack. You believe there is great fortune in it. Do not be deceived. Why do you think I was so willing to fight the unfortunate Dag."

Steiner's expression morphed from arrogance to irritation as he suddenly realized the women were probably nothing more than hustlers with Tone fighting unsuspecting men to earn enough for meals. The bag was nothing more than a ploy. Its heaviness was probably due to stones.

Smiling with only his lips, he dipped his head. "I understand. Well, good fortune to you then."

Tone smiled at him, pleased with the deflection as he turned around and became engrossed in conversation with his friend.

"What are we going to do?" Siv asked.

Tone glanced around the room. Either their presence was purposely being ignored or the two women had been reluctantly accepted as the surreptitious and overt glances diminished as men finished their meals and left.

Lowering her voice, she confided, "I like his idea of getting a boat. That's going to be the fastest way to Kaupang."

"Also the most dangerous," Siv pointed out.

"I know," Tone sighed, "but now that we're here, I'm not going to wait another three or four months to start again. We need to find someone we can trust."

"Easier said than done."

"We'll find him," Tone asserted, though not quite so convinced.

Chapter 11

I write this as a free man traveling north on business. I am full of joy at what has happened in my life. I have to remind myself that it was little more than six months ago that I was a monk on Lindisfarne, blind to the world around me. I see it now for what God had in store for me. What were the chances of an attack by these barbarians (I suppose I must learn to guard my tongue for I am now a citizen of these barbarians – does that make me a savage like them? May it never be. I will lead them to the true God and they and He will bless me for it.)

Yet I am not without guilt, especially when I see my former brothers toiling under the heavy yoke of slavery. I have seen Brother Hugh since my liberation. Though he says he is happy for me in my freedom, I can feel the looks he gives me behind my back. I saw it in his eyes when he asked me why I had renounced my faith. When I tried to explain that I had not renounced my faith but merely renounced my calling to the priesthood, he refused to listen, instead becoming too stiff-necked and stubborn, calling me names. It was there and then that I reminded him that he couldn't talk to me that way, that he forgot who I am now. I am a free man, a business man here in Kaupang and he was just a slave – that if he didn't watch his tongue, I'd have him punished. I am disappointed because I had liked Hugh. But I cannot let the past control my future.

When I saw his reaction, I knew I could not tell him that not only was I not going to become a priest, I was going to take a wife. Harek has seen the way Alvi and I are and sat me down to have a man-to-man talk. He came right out and asked me what my intentions were. I told him that I was going to be the best bead maker and business man (except for him, of course) that there ever was here because I was going to pay attention and learn all I could from him so that when he was ready to let go and enjoy his old age, I would be there to provide for everything he could want.

Naturally he was quite pleased. It was then he brought up Alvi and asked me what I thought of her. I told him she was the most beautiful and smartest girl I've ever met. I didn't tell him that I really haven't met a whole lot of girls. Being a monk does have its restrictions. But he was pleased and said that though there were other men who had approached him, he believed she and I would be an excellent match.

I immediately said I would be the best husband she ever had. He said something about hoping I'd be the only one she ever had and laughed. It didn't make sense to me because of course I would be the only husband she would have.

Once the agreement was settled, we had a family feast and he told me about my first business mission. Here I am traveling north to visit Jarl Halfdan's sister to show her some of the necklaces and bracelets I made as well as some that Harek made. I must admit that Harek has a gifted eye, for his jewelry is delicate and fine. Though he complimented me on my skills, I know I have a long way to go to match his talent.

December 21, 793
Hedeby

Tone stood and stretched. Warm and fed, she was ready to discover their options in getting to Kaupang. Glancing back at Siv who was sipping the last of her ale, she said, "The first thing we need to do is find men we can trust who would be willing to sail to Kaupang."

"You mean the first thing we need to do is find a place to stay," Siv corrected.

"Touché," Tone smiled. "The second thing we need to do is find men willing to sail to Kaupang."

"You won't find anyone here," the owner said, overhearing her. "Dangerous sailing this time of year."

"Why?"

"Ice," a patron interjected.

Tone turned to look at the speaker. He was a brawny red-head with a full beard, a little taller than she was.

"Ice?"

The man cocked an eyebrow at her. "Where did you say you were from?"

"Ulleval," Tone replied.

"Where is that?"

"In Vingulmork, north across the sea."

"And you don't know about ice floating in the sea, ice that can damage and sink ships?" He regarded her suspiciously.

Tone stared dumbly at him before understanding hit. "Oh, you mean icebergs."

"Icebergs?"

"That is what we call them – ice mountains. Very treacherous because what's visible is only a small portion of what is actually floating in the water. When you said 'ice,' I was thinking of the ice that some people put in their drinks to make them cold. Some even put ice in mead." She shook her head and curled a lip. "While I like my mead cold, putting ice in it ruins the taste."

The man relaxed and chuckled. "I have seen children put ice in their buttermilk."

"Me too," she said with a smile. "What has the weather been here? It was warmer than normal when we were traveling north.   Warmer weather usually means fewer icebergs."

"Ah," the man nodded in appreciation. "I see you do understand. But you are correct. The weather has been warmer, but that doesn't mean that men want to test the water. My suggestion is that you wait until the winter ends."

"I can't wait that long," she replied.

"Why not."

Tone gazed directly at him. "I have a husband waiting for me."

Erik stood outside his longhouse, staring across the water, wondering what Tone was doing right this very instant. Was she still asleep? Had she found a job? What was she making for breakfast? Was she still living in his house, their house? Did she still sleep on her side of the bed? Had someone else captured her interest?

His mood turned dark at the thought that someone else might be joining her in his bed. He immediately berated himself for thinking such thoughts, especially since they had pledged their eternal undying love for each other. But the thought nagged him, especially if Tone thought he was dead.

The door opened and Magnus emerged.

"See anything interesting?"

"Just wondering how long Torben's spiked fence will last," Erik lied.

Magnus looked over to where two docks jutted into a shallow inlet. Spiked stakes jammed into the seabed in a straight line began at each dock and ended at the shore line, the pointed tips just below the water line.

"How long does it need to last?"

"I don't know," Erik chuckled, "but it gave them something to do, something they felt was important."

Magnus smiled and nodded, shivering in the cold morning air. "I wonder what it would be like to live in a place where it was warm all the time."

"Like Jamaica?" Erik replied without thinking.

"Jamaica?"

"It's an island far away where the sun shines all the time and the water is so clear you can see down to the bottom even when you're far enough away in a longship that you can't see the person on the beach waving at you."

"And the women?" Magnus grinned, liking the story.

"Ah," Erik sighed. "All of them beautiful and desirable. All day long you sit on the beach, in a chair with a thin roof over your head to protect you from too much sun and the women bring you exotic drinks you've never heard of, sweet with strange delicious fruit in them. And when the sun is past midday, you stretch out on a soft cushioned table where the women massage your body. Finally, in the evenings, they build a fire and the women dance for you."

Magnus burst a laugh. "I should like very much to go to a place like this."

Erik grinned back at him. "Wouldn't we all."

"I have not heard this myth before."

Erik shrugged. "It's a place I've heard tales about, most of them too good to be true. Who knows? Maybe the island exists, though we'd probably have to sail far to find a place that's warm all the time."

"We'd have to leave all this behind." Magnus swept a hand at the surrounding farm.

"Which reminds me," Erik said. "We need to send out scouting parties beyond Hønefoss, especially along the western shore."

"What do we do if we encounter anyone?"

"We're hunting," Erik answered.

"How many on the patrol?"

"You decide, Magnus. Figure we need enough behind here to handle any problems that might surprise us."

"You want me to go or stay?"

"I'd prefer you to stay, but I'll leave that choice to you as you know best what should be done."

Magnus did his best to hide his pleasure with Erik's overt trust, so unlike Eystein who stuck his nose into everything, demanding it be done his way.

"I'll send Torben and several others."

"Torben again, eh?" Erik smiled.

"The man is taking great pains to be noticed and trusted. He's also responsible and the men like him."

Erik patted him on the shoulder. "Make it so, number one."

Magnus smiled and frowned at the same time, unsure what Erik meant.

The man frowned in astonishment at Tone. "Your husband let you go alone?"

"He goes alone when he goes raiding," she argued, "though to be accurate, he's not actually alone in the sense of being by himself. But he's alone as in without me." She stared intently at him. "My guess is that you don't think women can take care of themselves."

The man cocked an eyebrow, the answer obvious. "When it comes to fighting, of course not. Women aren't meant to fight. That's man's work."

"And all women are good for is making babies and cooking your meals," Siv goaded.

"Pretty much," the man agreed.

Siv sat back, shaking her head. "Did you not see her fight?"

"Yes, but she's not normal... I mean she's not typical. I've never met a woman who fights, let alone one who fights like she does."

"So who takes care of the farm or business when the men are off raiding?"

"The woman does."

"So she manages the farm while you're away, which means she has to be smart in order to take care of everything," Siv argued.

"I never said women aren't smart," he argued back. "I just said that war and fighting are men's work. Same thing when it comes to Idrótter, except maybe chess. Men will always surpass women in Idrótter. We are stronger so we can run faster, swim faster and longer, dive deeper, climb higher, shoot arrows better, throw spears farther and more. Let me ask you a question. Why are all the great scalds men?"

"Because you've relegated women to the hearth," Siv shot back. "While the men are sitting around getting drunk and making up poems and sagas, women are doing the work of feeding and caring for you oafs."

The man shot her a stern glare before morphing into laughter. "Are you married?"

Siv paused before self-consciously saying, "No."

"No wonder. You've got a mind of your own."

"And why shouldn't I?" she challenged.

The man held up his hands in defeat. "Never said you shouldn't." He turned to Tone. "Where did you say you were before here?"

"I didn't. But to answer your question, we were on a sort of pilgrimage down south towards the city of Rome. Wanted to check out this new god of the Christians."

"Why didn't your husband go?"

"He'd rather go raiding."

"Smart man."

Ignoring him, Tone turned to the owner. "Do you know a place where we can stay?"

"I have a room here."

"We can pay," she said then glanced around the room, "unless I can find another unsuspecting fool."

"How long will you stay?"

"As long as it takes to find a ship going north."

"That could be months," he said, counting on his fingers and adding up the cost.

"We'll see. Let's start with seven days."

"Perhaps I can help," the man interrupted. "My name is Hauk Mostrsson. I own a farm about ten days north of here. I have a longship that is in storage for the winter. I will make you a proposition. If the weather stays warmer like it is for the next ten days, I will offer my longship to take you across, provided you can pay."

Tone heart quickened. "We can pay, depending on how much," she quickly added.

"It will be fair."

"How do we know we can trust you?" Siv asked.

"First, because I am an honest man."

"I agree," the proprietor added with a quick head dip. "He is."

Hauk focused his attention on Siv. "Second, unlike those you hired before, I don't attack women. Obviously those men you hired were not Ostmen. We respect women and children."

"And if the weather doesn't stay warmer?" Siv interrupted.

"Then you can be my guests," he grinned broadly.

Tone glanced at Siv who barely ticked her head before turning to Hauk. "We accept. When do we leave?"

"Whoa," he laughed. "I got some business to settle first. We'll leave first thing in the morning."

Daylight had yet to rim the sky when Tone and Siv set out with Hauk and several of his men, including Dag whose cold glare said he had not yet forgiven Tone for his smack-down. Bundled up in warm clothing and a thick woolen blanket, Tone and Siv sat in the back of the second wagon as it lumbered away from Hedeby to the main cart path that ran north and south in Daneland.

"Where is your farm?" Tone asked Hauk who walked beside the wagon.

"It's in the Hornøg herreder."

Tone frowned at the unfamiliar term, wondering how she could find out without raising suspicion, when Siv came to her rescue.

"That's very far north, isn't it," Siv inquired, "north of Aarhus."

"Yes," he half- smiled at her, "though we pronounce it Arus. My farm is much closer to Aalborg. You can walk to the town quicker than it takes to milk a cow."

"That's pretty close," Siv laughed, noting the way Hauk looked at her with more than just polite interest. While Hauk wasn't bad looking, he didn't quite measure up to what she had in mind for her rugged handsome Viking.

"Who manages your farm while you're down here?" Tone asked.

"My children," he proudly replied. "My oldest son is nearly fifteen winters. He's old and strong enough now to go raiding."

"Will you let him?"

Hauk's look said it was a stupid question. "Of course. Why wouldn't I?"

"Possibility he could get hurt."

337

"He could get hurt around the farm," he pointed out. "Besides, all real men cut their teeth on raiding."

"What about your wife," Siv interrupted. "Doesn't she have a say in this?"

Hauk's face softened. "She died in the last childbirth five years ago, both her and the baby."

"I'm so sorry."

"No need to be," he kindly replied. "She left me with three wonderful sons."

"Has it been hard raising them by yourself?"

"At first, but then I figured they were my sons and they would turn out well enough. They work hard and they're obedient. Not like some of them other sons who think they're smarter than their Papa."

Tone gazed out over the flat terrain, devoid of color. A blanket of half-melted snow, frozen from the night before, spread out on both sides of the road.

"It's going to be a long ride," she commented with a resigned sigh, imagining ten days of this snail's pace, looking at the repetitive scenery.

"We'll pass the time getting to know each other," Hauk cheerily replied. "It'll make the time go by faster." He looked at Tone first. "So tell me all about yourself. Where are you from and where did you learn your fighting?"

Tone had rehearsed her cover story and as she began, it flowed with an easy comfort as though she were actually telling the truth.

"I'm from Ulleval like I said before. My father was a farmer."

"Was?" Hauk said.

"He was killed in one of the never ending foolishness of Idrótter."

"It's not foolishness," Hauk argued.

338

"It is when it gets carried away to extremes. Men have such pride that they can't stand to lose even if it is to a better man." She held up a hand. "Before you ask, I will tell you. He was the strongest of swimmers. Like a fish he swam, he was so fast. Strong arms and broad shoulders that would cleave the water like a longship."

"You are a poet," Hauk chuckled.

"I'll leave that to the skalds," she smiled. "But what happened was that a man thought he was better than my father and challenged him. The whole vil came out to watch. The result was embarrassment for the challenger, for he lost poorly. Unhappy with his glaring defeat, he and several friends ambushed my father and killed him. I was ten winters old when it happened."

"Were they caught and punished?"

"Three escaped before their foul deed was discovered. One man was the fool and thought that staying behind and pretending he knew nothing would absolve him. It was only a matter of time before the truth came out. He was dealt with. Since that time, I have spent it searching to find my father's killers and have my justice."

Hauk studied her a bit before asking, "Where did you learn to fight like you do?"

"I have traveled and studied various fighting styles and found one suited to my abilities."

Hauk nodded in appreciation. "Perhaps you should offer your services to a jarl. He might be able to help you find your father's killers."

Tone nodded in agreement. "I have thought of that, but it would mean being away from my husband for too long and I am unwilling to do that."

Hauk smiled in understanding then turned to Siv. "And what about you? What will you tell me about yourself?"

Siv shot a glance at Tone who gave her a nod of encouragement. "I'm from Bjerke, which is close to Ulleval. My parents own a large farm near the lake Maridalsvannet."

Tone sat back and listened, impressed with Siv's tale, though not as impressed as Hauk appeared to be.

Sitting by the fire pit in Kolga's house, Erik's eyes lit up when the door opened and a young man he recognized walked in.

"Pearson. It's good to see you." He noted the way the young man was dressed as well as the way he carried himself and knew immediately something good had happened.

Pearson was equally pleased and crossed the floor to Erik. "I was wondering why I hadn't seen you around Kaupang." He was about to add 'What are you doing here?' when he caught himself, knowing full well why Erik was with Kolga.

Remembering his manners, he turned to Kolga and respectfully dipped his head. "Lady Kolga. I am Pearson, Harek the bead maker's assistant. He sent me here to show you some of the latest creations."

"Assistant," Erik repeated with a smile. "Well done."

Kolga shifted a quizzical glance between the two men. "Obviously you two know each other."

"I had the good fortune of meeting Pearson when I went into Kaupang one day. He was working for Harek. At that time, he was just another worker." Erik saw Pearson tense up then relax when Erik specifically said nothing about this slave status. "That Harek made him his assistant is quite an honor."

"Thank you," Pearson said, obviously pleased.

"Not that I don't find jewelry absolutely fascinating," Erik said standing, "but I really do need to get back. When you're finished here," he said to Pearson, "stop by my place. You can spend the night before heading back tomorrow."

"You're leaving?" Kolga complained with furrowed brow, irritated this newcomer had interrupted what had been heading towards an intimate discussion.

"Yes," Erik replied with a smile. "I've got a farm to run and part of Halfdan's kingdom to protect." He turned to Pearson. "Kolga can point you to where I live. I look forward to visiting with you."

"Thank you," Pearson said, awed by Erik's graciousness.

Two hours later, Pearson arrived at Erik's longhouse and spent the evening relating the change in his status and fortune, the engagement to Alvi, as well as the disappointment to the reaction of the other brothers who castigated him for his renunciation of the faith.

"Remember who God chose," Erik said, imparting wisdom. "What happened to Joseph's brothers?"

Pearson thought for a moment before a smile curled the corners of his lips. "They came begging to Joseph for food."

Erik sat back, splaying his hands with a 'need-I-say-more' look.

Pearson heaved a sigh of relief. "Thank you so much for everything you've done for me."

"Now, now," Erik grinned, "let's not get carried away. All I did was point out the possibilities. You and God did the rest. You're a smart man and thankfully Harek saw that immediately. You have talent and the ability to go far. Don't let anyone hold you back, especially those who are jealous of your good fortune. Who knows, maybe there will come a time when you will provide for them."

Pearson nodded then shook his head, overwhelmed at the change in circumstances. "Some accused me of too easily abandoning my faith. I have thought long and hard about it.

It is true that I was happy where I was on Lindisfarne. Life seemed so simple and I believed I had a calling."

"Then everything changed just like that." Erik snapped his fingers. "Trust me, I know how you feel." *Not only did I lose a job, I've now lost the love of my life.* "Things happen and it's up to us to make the best of the situations. Whether you realize it or not, I was visiting the monastery when the attack happened. The only reason I am alive is because of my fighting skills. This isn't where I expected to be at this time in my life, but here I am, a wealthy farmer with Jarl Halfdan as a friend." He pointed to where Magnus sat and talked with several other hirdmen. "And I also have the friendship of that man and many others. So like you, I too am blessed. But tell me of the fair lady named Alvi."

Pearson's eyes brightened and he gushed, "She is the most beautiful woman I have ever seen."

While Pearson acclaimed the innumerable virtues of his love, Erik half-listened as he ruminated on the similarities and aching absence of his own true love.

It was well after the evening meal when the door opened and Torben entered, followed by three more hirdmen. Stamping his feet at the doorway, he searched to room for Erik, finding him talking to a young man better suited for farming than fighting. Magnus sat next to him.

"What news, Torben?" Erik called out.

"It's quiet," he said, walking over, "too quiet if you ask me."

"What's your gut feeling?"

Instead of answering directly, Torben explained, "We headed west once we got past Hønefoss, following the river that runs between the hills. After a while, we headed south into the forest and worked our way down towards Tyristrand just across the water from here, then back along the coast up to Hønefoss and back here. If someone was to ask me if I saw anything, I'd have to honestly say 'no.' But that's the problem. While we saw nothing, I got the sense that we were being watched. Maybe it's just my imagination, but I've got a feeling something's gonna happen soon."

"Good report," Erik complimented, "and I agree with you, which means we have to be even more vigilant. My thought is that they will attack when we least expect it. They'll come by land and wait until everyone's asleep then torch the place."

"How many will come?" Magnus asked.

"They already know how many we have here," Erik reasoned. "Figure at least twice that many."

"I don't think they will have that many," Magus politely disagreed.

"No?"

"They earn no glory if the fight is not equal, though I would not put it past them to want to burn the longhouse with us in it. My thought is that they will announce their presence and still burn the longhouse. While we all run out, they will fight us one at a time."

Erik glanced over to see Pearson's face flushed with fear. "Don't worry Pearson. They won't bother you. Oh," he said turning to Torben, "this is Pearson, a merchant friend from Kaupang."

Pearson's fears momentarily evaporated as he preened at the title as well as Erik calling him 'friend.'

"Merchant?" Torben repeated, puzzled. "What do you sell?"

"Necklaces, bracelets, things like that," Pearson answered.

"Don't see much of a demand for that here," Torben said, glancing around at the other hirdmen.

343

"I was here to show Kolga what we had. Tomorrow I'll go by Hønefoss before heading back home."

"Ah," Torben nodded. "Perhaps you could pass on to Halfdan our situation."

"Halfdan's already aware," Erik interjected, giving Torben a look that said not to meddle.

"We still have another group out scouting," Magnus said, redirecting the conversation. "They should be back in a day or two."

"Then we wait," Erik said, "until they come back. For now, fill your mug with mead and relax. In the morning, we've a lot of work to do while we wait."

Professor Johans Kallevig sat in his studio, puzzled to receive what looked to be an official letter from a lawyer's office in the United States. Opening the letter, his bewilderment turned to snarled anger when he read that Simon, Wellington & Romero had been retained by Tone Thorgilsdottir concerning the possession and use of all photographs taken during the month of December 2031. Their client exerted her rights per the signed agreement that no photograph of her may be used in any form or format without her express written consent. Any attempt to publish, display in any manner, share, or distribute said photographs constituted a breach of contract and would be subject to litigation.

His jaw clenched, Kallevig read the rest of the legal notification, immediately realizing that Tone had no intention of letting him publish the photos. The epiphany burst that not only was he out $2 million, there was nothing he could do about it. His first instinct was to go ahead and publish the photos and suffer the consequences. But he quickly nixed that idea, knowing full well that it would end up costing him more than the $2 million, not to mention the adverse publicity which would severely impact his future business.

Why would she do this?

Kallevig pulled up the model files on his desktop computer and scrolled down to Tone's file, opening up the contract file and rereading the agreement. It was just like all the other contracts except for the part that she added stating that she had to agree to the specific photos to be published. But it also added that they would keep taking photos until she found some she liked.

He sat back and smiled. Here was his payback. Contractually, she was lawfully required to continue posing until such time as she liked the pictures, which meant two things: first, she had to pose nude for him – on a regular basis – even if the pics were never published, and second, unless she wanted to pose indefinitely, she would finally have to agree to publish.

But why this absurd game? What was the point?

His questions were answered several days later with a phone call from TTI, requesting a meeting with a Meredith Allen, the VP for Marketing and External Affairs. She was flying in the next day.

"What is this about?"

"It will be explained in better detail tomorrow," the TTI rep stated. "But to give you a brief idea, it concerns your linguistic skills in Old Norse."

"Huh?"

"You do speak old Norse, correct?"

"Yes."

"Excellent. We look forward to meeting with you."

Kallevig wasn't sure what to expect, especially not the attractive brunette who showed up on his doorstep the next day. A likewise attractive assistant carrying a briefcase stood behind her.

"Mister Kallevig? I'm Meredith Allen." She stuck out her hand. "This is my administrative assistant Emma."

Kallevig shook hands, noticing the firm grim within soft hands. His photographer instinct took over and he quickly sized her up: height, about 5' 6"; slender; angular face with smooth skin, framed well by thick hair that fell to her shoulders; bright brown eyes that were too professional at the moment; the business suit was snug over medium sized breasts, most likely a 34-C; overall a nice figure. He wondered what she would be like nude. Would she still have this CEO all-business aura?

Emma, the assistant, looked and acted very much like her boss, causing him to wonder if there was anything sexual between them.

"May we come in?" Meredith asked, interrupting his reverie.

"Of course, please come in." He suavely stepped aside and opened the door. "Can I get you anything to drink?"

"Coffee if you have it."

"Emma?" he politely inquired.

"Coffee, if it's not too much trouble."

"None at all. Have a seat in the dining room. I'll be right back."

When he returned, carrying a tray with three cups, cream and sugar, Meredith and Emma were on one side of the table, a folder to the side of the briefcase.

"Let's dispense with the pleasantries and get down to why we're here," Meredith said, accepting the cup of coffee.

"Why *are* you here?" Kallevig sat opposite them, stirring the cream in his coffee.

"We're here concerning Tone Thorgilsdottir."

Kallevig sat up. "What about her?"

"She's gone back in time," Emma chirped, causing Kallevig's eyes to blink wide before settling into a scowl.

Meredith explained the episode of Tone's and Siv's scheme to go back in time to find Erik.

"That Bi —" he started then remembered his guests. "Pardon me."

"We understand completely," Meredith tersely said. "The reason we're here is that we want you to help us get them back."

Kallevig immediately understood. "Who else is going back?"

Meredith smiled and nodded appreciatively. The man had immediately grasped the significance of the mission.

"There will be four of you, two linguists and two facilitators."

"Facilitators?" Kallevig repeated with a grin.

"That's the euphemism we're using," she said, returning his smile.

"How's this work?" He took a sip of coffee. "From what I understand, trips only last a day. It's highly unlikely we'd find them in a day."

"You're correct," Meredith said. "However, the machine has the capability of remaining in place for an indeterminate amount of time. Second, we have a good idea where they might be."

"You do?"

"Kaupang, 793 CE,"

Frowning, Kallevig placed his coffee mug on the table. "How do you know that?"

"Because that's the location they put into the machine."

Kallevig tilted his head to the side as he pondered aloud. "Why Kaupang?"

"We don't know. We were hoping you might have an idea."

Kallevig shrugged. "My guess would be that after the raid, the Vikings went to Kaupang to trade, assuming the raiders were associated with the rulers in Skiringssal. But really, we have no way of knowing. What makes you think they're still there?"

"We don't but it's a starting point."

"Who's the other Norse scholar?"

"Not sure yet," Meredith evasively answered. "Do you have any suggestions?"

Kallevig thought for a moment. "A colleague of mine, Isak Mathison. He teaches runology. Very knowledgeable. Good linguist. Also physically fit."

"He was our next choice," Meredith smugly grinned.

"When do we leave and how will you work it out with the university? We both have classes this next session."

"Time of departure is TBD," she replied. "We'll work it out with the university. But you need to be available at a moment's notice."

Kallevig sat back, pleased with an opportunity few people experience as well as the satisfaction of seeing the look on Tone's face when he showed up. That was almost worth the $2 million.

"I understand you're a photographer," Meredith said, opening the folder containing the nondisclosure agreement and other contractual obligations.

The question surprised him. Just how much did they know about him? "Yes I am."

"I'm familiar with your work."

Now he was surprised even more. "You are?"

"I have your last book."

Kallevig frowned, struggling to remember her name, but with the sheer volume of subscribers, it was hard to remember everyone's name.

"It was superbly done," she complimented. "You perfectly capture innocence and sensuality."

"Thank you." He smiled at her, wondering where this was going and what did it have to do with Tone. Did she know about his photo session with her? The thought made him nervous, especially in light of the lawyer's threat.

"How do you choose your models?"

Still sorting out the direction of the inquiry, he said, "I look for women who are physically fit and have an aura about them that can be captured on film. Just because a woman is beautiful doesn't mean she can transpose that same aura to film. Simply look at all the narcissistic photos in the public domain, selfies and the like of women, and men, whose absurd posing and clothing is embarrassing. They clog the universe with their feeble attempts at sensuality."

Meredith listened and nodded agreement. Flipping the papers around, she slid them across the table to him. "These are the usual nondisclosure, privacy, and indemnity sort of stuff. The bottom line is that you are not allowed to tell anyone the reason for your travel nor the fact that you were allowed to travel. You can imagine what would happen if word got out that people were availing themselves of the time machine without having to enter the lottery."

"Of course." He read the pages, surprised at how brief each agreement was. Comparable to his own contracts in many ways, he saw nothing unusual and signed, sliding the papers back across the table.

Emma collected the pages, tapping the edges on the table to perfectly align them and placed them back in the folder.

"Now that the portion of business is concluded, Emma and I have another request. How much do you charge for a photo session?"

"Pardon?" he frowned.

"How much do you charge for private photo sessions?" She narrowed her gaze at him, an indulgent smile curling the corners of her mouth.

Kallevig blinked as he made sure he had heard correctly. This would be a first. He had always paid his models, but he had never had someone wanting a private session... and offering to pay for the session. What a great idea. He immediately extrapolated the possibilities as another means of extra income.

"It depends," he hesitated.

"Depends on what?"

My God the woman is direct. I wonder if I could capture that strength. "Depends on what you want and how many final pics you want."

"We want the same results that you achieve with your books."

Kallevig shifted his glance to each woman. They were certainly attractive and it wouldn't take long to capture pics that would satisfy them. Yet he would drag out the session simply for the fun of it.

"One other thing," Emma interrupted, her voice firm and confident. "We want to do it together."

Kallevig sat back with a knowing smile. This day was getting better and better.

Gene folded his arms and grinned with satisfaction. Ever since Tone and Siv had played him, he was focused on revenge and today that vengeance was just about to get some air time. He tapped the vid-screen on his computer.

Cooper's admin assistant appeared. She was a buxom blond with ruby lips, porcelain skin and pampered hair, an image completely at odds with her ruthless efficiency.

"Yes?"

"Tell Mister Cooper that I'm almost there," Gene proudly stated.

"Close only counts in horseshoes, hand grenades and nuclear bombs," she dismissively countered. "Call back when you actually have something."

The screen went blank, momentarily letting the air out of Gene's enthusiasm. Pursing his lips, he turned to his deputy, a young man in his early 20's.

"How long until we achieve time sync?"

"I'd say no more than a month." Using his middle finger, the man pushed his glasses up the bridge of his nose.

"What's the holdup?"

The man shrugged. "Same as it's always been, syncing the time and location. You know better than anyone else the difficulty of time variables and extrapolation; they're geometric. Now add spatial pinpointing and the –"

"You're not answering my question," Gene huffed. "What's the problem?"

The man took off his glasses and rubbed his strained eyes. "We're all tired. We've been at this 24-7 since before Christmas. Some of us haven't had a day off since then."

"Tell them they can rest when they're dead," Gene retorted. "Either that or they can search for employment elsewhere."

Crestfallen, the man turned to go when Gene spoke up.

"Tell them they'll get plenty of time off once we get the machine working like Cooper wants it. If you say we can do it in less than a month, then they should know they'll get a break after that."

The man turned around, a frown creasing his brow. "Why is it so important that it be done right this second?"

"Cooper wants it done," Gene pointedly replied. "That's reason enough."

The man was about to argue when he saw Gene's determined face. "OK."

It was after the man left his office that Gene wondered again if Cooper would let him go back and get Tone. The look on her face would be worth the trip.

Tone stood near the prow of the longship, the curved serpent's head towering above her. In the near distance, the landing point of her quest took form – Kaupang. Hauk had been true to his word and as the weather held mild, he had pulled his boat out of storage and rounded up enough men for the voyage.

The ship was small with only thirteen rowing positions, which meant a crew of twenty-six, each man sitting on his rowing/storage chest, stroking the oars in unison as they navigated around the numerous small islands and up to Kaupangskilen.

It had taken two days of sailing with the first leg of the journey landing them in what was known in modern times as the country of Sweden. From there they sailed and rowed along the coast until they rounded the small peninsula that led to the channel towards Kaupang.

The trip had been uneventful, the only disappointment coming from Hauk when Siv rebuffed his offers of marriage.

'I've a good farm," he argued, "and lots of servants and slaves. I'm a wealthy man." It was when he added, "And you're not getting any younger," that she politely thanked him and said, "I'll think about it."

"Don't think too long," he replied with a wink. "Lots of women would like to be where you're standing."

"I'll keep that in mind." Siv smiled sweetly at him before turning to Tone and in a voice only she could hear, "Shoot me if I even think about reconsidering."

Now, as the gangplank jutted out onto the pier and the two women prepared to leave, Hauk tried one more time.

"You sure you won't change your mind?"

"Yes, I'm sure," she answered. "But I know where you live should I decide otherwise. Thank you for the safe voyage. Best of luck to you."

Pearson arranged the necklaces on the table, his mind distracted. Since returning from Erik's farm and dutifully reporting Erik's dilemma to Halfdan, his mind was diverted with his approaching marriage to Alvi. He was giddy and nervous at the same time. Giddy that he was marrying the most beautiful woman in the world and nervous because he had no clue what to do in the marriage bed when the ceremony concluded.

He had sought Erik's counsel and was rewarded with a wealth of information, but the truth was that he had never seen a woman naked and the thought of copulating both excited and terrified him, for it produced babies and he wasn't ready to be a father. Still, his ignorance and inexperience plagued him. He had prayed daily, in fact several times a day that God would tell him what and how to do it.

So distracted he was that he barely noticed the two women enter the shop. Harek greeted them with enthusiasm though curious one woman was dressed like a man.

"Welcome, welcome. Might I show you some of our latest designs?"

"Actually, we're looking for a man," Tone said. "We've asked other merchants who have heard about him, but do not know where he lives."

"If you tell me his name, perhaps it would make it easier." Harek noted that her accent sounded familiar.

"His name is Erik."

"Erik?" Pearson squeaked.

"Yes. Do you know him?"

"We both know several Eriks," Harek answered, surprised at Pearson's startled reaction.

"This one is tall, handsome and an amazing fighter."

"Ah," Harek nodded. "We know the man and where he lives. Are you friends of his?"

Flooded with excited relief, Tone gave him a broad smile. "I'm his wife."

For the past several days, Erik's scouts reported little activity, causing a false sense of complacency among the hirdmen, which frustrated Erik because he had a gut feeling something significant was about to happen. So much was his unease that he took to spreading his hirdmen out among the various buildings around the farm in the evenings, leaving only himself and Magnus in the longhouse along with the slaves and servants. He made sure the men had plenty of firewood, food and enough ale to stay sober.

"I'm not sure how much longer the men are going to enjoy staying in the other buildings," Magnus observed. "I'm getting rumblings they had better comforts elsewhere."

Erik tugged up the collar of his cloak. The day was cold and bright with a biting wind coming off the water.

"I know, Magnus. We can't keep up this vigilance for too much longer. I know there's nothing happening and that's what concerns me."

Magus nodded agreement. "One would think that one of his spies would have nonchalantly strolled through to see if the number of men here had changed."

"Just a couple more days," Erik said. "Tell them a few more days then we can readjust. At least they're maintaining their swords and axes." Movement from the direction of Kolga's farm caught his eye: three people on horses in the distance were heading towards his farm. Squinting in the sunlight, he tried to make out who they were. One looked like Pearson, but why would he be back?

Tone saw two men standing in front of the longhouse and instinctively recognized the stance and posture of Erik. Kicking her horse to a gallop, she called out at the top of her lungs, "Erik."

Hearing his name upon the wind, Erik frowned, wondering who was on the horse, why was he approaching so fast, and how did he know his name? It was when the rider was within recognizing distance that Erik's heart leaped and he erupted.

"O my God. Tone."

Erik bolted away from the longhouse and raced to intercept her.

With 50 meters separating them, Tone jerked back on the reins, halting her horse and leaped off, racing to meet him.

When they crashed together, enfolding each other as though never to let go, their world exploded in a frenzy of smothering kisses and tears of unbridled joy. By the time they caught their breath, Magnus had arrived as did Pearson and Siv.

Impervious to the others, Erik caressed her cheek. "How did you know where I was?"

"The rune stone," she said, staring devotedly into his eyes, "and Pearson helped." She twisted her head to find him still sitting on his horse.

His arms wrapped around Tone, Erik glanced up at Pearson who grinned with pride then to a very attractive woman who had dismounted and stood by her steed.

Tone saw his look. "That's Siv. She's my best friend. She helped us get here."

"Thank you, Siv," Erik said with heartfelt gratitude. He looked back at Pearson. "Thank you, my friend."

"Who's this?" Tone asked, looking past his shoulder.

Erik turned his head to see Magnus standing close by, a smile on his lips. "That's Magnus, my closest and most trusted friend. Magnus, this is Tone."

"I had assumed something like that," Magnus said with a broad grin. "Since I've never seen you react this way before, I had to assume this was *the* Tone, the one you told me about." Though switching his gaze between Erik and Tone, his attention settled on the gorgeous creature who stood demurely by her horse. He dipped his head in a respectful nod. "Lady Siv."

"Magnus," she replied, taking in the handsome Viking. Though not as tall as Erik, he was certainly very attractive with a calm virility. Suddenly her options looked very good.

"Why don't we go back to the house?" Magnus suggested. "Besides being warmer, there's cold mead."

"Though I would prefer to stay here and enjoy your hospitality," Pearson said, "I need to get back. I left Harek in the middle of inventory." He smiled self-consciously. "And Alvi is waiting for me."

"I understand," Erik answered with a knowing grin. "Are you married then?"

"One more week," he sighed.

"Why the delay?"

"Harek wants a big marriage feast."

"Seems a waste of money," Erik observed.

"That's what I said," Pearson agreed with a shrug, "but Alvi is his only child and he wants to make an impression in the town."

Erik smiled at him. "Give my regards to him when you get back and thank him for letting you come here."

"I will." Pearson pulled the reins, guiding his horse to the right and back down the hill towards Kolga's farm.

Erik's gaze followed him for a bit when he saw another horse and rider approaching in the distance.

"Uh-oh."

Tone turned to see what he was looking at. "What's wrong?"

"Lady Kolga," Magnus solemnly answered.

"Who's she?"

"She owns the farm next to us," Erik replied, struggling to find a plausible explanation as to his and her relationship.

"So?"

"She has a… um, keen interest in Erik," Magnus said as Kolga approached.

"Are you lovers?" Tone asked, gazing up at him, searching his eyes, her heart skipping a nervous beat.

"We were never intimate," Erik said, "but we did enjoy each other's company."

"What does that mean?" She pulled away, raising an eyebrow.

"It means exactly what I said," Erik firmly stated. "I like her and enjoy her company. Though she wanted something more, I was not able to do that. We are friends, though she will not be happy you are here."

"Oh," Tone said, chastised and curious at the same time.

Kolga eased her horse around Siv's steed, slipping effortlessly down from the saddle. Her face a mask of social politeness, she smiled at Erik with only her lips.

"I noticed the commotion over here and decided to find out what was happening." She studied the woman holding Erik's hand. She was very pretty though dressed like a man, which caused Kolga to wonder why.

Before Erik could respond, Tone stepped away towards Kolga. "You're beautiful. I can see why he was attracted to you. I am Tone, Erik's wife."

"Wife?" Kolga took a startled step back then cast an accusing glare at Erik. "You didn't tell me you had a wife."

"I didn't?" Erik blurted, confused.

"You didn't or you didn't want to tell me," she snapped, whirling around and remounting her horse.

"Wait," Erik exclaimed. "It's not what you think."

"You don't know what I think," she seethed. She was about to kick her horse to a gallop when Tone's voice rang out.

"Wait. He's actually correct... to a point. We're betrothed, which is almost like being married."

Kolga's glare transferred to Tone. "Why didn't he tell me this?"

"Probably because he didn't think we would ever see each other again. Now if you'd get down off your proverbial high horse, perhaps we can explain it all."

Kolga hesitated, her anger fusing to overwhelming disappointment. "Why are you dressed like a man?"

"I'm a shield maiden," Tone said, irritated that people kept asking her that. They should know by now.

"You know how to fight?" Kolga's brow furrowed as she extrapolated the possibilities. Perhaps this woman would die in battle, leaving Erik no excuse.

"Yes," Tone confidently replied.

With a longsuffering sigh, Kolga dismounted. "I have heard his side of the tale. It will be interesting to hear your side. He said nothing of you being a shield maiden only that your parents were overprotective, refusing to let you marry."

Tone shot Erik an 'I'm-gonna-need-some-help-keeping-the-story-straight' look.

"I mentioned that nobody was good enough for you, that your parents were constantly trying to coordinate a better arrangement for you, or actually for them," Erik said, taking the cue.

Tone rolled her eyes. "Sheesh. Don't get me started."

"Come," Erik urged. "We can continue the tale back in the house."

Kolga positioned herself on Erik's left while Tone walked on his right, holding tightly onto his hand. Kolga struggled with the urge to hold onto his other hand then decided she had a right based upon their previous closeness and was surprised when Erik did not refuse. If Tone objected, she either chose to ignore it or didn't notice.

Walking behind them, Magnus leaned over to Siv and whispered. "What do you think is going to happen?"

Siv smiled and shook her head. "Tone is the most focused and purpose driven person I've ever met. Nothing will get in the way of what she wants."

Magnus nodded with a paternal smile. "I've heard the same about Kolga."

"Then it should make for some interesting fireworks," she chuckled.

"Fireworks?" he frowned.

Realizing her mistake, Siv quickly explained, "Things you throw into the fire that makes it different colors or cause it to leap up higher."

"Ah, I understand." He walked silently for a few steps. "You are Tone's close friend."

"Yes. She is like a sister to me."

"How long have you known her?"

On guard, Siv thought quickly and decided some of the truth would be easier to remember, hoping that Tone would tell the same tale. "I've only known her for half a year now, though it feels like I've known her my whole life."

"Then you knew she was betrothed."

"Oh yes. He was all she talked about."

"You are a good friend to leave your family behind to help her."

Siv immediately understood the line of questioning, praying that Magnus was not married. "There wasn't much family to leave behind other than parents and brothers."

"You are not married then?" he said, his hopes rising.

"No."

"How is that possible? Your beauty is one of sagas and poetry. Surely there have been plenty of men who have interested you."

"Yes, there have been plenty of men who were interested," she said, "but none were interesting. They were too preoccupied with puffing themselves up, thinking that running fast or wrestling better or some other feat of strength was sufficient to impress me. I'm not saying that those are not important, but I'm looking for a man who has brains inside that head of his. And what about you? Is your family here?"

"I do not have a family," he intoned. "I was one of Eystein's hirdmen until I heard about Erik and knew that I needed to switch my loyalties."

"Who is Eystein?" she asked with a sigh of relief.

"He is Halfdan's brother. He is the Jarl of Hedemark. The other brother, Sigfrig, rules in Raumariki."

"Where does Halfdan rule?"

"His longhouse is in Skiringssal, but he rules the Vestfold, Vestmar and Vingulmork."

"How long have you been with Erik?"

"Less time than you have been with Tone, but enough to feel the way about him as you do with her."

Securing the horses outside, Tone pulled off the saddle bags as they followed Erik into the house where the warmth of the fires was a welcomed respite from the outside cold. Arranging themselves around a table, Erik ticked his hand for the servants to bring the mead.

Turning to Tone, he said, "I told Kolga about how we met in Paris where your parents were plotting their various marriage arrangements within Charles' court and then how we got separated on Lindisfarne. You can fill in what happened after that."

Tone inhaled a deep breath, shaking her head. "I will never forget that day. At one point we were just pilgrims at a monastery and then suddenly we're fighting for our lives."

"I apologize for my brother," Kolga said with honest emotion.

"He didn't know," Tone replied, excusing and forgiving the attack.

"My guards hustled me away, even though I wanted to stay and fight. Erik stayed behind to give us a chance of escape." She turned to look at him, her eyes tearing up. "He stayed behind so that I could live." Wiping the wetness from her eyes, she turned back to Kolga. "We managed to escape across to the mainland, but I refused to go any farther. I had to find out what happened. When we saw the ships sailing away, we went back to the island. I searched among the bodies, but didn't find him. I knew then that he was still alive. I knew I had to find him. My problem was that I didn't know where to start."

By the time Tone finished, Kolga realized she was up against someone more determined and single-mindedly focused than she could ever be. Accepting that, for now, Erik was lost to her, she decided it was time to admit a temporary defeat. It didn't mean she couldn't pray that something would happen to her. Perhaps it was time to visit Folkvi the Volvur. Maybe she might have a spell or a potion that would get rid of Tone.

There was a lull in the tale and Kolga stood. "This has been a most revealing tale, but I really must back to my own farm before it gets too dark." She narrowed her gaze at Tone. "It was a pleasure meeting you, Tone Thorgilsdottir."

It was the way she said it that Tone knew she had not heard the last from Kolga. "It was nice meeting you too. Feel free to stop by anytime."

Kolga recognized the not so subtle barb. Yes, it was definitely time to see Folkvi.

Erik started to stand, but Kolga held up a hand to stop him. "You don't need to see me home... like you usually do. Your friends just got here. Have a good night."

Tone smirked with a silent *touché*. Instead she wiggled her fingers 'goodbye.'

Once Kolga left, the conversation resumed for a while until Magnus decided Erik and Tone needed some alone time.

"I know it's getting dark," he said to Siv, "but I can show you around the farm for a bit." Siv's quizzical look was answered with a tick of his head at Erik and Tone who were staring at each other.

"I'd like that," she answered, getting up.

"Where are you two going?" Erik asked noticing them both standing.

"He's going to show me some of the farm," Siv explained with an innocent smile.

Erik started to ask, 'Why now? It's too dark,' when he saw Magnus' intense stare at him. "Oh, ah certainly. Take your time."

"I need a hot bath," Tone smiled, noting the copper tub was big enough for two.

Ignoring the comment, Magnus said, "I'll alert the rest of the men to the presence of Tone and Siv."

"Thank you." Erik ordered the servants to prepare Tone's bath.

"I could use a hot bath too," Siv said.

"There's another tub in the training room," Magnus said. "I will have that one prepared for you."

"Thank you, Magnus," she sweetly replied, gently touching his arm and sending electric shocks of passion tingling up his arm.

When Magnus and Siv walked out and the servants bustled around heating water, Tone watched them for a bit before turning to Erik. "You said that you and Kolga were never intimate, but did you kiss her?"

Erik paused then said, "Yes."

"A lot?"

"No."

"Why not?"

Erik gazed into her eyes. "Because every time our lips touched, I thought of you. I was torn because I thought I would never see you again. But I was so hopelessly in love with you that I wasn't ready to give up, but I knew the only way for us to see each other again was all on you. I didn't know if you thought I was dead and decided to move on with your life."

Tone scooted closer and kissed him. "There will only ever be you."

"How did you manage to get back here?"

Tone explained about Gene and the time machine and her and Siv's trap for the man, causing Erik to burst a laugh.

"Wonder what's going to happen to him," he mused.

"I figure they're going to send someone after us. He knows we came back to Kaupang because that was what I entered into the destination. Unfortunately it dumped us near Hedeby. We can only hope the same thing happens to them, but we can't count on it."

"How could you afford to buy your way across the water?"

Tone lifted the saddle bags and plopped them on the table. Unlacing the top of one of the bags, she pried it open for Erik to look in.

"My God," he stammered, thrusting a hand in and feeling all the coins and bars. "Did you rob a bank?"

Now it was Tone's turn to pause as she sorted out how to tell him about Kallevig. "I… uh, stumbled upon a means of getting paid for something."

Hearing her evasive reply, he said, "Just tell me."

Tone inhaled then said in a rush, "I posed nude for a man who publishes nude art books."

Erik blinked and cocked an eyebrow. "OK?"

"Nothing ever happened, I swear it."

"He paid you all this just to pose nude?"

"Yes."

"How much?"

"Two million."

Erik sat back, stunned. "He paid you two… million… dollars to pose nude?"

"Yes," she replied, unsure of his reaction.

"Has the book been published?"

"No." She explained about her contract, her lawyers, and the other restrictions, which caused him to burst out laughing.

"He paid you two million dollars and he can never use the pictures." He continued laughing.

"You're not mad?"

"Of course not. What you did was for a greater purpose. I just pray that I am worthy of your love."

Tone flung herself into his arms, crushing herself against him. "O my God I was so afraid you would be mad."

364

Erik reached down and with a gentle knuckle under her chin, lifted her head to gaze into her eyes. "How could I be mad at you? Everything you did was for us. Even if you had robbed a bank or assassinated some country's leader or whatever, you always had me as utmost in your heart and mind. How could I ever be mad at you?" He squeezed her and implanted a deep longing kiss. "I have missed you so much."

"Not as much as I missed you," she teased.

A slave approached, distracting them. Tone glanced up at the attractive woman who looked to be in her late teens or early twenties. She had red hair and a smattering of freckles on her cheeks below her eyes, which were emerald green.

"You bath is ready, mistress."

Tone's first reaction was to ask Erik why he had slaves, but decided to wait. Instead, she extricated herself from his arms and stood, looking around the large longhouse. At one end was a large four-poster bed inside a demarcated area with half-walls topped with curtains that could be pulled closed for more privacy. The bathtub was located near the cooking fire. Steam swirled up from the water, collecting with the smoke-draft that snaked up to the ceiling and out the roof hole.

Tone twisted her head, silently counting the number of servants or slaves still in attendance. There were five and all were women, young attractive women. Her first thought was that they had all seen him naked. But then, Kallevig had seen her naked and even took pictures. At least there weren't any cameras here. But she did wonder if they were going to pretend to do something else while she bathed or were they going to play the voyeur.

"Do they all go about their business while you bathe?" she asked, feeling a little awkward.

"Pretty much," he smiled. "I'll be the only one intently watching you."

"I think you'll be joining me so that I can watch you too."

"Agreed. You'll want to have your clothes cleaned. We'll find something else for you to wear in the meantime."

"You've got women's clothing lying around here?" She cocked an eyebrow. "Something you need to tell me?"

"You never know when some gorgeous babe might drop by and need a change of clothes," he loftily replied.

"You got your gorgeous babe right here," she reminded him. "Take your clothes off."

Erik leaned back against the table. "You first."

"OK." She was glad to take off the clothing. Kicking off her shoes and woolen socks, she unwrapped the leg wrappings followed by the breeches then the kyrtill, leaving her in a linen undershirt that ended just below her butt.

Erik admired the shapely legs, waiting for the final piece of clothing to come off. "Need any help?"

"That would be nice," she purred, raising her arms.

Erik lifted the undershirt up, raising it over her head and dumping it on the pile of clothes on the floor. Stepping back, he sucked in a breath at her beautiful firm body, until she scrunched up shivering.

"It's cold and I'm getting in the tub." Sliding into the hot water, she uttered a soft moan of pleasure. "Hurry up, cowboy. A girl has needs."

Needing no urging, Erik peeled off his clothes and joined her.

Though the tub was big, it wasn't big enough for two to stretch out, which meant Tone ended up straddling Erik's legs and scooting up until she felt his arousal. Wrapping her arms around him, she kissed him.

"Someone's happy to see me," she smiled impishly.

"Very happy," he nodded. "In fact, so happy we need to hurry up with this bath."

With a large woolen towel wrapped around her, Tone followed Erik who had a towel wrapped around him from the waist down. Her heart fluttered as she thought he looked even stronger and more muscular than before. Upon reaching the 'bedroom', she patiently waited while Erik drew the curtains closed. Once the thin walls were in place, she pushed him down on the bed, flung off her towel and dropped to her knees onto the thick bearskin rug.

Once the final curtain was tugged into place, the five women slaves paused in their work to listen. The redhead commented in a soft whisper to another about Tone's unusual appearance; except for the hair on her head, there was not a hair on the rest of her body. A willowy blond grinned wickedly and elbowed the woman next to her, spreading her hands in front of her as though measuring Erik's erection.

Their smothered chuckles stopped when the cries of ecstasy erupted from behind the curtains. Expecting Erik and Tone to have consummated their passions, the women attended to their work only to stop again as Tone's pleasure moans continued. Impressed, they glanced at each other, smirking and nodding. Their admiration morphed to disbelief as the frolicking in the bedroom continued for some time.

By the time Erik and Tone emerged from the bedroom, the bathtub had been emptied, the floor swept, the fires stoked, clothes for Tone laid out, everything else put away and the women looking around for something to keep them occupied.

"We ought to check on Magnus and Siv," Erik said with a sigh of blissful contentment. He pointed to the clothes on the table. "Those should keep you warm enough until I can keep you warmer when we go to bed."

"I look forward to it." Handing the towel to the blond thrall, she traipsed over to the table and dressed, impervious to the subtle glances of the slaves.

Stepping outside, Erik paused and looked up at the bright moon-filled night, the light so bright that it illuminated the farm fields and sporadic clumps of trees. Walking to the end of the longhouse, he lifted his arm to point north to tell Tone Hønefoss was that way when he saw the faint flicker of a torch in the far distance.

"C'mon" he urged and ran over to where Magnus stood outside the training building.

"She's just getting dressed," Magnus explained with an indulgent grin. "We got to talking and lost track of time."

"They're here," Erik barked, "coming from the north. Alert the men."

Without a word, Magnus sprang into action and headed down to the outbuildings to rouse the hirdmen.

"What's going on?" Tone asked, surprised at Erik's abrupt change.

"We're being attacked."

"By who?"

"Don't have time to explain. Stay in here with Siv." He pushed to door open.

"I can fight," she asserted.

"Not like that," he countered.

"I can fight," she stubbornly insisted.

"Please," Erik begged, "just this once. Stay here and protect Siv." He pushed through the door to see Siv half dressed, with a look of confusion when it was Erik and Tone coming through and not Magnus.

"Hi," she said with a confused-smile. "What happened to my knight in shining armor?"

"We're being attacked," Tone said over her shoulder as Erik led the way to a side wall with a rack of weapons. Selecting his nunchuks, he pointed to the rest of the weapons.

"Choose whatever you want. With a little luck it won't last long." He grabbed her and kissed her deeply then hustled out the door.

"We're being attacked?" Siv exclaimed, speeding up her dressing.

"Yes," Tone calmly replied, scanning the swords, axes, knives and nunchuks neatly arrayed. Several Bo staffs taller than Tone rested against the rack. Selecting a set of nunchuks and a Bo staff, she handed the long staff made from oak to Siv. "Here. Play with this. In case any of the bad guys come through the door, we take 'em out before they get inside. If they do, whack 'em across the shins."

Outside, Erik's men were efficient and ready, arrayed in a semi-circle far enough away from the longhouse and down the hill so that the attackers would be silhouetted against the ridge. The hirdmen were patient and when the last attacker passed the point man of the semicircle, he silently passed back the number of attackers: 24, four with torches.

"You in the longhouse," a voice called out. It sounded familiar. "Send out the women and servants. They won't be harmed." The man waited and when no reaction came, he called out again. "You've got to the count of ten to get them out. One... two..."

As he was winding down the count, Erik motioned for the archers to get ready. When the man announced "ten," he uttered an exasperated grunt. "They had their chance," he told his men. "Torch the place."

At the same moment the four men raised their arms to fling the torches onto the roof, four arrows impacted in between their shoulder blades, the shaft penetrating so deep, the points protruded from three chests, the torches dropping harmlessly onto the ground.

"Now," Erik bellowed and the defenders leaped up the hill to the surprised attackers.

"Ambush," one of the attackers cried too late.

Erik's nunchuks whirled and struck, the metal bars crunching bone and flesh. Magnus' great sword swung in wide arcs and he severed heads and arms from reeling attackers.

One attacker ran to the training house to escape, bursting open the door. He was initially shocked to see two beautiful women, one holding a strange weapon of two bars linked with a chain, the other holding a long staff. Deciding they might make good bartering tools to enable his escape, he lunged for Siv only to be brought to his knees in excruciating pain when Tone whacked a nunchuk bar across his shins, followed by a chop to the neck.

"What do we do with him?" Siv asked, staring at the man stretched on the ground, his unseeing eyes staring at the far wall where wisps of steam still rose from the bathtub.

Tone glanced quickly around the room before prying him over onto his back and undoing the belt holding up his pants. "Guard the door," she commanded, pushing the man back onto his stomach. Wrapping the belt around one wrist, she pulled the arm behind him then folded the opposite leg behind him and tightly wrapped the rest of the belt around the ankle.

"That should hold him for a while," she said, pleased with her first foray into the world of fighting.

"Tone, it's me," Erik called from the outside as the door pushed open. "You two OK?" His gaze shifted to the prone attacker all trussed up. "I guess so," he chuckled.

"How'd we do?" Tone asked.

"Two wounded, but not severely. Eleven of them dead, five wounded, seven surrendered.

"What do you want us to do?"

"How bad is he?" Erik ticked his head at the man.

"He won't walk real well for a while, but he'll live."

"Alright. We'll leave him here for now. Help us collect the weapons in here and take them to the longhouse. We'll use this place as a holding area."

While Tone and Siv collected the weapons, the defeated attackers stumbled in, some limping, others aiding the wounded. The dead were left outside. Before morning arrived, they would be frozen stiff.

With the last weapon deposited in the longhouse, Tone and Siv hurried back to watch. Despite the size of the training building, it was crowded with the defeated seated on the ground and Erik's men surrounding them. Foremost among those seated was Kjell.

"You led this rabble here?" Erik demanded, knowing the answer.

"Yes," Kjell answered with a hint of defiance.

Erik scanned the rest of the attackers. "Who is next in command?"

There was a quiet pause before a middle aged man spoke up. "I suppose I am."

"Who are you?"

"I am called Arknell."

"Then Arknell, you will lead your men back to Thorsten."

"I'm his charge," Kjell snorted.

"You," Erik coldly said, "will be sent to Halfdan as a present for sacrifice."

Kjell's jaw dropped and his mouth went dry. "You can't do that. I'm Thorsten's man."

"You came here to kill me," Erik countered. "You lost. Now it's my turn to kill you. Instead of wasting your blood here, Jarl Halfdan can make use of it in Skiringssal."

"But...but... please... I was only obeying orders."

Ignoring him, Erik spoke to Arknell. "You will leave in the morning. We will feed you and give you your weapons back then. I expect you to act honorably and return to your own kingdom. You will take your dead with you."

"You have my word."

"That is enough," Erik solemnly intoned. Turning to one of his hirdmen, he said, "Go tell the women to bring mead for these men and for yourselves."

"Yes Erik," the man brightly replied.

Erik grabbed him by the arm and warned him. "Not too much."

"I understand, Erik."

Erik shifted a glance at Tone and smiled. "Welcome to our world."

Chapter 12

Cooper folded his arms and leaned back in the chair, listening to Gene extol the latest improvements. Holding a hand up for him to stop, he leaned forward, propping his elbows on the desk.

"So what you're telling me is that the machine is now accurate in both place and time back to the year 500?"

"Yes," Gene grinned with pride

Cooper turned to Meredith who sat in a chair to the side of Cooper's desk. "You have everything ready?"

"Yes."

"I'd like to go," Gene blurted.

"No," Meredith firmly replied. "It's too dangerous and you are of greater value here."

"But it's me she made an ass of," he half-pouted.

"Yes, she did," Meredith said, offering no sympathy. "Put that idea out of your head. Besides, you would only be in the way."

Frustrated, Gene consoled himself that he would get his revenge when they brought them back.

"Thank you, Gene," Cooper said, effectively dismissing him.

When the door closed behind him, Cooper turned to Meredith. "Who do you have?"

"We've got Johans Kallevig from the University of Oslo, Tone's former professor who seemed anxious to assist. While he did not elaborate, I have a feeling she and he were intimate at one point and that he was not happy with the way the relationship ended."

Cooper nodded. "Who else?"

"The other Norse expert is from the University of Minnesota, a man with a grudge against Erik Jonsson for winning a scholarship he believes was rightfully his."

Cooper shook his head, impressed. "How did you find these two?"

"The first one was easy," she chuckled. "We just went to where she was last. I then figured Oslo wouldn't let us have two Norse professors and decided to look closer to home. Digging into Erik's past I came up with Sven Olsen. The man's still pissed and that happened something like fifteen years ago. It's all over his net-page. I then learned it was really all about a woman, Erik's first wife, Linda. Apparently Sven was in love with her as well and he's been nursing that anger ever since she married Erik. The scholarship is just a cover for a broken heart."

Cooper lifted his hand and rubbed his thumb and middle finger together, signify the world's tiniest violin of sympathy. "When will they be ready to leave?"

"In a couple of days. Kallevig and Olsen are here in a waiting pattern. They know the mission. We're sending our two best escorts."

"Remember," Cooper calmly said, "alive… or dead, preferably dead by unfortunate accident."

"We've got that squared away. The two guards are carrying stun pistols with a jolt that'll lift a bull moose twenty feet off the ground and cook it to perfection."

Cooper smirked. "Talk to me about the machine itself. Sometimes Gene gets carried away and assumes everyone understands time physics. We've only ever had it in place for a max of two days. It's going to take a lot longer for them to find and eliminate the threat."

"Yes it is. In this instance, the machine stays in place for an indeterminate time. One of the guards carries a remote with a 100-mile range. If they see they're in serious trouble, he can remote the activate switch and send it back." She picked up her coffee mug from the side table, taking a sip. "Another concern was the possibility of some unsuspecting moron stumbling upon the machine and inadvertently activating it. To prevent that, we installed a cloaking device and force field. The machine will be effectively hidden and no one can get close to it unless the guard with the remote deactivates it."

"I assume there's a tracking device in the RC."

"Yes."

"Then let's get this show on the road."

It was snowing when Kallevig and Olsen stepped off the time machine, thick flakes that piled up in layers. The two escorts stepped out behind them, compacting the snow in a scattering of footprints. One guard, a compact man with broad shoulders, stepped away and pulled out the remote, pressing the cloaking button followed by the force field button. The force field was so strong that it pushed the four of them away, causing Olsen to lose his footing and tumble in the snow.

"Sorry 'bout that," the guard said though his tone said he was more amused than sorry.

Olsen picked himself up and brushed off the snow as best he could, glaring at the man.

"Let's get going," Kallevig urged, "before we get caught here." Taking in the surroundings through the falling snow, he saw they were in a small clearing, surrounded by forest. "Which way is the town?"

The RC guard held up the control, which contained a "You-are-here" dot and a matrix map. Zooming out he twisted the control until it pointed to Kaupang then raised an arm and pointed a finger. "That way."

Leading the way, the guard headed into the forest, the others falling in behind in single file. Ten minutes later the forest ended and farm fields spread before them. Just ahead lay the merchant town of Kaupang.

There was little activity on the street as they meandered into the town. Most merchants had their shops closed and were busy creating inventory. Kallevig took the lead and entered what he thought might be an ale house only to discover it was a leather shop.

"Sorry to intrude," Kallevig suavely said. "We're looking for the alehouse."

"In the middle of the town, two houses past Harek's bead shop," came the gruff reply of a man irritated by the interruption.

"Thank you."

After another false start, Kallevig entered Harek's bead shop, the others tumbling in behind him. Alvi was behind a table, piecing together a necklace. The woman's beauty immediately caught his attention.

"My apologies, fair lady," Kallevig said, using his most charming voice. "We were given directions to the alehouse and it seems we keep getting lost."

"I'm not surprised," she replied with a sweet smile, pleased that this tall handsome man had called her a lady, "what with all the snow. But you're close. It's only two more houses down on the right." She pointed a finger in the direction they were headed.

"You are so kind, thank you." Kallevig dawdled a moment. "That's a beautiful necklace. You have the eye of an artist."

Alvi blushed. "My Da makes the beads, I just put 'em together."

"Obviously your father is a superb craftsman. But it also takes someone with the gift of style to arrange such works of art into a larger masterpiece."

Olsen gave Kallevig's arm a tug. "C'mon. Let's go."

"You all go on ahead," he replied with a 'leave-me-alone' smile. "I'll be with you in a just a bit."

Olsen waffled for a moment then stormed back outside, the other two clueless as to what transpired.

"You'll have to forgive my friends," Kallevig cooed locking her eyes with his. "They're not used to seeing such beauty."

Alvi flushed once again, flattered by this man's smooth words, unlike so many of the other crude men that come into the shop. That was what she liked about Pearson. He was different, gentle, with a kind heart. What he lacked in physical character, he more than made up for with his intelligence and devotion. But this man was different. He reminded her a bit like Erik, confident and outgoing.

"May I admire your work?" Kallevig asked.

"Sure," she readily nodded, holding up the half-finished necklace.

Kallevig bent down as though intently studying the beads. He gently reached a finger to touch one of the beads, brushing her soft hand in the process.

Alvi felt a quiver of electricity in his touch, liking the way he made her feel.

"Not only do you exceed the beauty of the gods, you are an artist beyond equal."

Alvi's heart fluttered and she struggled to concentrate. "I've not seen you 'round here before."

"We're just passing through, though I could be tempted to stay a while longer if the women are as fair as you.' He stood up and shook his head. "But that's foolish. I imagine there is no one here who is as fair as you."

Alvi swallowed, flustered and flattered at the same time. "Where, where are you going?"

"We're looking for some friends of ours. The man's name is Erik. The other one came by here recently, a woman named Tone."

"I know them," she exclaimed. "They're really nice."

"They are. Do you know where they might be?"

"Oh," she said with a frown. "They don't live around here. They live farther north, a few days travel from here. My husband knows where they live."

Kallevig's shoulders slumped. "You're married? Of course you are. Who would not want to be married to such a fair lady? You said your husband knows where they live?"

"Yes."

"When might he be back?"

"I don't know. If you all are at the alehouse, I can send him to you there."

Kallevig placed a hand on his heart. "Not only are you beautiful, but you are sweet and kind. I would consider it an honor if you would inform your husband of our presence."

"Yes, sir."

"Oh please, you are much too polite. Call me Johans."

"OK, Johans. That's a nice name. I'm Alvi, Alvi Hareksdottir."

"And I am Johans Kallevig." Kallevig figured it was best to be honest. After all, there was little likelihood of being discovered.

"That's an unusual name, very nice though. I'll let my husband know."

"Thank you."

Kallevig stepped outside, smug with confidence. Not only had he found out where their prey was, he found someone to lead them there.

Inside Harek's shop, a scowling Pearson slipped out from behind the door. "I heard all that. What does he want Erik for?

"He said they were friends of Erik and Tone."

"Something's not right. He didn't even mention Siv and she's Tone's best friend."

Alvi frowned. "That's right."

"And he also didn't say anything about Tone and Erik being married. If they were friends he'd know that."

Alvi's frown deepened. "Why are you so angry?"

"I don't like the way he was ogling you and the way he talked. He was so smooth that butter wouldn't melt in his mouth. I don't trust him."

"I told him that you would talk with them."

Pearson folded his arms and started pacing. "I don't like it. Did you notice when the others were here with them, the two in the back looked ill at ease. I don't trust them. I've got to warn Erik."

"Now?" Alvi's eyes widened.

"Yes," Pearson resolutely replied, "now."

"But what about meeting them?"

"Tell them that I went to show some jewelry to Liv up in Skiringssal."

"But that won't take that long," she objected.

"Make something up," he blustered. "I've got to warn him."

"Oh Pearson, why? I know he's your friend, but I don't like you going out in this weather," she fussed. "It's dangerous. Can't you wait?"

"No, I can't," he resolutely said. "I don't trust this Kallevig fellow."

The door opened and Kallevig entered followed by the other three time travelers.

"Ah," he warmly smiled, ignoring Pearson's pained look. "Hopefully the man in question. Is this your husband?"

"Yes," Alvi said with a forced smile.

"Excellent." Kallevig said, taking in the mousy man, wondering how he managed to end up with such a beautiful wife. Perhaps it was a marriage of economics. The man probably owned the shop. *Maybe I'll bed the wench when I come back. She looks inexperienced enough to make it fun.*

Turning on the charm, he addressed Pearson. "I was telling your lovely wife – you're a very lucky man, by the way, to be married to a creature of such beauty – I was telling her that we were looking for some friends of ours, Erik and Tone. She said that you knew where they were."

"I do," he truthfully answered, studying the other men. Catching the attention of one of the guards, he asked, "Can I show you a necklace or a bracelet, something for your sweetheart?"

The man stared dumbly at him, his face affixed with the self-conscious smile or ignorance.

Pearson started to ask him again when Kallevig intervened.

"He doesn't speak our language."

"What language does he speak?"

"It's called English."

"Where is that spoken?" Pearson frowned.

"On a Saxon island to the west of Daneland," Kallevig replied, struggling to remember his 9th century geography.

"Why my husband –" Alvi began before Pearson interrupted, squeezing her hand.

"I have heard of it. We have had a few dealings with such men, though they spoke our tongue. Where in this Saxon land does he live?"

Kallevig thought quickly and spoke the first town that came to mind. "Jarrow."

Pearson's heart quickened and he knew the man was lying, for Jarrow was only half a day's walk from the town where he was born.

"Ah, never heard of it," Pearson blandly said. *May God forgive me this lie.* Forcing himself to relax, he asked, "How can I help you?"

"We were wondering if you could guide us to where Erik and Tone are staying."

"It's a four day one-way trip and I've a business to run," he replied, spreading his hands at the wares on the tables.

"Perhaps you could point us in the right direction," Olsen spoke up.

Kallevig flashed a glare of irritation at Olsen. "It would be better if you could take us. We are unfamiliar with the area and prefer not to waste time."

"What's so urgent," Pearson asked, "that you need my help?"

"We have messages from friends before we head back home."

"Where is home for you?"

"I too am from Jarrow," Kallevig said. "In fact, all of us are."

Pearson dipped his head, wondering how a man could lie with such ease. "I understand, but like I said, I do have a business to run."

"We can make it worth your while," Kallevig said, pulling out a small leather bag and dumping the contents on the table.

Alvi's eyes burst wide at the pile of thin gold bars gleaming on the table.

"Half now," Kallevig said scooping up half the pile, "and half when we return."

"He'll do it," Alvi blurted, much to Pearson's frustration.

"Excellent," Kallevig purred. "When can we leave?"

"When the weather breaks," Pearson said with a resigned sigh.

Tone smiled when she saw Siv and Magnus strolling together down towards the boatsheds. They seemed happy and she was glad that Siv found her handsome Viking. Tone liked Magnus because he seemed to genuinely favor Erik and acted the trusted friend.

Ever since the attack, the farm had been on alert, though more guarded than overt. Erik's reputation as a military leader was almost beyond belief. The men or hirdmen, as he called them, sang poems of praise for Erik's exploits, reminding her of the old Biblical verses of Saul killing his thousands and David killing his ten thousands. In this instance one could substitute Erik for David.

Erik. Erik was different from before, though not in a bad way. He always had those traits of leadership and teaching. Those were seen in the classroom. But here? There was no classroom of canned instruction here. Here was real life with the presence of death leering over one's shoulder. The folks on the farm trusted Erik to take care of them, even the slaves did, and he treated everyone with care and dignity.

But he was different and she had a hard time defining it. It was as though he was more confident, more self-assured... more at peace with himself. She remembered asking him if he wanted to go back to the present. They were snuggled together in bed after a wild ride of unbridled sex. Even the household slaves had managed to find something else to do outside to escape the raucous romp.

"Why?" He frowned at her as though the question was absurd. "What is there in the future-present that would make one want to live there? Sure there's all sorts of technology to help extend our lives, to make them more comfortable. But at what cost? Government controls everything. Besides, technology has brought out the narcissism of mankind. How many selfies does it take before we finally say 'We're tired of looking at you. Get a life.'

"And everything is sensationalized," he continued. "Everything is 'epic' or the 'best whatever you'll ever see.' Even the news is clickbait. People spend more time taking online quizzes to see what kind of vegetable they are rather than actually living. There's nothing in the future-present I need or want." He held her tight, gazing passionately into her eyes. "Everything I want is in my arms."

She had to admit that he was right. Since their reuniting, life had been sheer joy... well... aside from that first night when they were attacked, but even that was fun. She got to actually use the martial arts she had trained in.

Siv and Magnus were down at the edge of the first boathouse. Tone smiled though she felt like a voyeur when Magnus leaned down and kissed Siv, followed by Siv flinging her arms around him. When the kiss continued, she broke off her voyeurism and searched to go find Erik. Most likely he'd be in the training building... where she probably should be.

Now that things had settled to an almost routine, what was there to do to make life more exciting?

After nearly four days of traveling, Pearson still struggled to come up with a way of warning Erik. One thing he did know was the more time he spent with the man called Kallevig, the more intense his dislike. Part of him said it wasn't very Christian of him to have such thoughts, but as God was his witness, besides being a liar, there was something about Kallevig that gave him the creeps. It was obvious he was in charge, because the others deferred to him, but Pearson could tell they were not happy about their leader. And every time they stopped for the night, whether at a small vil or house, if there was a pretty woman, married or single, Kallevig would act the fool with honeyed words and exaggerated phrases, like he was courting.

Then the one called Olsen complained most of the time. He was too cold, or he was tired, or he was hungry. When he wasn't complaining about the weather or lack of food, he complained that his clothes didn't fit right.

Pearson shook his head. Whose fault was that? The man shouldn't have bought clothes that didn't fit.

And the two who didn't speak his tongue? They seemed totally lost, like they had been kidnapped and blindfolded somewhere else and dropped off here. Every now and then they'd jabber something in that tongue Kallevig called 'English' and Kallevig or Olsen would answer. That would shut them up for a while.

Yet the closer they got to Kolga's farm, the more apprehensive Pearson grew. There just had to be a way of getting word to Erik. He had timed it so that they would arrive at Kolga's farm after dark. He prayed that she would perceive the danger and somehow tell Erik.

"How much longer?" Kallevig asked. He was less than impressed with Pearson. The man had been cold towards him the entire journey and he knew why. The man's wife was obviously attracted to Kallevig and Pearson was jealous. Kallevig was tall and handsome compared to this wimp called Pearson. Kallevig had already decided he was going to seduce the young lass when they returned to Kaupang. What could Pearson or anyone else do? Once they were on the time machine, it wouldn't matter.

"We'll reach Kolga's farm tonight," Pearson answered. "Then we'll arrive at the farm where Erik is tomorrow."

An hour later, when the ink black night filled the sky, dogs barking announced their presence.

"Let me talk to her first," Pearson warned. "And remember your place. She is Kolga, the Jarl's sister. You would do well to respect her authority."

"Fine by me," Kallevig airily replied.

Sliding down from his horse, Pearson was halfway to the door when it opened and a tall farm hand stood silhouetted in the doorway.

"Who are you? Oh, it's you Pearson. Who's with you?"

"Good evening Reidmar. May I come in?"

"Of course." He opened the door wider and Pearson hustled in, Reidmar immediately closing the door behind him. Kolga sat at a small loom near the fire. She looked up as Pearson rushed over to her.

"There are men with me who claim to be Erik's friends, but it's not true. The one man called Kallevig said they were all from Jarrow, but he's lying because I'm from Jarrow and don't understand the language they claim we speak there."

"Slow down, Pearson," she said with a smile, "and start from the beginning."

Pearson related the story from the time the men showed up to now. "I don't trust them. Please, I beg you, send someone to warn Erik."

Kolga glanced up at Reidmar and nodded. "Send Gunnsten. Have him tell Erik that –" she looked at Pearson who said, 'Kallevig,' "that a man named Kallevig is here looking for him."

"And Tone," Pearson added.

"Yes," Kolga coolly agreed, "her too."

"Yes, Kolga," Reidmar said, dipping his head in respect.

Kolga glanced around the room. There were enough male farmhands inside to handle any unwanted requests. "Show them in, Reidmar."

Erik was surprised at the knock at the door. Before he could answer it, Magnus was already up and opened the door.

"Hallo Gunnsten," Magnus greeted him. "What brings you here?"

"Got a message from Lady Kolga for Erik and Tone," he awkwardly replied.

"What is it?" Erik asked, walking up.

"The message is this: there's a man named Kellywig looking for you."

"Kallevig?" Tone burst. "O my God, they're here."

Erik twisted his head to look at her standing behind the table, her face flushed with fear. Turning back to Gunnsten, he asked, "How many are there?"

"Four. Pearson's with them. He was the one that said they was bad men."

Muttering, "Thank God for Pearson," Erik frowned in thought then asked, "Can you tell us anything more about them?"

Gunnsten, who wasn't the sharpest knife in the drawer, shrugged. "I saw four of 'em. One of 'em did all the talkin', 'cept another fella who talked some. Them other two didn't say a word."

Erik immediately understood. "Thank you Gunnsten. Tell Kolga 'thank you' and keep this to yourself."

"Yes Erik."

Once the door closed behind Gunnsten, Erik walked over to where Tone nervously paced.

"They've sent them to take us back," she whispered.

"I know," Erik calmly and slowly nodded. "But we now have the advantage." Turning to Magnus, he said, "There are men here who were sent to take Tone back. I will not allow that to happen."

"Of course not," Magnus replied, his jaw set.

"We will set a trap for them."

"Of course," Magnus said with a wicked grin.

"Two of the four are probably the most dangerous," Erik mused.

"How do you know?" Magnus asked.

"That's the way they operate."

"They may not be using conventional weapons," Tone offered, walking up. She was calm again, irritated with herself for her sudden despair.

"That would be stupid," Erik said, pursing his lips, "but not outside the realm of possibilities, which means we have to eliminate them right from the start."

"Why not take them at Kolga's," Magnus suggested, "when they're outside, before they mount their horses?"

Erik's stern face slowly turned serene. "I have an idea."

"Thank you for your hospitality, Lady Kolga," Kallevig suavely said with a bow. "Tales of your beauty do not do you justice." He gave her his best smile, wishing he could take her back with him to photograph. She had that overt sensual superiority that was so difficult to capture on film, but he could have fun trying. He had wondered more than once during the night what she was like in bed.

Kolga stood outside in the morning sun, shielding her eyes with the palm of her hand as the four men mounted their horses. Pearson stood to her side. Though Kallevig was a handsome man, there was an arrogance about him that she found grating, that and his too smooth behavior. He had a glib answer for everything. Kallevig was the kind of man she detested, a man with an insincere honey-tongue.

"You are too kind. Erik's farm is not far. You can see it from here." She pointed across the water. "Just follow the road around the water."

The four men peered in the direction she pointed, noting the cluster of buildings in the far distance as well as the path that descended from Kolga's longhouse into a small forest that ran along the edge of the water until the fields of Erik's farm spread across the landscape.

"Thank you m'Lady," Kallevig gallantly said. "Ready, Pearson?"

"I've asked Pearson to remain because I have some business to discuss with him," she informed them before turning a stern glare at Pearson. "About those necklaces you last brought here. The beads are inferior and the necklace broke apart the first time I wore it, scattering the beads all over the floor."

"O my God," Pearson burst, horrified. "I... We'll make full restitution."

"Of course you will," she snapped. "Come back inside and let's see how much I paid for them. I expect to be compensated." She briskly turned to Kallevig. "Good day to you, gentlemen. And you," she pointed a finger at Pearson, "inside." Without looking back, she marched inside, Pearson offering profuse apologies.

Pearson was still groveling apologies when the door closed behind them. Kolga held a finger up to his lips.

"Shush. There's nothing wrong with the jewelry. I just needed to separate you from them."

Startled, Pearson's confusion turned to relief and admiration. "Thank you, thank you."

"Give them a little head start then you head back home, as quickly as possible."

"Thank you, Lady Kolga. Didn't I tell you there was something wrong with them."

"Yes," she answered, opening the door wide enough to see the men descend the hill. "I just pray that Erik is prepared."

Outside, Kallevig snorted a laugh at Pearson's nervous fear. "C'mon," he said to the others. "Let's finish this. I'm ready to get back to civilization with heating and indoor plumbing."

"And decent food," an escort chimed in.

"And traveling faster than a horse," the other escort said, shaking his head. "Just imagine how much quicker this could've been done if we had cars and topo maps."

"Technology," the first escort replied glancing around. "Why would anyone want to ever change the present for the past? Can you imagine *wanting* to live here?"

With Pearson no longer among them, the two escorts gave vent to their freedom to finally speak, most of it denigrating their present situation.

"So what's the plan?" Olsen asked. "I mean, we just can't go riding up and say, "Hi. We're here to take you back."

"We've got our orders," the first guard said. "Dead or alive."

"Dead's a lot easier," the other guard suggested.

"Yup," the first guard agreed with a nod.

"So what *is* the plan?" Olsen objected. "You two are the experts. Tell us."

"I don't want Tone killed," Kallevig stated. "She owes me money and I want to get it back. I don't care what you do with Erik, but Tone stays alive."

"We'll see," the escort airily replied.

"No we *won't* see," Kallevig snarled. "She stays alive."

The argument continued as the entered the forest. Midway through, their progress was interrupted when two men, armed with sword and battle ax stepped out of the forest and into their path.

"Good morning, gentlemen," Magnus said with an intimidating smile. At that moment, the forest shook as twelve men burst out onto the path, each armed with a bow, an arrow notched and ready to fire.

Kallevig's mouth went dry and he tried to speak. When he did, his voice squeaked. "We've nothing of value."

"I'll be the judge of that," Magnus said. "Place your hands on your head. If you drop your hands, your body will be filled with arrows. Get down off your horses."

"I can't get off the horse without using my hands," Kallevig complained.

"Do your best," Magnus cheerfully replied.

The four men managed to swing their legs up and over and slide clumsily down to the ground. One escort pretended to stumble and fall. As he curled into a roll, his hand went to his pocket and he withdrew the stun pistol. Rolling to his side, he took aim at Magnus. Just as he pulled back on the trigger, the first arrow pierced his side, followed by a half dozen more. But the finger closed the trigger and the bolts shot out.

The impact of the first arrow affected the man's shot and instead of hitting Magnus, the darts impacted the man next to him, lifting him off the ground in a quivering spasm. He was dead before the body flopped onto the ground.

Anger erupted and arrows would have flown had not Magnus stopped them with a curt command. Staring in shock at the wires attached to the hirdman, he followed them back to the gun in the escort's hand. Glaring at the three remaining intruders, he said, "I do not know what magic this is, but you are all dead men, just like him." He thrust a finger at the escort, his body pierced with arrows.

"I had nothing to do with that," Olsen wailed.

"Tie their hands," Magnus commanded.

While others guarded them, two hirdmen tied their hands, making no effort to be gentle.

"Leave them," Magnus ordered concerning the dead escort and hirdman. He pointed to a young man. "Stay here and warn anyone passing to stay clear of them. We will be back in a little while."

"It's not dangerous anymore," the escort said.

"What did you say?" Magnus demanded.

"He said it's not dangerous anymore," Kallevig answered.

"We shall see."

Erik, Tone, and Siv sat on stools outside, waiting. Erik saw them first, immediately knowing something was wrong. There were only three prisoners. He tallied the rest of his men and was one short.

"Damn."

"What's wrong?" Tone asked

"Looks like I lost a man."

Before long, the group stood before them.

"Hello Johans," Tone said, smiling sweetly. "What brings you here?"

"Vacation," he replied with a smug grin, believing he was safe from further harm. "Siv," he nodded in greeting.

"Hello Johans. Looks to me like you've gotten yourself into some trouble."

"What happened?" Erik asked Magnus. When Magnus finished, Erik ordered that everything in their pockets and saddle bags be emptied into a crate. "Everything. Strip them if you have to, but I want everything."

"What are you going to do with us?" Olsen whined.

"I'm half tempted to stake you out and let the wolves and bears have a meal."

"You can't do that," Olsen exclaimed. "You're a civilized man, not like these barbarians."

"You hear that," Erik said to his hirdmen. "He thinks you're barbarians. They come here to kill us and he thinks we're barbarians." His gaze rested on Olsen. "You look familiar."

His hands tied and his future less than secure, Olsen wasn't about to be insulting. Deciding that resurrecting an uncomfortable past might not be to his advantage, he shook his head. "I don't think we've ever met."

Erik saw one of the hirdmen pulled out the remote control to the time machine. "Here. I'll take that."

"What is it?" the hirdman asked.

"I'm not sure yet, but we'll find out. Be careful with that," he ordered when another hirdman pulled out the other stun pistol. "And don't point it at anyone. Give it here."

The hirdman was only too happy to give Erik the pistol.

With their belongings deposited into a wooden crate, the prisoners were led to the training house to sit against the wall opposite the weapons rack, with two hirdmen to guard them.

Outside, Erik and Magnus left to collect the dead hirdman while Tone and Siv decided to head inside the training room.

Standing above Kallevig, Tone folded her arms and shook her head. "What did you hope to accomplish?"

"You owe me," he said in English.

Pretending to not understand, she turned to Siv. "I am suspicious of his gibberish. He might be possessed by evil. We may have to burn him to kill this evil spirt."

"Very funny," Kallevig retorted, still in English.

"There he goes again," Siv said with mock concern. She caught the eye of the escort. "You. Are you too possessed?"

"He doesn't speak Old Norse," Kallevig answered for him, continuing in English.

Siv and Tone looked at each other. "All three must burn," Siv said.

They turned to go when Kallevig again spoke in English.

"You won't get away with this. They'll send more, you know."

Stopping at the door, Tone shook her head in feigned sadness. "To think," she said in a voice loud enough for Kallevig and the others to hear, "they are all consumed with evil and will burn. What a pity." She scrunched her nose. "The smell of burning human flesh stinks." Reaching for the door, she stopped when Olsen called out in Old Norse, "Wait."

Turning, Tone looked at him. "Yes?"

"I was forced here against my will. I never wanted to come."

"On please," Kallevig scoffed, reverting back to Old Norse. "You wanted to get back at Erik for stealing your girl away."

"It's not true," Olsen pleaded. "I've never met Erik before. I know nothing about him."

"Not only are you a liar," Kallevig sneered, "you're a bad liar." He glanced up at Tone and Siv. "You're making a big mistake. Release us and come back with us. Everything will be fine."

Tone chuckled dismissively. "Who's the liar?"

Erik bent down and pulled the gun out of the escort's hand, winding the wires around the barrel as he walked toward the dead hirdman. Yanking out the barbs, he shook his head in disgust.

"There will be more who come. We must be ready."

"What kind of weapon is this?" Magnus asked, awe in his voice.

"It is a dangerous weapon that thankfully few have."

"How do you know about it?"

"I have seen it before in my travels. I'm surprised to see it here. We will destroy both of them." He kneeled down by the dead hirdman, a young man of twenty winters. "Too young to be taken so soon. Fate is indeed cruel." Standing, he inhaled a deep breath. "Give him an Ostman's funeral."

"We will. What do we do with the prisoners?"

"I have an idea."

Kolga stood outside the door, her head tilted, staring out over the water towards Erik's farm. It had been two days since he and Tone and several others left with the prisoners. Magnus and Siv had remained behind. It would be at least another six days before Erik returned, plenty of time to get results. Wrapping her cloak around her, she mounted the horse that Gunnsten patiently held.

"I'll be back this afternoon."

"Yes, Kolga," he blissfully nodded then remembered to ask, "Where are you going?"

"I'm going to Hønefoss."

"Yes, Kolga."

Two hours later, she guided her horse to a small stoutly built house made of stone on a knoll in the woods to the east of Hønefoss. Smoke curled out the roof vent.

Ordering the two hirdmen to wait outside, she dismounted and knocked on the door.

"Come in," a pleasant voice answered.

Opening the door, Kolga entered a tidy home. The fire pit in the center of the house provided more than ample heat. A bed was placed against the far corner, though not too far from the fire pit. Dried herbs and flowers hung from the low ceiling. Except for the wall containing the door, the other walls were lined with shelves of stone jars, mortars and pestles, and various dried insects.

A small table nestled against a side wall. Sitting at the table, was a slender middle-aged woman with long thick blond hair. Her blue eyes sparkled with mischief and her smile revealed teeth perfectly white. Her skin was the pale white of one who spent more of her time indoors. Despite her age, she was attractive, unusual for a Volvur, the Ostman's word for seeress.

"I was wondering when you were going to come," Folkvi smiled, her voice warm and alluring.

"I don't know what to do," Kolga confessed. "I want Erik for myself, but I don't want to kill Tone."

"No," Folkvi agreed. "Doing that would drive him away. What you need is something to make him love you more."

Kolga's spirit rose. "Do you have something like that?"

Folkvi chuckled. "Of course." She motioned for Kolga to sit. "But there is one little concern."

"What?" Kolga slid out a chair and eased into it.

"It will only work on a man who has doubts about his love for the other woman. The advantage is that these doubts can be so small he does not even know he has doubts."

Kolga's eyes brightened. "Perfect."

Folkvi stood and retrieved a small vial from a shelf. "Pour the contents into his mead. It won't take long, so be patient."

"Thank you, Folkvi." She handed her a small bag of hack silver. "I will send a butchered stag as a token of my appreciation."

Folkvi dipped her head in a nod of thanks.

Halfdan was surprised, though pleased to see Erik. He was also surprised to see Tone, immediately understanding Erik's obsession with her, for she was beautiful. Still, he hid his disappointment, remembering Erik's story and knew his desire of a union between Erik and Kolga was not going to happen… unless something happened to Tone. But that was a matter for another time. Besides, if his sister really wanted this man, then she should fight for him.

"What brings you here?" he asked, pointing for them to take a seat at the table closest to the door.

"We've some useless baggage to get rid of," Erik replied, giving Astrid a wink, smiling when she blushed then pursed her lips when she saw Tone.

"Baggage?"

"It's a long story. More importantly, Thorsten is growing restless." He explained about the attack on the farm and their utter defeat. Astrid pushed aside the servant bringing the mead and brought it herself, ensuring Erik noticed her again.

Halfdan stroked his beard as he listened before noting Astrid was still standing here, long after the mead mugs were placed on the table. "Ach. Be gone girl. This is men's work." He swatted her butt with an affectionate tap.

"Oh, Papa," she bristled, marching off.

"Remember what I told you," Erik leaned forward, smiling at him.

"Don't remind me. I've got half a dozen offers as it is."

"She's a handsome lass. She'll make someone a fine wife." He took a sip of mead. "What do you want to do about Thorsten?"

"How many men do you have?"

"Not enough if he decides to send an army. I've enough to manage, but my thought is why don't we take the battle to him? Put him off balance? Give me enough men to protect the farm then we can start raiding his lands. You can always say that you didn't know about it. And it would be the truth to a point in that you wouldn't know when we raided."

Halfdan grinned at him. "You never cease to surprise me. Let me think on it. While I like the idea, I have to balance what it might cost in the long run. However, I will send you more men. If I send more than you expect, you'll know what to do." He turned to Tone and smiled. "I've heard his story. Tell me yours. According to him, he believed he was never going to see you again."

Tone impishly smiled. "At first I thought so too, but then love has a way of overcoming even the most stubborn obstacles."

Erik stood on the low platform in the central market space in Kaupang, Tone just behind him. Hands on his hips, he twisted his head back and forth in a slow regal sweep of those assembled, the bidders and the curious onlookers. Standing on the ground beside the platform, Kallevig, Olsen and the escort watched with growing apprehension.

The escort was the first one pushed onto the platform.

"What am I bid for this one here? Mind you, he doesn't speak our language, but he's strong enough to lift and carry." He slapped the man on the back.

"What good is he if he can't speak our language?" a voice called out.

"There's good and bad there," Erik grinned. "On the negative side, you'll have to be patient until he learns the language. On the plus side, he won't talk a whole lot and you won't have to listen to a lot of mindless jabber."

The crowd laughed and a voice called out, "One measure."

"I've got one measure," Erik announced. "Who will give me two?"

"One and a half," another voice offered.

"I've got one and a half," Erik repeated. "Two?"

Silence greeted the raised request.

"Sold for one and a half. You got yourself a bargain there."

Olsen was next, his legs quivering as he stood, bound with ropes, the leering faces determining his fate.

"This one is intelligent, speaks our language, but that's about it," Erik said. "Part of me thinks he'd be better used as a sacrifice, but then someone might think of a better use."

"O God, please no," Olsen pleaded. "I can cook and I can clean."

"Cook?" A voice called out. "I'll bid a measure."

"One and a half," another countered.

"Two."

"Two and a half."

By the time bidding ceased, Olsen went for three and a quarter measures.

"Last is this specimen here," Eric announced as Kallevig was lifted up to the platform. Tone jumped up onto the platform, winking at Erik.

"Mind if I do this one?"

"Be my guest," Erik gallantly replied with a sweeping bow.

"You'll never get away with this," Kallevig seethed in English. "They'll come looking for me. And when they do, your game is over."

Tone stared blankly at him before turning to look at the crowd. "Anyone know what he said?"

"You sure he's not got some evil spirit?" a man's voice exclaimed.

"That's a possibility. Tell you the truth, he's done a lot of that gibberish since we captured him. He'll be talking like us one moment and the next he's spouting stuff I've never heard and I've done a lot of traveling. But besides that, he's reasonably smart, but I wouldn't trust him with your daughters."

"That's a lie," Kallevig bellowed. "She knows damn well what I'm saying because she can speak it too. Go ahead and ask that other slave there." He indicated Olsen who turned around.

Shifting a look from the smiling Tone to Erik whose look said that 'you say anything and you are a dead man', Olsen shook his head. "I don't know what he's talking about."

"Damn you," Kallevig shouted, turning to the crowd. "Don't you see? They're pulling the wool over your eyes. They're in this together."

"And that's why I sold him to be a cook," Erik grinned at the crowd. Shaking his head, he shrugged. "I don't know if anyone's going to want you now."

Deciding he had nothing left to lose, Kallevig spouted, "They're both from the future. I'm from the future. I was sent here to take them back."

Tone's shocked look and Erik's mocking face caused the crowd to roar with laughter.

"It's true I tell you," Kallevig sputtered. "It's true."

Erik signaled for Kallevig to be gagged as Tone continued. "Well friends. Since he's revealed our secret, I'll demonstrate that I'm from the future by predicting the weather for tomorrow." She paused for effect, gazing over the crowd and bent forward. "It's going to be… cold."

Laughter burst and the crowd applauded.

"Seriously my friends, what are we going to do with him? It's obvious he's touched in the head. What do you suggest?"

"We need a sacrifice for summer planting," a man suggested, receiving grunts of agreement.

Kallevig's eyes expanded with terror.

"Not a bad idea," Erik mused aloud. "We're not taking him back with us because it's an eight-day journey round trip, so someone will have to provide for him."

"I'll give you a measure for him," a deep voice spoke.

Erik looked to where the smithy stood. He was heavyset with thick powerful arms. His face had a streak or two from charcoal.

"I can use someone to haul and pump."

"You want him to keep or sacrifice?" Tone asked.

"I'll make that choice as time goes on."

"A wise decision," Erik said with a smile.

Cooper paced the office when Gene walked in. Meredith sat in her usual spot. Seeing his whiz-kid framed by the doorway, he jerked to a stop.

"Where's my damn machine?"

"It's still in Kaupang," Gene replied, the answer obvious.

"Why? They should be back by now."

"Maybe something's gone wrong on their end," he said with a limp shrug.

"No kidding," Meredith snapped. "What's the safety protocol for getting our machine back?"

"Uh, we set the return timer for a three-month delay, but –"

"Three months," Cooper burst. "We can't wait three months. We've got travelers to send back. Bring back that machine, now."

Gene inhaled a deep breath, preparing for the ass-chewing he was about to receive. "I can't. The escort has the remote and unless he activates the remote, the machine will stay there for the entire time. If you remember, we had agreed on this based upon the assumption that the trip wouldn't take this long."

"Get out, damn you," Cooper thundered, "and don't come back here until you have my machine."

Tone and Erik had yet been a day back home when Kolga's invitation arrived via Gunnsten.

"Kolga says to come to the evening meal." His gaze remained on Erik.

"I'm not invited?" Tone said, folding her arms across her chest.

"Well yes," Gunnsten replied, confused why she thought that. "You and Magnus and Siv."

"Thank you," Tone's smile returned. "We'll be there."

Tone was immediately on guard when Kolga was overly solicitous and kind, offering compliments to Tone's hair, figure and dress, as well as favorable praise for Siv. She wondered if Kolga finally accepted that Erik would never be hers as long as Tone was there, which immediately conjured up all sorts of evil possibilities, like being drugged and sold off to other Vikings as a slave.

Dismissing the negative thoughts, she watched as one of the servants handed out mugs of mead, noting that Erik and Magnus were given drinking horns. Kolga raised her mug in toast.

"To the success of past and future battles. May our children grow old on these farms."

While Kolga took a small sip, she inwardly smiled at Erik's deep swallow. Her glee increased when he raised his horn and offered another toast.

"To a relaxed and enjoyable evening. Thank you for your hospitality."

This time, Erik drained his horn, much to Kolga's delight.

Tone noticed the elevated change. While Kolga was pleasant and sweet before, she was downright friendly now... almost intimate like they had been best friends forever.

Yet as the night wore on, despite the excellent meal of fish and potatoes and plenty of mead, Kolga's mood seemed to sour by degrees. By the time the meal was over, the plates cleared, and the after dinner stories started, she had fallen into an irritable gloom, so much so that Tone knocked her knee against Erik's leg, getting his attention and ticking her head towards the door.

Immediately understanding, he caught Magnus' eye who had already determined he was ready to go home.

Pushing away from the table and standing, Erik inhaled a tired breath. "Thank you for an enjoyable meal, Kolga. If you don't mind, I think Tone and I are still a little tired from all the days of travel, so we'll say our 'goodnights.' Thank you again."

"Yes, I understand," she curtly answered. "Thank you for coming. It was a... an unusual evening. Be careful going home."

Once outside, Tone chuckled. "Why do I get the feeling we were just given the bum's rush out of a bar?"

"What happened?" Siv asked. "She was so sweet in the beginning and then Mister Hyde took over."

"Haven't the faintest idea," Erik shrugged. "C'mon. Let's go home."

Inside, Kolga brooded, remembering Folkvi's warning: *It will only work on a man who has doubts about his love for the other woman. The advantage is that these doubts can be so small he does not even know he has doubts.*

Flinging her empty mug against the wall, she snarled then inhaled a slow deep breath, calming herself. She would wait. Erik would be hers one way or another. She was used to winning and this was not going to be an exception.

The morning was unusually warm for the middle of February, or the beginning of Góa in the Viking Calendar. Tone and Erik stood down by the water opposite the island of Frognøya, the box of possessions from Kallevig and the others on the ground next to them. Reaching in, Erik retrieved the stun gun with the wire wrapped around the barrel. Rearing back, he flung it as far as he could into the water. He did the same with the other stun gun, silently praying the weapons would rust and decay over time or that silt would eventually cover them and that no one would ever find them.

Tone picked up the remote. It was flat, the size of a cellphone.

"What's that?" Erik asked.

"Looks like a TV remote." She glanced up at him. "I bet the time machine is still here. This is their ticket to get back."

"Or for them to come here," Erik smiled, "though they have to have some sort of failsafe measure on it. I can't see them sending the machine into the past without a guaranteed return."

"Let's make it more difficult for them." Kneeling down, she picked up a rock and smashed the remote, again and again then tossed it to Erik who flung it out into the water.

Pushing herself to standing, she slipped an arm around his waist while he wrapped an arm around her shoulder. Peering out over the water at the forested island and then at the wide vast lake, they breathed deep the fragrance of freedom.

"Thank you for coming back for me," Erik said, kissing the top of her head.

"Thank you for not giving up on me." She squeezed against him.

Silence drifted around them and a circling hawk caught their eyes.

"Think they'll come back for us again?" Tone wondered.

"Wouldn't be surprised if they did. I say we need to plan for it."

"At least they still don't know where we are," she chuckled.

"Which means we need to enjoy what we have." He turned her to face him, his hands resting on her shoulders. "We were never officially married in the future, but I don't need a ceremony or piece of paper to satisfy me or anyone else. You are my wife and that's all there is to it."

"Yes sir," she grinned and saluted then leaped in his arms. "I love you more than anything. Nothing will ever separate us again."

A voice haled them from behind and they turned to see Torben striding happily towards them, Magnus and Siv in tow, hand-in-hand.

Erik chuckled, shaking his head. "Now what?"

"Erik," Torben called out. "I'm writing a poem about you. Thought you all might like to hear it."

"A poem about me," Erik laughed. "I can think of better topics, like both of these fair ladies here."

Torben mused for only a moment. "Yes. That would be good too. After I finish this one."

Magnus placed an arm around Siv who snuggled into him. "Come Torben. Let's hear the beginning of this saga."

"I don't have a title yet," Torben said by way of introduction. "But this is what I have so far." He cleared his throat and in a strong voice began his poem.

"The spinner of fate is cruel to me.

Hands bound, chained by the Pines
of the sea's golden moon,
on too many ships; the bringer of
battle is hard at work.

I have traveled on the sea-god's steed
a long and turbulent wave-path,
though none have I seen
like this Maker of War.
The soul-cleavers whirl in his two strong fists,
a thirst for bone and Odin's fury,
a god of the quick flying weapon
until he dealt out mortal wounds.

There thirteen men fell,
clad in a cloak of blood.

Stain wolf's teeth with blood

Wolf and eagle stalk,
Over the dead
in praise of the feeder of ravens"

"O my God," Tone burst. "Erik's Tale." She snapped
her head to gaze in wonder at Erik, remembering that day in
class when she first asked him to go out with her.

Torben furrowed his brow and nodded. "I suppose
'Erik's Tale' is as good a title as any other."

"Friend Torben," Tone sweetly replied. "Your poem
will be remembered for a thousand years and more. Be sure
to write it down so that all may enjoy it."

Flattered, he flashed a broad grin and spun around to
head back to the house to work on his poem.

"That was a nice thing to say," Magnus observed with a raised eyebrow. "But really... a thousand years?"

Epilogue

When Tone smashed the remote, it disconnected the active locator link to the Time Machine causing the Machine to start the return process. Before Erik had tossed the remote into the water, the machine was back in the present.

Gene whooped a war cry when the machine whirred into place. His glee was muted when he saw no one aboard. Still, the machine was back and he was off the hook. Racing down the hall and impatiently waiting for the elevator to take him to the top floor, he burst through the doors to Cooper's office.

"He's in conference," Cooper's admin assistant shouted as he brushed past her. "You can't go in there." Leaping up she tried to stop him but was too late as he flung the doors open, discovering Meredith sitting on Cooper's lap, her arms around his neck, their heads snapping back from the kiss.

"What the hell," Cooper snarled. "How dare you come in here."

"It's back," Gene said, ignoring Meredith rapidly dislodging herself from Cooper's arms. "It's back. The Time Machine is back."

Cooper stood up, his indiscretion momentarily forgotten. "And the team?"

Gene shook his head. "No one returned. What do we do?"

"Damn," Cooper huffed. "This is *not* good." Morphing to professional boss, he shot a look at Meredith. "We're going to have to come up with some explanation for the two Norse guys."

"We can't leave them there," Gene pointed out. "Their presence could affect all sorts of future events, not to mention if any of them have children."

"I know, I know," Cooper said with a flip of his hand. "Recommendations?"

"Truth is, we don't know what happened. For all we know, the team could have been attacked and killed."

"That's too much to hope for," Cooper replied without thinking. "We have to assume they're all still alive."

"So we send a larger team?" Meredith suggested.

"We still need the linguists," Gene reminded them. "How many Old Norse folks are out there?"

Cooper twisted his head to look at Meredith. "Find some. Put together a team that can sustain itself. I don't care how long it takes. But we're going to get them, all of them, especially that Tone Thorgilsdottir. The woman has been nothing but a giant headache. I don't care if the rest are killed or already dead. I want her alive, back here. She's going to pay for all the trouble she's caused."

The adventure continues in Book 2 of the Viking
Time Travel Romance – *Hidden in Time*

OTHER BOOKS

Thank you for choosing to read this story! If you enjoyed this book, please leave an online review.

Thanks for reading!

-pdmac

WEBSITE
www.pdmac-author.com

FACEBOOK
www.facebook.com/pdmacauthor/

The Misfits of Gambria

Berserker of Gambria
The Voice of Thunder
Ghost in the Desert
A Wizard of Sorts
No Rest for the Wicked
A Noble Rebellion
No Loose Ends
Quest for a Throne
A Queen Most Evil
Warlord of Gambria

Teen & Young Adult Coming of Age Fantasy:
The Wyvern Master Chronicles
The Sixth Kingdom
A Spy in the Court
Raising the Dead
Wizard King

Bridge Quest: A GameLit Adventure Series
Bridge Quest
Orc's Bane
Lord of Innis Torr

Steampunk Western: Tombstone Duology
Fool's Gold
An Ounce of Lead

Viking Time Travel Romance
Beyond Her Touch
Hidden in Time

A Dystopian Novel
Rebirth of Angels

A Time Travel Novella
Ctrl Z: The Do Over Stone

Poetry
a young man no more

CO-AUTHORED BOOKS

Teen & Young Adult Coming of Age Fantasy:
Dragons of Isentol
Throne of Deceit
Rune Marked
Empire of Serpents

www.ingramcontent.com/pod-product-compliance
Lightning Source LLC
Chambersburg PA
CBHW030549020726
47494CB00005B/1539